Asleep In The Light

An Historical Novel About The
Cultural Revolution in America

By

THOMAS A. WALSH

All rights reserved. No part of this book shall be reproduced or transmitted in any form or by any means, electronic, mechanical, magnetic, photographic including photocopying, recording or by any information storage and retrieval system, without prior written permission of the publisher. No patent liability is assumed with respect to the use of the information contained herein. Although every precaution has been taken in the preparation of this book, the publisher and author assume no responsibility for errors or omissions. Neither is any liability assumed for damages resulting from the use of the information contained herein.

Copyright © 2013 by Thomas A. Walsh

ISBN 978-0-7414-8331-7 Paperback
ISBN 978-0-7414-8386-7 eBook

Printed in the United States of America

This is a work of historical fiction. Names, characters, places, and incidents either are the product of the author's imagination or are used fictitiously. Any resemblance to actual events or locales or persons, living or dead, is entirely coincidental.

Published March 2013

INFINITY PUBLISHING
1094 New DeHaven Street, Suite 100
West Conshohocken, PA 19428-2713
Toll-free (877) BUY BOOK
Local Phone (610) 941-9999
Fax (610) 941-9959
Info@buybooksontheweb.com
www.buybooksontheweb.com

Table of Contents

Table of Contents	i
Acknowledgement	ii
Dedication	ii
About the Cover	ii
Disclaimer	iii
Credits	iv
Introduction	v

Chapter	Title	Page
1	Small Town Roots	1
2	Introduction to Parish Life	27
3	First Holy Communion	52
4	A Looming Problem	62
5	Fighting Back	83
6	Soldier of Christ	107
7	Blackout Drill	130
8	Life on the Farm	151
9	An Angry Young Man	166
10	Summer Camp	182
11	Boarding School	189
12	Anything Goes	206
13	A New Beginning	224
14	Cultural Convergence	235
15	Meltdown	248
16	Sex, Drugs & Danger	263
17	Summer of '42	276
18	Mr. Big Stuff	284
19	Blind Ambition	307
20	Lazy Daze	328
21	Love Unlimited	352
22	Flying High	370
23	Wilderness Survival	395
24	Amazing Grace	410

Acknowledgements

I want to thank God, my family and the many friends and acquaintances whom I have had the privilege of walking with over the years. You have helped me to follow my quest.

Dedication

I dedicate this book to my beloved son Benjamin.

About the Cover

Some of the most beautiful places on earth are also the most forbidding. This picture of the Grand Teton National Park shows majestic snow covered peaks and a serene view of the Snake River. While it is a tranquil scene, anyone who has ever camped on a snow covered peak or run the gauntlet of whitewater, knows that these action packed adventures are potentially lethal. Socrates once opined, "The unexamined life is not worth living." In the sunset of our lives we will have the opportunity to quietly contemplate those events that may have been impossible to assess during the frantic paddling of our youth. Will we learn from the journey and repent of our sins? Or will we find ways to distract ourselves from the painful realities and descend into the emptiness of a self-induced coma? It takes courage to accept responsibility for how we have lived our lives and it takes humility to accept God's forgiveness; but once we are redeemed, we are promised a glorious eternity in heaven and an abundant life here on earth; which is why Archbishop Fulton J. Sheen reminds us, "Life *is* worth living."

Disclaimer

This is a work of historical fiction; therefore some public figures and events are referenced. However, all the other characters, which are portrayed in this book, are either purely fictional or composite characters derived from the traits of multiple subjects. Any resemblance to specific private persons, whether living or dead is purely coincidental.

Credits

Volunteers – I would first like to thank my parents; my mother for affirming and encouraging my writing and my father for supporting my efforts in the process. My friend Scott Reichley suggested I publish *The Wild Man's Journal*, which served Catholic men of action for over seven years and led me to write on a more consistant basis. My mentor Dorothy Ireton purchased the first subscription of that journal and assisted me with the marketing in my first publishing endeavor. This wise woman kept me honest with myself and encouraged me to do the right thing, while not ignoring basic common sense. A special thanks goes out to the Reimer family who shared their home with me when I needed a quiet place to edit. My brothers John and Michael Walsh listened to me for countless hours, as I tried to make sense of my life and this topsy turvy world of ours. My sister-in-law Bridget Walsh, Sharon DeVan, Amelia Ickinger and Mike Hansberry generously provided editorial feedback, comments on story line and help with fact checking.

Douay-Rheims Catholic Bible – was used for all Sacred Scripture quotes and references. This faithful online source is a translation of the Bible from the Latin Vulgate. It was translated in the service of the Catholic Church, by members of the English College at the seminary in Douai, France. www.drbo.org

Wikipedia – unless otherwise stated this online encyclopedia is the origin of information used in footnotes; however much of the source documentation has been modified for the sake of brevity and/or merged with my own added information. www.wikipedia.org

Introduction

Thomas Jefferson once said, "Eternal vigilance is the price of liberty."

Not all that long ago, President George H.W. Bush used his inaugural address to usher in, "A New World Order". After the collapse of the World Trade Center, his son demanded an unquestioning loyalty for his War on Terrorism. Anyone who dared to oppose him was branded an "Enemy of the State". What followed was the USA Patriot Act and it dramatically reduced individual freedom and multiplied the tools of law enforcement. The stock market tanked in 2007 and with his message of "Hope and Change," our first black president was catapulted into office. Barack Obama used the looming crisis to expand federal power on an unprecedented scale. He bailed out banks, nationalized car companies and took over healthcare.

In a rapid response that was reminiscent of the 1773 Boston Tea Party, irate citizens began confronting the government with a modern day Tea Party of their own. Angry citizens began by protesting at hall meetings, but the movement soon spilled out onto the streets like a wildfire and patriotic rallies were soon being held from sea to shining sea. In 2010, Tea Party candidates took over the House of Representatives and won major victories in their respective states, but these same patriots were unable to take back the Senate and the President was also reelected. Obsessed with a progressive agenda; Obama threatened to take away our guns and bypass Congress if he didn't get what he wants.

What happened to the America that our ancestors knew and loved? Do we even know or remember what a limited Constitutional government looks like? When did everything become so corrupt? Can we ever get that freedom back?

Although today's tyrants make easy targets for our anger; this present darkness that we find ourselves living in is actually spiritual in nature. Founding Father and former President John Adams once warned us that our Constitution was "designed strictly for a self disciplined, moral and religious people." He went on to remind us that our Republic is, "completely inadequate for the governing of any other." So what is the unvarnished truth about our own personal adherence to moral values and the faithful practice of our glorious religion? Have we reaped what we have sown?

Patrick Callahan was baptized a Roman Catholic and raised in a small peaceful town outside the city of Camden, New Jersey, by parents who loved him. Although Patrick began life with the benefit of loving parents and a faith filled community, the entire American culture was *Asleep in the Light*. The child grew up enjoying all the freedoms America had to offer, but he eventually fell prey to the siren songs of the sixties and nearly lost his country along with his faith in God. Listening to him tell this intimate tale is something akin to being a fly on the wall. Transported back in time; Patrick takes us with him, as he navigates a wild and dangerous ride down the rapids of change, right smack in the middle of the Cultural Revolution in America.

Some of his reflections sound delightfully familiar, while other passages are not nearly as pleasant and a few of the stories are downright indecent. **This book is *not for children***, nor is it for those who are quick to condemn. The mythical memoir will speak to those curious souls who are willing to learn, ponder and grow, while reflecting upon their own experiences of growing up in America. Although a work of fiction; Patrick Callahan reveals a world seldom shared with this level of candor and reflection.

The Greatest Generation lived the rough and tumble life of freedom and clearly understood their duty toward God, their family and the country. Many of them have since passed away, but their children received the benefits of their grit and wisdom. In addition they grew up during the Great Depression and because times were tough, their large families were very close knit, faith was central and freedom was still a lived experience. The phenomenal economic growth that followed WWII made life easier for most Americans and the Fifties were considered to be a golden age. Tragically, Kennedy's assassination brought an end to the innocence of Camelot and by the end of the Sixties, a cultural tsunami had transformed America's dominantly Christian nation into a pagan one. Generations X, Y & Z have never known the economic deprivation of their ancestors and are very adept at gaming the system. However, spiritually they are steeped in a kind of religious relativism; they confuse tolerance with indifference and license with liberty. Today vast numbers of Americans routinely give up their rights for the intoxicating illusion of security. People from almost every age group believe they are entitled to something from the government, but most fail to grasp the relationship between freedom and individual responsibility.

Our faith, our morals, our system of government and even our economy bear the scars of our anarchistic lifestyle and the consequences continue to unfold. Despite his tragic and sinful journey, Patrick Callahan remains optimistic and his naked confession reveals the reason behind his faith.[1] This once great nation of ours now teeters on the brink of economic, political and moral collapse. Men of inspiration and vision once designed and built a shining city on a hill. America's dream of freedom is real and some of us have lived that dream; but we are losing it because we have been *Asleep in the Light*. The life of Patrick Callahan can show us the way to recapture that vision and rebuild our country.

---

[1] *1 Peter 3:15* – "But sanctify the Lord Christ in your hearts, being ready always to satisfy every one that asketh you a reason of that hope which is in you."

Chapter 1

Small Town Roots

Sacred Heart Church stands like a fortress at the corner of Broadway and Ferry Avenue in the once thriving city of Camden, New Jersey. The traditional parish sanctuary with its thick black stone walls is still located about five miles down the road from Saint Peter's Church in Merchantville. Many years ago a young woman knelt down at the white marble altar rail and fingered the beads of her rosary. She was praying for the grace to be a good wife and mother. At a nuptial Mass held on February 7th 1953, Tom Callahan and Theresa Fitzgerald were married at Sacred Heart Church. Life would not begin easy for the young couple, but the bride's request would eventually be granted. After suffering the heartache of a miscarriage, the doctors at Cooper Hospital[2] presented the young newlyweds with their first born son on the first of April. The birth of the lad brought healing to the family and also the humor of April Fools Day jokes. On April 18, 1954 Patrick Michael Callahan was baptized in the font of the Sacred Heart.

Two months later Tom Callahan lost his father to a heart attack. Shannon Callahan was only fifty-five years old, but on June 4, 1954 he was pronounced dead at Shore Memorial Hospital.[3] There would be little time for grieving, since the family business was willed to the children. The Monday following the funeral, Tom, his brother and his sister's husband took over the day-to-day operations of the Callahan Machine Company. Motivated by the urgency of the situation, Thomas Callahan quickly finished up his Associates Degree in Engineering at the Spring Garden

---

[2] *Cooper Hospital* – in 1887 Richard M. Cooper, M.D., & members of his family donated money & land for a hospital that would provide medical care for the people of Camden, NJ.
[3] *Shore Memorial* – is a community hospital in Somers Point, New Jersey.

Institute, where he achieved the highest overall grade in his class.

Although America had survived The Great Depression and World War II, the pace and stability of American society had been significantly altered. New discoveries in medicine,[4] groundbreaking inventions[5] and high-tech advancements,[6] changed the way of life even further. When Burger King[7] and McDonald's[8] opened their doors, even the way we ate our meals changed. Many innovations contributed positively, but some were both deceptive[9] and immoral,[10] while others produced unintended consequences. When the Supreme Court ruled that segregated schools were unconstitutional,[11] the decision removed local control from school boards and transferred their authority to the federal government. The ruling produced a firestorm of legal battles over bussing and rendered parents politically unable to control the curriculum of their own children.

---

[4] *Jonas Edward Salk* – was an American medical researcher & virologist, best known for his discovery & development of the first safe & effective polio vaccine. (1914-1995)

[5] *Transistor Radio* – Texas Instruments & (I.D.E.A.) Industrial Development Engineering Associates produced the world's first commercially produced transistor radio, the Regency TR-1 went on sale in November 1954 & sold almost 100,000 units.

[6] *Color Television* – on January 1, 1954, NBC made the first coast-to-coast color broadcast, of the Tournament of Roses Parade.

[7] *Burger King* – was founded in 1953 in Jacksonville, FL, as "Insta-Burger King". Kieth J. Kramer & his wife's Uncle Matthew Burns used equipment known as the Insta-Broiler. In 1959, the company was purchased by the Miami, FL franchisees James McLamore & David R. Edgerton, who renamed the company Burger King.

[8] *McDonald's* – began in 1940, with a restaurant opened by Richard & Maurice McDonald, in San Bernardino, CA. The "Speedee Service System" in 1948, established the principles of the modern fast-food restaurant. Ray Kroc, purchased it on April 15, 1955 & renamed it.

[9] *The Kinsey Reports* – are two books on human sexual behavior, Sexual Behavior in the Human Male (1948) & Sexual Behavior in the Human Female (1953), by Dr. Alfred Kinsey, Wardell Pomeroy & others & published by Saunders. Critics have raised concerns about the methodology used to collect data, including that data in the reports could not have been obtained without the collaboration of child molesters.

[10] *Playboy* – in December 1953, 27-year-old Hugh Hefner published the very first Playboy magazine. This 1st edition was 44-pages long & had no date on its cover because Hefner wasn't sure there would be a 2nd edition. In that first run, Hefner sold 54,175 copies of Playboy magazine at 50 cents each. www.history1900s.about.com/od/1950s/qt/Playboy.htm

[11] *Brown v. Board of Education of Topeka* – was a landmark decision of the US Supreme Court that declared state laws establishing separate public schools for black & white students denied black children equal educational opportunities & were unconstitutional.

Patrick's sister Sarah was born on April 19th and the date of her birth heralded the arrival of a politically powerful patriot.[12] As an adult, Sarah would not only sit on her local school board, fighting to hold down taxes and block federally mandated sex-ed programs, but her quest for local control over her children's education would one day land her on the Larry King Show.[13] Like that first shot heard round the world in 1775, her revolutionary defense of conservative moral principals would one day be heard around the world on the airways of CNN. Alas, all that would be in the future. For now, Patrick was happy to help his mom take care of his precious new baby sister Sarah.

The truly positive changes in the American culture were not the result of armed conflict or even governmental action. They were the consequence of courageous individuals. Rosa Parks, the genteel black woman who refused to give up her seat on a bus was one such individual.[14] Inspired by this woman's pluck, clergyman Dr. Martin Luther King Jr. decided the timing was ripe for organized action. Along with several other black ministers, he formed the Montgomery Improvement Association.[15] Their support of Miss Parks eventually led to the U.S. Supreme Court ruling against segregated seating on public buses in 1956.[16] So far so good, but the racial equality movement was about to be co-opted,

---

[12] *April 19,1775* – the proverbial first "shot heard round the world" was fired during an armed stand-off between British forces & the local militia in Lexington, Massachusetts. It marked the beginning of the American Revolutionary War. The conflict then escalated into engagements at the Old North Bridge in the battle of Lexington & Concord, when British troops tried to confiscate guns & ammunition. British officers were confused by the unexpected resistance, so they returned to Lexington for new orders. On their way back, British regulars were picked apart by local snipers & thousands of colonists subsequently volunteered for the *Continental Army*.
[13] *Larry King Live* – was a talk show hosted by Larry King on the Cable News Network. It debuted in 1985 & was CNN's most watched program, with over 1 million viewers nightly.
[14] *Rosa Parks* – was born in 1913, the same year Harriet Tubman died. She was arrested in 1955, for refusing to relinquish her seat on a bus to a white man, in violation of local Jim Crow laws. Her courageous act inspired the Civil Rights Movement.
[15] *MIA* – the Montgomery Improvement Association was established to oversee a boycott, following Rosa Parks arrest & a young minister was elected its chairman. His name was Rev. Martin Luther King, Jr., who became the iconic leader of the Civil Rights Movement.
[16] *Browder vs. Gayle* – declared segregated bussing unconstitutional.

turning the race issue into a ticking time bomb. Quaker and Episcopal businessmen (think former British landowners) working in tandem with Jewish Realtors, engaged in a practice called blockbusting in many northern cities. They simultaneously funded what were euphemistically called Freedom Buses, to entice large black populations to move north. The purpose behind these massive manipulated migrations was to secure cheap black labor from the South to replace Catholic immigrants, who were now daring to form unions in the establishment's northern factories.[17]

While these events were clearly reshaping the country, most people were busy watching the boob tube. The masses were blissfully unaware of these looming problems and the Callahan family was no different. Every morning Patrick watched his cartoons on Captain Kangaroo.[18] In the evenings mom and dad enjoyed the latest episode of The Honeymooners.[19] But not everyone was *Asleep in the Light*. Thomas Callahan paid strict attention to the news; especially the political broadcasts. Since he worked in Philadelphia, he knew about the racial tensions developing in the city. He also listened with interest to Eisenhower explain how close we had come to a German invasion during the war. Therefore he understood why the president was calling for an Interstate Highway System.[20] Mr. Callahan also opposed Margaret Sanger[21] who was pushing birth control, in direct contradiction to the directives of the Church and of the Holy Scriptures.[22] He also worked diligently with the Knights of

---

[17] From the book *The Slaughter of Cities: Urban Renewal As Ethnic Cleansing*, by E. Michael Jones, published by St. Augustine Press. ©1995
[18] *Captain Kangaroo* – was a children's television series, which aired weekday mornings on CBS from 1955-1984, making it the longest-running children's TV program of its day.
[19] *The Honeymooners* – was a situation comedy television show, based on a 1951–'55 sketch of the same name, which originally aired on CBS. It was created by Jackie Gleason & shot before a live audience.
[20] *National Interstate & Defense Highways Act* – became law on February 29, 1956.
[21] *Margaret Sanger* – was a fallen away Catholic & a birth control activist, an advocate of eugenics & the founder of the American Birth Control League, which later came to be known as Planned Parenthood. (1879-1966)
[22] *Genesis 28:3* – "And God almighty bless thee and make thee to increase & multiply thee: that thou mayst be a multitude of people."

Columbus, to get the phrase "under God" inserted into the Pledge of Allegiance.[23]

Little Patrick and baby Sarah were blessed with a prayerful mother and a principled father. The two toddlers felt all the warmth and security that God intends for little children to know. Thomas Callahan provided a safe comfortable place in which to live and corrected Patrick when he needed guidance or discipline. Theresa cleaned the house, cooked the meals and occasionally fussed over her children. Several times a day she sat Patrick down beside the bassinet, while she changed Sarah's diaper. Thanks to this daily attention, Patrick soon became very attached to his mother.

The cognitive development of two-year-olds includes: episodes of staring for several minutes at something or someone, in order to discover the cause and effect of things, like recognizing a point of pain or finding the ball that rolled behind the sofa. According to Piaget,[24] a child in this stage of development uses magical thinking to believe, for instance, that his teddy bear is real. Since he makes linguistic advances during this period, he can also tell you what he is thinking. Although its early in his life, Patrick is now aware of his surroundings and capable of communicating with others. I think its time we let him speak for himself.

Patrick Callahan tells his own story.

I have many more questions than answers. Like why does mommy put pins in her mouth when she changes Sarah? I

---

[23] *Under God* – Louis A. Bowman (1872–1959) was the first to initiate the addition of "under God" to the Pledge of Allegiance. In 1951, the Knights of Columbus, the world's largest Catholic fraternal service organization, also began including the words "under God" in the Pledge of Allegiance. The Knights of Columbus worked closely with Congressman Louis Rabout. The Democrat from Detroit was a long-time member of the House Appropriations Committee, but he was also a devout Roman Catholic. One of his sons became a Jesuit and two of his daughters became Catholic nuns. A Joint Resolution of Congress incorporated "under God" into the Pledge on June 14, 1954.

[24] *Jean Piaget* – was a Swiss developmental psychologist & philosopher known for his theory of cognitive development. (1896-1980)

think daddy must work a lot, because after he closes my door at night, I don't see him again till he comes home for dinner. Who is the little boy mommy is holding in the mirror? And why does it hurt so badly when a bee stings me?

The other day, while she hung up the laundry, mom sat me down on the ground in our backyard. The sun was real hot and it was so bright it blinded me. Looking down at the dark green grass, I noticed something like steam and it made me hot and yucky. I wanted to crawl around and cool off, but I couldn't move. The little white flowers on the clover smelled sweet, but the bees liked it too and they were buzzing around me. Since I don't know how to talk yet, I couldn't tell mommy I was afraid of being stung. She was so busy; she didn't seem to notice me or the bees.

Although not always protected from things like bees, I felt welcome and loved in our family. I often helped mommy to take care of Sarah and I look forward to meeting a new baby that I hear is on its way. Mom seems especially close to me now. She makes me happy and curious about the mysteries of life when she places my hand on her stomach and I can feel the baby kick. The day before my little brother Sean arrived, I saw mom standing on a chair in the hallway trying to hang a picture. I was so afraid she would get hurt I blurted out, "Don't fall mommy." As the radio faintly played Love Me Tender,[25] in the other room mommy smiled at me with her beautiful blue doe eyes. Life with mom is all warm and fuzzy!

Sadly, all that coziness would soon disappear. Although I had looked forward to the birth of my new baby brother, I didn't understand that mom had to go away to have Sean. The night she left, I tearfully begged and pleaded with her to stay, but she went away anyway. Standing at the back door, I

---

[25] *Love Me Tender* – was a song sung by Elvis Presley & adapted from the tune of "Aura Lee" a Civil War ballad with music by George R. Poulton & words by W.W. Fosdick. It was released under the RCA record label on October 6, 1956.

screamed and sobbed for over an hour. Despite her best efforts, my babysitter, who had been called in at the last minute, was unable to console me. Not only did mom leave me, but dad departed the following day to pick up a new trailer. After being abandoned for several days, it dawned on me that mommy and I would never be the same again.

Near the end of the year, I had had it with all the attention Sean was getting from mom. Mommy still sat and read books like The Cat In The Hat[26] to Sarah and me, but when Sean cried story time was over and we had to wait till his bottle was heated or the diaper was changed. Sometimes she even forgot about reading to us altogether. Adding insult to injury, it became my assigned duty, to place the ammonia drenched cloth diapers in the hamper for the Dy-Dee Service.

Once I started thinking and talking, there was almost no stopping me. Dad took me down to the trailer in the Pines[27] at a place called Fred's Folley and when it came time for us to leave I told him, "The trailer is very tired because Patrick was there. It has to go to bed." One day grandmom Cunningham came over to visit. I asked her, "Where is grandpop?" She said that grandpop was in Heaven with God. Pondering over what she said I asked, "Where is Heaven?" She looked up at the clear blue sky and said, "Its way up high in the air. We can't see it from here." Soon afterwards my mother discovered me on the way up to the attic. When she asked me where I was going I said, "I'm going up to find grandpop and God." Besides being inquisitive, I also found ways to express a growing resentment towards my brother.

---

[26] *The Cat in the Hat* – is a children's book by Dr. Seuss.©1957 The cat is perhaps the most famous, featuring a tall, anthropomorphic, mischievous cat, wearing a tall, red & white-striped hat & a red bow tie. He also carries an umbrella. Through his books, Dr. Seuss promoted both his name & the cause of elementary literacy in the USA.

[27] *Pines* – refer to the Wharton Tract State Park. It encompasses 115,000 acres of Pinelands & is named for Joseph Wharton, who purchased the property in the 19th Century in the hopes of providing a source of clean drinking water for Philadelphia; but New Jersey quashed the plan by passing a law that banned the export of water. New Jersey eventually bought the land from Wharton's heirs in the 1950s.

When my cousin Kathleen Fitzgerald was born, I put in my request. "Mommy, will you please send our Sean one back and get a Kathleen one?"

No longer the center of attention, I began playing alone. Dad brought home one of those new Wham-O Frisbees,[28] but at three years old, I wasn't able to do very much more than send it rolling across the yard. One day a TV repairman came to the house and took the access panel off the back of the set. When he pulled the television away from the wall, it revealed a crawlspace door that led to an indoor sandbox under our living room. I got in lots of trouble for tracking in sand, but even more so, for disappearing without telling mom where I had gone. I eventually got banned from the crawlspace, leaving only the TV set for entertainment.

Technology in and of itself is neither good nor evil; it's simply a tool and the television was quickly becoming a fact of everyday life in America. To aid Catholics in the proper use of this novel innovation, the Pope held out St. Clare[29] as the Patron Saint of Television. Ironically, or perhaps prophetically, the first Catholic international cable company EWTN[30] would later be founded by a Poor Clares nun[31] named Mother Angelica.

---

[28] *Wham-O Frisby* – was a pie plate style toy, manufactured by a company founded by Richard Knerr & Arthur "Spud" Melin, who were USC graduates unhappy with their employment. They began their company in 1948 as "WHAM-O Mfg. Co." & started out in Knerr's garage. Their 1st market idea was the Wham-O Wrist Rocket slingshot, which they developed while hurling meat in the air to train a pet falcon. The name Wham-O came from the sound effect upon releasing the sling. In 1957 they hit pay dirt with the Hula Hoop, which was copied from a bamboo exercise hoop in Australia & the Frisby, originally called the "Pluto Plate" was purchased from its inventor Fred Morrison.
[29] *St. Clare of Assisi* – was designated the "Patron Saint of Television" on October 9, 1958, by Pope Pius XII. His reason for selecting her is that when she was too ill to attend Mass, she used to see & hear a vision of the Mass on the wall in her room.
[30] *EWTN* – the Eternal Word Television Network is an American cable TV network, which presents Catholic-themed programming. It was founded by Mother Mary Angelica of the Annunciation (born Rita Antoinette Rizzo) in 1980, on the grounds of Our Lady of the Angels monastery in Irondale, AL, a suburb of Birmingham. www.ewtn.com
[31] *The Poor Clares* – is a Franciscan order for women established in the Roman Catholic Church. Saints Clare of Assisi & Francis of Assisi founded it on Palm Sunday in the year 1212. As of 2004 there were over 20,000 Poor Clare nuns living in over 76 countries.

I especially enjoyed watching Leave it to Beaver[32] and quickly identified with how the Beaver's innocent curiosity got him into all sorts of trouble, with his kind and wise, but often preoccupied parents. Somehow I could relate. TV was a powerful medium and my worldview was pretty much formed by the shows that I watched. Besides cartoons like Buggs Bunny and Huckleberry Hound, the Mouseketeers on the Micky Mouse Club[33] not only entertained me, but gave me the feeling that I was not alone. Walt Disney also opened the door to more serious drama shows like Johnny Tremain,[34] which helped to form my moral character and cemented an emotional bond between me and The American Revolution. Shows like Wagon Train[35] held out good sturdy men and women of the West, as role models and I was particularly enamored with the wisdom, strength and courage of the Wagon Master. These characters gave me a pioneering spirit and increased my love for exploration and adventure.

For a several years a vendor had been dropping by to see my father at his shop. In addition to discussing business, the salesman enthusiastically spoke of his love for aviation and invited my father to go flying with him. On Saturday October 22, 1957 dad took him up on the offer and they spent over an hour in the air, going through all kinds of exhilarating aerobatics. Before returning to Buhle Field[36] they flew over our house in Pennsauken and dad's boyhood

---

[32] *Leave It to Beaver* – is a 1950s & 1960s family-oriented American television situation comedy about an inquisitive, but often naïve boy named Theodore "Beaver" Cleaver & his adventures at home, in school & around his suburban neighborhood.

[33] *The Mickey Mouse Club* – is a long-running variety TV show that began in 1955. Produced by Walt Disney Productions & televised by ABC, it featured an ever-changing cast of teenage performers called Mouseketeers.

[34] *Johnny Tremain* – is a 1957 film created by Walt Disney Pictures, based on the 1944 Newbery Medal-Winning children's novel of the same name by Esther Forbes. The film & a later TV series retold a story about the years in Boston, Massachusetts. prior to the outbreak of the American Revolution.

[35] *Wagon Train* – is an American Western TV series that ran on NBC from 1957–1962 & then on ABC from 1962–1965. The show was based on the 1950 film Wagon Master, which was directed by John Ford.

[36] *Buhle Field* – was a small private airport, located along the Delaware River in Philadelphia, Pennsylvania, just south of the Tacony-Palmyra Bridge.

home in Maple Shade. Dad was hooked and he began taking lessons the next weekend at Echelon, Airport.[37]

Although my father was having the time of his life, he was also witnessing the world around him unraveling on the television news. Fidel Castro and his Communist Revolutionaries invaded Cuba and the Russians launched the Sputnik satelite, which scared the United States into entering the space race with avengence. About the same time that Special Forces Captain Hank Cramer, became the first American to die in Vietnam,[38] The Gaither Report[39] called for the production of more missiles and fallout shelters. Stories about corruption and scandal like the FBI arresting Teamster's boss Jimmy Hoffa[40] on bribery charges, dripped through the portal of the one-eyed monster like a Chinese water tourture. Although dad paid close attention to all of these geopolitical events, which would one day dramatically effect my life, he also kept me physically safe, emotionally entertained and blissfully unaware of the danger. But my universe was about to expand beyond the safety zone.

Despite all reasonable disciplinary measures, my routine of disappearing into the crawlspace, gave my mother the illusion she knew where I was playing. However, the winter wonderland outside was simply too inviting and I frequently snuck outside to go sledding in the back yard. When spring arrived, my sister and I often accompanied mom with the baby carriage, as she walked Sean around the neighborhood. These little excursions made me anxious to explore the

---

[37] *Echelon Airport* – was a simple grass airstrip with some tie-downs & a few hangars. It was closed in 1965 & is now the home of the Echelon Mall, in Voorhees, NJ.
[38] *Harry Griffith Cramer, Jr.* – was killed on October 21, 1957, making him the first United States military casualty in Vietnam. Citation from www.westpoint.org
[39] *Deterrence & Survival in the Nuclear Age* – was a report recommending significant strengthening of U.S. strategic offensive & defensive military capabilities. Nov. 7, 1957.
[40] *Jimmy Hoffa* – was the President of the Teamsters union from 1958–1971 He built up the trucker's union, into a powerful force & was beloved by his members. Unfortunately, he was also convicted of jury tampering & bribery, thanks to his alleged association with the Mafia. Richard Nixon, pardoned him in 1975, but he mysteriously disappeared on July 30, 1975, somewhere in Michigan and is now presumed dead.

unknown territory beyond my back yard, but they also made me cautious and fearful. About a block away from our house was a fenced in yard with four million aggressive Chihuahuas.[41] OK, so maybe it wasn't quite that many, but these miniature Mexicans were the loudest, meanest, barkenist creatures I had ever seen. Whenever we walked by with the stroller, a whole pack of the tiny terrorists came running over to the fence and would scare the living daylights out of me. I can only imagine what Sean must have felt. Other than the dogs, our neighborhood seemed like a pretty quiet and friendly place. So I soon began venturing out on my own, albeit in the opposite direction of the dogs. The first kid I met was Richard Rubin.

Richard lived only a couple of doors down and was not a nice guy, but he knew lots of other kids in the neighborhood. Richard Rubin loved to brag about how many toys he had and took anyone who would follow him down into his basement, to show off his possessions. Entering the cellar was like hitting the mother load. Richard had toys; lots of toys! Besides tricycles and cars, he had fire engines and trucks. I'm not talking little stuff, but vehicles you can ride. Round and around his basement we rode and at break-neck speed too! Compared to being at home, it was a blast!

The only fly in the ointment is that Richard Rubin was a very selfish little brat. While he loved to brag about all his toys, he never wanted to share them. If one of us got into a car, he would want to ride the same car. I knew they were his toys, so I would just get out of the car and climb into a truck. But when he saw me riding the truck, he suddenly wanted to ride the same vehicle. Since it was his house, I got out of the truck and tried out the fire engine, but even that didn't satisfy him. I had had enough and drew my line in the sand. Running upstairs he went crying to his mommy. Mrs. Rubin

---

[41] *Chihuahua* – is the smallest breed of dog & is named after the state of Chihuahua in Mexico. They are noted for their nervous temperament & diminutive appearance.

came running down the stairs and made me get out of the fire engine. It was completely unfair and it happened day after day. It was getting old fast and although I tried telling mom, she just told me to be nice to him. I even tried explaining the situation to Richard's mom, but no matter what I told her, she always sided with her son.

No adults seemed willing to listen, believe me, or do anything about it. So when summer came along, I stopped playing in the basement and brought my own Tonka Trucks[42] over to play with the other kids in his back yard. Things were going along pretty well until Richard tried taking one of my trucks. When I held the bulldozer tight, he ran into the house crying. Once again his mommy came out to defend her boy. I told her what he did, but she still insisted I give him my yellow truck. I gave him a dump truck, but as soon as she went back into the house, Richard smirked and pushed me onto the ground. He had taken things way too far. Something deep inside filled me with rage. I saw red and picked up a large stone from the edge of the garden and threw it at his stomach.

His mother, who had been watching from the kitchen window, ran out the back door screaming. She dragged me home to my mother and told her what I had done. Mom was horrified, and looked at me as if she had no idea who I was, or what kind of monster she had created. When she asked me why I had done such a thing, I just looked down at the ground feigning a guilty embarrassment even though my heart was still on fire. Not only did I have no remorse, it was I who was disgusted with her. I felt completely justified in my actions. I had told mom about Richard. I had told his mother. I had even spoken to dad about it the night before,

---

[42] *Tonka Trucks* – the Mound Metalcraft company was founded in Mound, MN. on September 19, 1946 by partners: Lynn Baker, Avery Crounse & Alvin Tesch. They started manufacturing garden implements, but metal toy trucks, which started out as a sideline, soon grew into a successful product line. On November 23, 1955, they changed the company name to *Tonka Toys Inc.*, which is a Dakota-Sioux word meaning great or big. After design changes & a new logo Tonka became a household name.

but none of them had lifted so much as a finger to help me. Every adult thought I had done something terrible, but all I had done was to stand up for myself. How dare they be mad at me! What else was I supposed to do? They were the ones charged with protecting me and I was the one taking the bull by the horns and solving the problem. Nothing I could say would improve my situation, so I stared at the ground in stoic silence.

Obviously, I was no longer allowed to hang out at Richard's house. However I now had new playmates who knew the score, even if the adults were clueless. My best buddy was Josh Cooper. Josh was a couple of years older than I, so naturally he was the cool one. The Coopers lived in a light blue house on the corner and Josh didn't hang out with Richard anyway, so every day I cut through Rubin's backyard for a visit. My trespassing infuriated Richard, but it was fun for me, since I knew there was nothing that spoiled little control freak could do about it. Josh told me about a place we could explore, but we would have to cross Homestead Avenue to get there. This all sounded pretty exciting to a kid who had never actually traveled more than a few of doors from home. Unfortunately, I was not allowed to cross the street.

If Josh Cooper was the Huck Finn of our neighborhood, I was Tom Sawyer. Josh was the experienced guy who knew the score, because he had been out there. He was the one showing me the ropes. Because he was older, my mother gave me permission to cross the street, as long as Josh crossed with me. Once across the street we watched high school boys race around a track, throw the Javelin, or jump using a poll vault. A couple of times we stopped to watch two heavyset guys throwing the shot put or spinning around in circles to throw the hammer.[43] It was impressive to watch

---

[43] *Hammer* – the modern or Olympic hammer throw is an athletic throwing event where the object is to throw a heavy metal ball attached to a wire or chain with a handle at the end.

the men spin around like tops and then throw the hammer or shot so accurately.

Along side the track and field fence was a foot path that led back behind some houses and disappeared into a dark wooded swamp. Keeping our voices low as we slinked along the trail, only added to the excitement of our adventure. When Josh issued a hand signal we slowed down to an almost reverent pace, as we entered the dense vegetation of the mysteriously wet wonderland. Here was a portal to another world.

Although the marsh was a very scary place, for some reason it was equally inviting. There were tall trees with moss and vines hanging down from the branches. The swamp was filled with cattails and clumps of yellow grass just above the water line. There were wild birds, frogs, fish and spiders. What else could a young boy want? In reality, our magical realm was nothing more than a vacant wetland that was occasionally used as a dumping ground. Old refrigerators, skids and mattresses, became raw material for our projects. In the winter an old freezer door became a sled and in summer a beat up old skid was transformed into a raft on the Big Muddy Mississippi. We spent hours exploring the forest, catching minnows and working on building projects, with the seriousness of professional engineers. Until one day it all came to an abrupt end.

Sometime after my brother Sean was born, mom and dad went on a vacation trip to Bermuda. They hired Mrs. Fletcher to baby-sit for us while they were gone. Supposedly she came highly recommended and did seem competent enough, but she ran our home like a boot camp. If we didn't jump when she barked, she began yelling at us with a gruff, booming voice making her sound like a drill sergeant. Sarah and I were scared to death of the old hag. Except for a when the grouch hung laundry; we were forbidden from going out doors. We felt like prisoners under house arrest. Whenever

Mrs. Fletcher went into one of her tirades, she reduced my poor sister Sarah to tears. I was so angry with how she was treating my little sister that I no longer feared her. I was just mad about her criminal capacity for cruelty. The minute mom and dad returned, Sarah let loose with a boatload of tears relating stories about the mean old woman's tyranny. I concurred with her assessment; supplying graphic examples of why we never wanted see her again. Although we never did, mom and dad frequently threatened to bring her back, if we ever gave any other babysitter any grief. It was a covenant that worked for all of us.

Our house became even more hectic in the Spring, when my other brother Murray was born. Still not getting along very well with Sean, I played outside as much as possible. I figured mom didn't so much need my help taking care of the other kids, as she needed me out from under her feet. I was more than happy to oblige, so long as I could hang out with Josh Cooper in the swamp. But one day when I went over to play with him, Mrs. Cooper said he was sick, which meant I would not be allowed to cross the street. Not wanting to return home, I decided to take my chances. After looking up and down the silent street several times, I zipped across the cracked concrete pavement and disappeared into the bushes. Feeling like some kind of commando hiding out behind enemy lines, I kept out of sight until I reached the safe haven of the swamp. I had a wonderful time climbing trees, exploring and gathering more building materials for the tree fort. At the end of the day I felt a sense of pride about my accomplishments and about my independent decision. I walked home with my head held high, enjoying the ecstasy of freedom.

Hanging out in the swamp alone gave me time to reflect. The solitude helped me to focus and organize my thoughts. Being alone wasn't lonely; it was fulfilling and fun. This silent place afforded me the opportunity to ponder things in life and come to reasonable conclusions about them. Stepping back from the drama, I started forming my own perspective.

I began to see that people were different and not everyone was equal. Some guys like Richard Rubin were boring, selfish and mean, while other kids like Josh Cooper were adventurous, helpful and friendly. Parents too were unique. Mrs. Cooper was firm; she knew the score and was fair with her son Josh. Mrs. Rubin, on the other hand, was easily conned by her son Richard and blind to his character flaws. Although my parents were well intentioned, they also seemed overwhelmed with the responsibilities of a growing family. In spite of the facts, mom thought that all adults told the truth and that the word of children was suspect. The idea that a child would be deliberately evil seemed far-fetched to her and the prospect of an adult telling a lie was simply beyond her comprehension. This blindness affected my credibility and pleas for help often went unanswered. So I realized early on that I was on my own.

The lessons I learned from television personalities like Johnny Tremain, the pioneers on Wagon Train, or the Cartwrights on Bonanza,[44] all seemed to be saying the same thing. Freedom isn't free! The path pointed out in these petite parables connected with real life. Fear of bees left me paralyzed as an infant, yet braving spider webs in the crawlspace gave me the freedom to play with my trucks in the sand on rainy days. Submitting to an incompetent authority that was either unwilling or unable to defend me was emotionally crushing, but facing down the bully freed me up to hang out with another friend who treated me much better. Finally, fear of being alone only led to loneliness, while embracing solitude permitted me to participate in the pleasure of my own company. It was a good beginning, but soon there would be larger issues to ponder.

---

[44] *Bonanza* – is an American western TV series that ran on NBC from 1959-1973. The story about Ben Cartright & his 3 sons living on the Ponderosa is 2nd only to Gunsmoke among westerns, starring Lorne Greene, Pernell Roberts, Dan Blocker & Michael Landon.

I was about to enter the world of business. It began on an extremely hot day in August. Even though it was only eight in the morning, the thermometer was already approaching ninety degrees. I used a card table for my Lemonade Stand. Mom set me up with a pitcher, some powdered drink mix and a stack of paper cups. Then she taught me the mechanics of getting the ice cubes out of the aluminum trays. Once everything was in place, I taped my sign to the table and waited... and waited... and waited, in the heat of a broiling hot sun. Despite my excitement and patience, no one bought the lemonade. Were it not for mom and Mrs. Yadin, our next-door neighbor, I would have sold nothing at all.

Jay Miller came by at about eleven and asked me how I was doing. Lowering my head in shame before the older kid from next door I murmured, "Not so good." Giving my stand the once over he asked for a taste. Thinking I was about to make a sale, I happily complied with his request. After a long pause he looked back at me and said, "How would you like to form a partnership?" When I asked him what a partnership was, his face lit up with the excitement of a televangelist. He explained that we could both go into business together and then split the profits fifty-fifty. Although I didn't quite understand the accounting intricacies, I saw no down side to his proposal. So I smiled and said, "Sure!"

Jay Miller immediately started yelling, "Lemonade! Get your ice cold Lemonade!" He screamed it at the top of his lungs. He flagged down every car that passed by on the street. He even walked up and down the sidewalk, ringing the doorbells of every house in the neighborhood. It didn't take long for us to run out of Lemonade, with this huckster on my side. Periodically I had to run back in the house, to fill up another pitcher. Meanwhile my exuberant partner was encouraging our customers to send back their family and friends, as soon as they returned home. Like a miracle, they came! By the end of the day we had made over sixteen dollars. My partner was happy and I was thrilled. We then shook hands and agreed to return the next day, to repeat our success.

I couldn't wait for dad to get home. I knew he would be happy for me, proud of me and thoroughly impressed with our success. As soon as he pulled in the driveway, I ran up to the side of his car. I told him about the lemon aid stand and showed him the money. Although a little bit preoccupied, he smiled as we walked up the sidewalk together. When I opened the front door for him he said, "Great! Tell me all about it." He seemed real interested as I told him about how mom helped me mix the lemonade and taught me how to get the ice cubes out of the tray. When I told him that I was not doing very well at first, his eyes were filled with compassion and he seemed to understand the difficulties of being in business. However the expression on his face fell when I told him that Jay and I had formed a partnership. He wanted to know why Jay Miller was getting half the profits when I was supplying the table, the cups and the lemonade mix. I told him Jay shouted, "Get your Ice Cold Lemonade", how he had flagged down cars in the street and that because of him our sales had dramatically improved, but he still thought it was unfair. He concluded our conversation by informing me that I was not allowed to sell any lemonade, unless I did it all by myself.

I was confused and disappointed with his reaction. Dad seemed to overlook how much fun I was having. The real reason for his objection was that the Miller family was Jewish. Jay's father Nathan played the violin for The Philadelphia Orchestra.[45] I saw in Jay a talented friend, but what dad saw was a Jewish con artist. There was no way he was going to let some Jew take advantage of his kid. Dad rejected all requests to reconsider and I was forbidden to sell

---

[45] *The Philadelphia Orchestra* – is among the world's leading symphony orchestras. Founded in 1900 and based in Philadelphia, Pennsylvania it is one of the "Big Five" American orchestras and is renowned for its artistic excellence. The orchestra has excited audiences with thousands of concerts both in Philadelphia and around the world.

the lemonade with Jay. Embarrassed and ashamed, I met with him on Saturday morning and told Jay I was not allowed to be his partner, but I left out the part about him being Jewish. It seems that no good deed goes unpunished. Although tragic, everyone had acted with good intensions. Mom wanted to help me get started in my first business. Jay saw a win-win situation and helped me with his gift of salesmanship. Dad was defending me from what he perceived to be usury. Despite the best of good intentions that night there were Tears on my Pillow.[46]

On October 28, 1958, Pope Pius XII died and Pope John XXIII succeeded him as the 261st Pope. Good Pope John began his reign by encouraging the flock to face the root causes of human behavior saying, "Consult not your fears, but your hopes and your dreams. Think not about your frustrations, but about your unfulfilled potential. Concern yourself not with what you tried and failed in, but with what it is still possible for you to do." Shortly thereafter, Monsignor announced that a Parish Mission led by The Precious Blood Friars would be held at Saint Peter's Church. From the Vatican to the local parish, God's people were being encouraged to build up their faith and to live it out with passion.

During the Fifties, faithful Catholics had reached a pinnacle of holiness in the practice of their faith. However, the way it was being lived out had become somewhat stoic and disconnected from certain aspects of daily life. From the aerial vantage point of the Chair of Saint Peter, a weakness had been spotted in the areas of Faith and Obedience. Catholics worldwide had been following the letter of the law, but their passion for evangelism seemed to be on the wane. To address this vulnerability, Pope John XXIII called for the opening of the Second Vatican Council.

---

[46] *Tears on My Pillow* – is a doo-wop song, written by Sylvester Bradford & Al Lewis in 1958 and first recorded by Little Anthony and The Imperials on End Records.

Guided by the Holy Spirit, the Pope was apparently seeing things accurately and my life was a good example. Corinna and Ariel Yadin were ready-made babysitters that lived next door. One day I refused to put away my toys and Ariel told me to stand in the corner. Unhappy with her discipline, I ran up the stairs to my bedroom and slammed the door. She came running up behind me and tried prying open the door, but I held it fast. She kept pushing on the door and I pushed back with all my might. Something had to give and it did; I broke my arm! Poor little Ariel, who was only about fourteen, was beside herself with remorse. She rushed in and cradled me saying, "Oh, I am soooooooo sorry. I didn't mean to hurt you. Are you all right?"

The young woman was scared, concerned and totally devastated; but was I compassionate about her situation? Absolutely not! Even though I would not read The Prince[47] for another fifty years, I seemed to instantly earn a dishonorable doctorate in Machiavellian modus operandi. "Now you're in trouble." I sneered. "Wait till my mommy gets home. Then you'll really be in trouble." I was sure that I could manipulate mom into punishing this sweet sensitive girl and I looked forward to a shift in the balance of power, but I had become just like my nemesis, Richard Rubin. Fortunately for Ariel, I was unable to manipulate my mom in the same way that Richard had done with his mother. She intuitively knew that Ariel had done nothing intentional to hurt me.

Unfortunately, I was not the only Machiavellian loose on the planet. Corruption was putting our republican form of government in jeopardy, and the Communists were toppling one government after the other around the globe. This

---

[47] *The Prince* – is a book written by Niccolò Machiavelli. Originally written in 1513 A.D. it advocates "the employment of cunning & duplicity in statecraft or in general conduct". Some believe it is a plagiarized version of *The Art of War*, by Sun Tzu, circa. 476-221 B.C.

prompted Robert Welch,[48] a retired candy manufacturer, to found the John Birch Society.[49] He would not have to wait long for Americans to see the need for such an organization. In Cuba, President Batista escaped from Havana just prior to rebel forces sacking the capital. Shamefully, within a week the United States recognized the newly formed Communist government of Fidel Castro. A week after the invasion this ruthless dictator executed seventy-one of Batista's men. Birchers began circulating literature, which exposed the communist conspiracy and by March of 1961 the thirteen-member Birch Society had grown to almost one-hundred thousand members. Mom and dad both attended meetings, but dad declined to become a member for fear of getting his name on some kind of government list. Although engaging in political battles was important to my parents, equipping our family to fight the principalities of the air seemed even more necessary.[50]

Holy Thursday was a big deal in our home and mom made a special dinner with a leg of lamb, to commemorate the Passover. Dad shared the story of how Moses led the Israelites out of their bondage in Egypt and how he parted the Red Sea at God's Command. The ritual meal also included unleavened bread, bitter herbs and wine, just like the first Passover and dad explained the meaning behind each item of food. When given a taste of wine I remarked, "Oh, this tastes awful, but it's good!"

Good Friday was a sad day at our house, as we mourned the death of our Savior. Mom drew a picture of Jesus, which she hung on a wooden cross. She sent all the kids out to collect

---

[48] *Robert Welch* – was an American successful businessman, political activist & author. Following retirement he used his wealth to co-found the *John Birch Society*. (1899–1985)
[49] *John Birch Society* – was founded in 1958 to promote the ideals of Americanism in order to battle an overwhelming wave of communism, which was taking over many countries at the time and having a prominent influence in America. It was named after John Birch, who was the first American killed by Chinese Communists. www.jbs.org
[50] *Ephesians 6:12* – "For our wrestling is not against flesh and blood; but against principalities and power, against the rulers of the world of this darkness, against the spirits of wickedness in the high places."

rocks, which were used to build a tomb. In the evening we buried the cardboard image of Jesus inside. On Holy Saturday, out of reverence for the sacrifice Christ had made for us, we had to play very quietly. Upon rising on Easter morning, we found the entrance stone rolled away and a cardboard image of the risen Christ standing atop of the rocks. These simple little Catholic family traditions, along with a hunt for the Alleluia Egg, are how we first learned our faith.

Learning about the faith also meant being corrected for breaking the rules. Dad was the disciplinarian and he backed up mom's authority. Whenever I disobeyed her she would say, "You just wait till your father gets home." Depending on the severity of my crime, I either got the belt or had to stand in the corner. I knew daddy loved me, but I didn't always make the connection between the punishment and its intended objective. Knowing him to be a nice guy I once asked him, "Daddy, when you send me to the corner, please let me sit down, because I get tired standing." His refusal was swift and stern, but he probably chuckled too.

The Nun's Story,[51] staring Audrey Hepburn, highlighted a struggle our nation was having between trying to be civil in our dealings with other countries and the incredibly evil forces at work in the world. Our country had been involved a cold war ever since Korea, but now the Communists were drifting toward a much more heated confrontation. In order to concretize our strategic military advantage around the world, Alaska and Hawaii became the forty-ninth and fiftieth states respectively.[52]

---

[51] *The Nun's Story* – is a dramatic film released by Warner Bros. in 1959, based upon the 1956 novel, by Kathryn Hulme. The story tells of the life of Sister Luke (Audrey Hepburn), a young Belgian woman who decides to enter a convent and makes many of the sacrifices required of her, but at the outset of World War II, she finds she cannot remain neutral in the face of the abject evil of Hitler's Germany.

[52] *Alaska Statehood Act* – was signed into law by Dwight Eisenhower on July 7, 1958. On January 3, 1959, *Alaska* became our 49th state & on August 21st *Hawaii* became our 50th.

Aviation played a big role in our nation and would loom large in our family as well. Dad became a Flight Instructor based at Echelon Airport and gave flying lessons on the weekends.[53] In addition to flying, dad was periodically invited to parties at the homes of the other pilots. Even mom got into the act. She took flying lessons and even attracted the attention of The Courier Post.[54] One of their articles began, "The airplane settled lightly onto the runway, drifted to a stop and turned toward the parking line. The pilot stopped the engine and returned the waves of the spectators on the ramp. It was not a daring Lindberg arriving at Paris, or the pilot of a giant transcontinental airliner, or a record-breaking jet flight. It was the petite mother of four, greeting her family after finishing another Sunday training session in the family airplane. [Theresa] is not unique... Hundreds of women have joined their husbands in the cockpit of the family airplane, not just as passengers, but as the pilot."[55]

Soon I too would be flying the coop. On September 7, 1959 I left the security of my home to enter Kindergarten at Roosevelt Elementary, but my solo flight would not be without incident. I had been told school would be lots of fun and I was looking forward to my first day in class. While cheerfully ascending the granite stairs of the mammoth school building, I suddenly realized my mother was not coming inside with me. I instantly flashed back to the time when she went away to have my brother Sean. Thinking I was about to be abandoned again, I freaked out! Falling to the pavement sobbing I cried out, "I want to go home. I don't wana go to school." I was absolutely hysterical, until the teacher came out. Without breathing a word Mrs. Adams pulled me away from mom and led me inside. I had never seen so many kids. They were all working in front of easels

---

[53] *Echelon Airport* – closed in 1965 & is now the home of Echelon Mall in Voorhees, NJ.
[54] *The Courier Post* – is a morning daily newspaper that serves South Jersey. It is based in Cherry Hill, NJ and serves most of Burlington, Camden & Gloucester counties.
[55] From the article *Many Husbands, Wives Becoming Flying Teams*, by Edmund C. Glowka, published by the *Courier Post* on August 15, 1959.

and doing something they called finger painting. I was shy and intimidated by the multitude of children, none of whom seemed to be nearly as bashful as me. Mrs. Adams introduced me to a cheerful little red headed boy named Jimmy MacDonald, who showed me what to do. I soon discovered the joys of finger painting and realized I hadn't had this much fun since my terrible twos, when I smeared my own feces all over the bedroom walls. As it turns out my new found friend lived only a few blocks away from our family home. He invited me over to his house that very afternoon to watch The Quick Draw McGraw Show[56] on TV.

After school mom took me over to Jimmy MacDonald's house, so that I could watch cartoons with him and so that she could meet his parents. Mrs. MacDonald was a beautiful, energetic woman, who dearly loved all seven of her redheaded children. Come Saturday, Sarah and Sean tagged along with me to play with the MacDonald kids. There were always plenty of things to do at their house and lots of peanut butter and jelly sandwiches to eat. I often wondered if it was all they ever ate. In any event, it was fun running around outside with a bunch of wild Indians and playing hide-n-seek with them in the house on rainy days.

Just before Christmas, Brennan became the fifth member of our growing family. Shortly after his birth, Doctor Wakefield raised some concerns about his eyes. We all watched with fascination, as our brother's baby blues tracked the physician's finger while he diagnosed the infant. The precious little tyke was born with a lazy eye. After the doctor left the room, Sean and I took turns imitating the doctor's exam and watching Brennan go cross-eyed. Sarah quickly ran off to tell mom what we were doing and got us in lots of

---

[56] *The Quick Draw McGraw Show* – was the 3rd cartoon TV production created by Hanna-Barbera starring an anthropomorphic cartoon horse named Quick Draw McGraw. This cartoon followed their success with The Ruff & Reddy Show & The Huckleberry Hound Show. It debuted in syndication in the fall of 1959 and was sponsored by Kellogg's.

trouble. Although his condition had nothing to do with our little prank, we all thought it did and felt guilty for years.

When I turned six, I saw Toby Tyler.[57] I loved that movie and especially liked the scene where Toby and his puppy love girlfriend joined hands, while standing on the backs of two galloping horses. Included in the story was a great message about being loved even when you think your family doesn't care. I thought of that flick every time I felt unloved, but the film also turned me off to carnivals, fairs and amusement parks. Every time I went to one, I thought of all the sad and lonely people that traveled with the circus.

The best thing about school was recess. Every morning all the kids lined up behind a big tree that was shaped like a "Y" and pretended to be on television. During lunch I played marbles with the other boys on white sand at the edge of the parking lot. Charcoal marks on the knees of my school clothes got me in trouble with mom, but I never understood how white sand made black marks. Every afternoon I rushed home to change my clothes, so that I could go over to Jimmy MacDonald's house and play in his back yard. On rainy days we watched cartoons in his frequently wrecked recreation room. Although Kindergarten was lots of fun, the summer was coming and my world was about to change.

Our split-level home in Pennsauken was becoming too small for the Callahan clan. We had now grown to a household of seven and another child was on the way. Our family needed larger accommodations and the time was fast approaching for me to be registered in the Catholic School. Dad bought

---

[57] *Toby Tyler* – is a film that was released on January 21, 1960 by the Walt Disney Company and was based on the 1880 children's book Ten Weeks with a Circus, by James Otis Kaler. Angered at a stern Uncle, Toby Tyler runs away from his foster home to join the circus, where he soon befriends Mr. Stubbs, a frisky chimpanzee. However, the circus isn't all fun and games. When Harry Tupper, an evil candy vendor, convinces Toby that his Aunt Olive and Uncle Daniel do not love him or want him back. He resigns himself to circus life, but when he finally realizes that Tupper lied to him and that his Aunt and Uncle truly love him, Toby happily returns home again.

an old three-story Victorian house in Merchantville, just two blocks from Saint Peter's Church and its parish school.

Once again my world was about to expand, but I had no say in the matter. Mom and dad said absolutely nothing about the move before it happened. There would be no time for looking back, grieving or even saying goodbye to my friends. The day after kindergarten ended, dad called all of us together and told us to pile into the station wagon. I called out to Jimmy, as we passed by the MacDonald house and tried to say we were moving, but how much can you communicate in a drive-bye? Besides, I didn't even know why we were leaving Pennsauken or where we were going. Jimmy just waved back with a puzzled look on his face.

Chapter 2

Introduction To Parish Life

Prolific families like mine were altering the demographics of America. The resultant population explosion created a dramatic increase in Catholic political power. Senator John F. Kennedy won his party's nomination for president at the Democratic National Convention in California and would soon be leaving Boston to take his place on the world stage. He was not alone in this ascendancy. In 1963 James Tate became the first Roman Catholic Mayor of Philadelphia,[58] but not before New York City,[59] Chicago,[60] Baltimore,[61] Boston[62] and Detroit[63] had all made similar coups d'états.

Like millions of other Americans, who were used to the stability of staying in one location for a lifetime, I too was leaving the familiar and found myself in an utterly unfamiliar environment. In the summer of 1960 our family moved to a new house at 14 Lexington Avenue in the boro of Merchantville, New Jersey. Although the deracination was a complete surprise to me, my parents had been planning this move for over a year. Within the week, they enrolled me in Saint Peter's parish school, where I would soon be given a crash course in Catholic education and the associate social discipline of the parochial school system.

Compared to my previous domicile, the new place felt like a mansion. Attached to the three-story Victorian was a huge

---

[58] *James Tate* – was the first Roman Catholic to serve as Mayor of Philadelphia. Tate was elected in 1963 & defeated District Attorney Arlen Specter in 1967. (1910-1983)
[59] *Vincent Impellitteri* – was a Catholic Mayor of NYC from 1950-1953. (1900-1987)
[60] *Richard Daley* – was a Catholic Mayor of Chicago from 1955-1976 & is considered the "last of the big city bosses." He played a major role in getting JFK elected. (1902-1976)
[61] *Joseph Grady* – was a Catholic Mayor of Baltimore from 1959-1962. (1917-2002)
[62] *John Collins* – was a Catholic Mayor of Boston, from 1960-1968. (1919-1995)
[63] *Jerome Cavanagh* – was a Catholic Mayor of Detroit, Michigan from 1962-1970. He was seen as the next JFK, until his reputation was doomed by the 1967 riots. (1928-1979)

wrap-around porch and the big house sat to one side of an oversized lot in a quiet peaceful neighborhood. In the center of the yard, stood a huge tree with massive overreaching branches. The big Elm covered half the yard and shaded both house and yard like a big umbrella. I couldn't wait to climb it.

At the end of our street was a set of railroad tracks. Not only did they beckon me like a pied piper, but they stretched out east and west all the way to the horizon. There were dozens of things to do and see along the way. I put pennies on the track and waited for the trains to come by and flatten them into the size of quarters. I balanced myself on the rails like I was walking on a tight rope. I could explore for miles and still find my way back home with the aid of twin steel ribbons to guide me home. Getting home in time for dinner was never a problem, because every night at five o'clock, the Niagara Fire Company blew an old air raid siren and mom always had dinner ready for us by five-thirty. However, if I ever was late for dinner, I had to go straight to bed without any supper.

Almost everything was within easy walking distance of home. On sunny Sunday mornings our family strolled together on our way to Mass. On weekdays I made my way to school on foot and as soon as school let out I ran home to play. Occasionally I walked down to Kay's Pharmacy with some of my classmates, where we split ice cream sodas and bought baseball cards. If ever I wanted to work on a construction project, dad would drive the car down to J. Collins & Son's hardware store. Workers in the yard loaded the lumber into the back of our station wagon and we looked for nails in steel bins organized by type and size. Gathering them up in handfuls we weighed them out and stuffed them into brown paper bags and paid for them by the pound.

Much as I missed exploring the swamp with my friends back in Pennsauken, Merchantville was looking like a pretty cool town. Mom and dad seemed to know lots of people at Church and introduced us to several of them every week. The Nave[64] and the Sanctuary[65] of the Church were shrouded in absolute silence, but as soon as Mass was over we gathered together in the basement. The adults stood around talking and drinking coffee, while the kids ate donuts and played tag with the other children. We made lots of friends there and were often surprised to discover that many of them lived in our neighborhood, so we invited them over to play with us.

Unlike the services of other religions, the focus of a Catholic Mass had precious little to do with fellowship and everything to do with the worship of God. The Sacrifice of the Mass was quiet, reverent and mysterious. Once the Eucharistic Celebration began, the priest averted his eyes away from parishioners and focused all of his attention on the presence of Jesus in the tabernacle. Clothed in majestic robes, the priest led us in a solemn procession toward the worship of our Sovereign King.

Don't get me wrong, there was plenty of fellowship; it just didn't take place during the same time that was set aside for worship. Our parish[66] was like a spiritual family traveling together in a caravan through a strange land. We were being tested along the way, as we make our way back home to heaven. The kids we met at Church soon became our classmates and playmates. The ladies my mother saw at Church on Sunday were the same ones she ran into at the

---

[64] *The Nave* – in Roman Catholic Churches, is the central approach to the high altar, or the main body of the church. In Latin *navis* means ship and refers to the keel shape of the vaulted ceiling. Like Noah's Ark, the Catholic Church is the Ark of Salvation.
[65] *The Sanctuary* – is the most sacred area of a Catholic Church. The area encompasses within it the tabernacle and the altar. Sanctuary means a place of safety.
[66] *Parish* – the Catholic Church organizes the faithful inside geographical boundaries called parishes, several of which are placed within each diocese. A bishop is in charge of the diocese and a pastor has authority over his parish. Most parishes include a church, an elementary school, a rectory for the priests and a convent for the sisters who teach in the school. The word parish actually means, "An earthly life as a temporary abode."

Acme.[67] Men who shared donuts with my father had families of their own. These men did business with dad and walked door-to-door with him during political campaigns. Owing partly to its geography, Parish life was community!

The Gague family was one group of kids that we met. Robert, Alanna and Elliot lived directly behind our house in back of a very tall hedge. They became our most frequent guests, after dad bought us a four-foot deep above ground pool. Our two families spent countless hours swimming together and grew very close. So close in fact that one day Alanna asked me to kiss her. I liked her very much and was excited about her proposal, but I was also still very young and embarrassed, so we kissed under water. I treasured her innocent and intimate affirmation of our friendship.

Patriotism was a hallmark of our family. On the Fourth of July we all celebrated our independence from Great Britain. All year long a large American flag flew from one of the white columns on our front porch, but on Independence Day I was allowed to carry the big flag in our own private parade. The entire family marched up and down the sidewalk in lock step, with each kid waving little American flags. After the march, mom gave us red, white and blue crepe paper, which we used to decorate our bicycles. Dad gave us clothespins so we could attach baseball cards to the bikes and make them sound like they had engines. As soon as they were all decorated we took them up to Maple Avenue. The Mayor of Merchantville drove by in a convertible leading the Fourth of July parade. Then the fire engines passed by with their red lights flashing and the sirens screaming. Next were the Boy Scouts, Girl Scouts and Veteran Soldiers. Finally we all followed the parade on our bikes and each bike was judged by the Mayor, based on creativity and a patriotic theme.

---

[67] *Acme Markets* – is a supermarket chain owned by Eden Prairie. It was founded in 1891 by Samuel Robinson & Robert Crawford in South Philadelphia & now operates about 130 supermarkets, in Delaware, Maryland, New Jersey & Pennsylvania under the name Acme.

When we returned home, Sean reenacted the Famous Ride of Paul Revere,[68] by saddling up on his make-believe mighty steed. In reality, the horse was mom's kitchen broom and a piece of close line rope substituted for the reins. Sean galloped up and down the sidewalk shouting, "The British are coming. The British are coming." and I stood atop the railing of our front porch, swinging a kerosene lantern back and forth, to signal my compatriots that the British were on their way.

Just because the sun went down did not mean the festivities were over. We all ran around the yard with sparklers, while dad set off penny firecrackers and even let some of us throw a few, but we were strictly instructed not to touch any duds until the following morning. Our neighbors were setting off their own firecrackers and lighting Roman candles, but dad was not about to be out-done. Bracketing the front porch steps were a pair of brick walls and dad set up a Big-Bang Cannon[69] on the top of one of them. When he fired it the whole neighborhood shook. So many people were setting off big firecrackers that it seemed like the Revolutionary War itself was starting all over again. Competitive to the end, dad was fully prepared to best his neighbors. He pulled out a brown paper bag filled with T-bombs,[70] which were almost as loud as the cannon. We all banged pots and pans together as midnight approached. The finally reached a crescendo,

---

[68] *Paul Revere* – was a silversmith & a patriot in the American Revolution. He is celebrated for his role as the messenger who alerted the colonists that the British were coming prior to the battle of Lexington & Concord. Henry Wadsworth Longfellow later dramatized his "midnight ride" in the poem *Paul Revere's Ride* and he has become a legend in American history. Revere was a prosperous & prominent Bostonian craftsman, who helped organize an intelligence & alarm system to keep watch over the British military. (1735-1818)
[69] *Big-Bang Cannon* – is an early 20th century American toy that is still manufactured today. Numerous consumer fireworks injuries prompted a physics professor at Lehigh University in Bethlehem, PA, to patent a "Gas Gun" in 1907. The manufacturing of carbide cannons started in 1912. The cannon uses calcium carbide, which mixes with water in the chamber of the cannon, producing acetylene gas. A few seconds after the gas forms, a spark is ignited, which results in a very loud "bang" or "boom".
[70] *T-bombs* – are "T" shaped pyrotechnics with the fuse coming out of the side of the firecracker & having the firepower equivalent of an 8th of a stick of dynamite.

when dad emptied his .45 caliber pistol into the ground. Then with a few exceptions, the neighborhood fell silent.

The neighbors did not begrudge us the win. We all celebrated our freedom together and unlike today, no one called the cops. Other than a couple of sparkler burns, which only served to reinforce the credibility of our parent's cautionary warnings, no one was ever seriously hurt. The next day started out almost dull in comparison, except for breaking the dud penny firecrackers in half and lighting what we called fizzers.

Since our garage was more of a workshop for projects than a shelter for cars, we kept our station wagon in the driveway. Imitating my father, I climbed into the car and pretended to drive. I began pushing and pulling every button and switch in sight, but when I pulled on the column shifter, the automatic transmission dropped into neutral. The car started rolling backwards and was headed for the street. Dad sprang from his chair on the front porch and sprinted across the yard. Throwing open the driver's side door he attempted to muscle the car to a stop, but it had way too much momentum. Jumping into the front seat, he pushed me out of the way and jammed the lever back into park. The car made a horrible grinding sound, before coming to a rocking stop. Once dad saw that I was all right he apologized for scaring me, but then scolded me for messing with his car. While never physically damaging, his discipline was often fierce, but as soon as the danger was past or the lesson concluded, all was forgotten and he made sure I knew that he loved me.

One evening dad brought home a baseball glove, to teach me how to catch. The beautiful leather pitching glove was way too big for my small hand, but I learned how to catch with it anyway. Little did I realize that I would still be using the same glove in high school. Dad started me out with a softball, but within a couple of weeks I graduated to a hard one. Every day after school let out I played an abbreviated form of baseball in the side yard with Sarah and Sean. We used just about anything for bases; pie plates, paper plates, scraps of wood or even our jackets. Soon baselines were worn into the grass and a there was a big puddle of water where the pitcher stood. One Saturday morning, dad dug up some sandy clay soil from behind the garage. He brought the dirt over to our baseball diamond in a wheelbarrow and built up our pitcher's mound, so that the spot wouldn't fill up with water when it rained.

Ever since my grandfather died, dad found it necessary to spend more and more time working at Callahan Machine Company. He left the house before dawn and returned home long after we were all asleep. In addition to putting in a full day in the shop running machines, he and his partners went out to a local sandwich shop to discuss the direction of the business and make decisions. The rest of his evening was devoted to paperwork. Dad's primary responsibility at Callahan Machine Company was to manage the men in the machine shop. Uncle Ray[71] took care of sales. Uncle Frank[72] did the accounting. And Uncle Leon[73] took care of everything else. My father wasn't home very much during the week and when he was home, he seemed exhausted. All he wanted to do was to read the Courier Post, watch the evening news and zone out. Our living room was off limits and became the man cave where my father hid out.

The rest of our family hung out in what was called the Breakfast room. I'm not exactly sure what a breakfast room is supposed to be or why you would need one if you already had a dining room, but that's what the realtor told us when

---

[71] *Uncle Ray* – was my dad's older brother & a partner in *Callahan Machine Co.* He was also my Godfather and the salesman for the company.

[72] *Uncle Frank* – was a title of endearment given to Francis Smith. Although not really my uncle, he was a friend my Uncle Ray met while going to college at Villanova. He was brought in as a partner to handle the accounting for *Callahan Machine Co.*

[73] *Uncle Leon* – married dad's older sister Mary, which is how he became a partner in *Callahan Machine Co.* He took care of things like taxes, healthcare benefits, machine purchases, legal matters & developed a profit sharing plan for the workers in the company.

mom and dad bought the place. We may have been better off than some, but for an Irish Catholic clan only a few generations removed from the mother country, it sounded a bit too hoity-toity for us so we quickly renamed it the family room. It contained a brand new Console Color TV and every Sunday evening, as soon as we got into our pajamas, we were allowed to watch The Wonderful World of Disney.[74]

Dad paneled his den and kept the old black and white TV along with its rabbit ears, so that he could watch the news. He painted the ceiling with a bright white sand textured paint, which accented the dark wooden beams in his regal little retreat. From the comfort and solitude of his lair, the patriarch of our family watched Kennedy get the Presidential nod at the DNC[75] and saw Nixon get upstaged by *Mister Conservative*, at the RNC.[76] He also kept an eye on Castro and tried to understand what was behind the black protests in the South. As an avid boxing fan, he also developed a keen interest in a young pugilist named Cassius Clay.[77] He first noticed the man, who would later change his name to Mohammed Ali, while observing the Olympics on ABC's

---

[74] *The Wonderful World of Disney* – premiered on ABC on October 27, 1954 under the name Disneyland. The same basic show has since appeared on several networks under a variety of titles & ended in 2008. The show is the second longest showing prime time program on American television, behind its rival, the Hallmark Hall of Fame.

[75] *DNC* – the 1960 Democratic National Convention was held in Los Angeles, California delivering the Kennedy-Johnson ticket.

[76] *RNC* – the 1960 Republican National Convention was held in Chicago, Illinois, at the International Amphitheatre. Vice President Richard M. Nixon of California was nominated for President & former Senator Henry Cabot Lodge, Jr. of Massachusetts for Vice President. The highlight of the convention was a speech by Senator Barry Goldwater of Arizona. Known as "Mr. Conservative" he had removed himself from the race, but then called on the Conservatives to take back their party, from the so-called moderates.

[77] *Muhammad Ali* – was born Cassius Marcellus Clay Jr. & is a retired American boxer & World Heavyweight Champion, who is widely considered one of the greatest heavyweight championship boxers of all time. As an amateur, he won a gold medal in the light heavyweight division at the 1960 Summer Olympics in Rome. After turning professional, he went on to become the 1st boxer to win the heavyweight championship 3 times. Ali changed his name after joining the Nation of Islam in 1964, subsequently converting to Sunni Islam in 1975. In 1967, Ali refused to be inducted into the U.S. military, based on his religious beliefs & opposition to the Vietnam War. He was arrested & found guilty on draft evasion charges, stripped of his boxing title & his boxing license was suspended. He was not imprisoned, but didn't fight again for nearly 4 years while his appeal worked its way up to the U.S. Supreme Court, where it was successful. (1942-Present)

Wide World of Sports.[78] This gifted, cocky, playful and entertaining gladiator held dad's interest throughout the young man's career.

While dad had his own interests, he never forgot the needs of his children. Like a cowboy from the great state of Texas, dad was always trying to do things bigger and better than anyone else. He built us a sandbox that held six tons of sand and bought me a two foot long skateboard called "Big Daddy." Although he meant well, the board was so big I was embarrassed to use it around my friends and never did developed even a modicum of competence in the sport.

The lazy days of summer were fun and relaxing, but they came to an abrupt end on September 5, 1960 when I entered the first grade at Saint Pete's parish school. Sister Mary Catherine became my teacher and Sister Mary Francis was the Mother Superior and Principal of our grade school. They were both consecrated virgins who belonged to the order of the Franciscan Sisters of Allegany, New York. In my particular classroom there were eighty children and the desks were so tightly crammed into the relatively small classroom that whenever we needed to get in or out of our seats, the entire class had to stand up one row at a time and shuffle the desks to create an aisle. Sister wasted no time in organizing us into a crack military regiment. She taught us the rules and let us know how strictly those rubrics would be enforced. She began by teaching directly from the Baltimore Catechism.[79]

---

[78] *ABC's Wide World of Sports* - is a sports anthology series on American TV that ran from 1961-1998 & was originally hosted by Jim McKay.

[79] *Baltimore Catechism* – was a Catechism of Christian Doctrine, Prepared & Enjoined by Order of the 3rd Council of Baltimore & was the standard Catholic school text in the U.S. from 1885 to the late 1960s. It was the 1st such catechism written for Catholics in North America, replacing a translation of Saint Bellarmine's Small Catechism. It remained in use in nearly all Catholic schools until many moved away from catechism-based education, though it is still used up to this day in some. These questions & answers are taken from where we began our education, Lesson #1, "The Purpose of Man's Existence"

Who made the world?
God made the world.

Who is God?
God is the Creator of heaven and earth, and of all things.

What is man?
Man is a creature composed of body and soul, and made in the image and likeness of God.

Why did God make you?
God made me to know Him, to love Him, and to serve Him in this world, and to be happy with Him forever in heaven.

What must we do to save our souls?
To save our souls, we must worship God by faith, hope, and charity; that is, we must believe in Him, hope in Him, and love Him with all our heart.

How shall we know the things, which we are to believe?
We shall know the things, which we are to believe from the Catholic Church, through which God speaks to us.

Our education was to come from God Himself, by way of the Baltimore Catechism. As Sister Mary Catherine explained the need for salvation, we learned that there were only two possibilities: heaven or hell. Since God was all-powerful it would be up to Him whether we would be going to a place of eternal bliss or one of horrible torture. Furthermore, since God was communicating to us through the Catholic Church and by way of inference through Sister, we had better obey her or we would be risking eternal misery. I also instinctively knew that if I did not behave in school, there would be hell to pay when dad arrived home at night. There was no need for Sister to back up her words with harsh treatment. The Catholic Church had a hierarchy and it included those in religious orders. If there were any problems Mother Superior would stand behind sister and beyond that, God Himself would deal with me when I died. The good sister's authority had been clearly established and discipline in a class of eighty children would not be a problem.

Once the religion lesson was completed, I began learning my letters and numbers. Soon I would be taught from Fun With Dick And Jane.[80] I enjoyed learning and was carrying a "B" average, but the book seemed simplistic to me and the repetition was boring. I began to talk in class. Just as absolute silence was required in Church, it was also compulsory in the classroom. It was a reasonable rule in light of the class size, but no matter how hard I tried, I couldn't keep my mouth shut. Soon I was being sent to the principal's office on a daily basis. First I received a strong verbal warning, then I was threatened with a spanking, and finally I was actually spanked. Sometimes I stopped talking for a while, but the next thing I knew I was back in Mother Superior's office again. Mother Mary Francis was a big woman and I was just a small skinny kid, so she was quite intimidating. I felt guilty for talking and truly intended to stop my bad behavior, but every time boredom set in, I made comments and asked questions of my classmates. Actually my biggest problem wasn't the dicipline, it was cutting through the "B" class on my way to the office.

Our classrooms were split up between those whom the nuns considered smart enough to go on to college and those destined for the trades. The smart kids were put in the "A" class and the rest were put in the "B". Since the 1st & 2nd grades were housed in the old section of the building and there were no hallways leading to the newer part of the

---

[80] *Dick and Jane* – were the main characters in popular basal readers written by William S. Gray & Zerna Sharp & published by Scott Foresman, that were used to teach children to read from the 1930-1970s in the US. Gray's vision was to tie "subject area" books in health, science, social studies, etc with the vocabulary mastered in the basic readers, thus vastly improving readability in these same areas. The books relied on whole language theories (or "whole word reading") & repetition, using phrases like, "Oh, see. Oh, see Jane. Funny, funny Jane," but they didn't totally ignore phonics. Although not the primary focus, phonetic analysis was part of each reading lesson.

school, I had to ask permission of the "B" class teacher, to pass through a big heavy fire door, at the back of her class. The teacher became quite annoyed with me interrupting her lessons day after day and would roll her eyes to let me know it. The kids in the "B" class, on the other hand, were all too happy for the break in the action and loved the chance to ridicule one of the so-called smart kids. I would just about make it through the social gauntlet, when I would have to struggle to slide the big fire door open. The thick metal door was much too heavy for a skinny little first grader and the whole class jeered me, as I grunted and groaned my way through the task. After making it through to the office, I had to return and go through the entire humiliation all over again.

Dad didn't get to spend much time with his father when he was a kid, so he wanted something better for his own children. Therefore even though he spent a lot of time at work during the week, he made it a point to take Saturdays off and spend time with us. We all pitched in to straighten up the workshop, or pick up sticks while he mowed the lawn. My father had some kind of vision about what the garage was supposed to look like. Although he didn't always share the vision with us, each weekend the place got cleaner and more organized. Despite being task oriented, he spent lots of time with us and gradually brought his plan to fruition.

On rainy days we stayed indoors and watched television programs like: The Andy Griffith Show,[81] Bugs Bunny[82] and

---

[81] *Andy Griffith Show* – was a 1960 CBS sitcom, staring Andy Griffith who played a widowed sheriff in the fictional small town of Mayberry, NC. His inept but well-meaning deputy, his aunt, temperamental girlfriends & a young son complicated his life. The actors enjoyed stellar careers & Ron Howard went on to become an accomplished director.

[82] *Bugs Bunny* – was a fictional rabbit that appears in the Looney Tunes & Merrie Melodies series of animated films produced by Jublee Productions, which became Warner Brothers Cartoons in 1945 & Bugs is now its cartoon mascot. The mischievous rabbit starred in 163 shorts in the Golden Age of American animation. Tex Avery first created him in 1940 & Robert McKimson created the definitive character design. His signature voice has a Flatbush accent, which is an equal blend of the Bronx & Brooklyn, NY dialects. His catchphrase is a casual "Eh...what's up, doc?" usually said while chewing a carrot & other popular phrases "Of course you realize, this means war" & "Ain't I a stinker?".

The Flintstones.[83] We probably would have watched cartoons non-stop every day of the week, were it not for our mother chasing us out of the house on sunny days. Whenever we were shooed out of the house, nature became our entertainment as well as our teacher.

Our yard was full of red-breasted robins looking for food and I spent quite a bit of time alone watching them with interest to see how they survived. The birds would often cock their heads to one side and seemed to be listening for worms. Whenever they found one, they would poke their beak into the ground and pull out a squirming little worm and fly away. Blue jays were fast and beautifully colored, but I didn't like these mean spirited birds, because they also pecked into the pale blue eggs of baby robins and ate them. So I felt a sense of justice whenever I saw several robins ganging up on the jays, to chase them away from their nests. The lush branches of the elm tree in the center of our yard covered everything like a big green umbrella. The tree was so large it blotted out the sun and along with a small cedar tree in the corner of the yard, it became a habitat for hundreds of birds. Squirrels were the only other wildlife in the area, but there were plenty of them. I would often lie down on our redwood picnic table and watch them scamper around for hours. They were fun to watch, as they chased each other around and took incredible risks jumping from one branch to the other. These agile creatures made trapeze artists look like amateurs. Although nature had much to teach me, some of her lessons were painful. Behind our garage was an old asparagus patch. Dad had no use for the garden and mowed it down. However the shoots dried out and became as stiff as punji sticks.[84] One day I was running

---

[83] *The Flintstones* – was a 1960 ABC animated TV sitcom produced by Hanna-Barbera. The cartoon series is about a working class Stone Age man's life with his family & his next-door neighbor & best friend. This prehistoric Honeymooners popularity, rested on its juxtaposition of modern-day concerns in a Stone Age setting.
[84] *Punji Sticks* – are a type of booby-trapped stake. It is a simple spike, made out of wood or bamboo & generally placed upright in the ground. They are usually deployed in substantial

around in my bare feet and one of the spikes sliced right through my foot!

Now that I was in school, I no longer sat with my family during Mass on Sundays. Instead I joined my classmates in the lower Church. A wooden altar was erected on the stage of our basement auditorium, complete with a portable altar rail. Folding wooden chairs were neatly arranged in rows, with a wide aisle down the center, separating the boys from the girls. There were also crosswalks in between each of the grades. The first grade class made up the front block while the tall eighth graders sat in the back. There was no such thing as a Children's Mass, like some renegade parishes have today. The Latin Liturgy was identical to the one upstairs, with a singular exception. The priest's homily was geared to topics better suited for the children. Father often taught us about obedience to our parents and teachers, as well as how to get along with our brothers and sisters. All the nuns had crickets,[85] which they used to alert us when it was time to sit, stand or kneel. Their instructions were strictly enforced, and we learned to respond to the different parts of the Mass in lock step.

When the Mass concluded, we folded our chairs and carried them to the back of the room, where the older boys stacked them against the wall. Then we were free to talk with our friends and wait for our parents. While the big kids set up tables and brought out coffee urns, cheerful Knights of Columbus brought in trays of donuts from a local bakery. Everyone knew their job and did it to the best of their ability. No one shouted orders, it all just seemed to work and everyone had a good time.

---

numbers & were often found in the bottom of holes in Vietnam. The Viet Cong smeared the tips with human feces, causing many of our soldiers to have infected wounds.
[85] Cricket – is a small metal toy with a flat metal spring that snaps back & forth with a clicking, cricket-like noise when pressed. The religious sisters used them as a signal, to train children when to sit, stand & kneel in Church.

After donuts, we headed home and changed out of our Sunday clothes, so that we could all go out and play. Dad retired to his newly paneled den to watch Meet The Press[86] while mom started getting lunch ready. Many men watched the American Football League[87] on Sunday afternoons, but my father wanted to increase his knowledge and understanding of world events. So instead of watching football, he watched the first televised presidential debate.[88] He also learned of Dr. King's bogus arrest for a traffic ticket in Atlanta and acquired the back-story on how Bobby Kennedy[89] had intervened with the Governor of Georgia to get King released.[90] The times they were a changing and dad felt it was his civic duty to stay informed.

When I returned to school on Monday, I learned that the parents, teachers and priests were not the only people with authority. Safeties were upperclassmen that looked after the younger kids on their way to and from school. These junior cops wore wide yellow belts with sashes and silver badges. Although sometimes annoyed with their bossy style, my classmates and I also admired them and looked forward to the day when we could hold the same status and wear the same uniform.

---

[86] *Meet the Press* – is a weekly TV news & interview program produced by NBC. It is the longest-running show in worldwide broadcasting history, having made its debut in 1947.
[87] *American Football League* – on ABC was a TV program that broadcast professional football games of the then fledging American Football League. ABC broadcast AFL games from the leagues very first season in 1960 until 1964, when NBC took over as the league's primary network television broadcaster.
[88] *Presidential Debates* – in 1960, an estimated 80 million viewers watched the 1st of 4 debates. Most people who watched the debate on TV believed Kennedy had won while radio listeners believed Nixon did. This was the 1st time TV was used as a medium in a presidential race & political observers believed that Kennedy won the debate on style, while Nixon prevailed on issues, but TV had changed the paradigm.
[89] *Robert Kennedy* – was the younger brother of President John F. Kennedy. Bobby served as his brother's presidential adviser & was appointed U.S. Attorney General. (1925–1968)
[90] *Bogus Traffic Ticket* – on 10/25/60 Dr. Martin Luther King was sent to Reidsville State Prison in Georgia for a parole violation stemming from his 5/4/60 arrest for driving without a license. On 10/26/60 Robert Kennedy called Georgia Governor Ernest Vandiver seeking King's release from Prison. http://www.ourgeorgiahistory.com/ogh/Martin_Luther_King

Each evening mom made me a sandwich for lunch the next day and gave me money to buy milk. At school we ate lunch in the cafeteria, which was located in the basement and then went outside for recess, where I was getting to know the other kids in my class. The schoolyard, which doubled as a parking lot for Mass on Sundays, provided plenty of space for games like my favorite *Jail Break*. In my dad's day, he called it *Cops and Robbers*; since half the players were cops and the other half were robbers. Once a cop tagged a robber he was brought back to the jail, which in our case was the steps that led up to the side door of the school. All prisoners had to remain in jail with at least one hand touching the brick railing, until another robber came running past and tagged your hand. Then all of us would execute our escape and run away from the cops. Jail Break was a high-speed game of tag that often involved dangerous velocities and occasionally even bloody consequences. In one such incident, I was running away from Andy Mallo at break-neck speed, when he aggressively slapped my back with both of his hands. I flew forward from the impact and landed head first on the macadam. Blood gushed out of my forehead and I was immediately walked over to the nurse's office. To this day I still have a T-shaped scar on my forehead, but it never stopped me from enjoying this lightning fast game.

Pitching baseball cards didn't take the same level of energy, but it was no less competitive. Boys took baseball cards and flung them up against the back wall of the school, to see which card could land the closest to the building. The loser had to give both cards to the winner. Everyone tried to use up the cards with pictures of the lesser-known players while attempting to get really valuable cards like Mickey Mantle[91]

---

[91] *Mickey Mantle* – was a legendary baseball player, who played his entire 18-year major-league career with the Yankees, winning 3 MVP titles & playing in 16 All-Star games. He helped win 12 pennants, 7 World Series & still holds the record of 18 home runs in a World Series. Mantle is regarded as the greatest switch hitter of all time, one of the greatest players in baseball history & was elected into the Baseball Hall of Fame. (1931-1995)

or Babe Ruth.[92] I had no cards of my own, but purchased some down at Kay's Drug Store in town. The sealed packs included random cards of baseball players, so you never knew which ones you were going to get, but there was always a stick of bubble gum in the pack, so I never felt like I got ripped off. Soon I had my own baseball cards and was in on the game, acquiring tossing skills and building up a halfway decent collection.

The girls spent their recess a little bit differently than the boys. They sang rhymes while clapping their hands together and jumped rope to similar cadenced tunes. They looked so sweet and innocent in their yellow blouses and green jumpers. Some of the younger girls jumped rope silently by themselves, while others were being taught by the older girls. The more experienced girls had extremely complicated hand-clapping routines and often used two ropes for jumping, which was a practice they called Double Dutch.

Even though I had no interest in joining them, I admired their skills, which seemed so much more complicated than what the boys were doing. Most of the girls seemed to get along with each other, but every once in a while I noticed one that was being left out. Since I couldn't get in trouble for talking outside during recess, I began talking with Charlene Russo, who was one of the prettiest little wallflowers. I don't remember what we talked about, but we must have achieved some level of intimacy, because one afternoon I came home and announced, "Mommy, there's a girl in my room named Charlene and I like her so much that every time I see her in the school yard, I take her in back of a big tree and what I do is a secret that I'll never tell anybody." It was all very

---

[92] *Babe Ruth* – was a legendary baseball player from 1914–1935. George Herman Ruth, Jr., originally broke into the majors with the Boston Red Sox as a pitcher, but was sold to the Yankees in 1919, where he converted to a right fielder & became one of the league's most prolific hitters. "The Sultan of Swat" was a mainstay in the Yankees' lineup & won 7 pennants & 4 World Series titles. After a short stint with the Boston Braves in 1935, "The Bambino" retired in 1936 & was elected to the Baseball Hall of Fame. (1895-1948)

innocent and a precious moment. Not counting the one next door; she was the first girl I kissed.

Recess was run at full throttle. It was loud, it was rough, it was playful and it could even be romantic, but when the deafening fire bell rang, we had to stop what we were doing and gather on the white painted lines. Each grade had one line for the boys and another for the girls. We organized ourselves according to height and when we were completely silent, our teachers led us back into the classroom. There was an appointed time for everything under the heavens.[93] The time for fun was over and it was time to get back to the serious business of learning.

Each day held out something new, while still keeping a certain routine about it. There was even a comfort in discipline and in knowing what was expected of me, but there was also an excitement about learning new things. Religion and Mathematics were my favorite subjects and for some of the same reasons. Mathematics taught me about structure and limits while religion opened my mind and heart to the wisdom of our ancient religion and the myriad forms of God's love. I couldn't wait to learn more about God and was proud to belong to His Church.

Despite frequent trips to the principal's office, I generally liked Sister Mary Catherine and enjoyed most of my subjects. The only thing that aggravated me was when a punishment didn't fit the crime, or when my intentions were misinterpreted. One day after running the gauntlet of the "B" class, I walked down the long hallway and sheepishly entered the Principal's office. Mother Mary Francis was having a discussion with the pastor. The two of them were

---

[93] *Ecclesiastes 3:1-5* – "All things have their season, and in their times all things pass under heaven. A time to be born and a time to die. A time to plant, and a time to pluck up that which is planted. A time to kill, and a time to heal. A time to destroy, and a time to build. A time to weep, and a time to laugh. A time to mourn, and a time to dance. A time to scatter stones, and a time to gather. A time to embrace, and a time to be far from embraces"

involved in a deep conversation of some import, but they stopped talking when I entered the room. Monsignor greeted me and after a short pause Mother Superior asked why I had come. When I told her I was talking in class, she rolled her eyes and groaned, "Again?" After a quick glance toward Monsignor, her eyes narrowed and she told me to drop my pants. Father turned his head and looked out the window. "Your underwear too" she commanded. I turned beet red, as I dropped my drawers to receive six swats from her wooden ruler. I quickly retrieved my pants and returned to the classroom. On my way out the door, father looked up at me with a strange combination of tender compassion and white knuckled restraint in his eyes.

If Mother Mary Francis was trying to demonstrate how well she was handling discipline in the school, she made a serious miscalculation. Judging from the look on Monsignor's face, he was angry and unimpressed. I'm sure that one incident did not make up Monsignor's mind, but the mercenary style of the Franciscan Sisters would soon be replaced by the warm hearted Religious Teachers Filippini.[94]

Over the top corrections were rare, but they did happen. Much more common were misunderstandings about motive. One cold rainy morning, the sky was filled with unusually dark swollen clouds and it had been pouring since before breakfast. In art class we were each given coloring books and instructed to stay within the lines. When I opened my workbook, I turned to a picture of an airplane. Since it was raining out, I colored the clouds black. Upon observing the ebony clouds, Sister asked me why I had chosen black for

---

[94] *Religious Teachers Filippini* – are a teaching order of sisters founded by Lucy Filippini & Cardinal Mark Anthony Barbarigo. In 1692 they had a vision to fulfill, which included a generous, ardent & profound mission of faith & charity. At first they established schools of Christian Doctrine for girls in Italy that were intended to promote the dignity of womanhood & to help influence a healthy family life. St. Lucy Filippini also ministered to the poor & the sick, conducted retreats & guided women who were preparing for marriage. In more recent years the Catholic teaching order chose to blend a contemplative life of prayer with a life of ministry educating both boys and girls.

the clouds. Although I attempted to tell her my reason, she didn't buy the explanation. Thinking I was just being a wise guy, she made me stand in the corner.

It seems to go with the territory, that when Catholics meet other Catholics or alumni get together, they often tell war stories about their experiences in Catholic Schools. It's one of the things that ironically bind us together, even if we're total strangers. However, that same competitiveness that fueled our games in the schoolyard also animates our conversations. Each time a tale is revisited; there exists an intense pressure to raise the ante. It usually starts out something like this, "Oh that ain't nothin. One time Sister Gwendolyn…" With the increased wattage, which is often more heat than light, the myth eventually overrides the truth. Veterans of parochial schools all recognize these exaggerations and they do no real harm. The recycled stories actually serve to heal the few genuine wounds we actually did receive. Unfortunately, this phenomenon also provides social and legal cover for those who actually did abuse students and perpetuates the commonly held misconceptions non-Catholics have about what goes on in Catholic schools, since they have no idea that these stories are being exaggerated. Most Catholic school children experienced some kind of injustice along the way, but for the most part, the teachers in the Catholic school system were good, holy men and women. Much of what I experienced was good, even if some very bad things did happen to me and the incidents of unfairness were all a part of the package. Mother Superior apparently used me to play parish politics, but Sister Mary Catherine was a wonderful teacher. She cared deeply about her students and had she not had to deal with eighty of us, she may have seen clear to understand my innocent motives, but life is messy like that sometimes.

The leaves were falling and all the conversation at school was about Halloween. Many of the kids talked of dressing up in scary costumes and going door to door with grocery bags to collect free candy. As soon as I got home I told Sarah and Sean about the holiday. We asked mom and dad if we could join in on the festivities, but when they looked at each other a strange look came over their faces. Mom said she would let us dress up as saints, but not as pirates or anything scary. She even offered to make our costumes, but she said that as Catholics we should never celebrate the devil or bad people like pirates. Dad added that we were not allowed to go out on mischief night. He said that bad kids sometimes soaped up windows and did mean things to people who had not given them candy last year. He explained that *Trick-or-Treat* meant, give me a treat or I will trick you and that since we were Catholics, we could not to be nasty to people. Mom and dad told us a story of how St. Francis used to go up to homes and beg for food and money, so he could give it to the poor people who needed it. Dad said that in the old days these gifts were called alms. So instead of saying, "Trick-or-Treat", we were required to say, "Alms for the poor".

Mr. and Mrs. Douglas lived next door and spent their retirement years landscaping. The leaves from our giant elm tree were now distributed all over their fine trimmed lawn. It must have been pretty frustrating for them, to watch the cold autumn winds cover the green grass with the yellow and brown clutter from our gigantic elm and the commingled mess coming from the maple, beech, holly, oak and apple trees of our less finicky neighbors. Fall made the old couple cranky, but others in the neighborhood found it a time of great joy and I would soon learn why.

Dad brought home several large fan rakes and our entire family was put to work raking up the leaves. It required a great deal of labor and seemed a bit futile to me, since the autumn winds often blew the leaves back, as soon as we raked them into piles. So I asked my father why we did it. He explained that the rain and snow matt down the leaves over the winter months and they cut out the sunlight and kill the grass. All that made sense, but it seemed as if there was more to it than that. Everyone on our street came out to join in on the project. Dad had us amass one great big pile in the side yard and then picked each one of us up to throw us into it. We lined up to go again and again. The laughter and excitement continued, until dad's arms got tired. Eagerly wanting to continue, we brought out a chair and took turns jumping into the fluffy pile by ourselves and soon other kids came over to join us. When the novelty wore off we got back to the work at hand.

Sweeping the piles onto large canvas tarps, we pulled the heavy loads to the curb where they were set on fire. Watching any fire can be fascinating, but the smoke gave off a distinct aroma that somehow seemed to fit the brisk temperatures and celebratory mood. Mom brought out a jug of hot cider and her snack provided a break in the action. We savored the moment, inhaled the incense and shared a tasty drink with our friends, as we watched the flames leap skyward. All up and down the street there were mountains of brown leaves glowing orange fires and billowing gray smoke. In this surreal aerial paradise, we lunged headlong into an aerobatic fantasy. One by one, we spread our arms out like wings and flew through the clouds. We were no longer children; we were fighter pilots flying in formation. Tipping our wings and executing serpentine maneuvers, we soared high and low, swooping in gentle banks that followed each WWI ace to his inevitable demise. When the fliers returned to base, the flames had been reduced to embers and we gathered by our campfires in quiet contemplation. Placing single leaves on stacks of paper-thin coals, we watched them burst into momentary flares before curling up into a black and gray ash. When the fire died down to a glowing orange, mom surprised us with a big bag of marshmallows. Dad sent us out to look for roasting sticks and attempted to teach us about the fine art of balance, by baking his marshmallow to a crisp golden brown. We tried to imitate his fine-tuned skill, but one by one we justified our incompetence, as the treats burst into flames, by claiming to like them burnt.

Our home, neighborhood, church and school, were all part of our parish community. Although there were some personal adjustments to be made, I was happy to be living in Merchantville. Every day I learned more about God in school and seasonal activities like this one introduced me to my neighbors and demonstrated how safe, secure, exciting and enjoyable living in a small town can be.

Christmas was just around the corner and in school we were learning all about Mary, Joseph and the birth of Christ. I watched dad put up Christmas lights back in Pennsauken, but had been too young to help out. Now that I was older, I was hoping things would be different. The prospect of putting up lights with my father was something to look forward to and the anticipation was driving me nuts. I kept nagging him about when we would put them up and finally he told me that we would begin on Friday afternoon. When recess began, I left the schoolyard and headed straight home to help my father. After lunch, Sister Mary Catherine took attendance and soon discovered I was missing. Alarmed, she phoned my mother and exhaled a grateful sigh of relief when she learned I had been located. I had left school in all innocence, absolutely sure that my father would be waiting for me when I got home. The misunderstanding earned me a couple of swats with the belt, but I was still allowed to help put up the lights. I also discovered that December is a really cold month and that putting up Christmas lights in the wintertime was not nearly as much fun as I thought it would be. I had raised Sister's blood pressure and the incident taught me to ask people in authority for permission, before I go changing my routine.

On Christmas Eve, we put up our tree and watched a couple of movies on television. The first was called The Spirit of Christmas and the second was called A Visit from St.

Nicholas.[95] Both feature films used marionette puppets to act out the Christmas story about the birth of Jesus and an endearing tale about Santa's nocturnal visit. Our family loved the stories and watching them became a Christmas tradition for years.

Misunderstandings seemed to follow me and I didn't always learn my lessons quickly. Our family had a large Nativity situated on the top of a table in our living room. The scene of the Holy Family faced the street in our picture window and dad put a spotlight on it, so that all who passed by could see it. Mom used thumbtacks to place a skirting around the table, which also made it the perfect hiding place. When bedtime rolled around and the rest of my siblings went to bed, I hid under the Nativity so that I could spy on Santa. Predictably I fell asleep. Mom and dad were busy wrapping presents, assembling bicycles and placing batteries in the new toys. Finally finishing at two in the morning they went upstairs to do a bed check and I was no where to be found. Like Mary and Joseph,[96] my anxious parents searched everywhere they could think of and finally found me safe and sound in the house of the Lord, or at least underneath it. Although they listened to my explanation, mom let me know how worried they had been and dad used the opportunity to show me that there are consequences to my disobedience.

The day after Christmas, our family went to the Drive In Theater and saw The Swiss Family Robinson.[97] From that moment on, I began dreaming about building tree forts with

---

[95] *The Spirit of Christmas* – was a Christmas television special performed mostly by marionettes. It was first aired in 1950. Its half-hour showing time is divided into two segments, one dramatizing "A Visit from St. Nicholas" & one the story of the Nativity.

[96] *Luke 2:46-48* – "And it came to pass, that, after three days, they found him in the temple, sitting in the midst of the doctors, hearing them, and asking them questions. And all that heard him were astonished at his wisdom and his answers. And seeing him, they wondered. And his mother said to him: Son, why hast thou done so to us? behold thy father and I have sought thee sorrowing"

[97] *Swiss Family Robinson* – was a 1960 film of a shipwrecked family building an island home. The screenplay by Lowell S. Hawley is loosely based upon the 1812 novel Der Schweizerische Robinson by Johann David Wyss, directed by Ken Annakin in Tobago.

all sorts of cool contraptions in them. The following week we returned to the Drive In to see 101 Dalmatians.[98] Upon returning from the theater we lobbied for a puppy, but dad wouldn't hear of it. He told us we had a lousy track record regarding chores and were not responsible enough to take care of a dog. Christmas vacation was over. It was time to get back to school.

---

[98] *101 Dalmatians* – was a 1961 animated Walt Disney film based on the novel The 101 Dalmatians by Dodie Smith. It was the 17th in the Walt Disney Animated Classics series & released to theaters in 1961 by Buena Vista Distribution. The plot centered on the fate of kidnapped puppies, Pongo & Perdita by the villainous Cruella de Vil.

Chapter 3

First Holy Communion

After Christmas vacation, Religion classes took on a whole new dimension. Instead of just learning an abstract theological belief system, Jesus became intimately personal to me. I was preparing to receive the sacraments of Confession[99] and First Holy Communion.[100] Once again, our lessons came straight out of the Baltimore Catechism. In addition to the familiar question and answer format, the book also included easily understood illustrations. Sister Mary Catherine clearly and cheerfully answered any questions we had. Suddenly, all my other subjects seemed to pale in comparison. I eagerly looked forward to meeting Jesus in person and wanted to be real good, so that the baby Jesus would have a nice clean warm place to stay when he visited my soul.

Initially we learned about the Mass. Although I had been attending Church every Sunday with my parents, I never really understood what was going on. Sister Mary Catherine spoke with awesome wonder about the Eucharistic Sacrifice and broke open each of the mysteries like the petals of a rose. The more she taught us, the more interested I became. I learned that with God there is no time and when we attended Mass, we were literally being transported to the foot of the cross. We could observe His crucifixion in the ever-present moment of now. Standing beside us were all of the saints and

---

[99] *Confession* – is one of the 7 sacraments, also known as Penance or Reconciliation, in which the priest (who stands in the place of Christ) uses the delegated powers of Christ & of His Church to absolve the sins of the penitent & reconciles him or her to both God & His Church. In order for a person to be forgiven, they must not only confess their sins, but they must intend in their hearts to avoid those sins in the future.

[100] *Holy Communion* – is another one of the 7 sacraments. Also known as the Eucharist, it is the Body, Blood, Soul & Divinity of Christ Himself. During the sacrifice of the Mass, the host & the wine in the chalice, cease to be bread & wine & are transformed into the Most Precious Body & Blood of Christ.

the angels. To my utter amazement, I learned that during the Mass the priest actually became Christ.[101] Ordained Catholic priests are the only persons who can change bread and wine into the Body and Blood of Christ. The Catholic Mass literally allowed us to experience heaven, if only for those few precious moments.

Much was made of the importance of going to Confession. We were taught to take advantage of the sacrament on a regular basis, but especially if we had committed a mortal sin. We learned that mortal sins killed our relationship with God and if not confessed would sentence us to an eternity in hell. Even venial sins were to be avoided. They wounded our relationship with Christ and eventually led us into more serious sin. To prepare us for the Sacrament, Sister took us over to the Church, opened up the doors of the confessional and let us look inside.

In all our classes, Sister Mary Catherine never shied away from using big words. She simply explained what they meant and we seemed to get it. Some of what she taught was admittedly deep theology, but she explained it in such a way that we understood it. She presented it with such reverence that we walked away marveling at the majesty of God.

Every class began with rote prayers, but we were also encouraged to talk with God on our own. I wanted to spend more and more of my time alone with Jesus and talked with God every night in my bed before drifting off to sleep. I also held lengthy conversations with Him, while hiding out in the privacy of our crawlspace, which was underneath the kitchen. Eventually the big day came for my First Holy Communion. Sister gave the boys bright white suits to wear, including a matching white tie and saddle shoes. The girls wore white dresses with veils. Finally kneeling at the marble

---

[101] *Persona Christi* – the Catholic Church understands the priest to be an alter Christus or "another Christ" who acts in Persona Christi, which is Latin for "in the person of Christ".

rail, I laid my hands humbly across my chest and received Baby Jesus on my tongue and into my heart. Christ was no longer outside of me. I dearly loved my Lord and Savior, but there was not that sense of chumminess with Him that I hear spoken of today. I was awed in the Presence of my Sovereign King. After all, He was the King of Kings and Lord of Lords! He was visiting His lowly creature and I was grateful for the privilege.

With five children in our family and one on the way, mom became overwhelmed with the workload. So at a parent teacher conference, she asked Sister Mary Catherine, if she would suggest a responsible teenage girl that could help her out. Sister offered to look into the matter and in about a week gave mom her recommendation. Clara Riley, the school nurse, had a daughter who was both capable and responsible. Rachel Riley was sixteen years old and would be able to fit the bill nicely. The following Saturday, mom and dad took in a movie and called on Rachel to baby sit for us. The family was told to behave for her or they would bring back Mrs. Fletcher. So we all remained on our best behavior.

Rachel was nothing like Mrs. Fletcher. To keep things simple mom recommended a meal of hot dogs and beans. Luckily for the inexperienced young lady, her first meal became an instant hit and a repeated Friday night favorite. Rachel was a thin, athletic and energetic young woman. She loved playing with us and seemed to have just as much fun as we did. We were all very good the first night, but it wasn't long before I would attempt to test her metal. No stranger to confrontation, she was quick to nip my nonsense in the bud. Her firm boundaries actually impressed me and I quickly grew to love and respect our beloved new babysitter. Mom and dad never again had to threaten us with bringing back Mrs. Fletcher, since we always gave them good reports about Rachel Riley.

Only having one car, mom often walked into town to buy groceries. Dad would then pick her up on his way home from work. In addition to baby-sitting while mom went shopping, Rachel also helped out on the weekends. She did dishes, washed laundry and even assisted us with our homework. When we went camping, Rachel came with us. When we shopped for new shoes, she tagged along to keep us in line. She was like an intimate member of the family and took care of us like a big sister.

Rachel Riley occasionally even joined us on Sundays at Saint Peter's. Like every other Catholic on earth, we attended the Tridentine Mass,[102] although we called it the Latin Mass. Despite its minimal usage, Latin still remains the universal language of the Catholic Church. The mystery and reverence experienced in the sacrificial rite of the Tridentine Mass is absolutely majestic and stands in sharp contrast to the pep rally style celebrations held in the sterile buildings of today's evangelical liturgics.

Unlike many of today's faith communities, Mass had little to do with fellowship and everything to do with worship. Two prodigious dark stained oak doors opened the back of our Gothic styled Cathedral and shut out the busyness of the world around it. The vaulted ceiling above created a sacred space that was ever silent and always inviting the presence of God. Beautiful and detailed artwork graced the walls. Statues of saints sat atop marble pedestals. Sunlight penetrated ornate stained glass windows and told of ancient bibilical stories and the early history of the Church. Walking through the holy portal, I blessed myself with holy water and took my place in one of the pews. The entire ensamble created an

---

[102] *The Tridentine Mass* – is the name of the Roman Rite Mass, contained in the rubrics of Roman Missals that were published from 1570 to 1962. During this time period, it was the most widely celebrated form of the Catholic liturgy. The term *Tridentine* came from the Latin word *Tridentinus*, which means "related to the city of Trent, Italy". In response to a decision by The Council of Trent, Pope Pius V promulgated the Latin liturgy through the apostolic constitution *Quo Primum* on July 14, 1570. The order standardized the Traditional Rite Mass and with very few exceptions, was mandatory throughout the Western Church.

atmosphere that was perfectly condusive to worship. I knelt down on the padded leather kneeler, folded my hands, bowed my head and asked Jesus to come into my heart. The distractions of life seemed to drift away and they were soon replaced with an overwhelming sense of awe before the tabernacle. I was keenly aware of being in the presence of God.

When the entrance bell rang, we all rose to our feet and watched a pageantry of altar boys, who exited the sacristy with white lace surplices, which overlaid black cassocks. The acolytes[103] carried lighted candles and were followed by the priest. He held a covered chalice in his hands, was vested in the color of the day[104] and wore a black biretta. Reverently ascending the marble stairs in a solemn procession, they all genuflected in unison before the tabernacle. The priest then removed his biretta and kissed the relic in the altar.[105] Although it was all done at a snail's pace, each movement was choreographed with the precision of a crack military drill team. Making the sign of the cross three times, the priest began the Mass with the words, "In nomine Patris, et Filii, et Spiritus Sancti, Amen."[106] From that point on, the wonders of heaven opened up for me and I was quite literally, transported from this earth into another dimension. When it came time for Holy Communion, nothing could equal the intimacy I felt with Jesus. Although Daily Mass is available to all the faithful, our family rarely took advantage of it and we only participated on Sundays and Holy Days. But during Advent and Lent, the sisters at school required us to attend

---

[103] *Acolyte* - is a cleric promoted to the 4th and highest minor order in the Church, ranking next to a sub-deacon. The duties of the acolyte or altar boy in liturgical services are detailed in the manuals of liturgy, e.g. Pio Matinucci, "Manuale Sacrarum Caeremoniarum" (Rome, 1880), VI, 625; & De Herdt, "Sacrae Liturgiae Praxis" (Louvain, 1889), II, 28-39.

[104] *Vestment Colors – White* – Easter, Christmas & special feasts. *Red* – Palm Sunday, Good Friday, Pentecost, Apostles, Evangelists & Martyrs. *Violet* – Advent & Lent. *Black* Funerals. *Rose* or *Gaudete* - (3rd Sun/Advent) & *Laetare* (4th Sun/Lent). *Green* – all others.

[105] *Relic* – in most Catholic Churches a splinter of the true cross is placed in the altar upon which they celebrate the Holy Sacrifice of the Mass.

[106] *English Translation* – of the above Latin text is "In the name of the Father and of the Son, and of the Holy Ghost. Amen."

Mass on a daily basis. Surrounded as I was by holy ritual, it was not long before I began to consider a vocation to the priesthood.

When I first started to play the part of a priest, friends and family joined in on my mock liturgical celebrations, which were anything but mocking. Mom sewed priestly vestments for me to wear and I found an old wooden hutch, which became the perfect altar for Mass. Pressing a shot glass like a cookie cutter into slices of Wonder bread,[107] my sister Sarah played the part of a nun, making hundreds of hosts for holy communion. My brothers became altar boys and my father further encouraged me by bringing home an aluminum cylinder from work and then teaching me how to machine it down into a chalice on his lathe in the basement.

A priest also administers the Sacrament of Confession, so mom made a purple satin stole for me and Sean helped me retrofit an old wardrobe into a confessional in the basement. One by one Sarah, my brothers and even kids from the neighborhood lined up to confess their sins to me. I took the seal of confession[108] very seriously and never revealed what was shared in the booth. However, it did give me tremendous familial and neighborhood insights.

My love for Jesus was growing and my knowledge of the Catechism was increasing, but I was not doing so well in other areas of my life. For centuries children learned how to read and write through rote memorization and drill. While not without its controversy, a new method of teaching called

---

[107] *Wonder Bread* – was a bakery based in Norristown, PA, which sold whole loafs of bread beginning in 1925. In 1928 W.E. Long, pioneered & promoted the packaging of sliced bread, under the Holsum Bread brand, which was used by various independent bakers around the country. In 1930 Wonder Bread began marketing sliced bread nationwide.

[108] *Seal of Confession* – is the absolute confidentiality that must be maintained by Catholic priests, regarding anything they learn from penitents during a sacramental confession. The church considers this matter so serious that if a priest breaks the seal, he is immediately excommunicated & the excommunication can only be lifted by the Pope himself.

Phonics[109] was being introduced. Unfortunately, our class happened to provide some of the first Guinea pigs for the program. The new methodology deleted spelling in favor of sounding words out. The experiment failed miserably and in subsequent years spelling would be reintroduced, but the damage was done. As a result, I can sound out and pronounce almost any word in the English language, but can't spell for beans. The dichotomy between what I thought I could accomplish and how I was actually performing, shook my confidence to the core. Was I just not that bright? No. Reckless social engineers at progressive teaching colleges were deliberately designing programs to dumb down American kids, because an illiterate population is politically easier to manipulate.[110]

Fun With Dick and Jane was boring and I continued to get in trouble for talking. I was weary of the humiliation I experienced walking through the "B" class and afraid of Mother Superior, so I began getting creative with the excuses I gave Sister. Necessity being the mother of invention, I came up with all sorts of clever ways to justify my actions. Sister Mary Catherine thought I could talk my way out of anything and was so impressed with my creative excuses, she told my parents I would probably become a Philadelphia lawyer.

When school let out, dad reopened our above ground pool. In four feet of heavily chlorinated water, we held our breath, dove for quarters, engaged in splash fights and played water polo. From the top of the ladder we terrorized each other with cannon balls and dunked each other, until our eyes were so cloudy and red, we could barely see where we were going. Time-out was the expression we used to describe a break in

---

[109] *Phonics* – taught children the connections between letter patterns & the sounds they represent. Students were taught to sound out words instead of memorizing lists of words.
[110] *None Dare Call it Education: What's Happening in Our Schools*, by John A. Stormer, published by Liberty Bell Press, Florissant, MO. ©1998

the action, not the pathetically ineffective form of correction it denotes today.

Every afternoon, an ancient man with dark brown skin painfully peddled his homemade cart up Lexington Avenue. In spite of the hot summer sun, which seemed to persecute his poorly clad lanky frame, this kindly old gentleman wore an ear-to-ear smile on his leather textured and deeply lined face. Whenever we heard what sounded like Santa's sleigh bells, our mouths began to water like Pavlov's dogs[111] and we scrambled out of the pool to ask mom for some money. The homemade contraption, this independent peddler had constructed, was adorned with a fresh coat of white enamel paint and it sat on an axle that was book ended by a couple of bicycle tires. A hinge near the bottom of the cart allowed for a change in direction and was attached to the back half of an old rusty bicycle. His legs provided the power and he steered with handle bars that were mounted on the back edge of the box. A shiny chrome handle was bolted to an insulated door on the top of the ice chest and the hatch released a mysterious gray vapor from the dry ice, which kept things cold. Inside his dark treasure chest, were the frozen orange creamsicles we desired. Some of the most enjoyable experiences of summer were the time-outs!

After some more swimming and dinner, the time-out ritual entered phase two. Pre-recorded chimes amplified through loud speakers proclaimed the arrival of a much younger man. He came in a truck and wore a clean white uniform. Dad readily gave us the cash we needed for the Good Humor man, but he also took a bite out of each one of our chocolate dipped vanilla ice cream bars. He wanted to make sure they were not poisonous. Although this inspection involved great personal risk, he was happy to perform the selfless sacrificial duty, in order to protect his family. Once he knew the

---

[111] *Pavlov's Dogs* – refers to a group of experiments conducted by Ivan Pavlov that demonstrated Classical Conditioning. He noticed that dogs would salivate at feeding time as soon as the lab technician who fed them entered the room, whether he had meat or not.

product was safe; he gave us the green light, handed one to my mother and consumed two additional bars himself.

After dad installed a flood light on the top of a pole, we could go swimming after dark. One by one dad picked us up and swung us around like airplanes. He also threw us into the water like watermelons. Frenetically we rode on his back like a bucking bronco, as he tried to throw us off in the churned up water. While it was a blast playing with our father, every evening came to a screeching halt when he threw out his back. Years before dad had hurt his back, while working as a lifeguard in Strathmere.[112] Tragically, the injury created a life long weakness in his spine. Seems some reckless kid flipped over a motorboat in the bay and dad dove off the bridge to save him. Whenever dad threw his back out, mom broke out a tube of Ben-Gay[113] and gave him a rubdown in the den. Dad enjoyed getting the massage and mom liked taking care of her man, but the ointment really reeked and as soon as we knew he was ok, we marched off to the family room holding our noses. Finding a place on the couch we watched TV shows like My Three Sons[114] until it was bedtime.

On July 17, 1961 my father received his Flight Instructor Airman Certificate. Now, instead of just getting a ride, I was allowed to hold the stick and take lessons. Although nothing was truly at risk, I believed I was flying the plane and when I pulled back on the stick during take-off, dad said nothing to dissuade me from thinking I had actually made the plane lift off the ground. What bragging rights!

---

[112] *Strathmere* – was originally known as Corson's Inlet and is located in Cape May County at the Jersey Shore. It was annexed to Upper Township in 1905 and then renamed Strathmere in 1912. Shannon Callahan owned a summer place in the sleepy shore town.
[113] *Ben-Gay* – is a strong smelling analgesic heat rub used to relieve muscle & joint pain.
[114] *My Three Sons* – was a situation comedy about a Scots-Irish-American family. It chronicled the life of widower and aeronautical engineer (Fred MacMurray), raising his three sons. The series ran from 1960-1965 on ABC and was television's 2nd longest running (live-action) family sitcom.

In August my brother Art was born and there were now six of us in the Callahan clan. In preparation for entering school in September Sarah and I went with mom to see Doctor Wakefield who gave us our booster shots. Getting a needle was stressful, but the experience would not be nearly as disturbing as the tyranny of my second grade teacher.

In the early sixties small towns were much safer than they are today. Cops were the good guys, neighbors looked out for each other and every adult took care of little children, as if they were their own kids. Older boys were expected to look after their younger brothers and were duty bound to protect a sister of any age. Although I was only seven, I walked Sarah to school, introduced her to some of the other kids and helped her through the social minefield we called our schoolyard. Since it was her very first day at school, I showed her the line she had to stand on when the bell rang. Sarah was pretty sure of herself and once she understood where the starting point was, she felt pretty confident she could take it from there. Even so, I took the responsibility of looking after my little sister very seriously and relished the honored role of being her big brother. Summer vacation had been relaxing and fun, but I was looking forward to second grade and happy to be back in school.

Chapter 4

A Looming Problem

The ringing of the school bell might as well have been the opening round of a prizefight. Mother Mary Francis was still our principal and a young single woman, by the name of Miss Looming was assigned to be my second grade teacher. Transitioning from a religious instructor to a lay teacher would be an adjustment for me, but not the only one. It was the last year of service for the Franciscan Sisters at Saint Peter School. Although the decision had already been made, the changing of the guard would not take place until the following summer. Within a year the Religious Teachers Filipini would be replacing the Franciscans, but for the time being the mean spirited principal was still in charge. This year however, she would be the least of my problems.

The first few days of class were easy enough. We began by reviewing the subjects from first grade. I enjoyed tackling some of the more challenging material in second grade and was happy to be back in school with all the other kids. Since Religion was my favorite subject, I enthusiastically sailed through my catechism classes. First grade math had been a breeze and I completed the review with relative ease. Thanks to Phonics, the only difficulty I really had was with spelling. It affected my reading and writing skills, but here too there was reason for hope. Local educators had recognized the flaws in the Phonics experiment and reintroduced spelling along with the practice of sounding out vocabulary words, bringing balance to the learning program. New to our curriculum was the Palmer Method[115] of Penmanship.

---

[115] *Palmer Method* – is a form of penmanship instruction that was developed & promoted by Austin Palmer in the late 19th & early 20th centuries. It soon became the most popular handwriting system in the US. Students were taught to adopt a uniform system of cursive writing with rhythmic motions & left-handers were told to use their right hands. The

Although mastering the graceful strokes of cursive writing became a great source of personal pride, it also set me up for my first political nightmare.

Across newsprint paper that was printed with solid and dotted light blue horizontal lines, our class spent hours drawing zigzag slanted lines and circles. It was kind of boring, but it was also amusing and artful. I practiced without complaint and worked diligently to match my penmanship to the examples in our book. Miss Looming was an inexperienced teacher who was having some trouble getting the concept across to our class that cursive letters had to be written on a slant. Sitting near the back of the room, I watched one student after another attempt to form the fancy new letters on the blackboard. The first few students wrote their letters straight up and down. After some repeated instruction, a timid little girl slanted her letters to the left. Frustrated and annoyed, Miss Looming drew another example on the board and raised her voice while instructing the students to slant to the right. A second girl walked up to the front of the class and did finally slant her letters to the right. The teacher affirmed her work, but said that the slant needed to be more pronounced. One bashful boy followed her, but he slanted to the left again. The youthful lay-teacher threw up her hands and bellowed, "No! No! No! ... to the right!" Overwhelmed with confusion and fear, the rest of the kids angered her even more. Some drew straight up and down, others to the left and still others just a little bit off to the right.

It didn't take me very long to figure out what she wanted. I raised my hand and confidently walked up to the front of the class to demonstrate my proficiency. Boldly writing my cursive letters on the blackboard, I totally exaggerated the

---

method developed around 1888 & was introduced in his 1894 book Palmer's Guide to Business Writing, which sold 1M copies. The Palmer's style won many awards, but fell out of popularity & many believe it has been responsible for a decrease in the overall legibility of modern American handwriting, although now it is experiencing renewed attention.

slant to the right. Miss Looming was so ecstatic that someone finally understood what she was trying to communicate, she shouted, "YES! YES! YES!" Turning to the rest of the class she said, "That's what I've been trying to show you. Now I want you all to do what Mr. Callahan has just done." Proudly marching back to my seat, with a big smug smile, I exhaled on my knuckles and pretended to polish a gold medal on my puffed up chest. I had accomplished what no one else seemed able to do. It had given me stature in the class and I strutted around like a peacock for the rest of the semester. Although momentarily happy with my successful demonstration of penmanship, the teacher was not at all happy with my arrogance. Miss Looming saw pride as a character flaw and set out to annihilate it. But instead of confronting me about my conceit, she determined to break my spirit by ratcheting down my grades. No matter how well I did in class, my grades continued to fall like the autumn leaves outside the classroom window.

Unlike Sister Mary Catherine, it was rare for my teacher to send people to the office for small offenses like talking. Miss Looming prided herself in her ability to take care of things on her own. Every morning and each afternoon we had a bathroom break. There was a strict rule that we were to remain totally silent while lining up in the hallway. One day, while being metered into the lavatory, two students at a time, the teacher caught me talking. She pulled me down the hall by my ear with her long, sharp, shiny red fingernails and lacerated my ear lobe. I told mom about it as soon as I got home, but she said I must have deserved it and shouldn't have been talking in the first place. Floored by her lack of concern and compassion, I pointed to the scab and screamed, "She ripped my ear off!"

It was like that with everything, including my grades. Teachers were always right and kids were constantly condemned for trying to get away with stuff. If I persisted in my defense when dad got home, he would give me an additional punishment. The diabolical plan of Miss Looming, to bust my chops by incrementally lowering the grades on my report card, got me into a lot of trouble with my father. After the first marking period ended, I was grounded from leaving our property and had to have all my homework done, before I could go outside to play in the yard. Worse than any punishment was the look of disappointment on my father's face, as he looked over the report card. No matter how hard I studied, labored over my homework, or participated in class, my grades continued to sink into the netherworld.

Being grounded would probably have become unbearable, except for the fact that I met a friend on the way home from school. Tom Reeves came from a large musically inclined family. They lived in a big Tutor house across the street from the school, which also housed his father's business, The Sonata School of Music. Each afternoon Tom rushed through his studies and then walked over to my house to play. His timing was perfect and he always seemed to arrive just as I was finishing up my homework. Tom's favorite subject was science and one day there was a solar eclipse. Our teachers had cautioned us not to look directly at the sun, because they said it could blind us. When Tom came over we looked up solar eclipse in the encyclopedia and found out that we could make a viewer out of a cardboard box. The sunlight was supposed to come in through a pinhole in the back and project like a movie onto a piece of white paper taped on the opposite side of the box. Tom and I tried it, but it didn't work very well, so we modified the design by cutting a one-inch hole in the back of it. The change solved our problem and we got to watch the eclipse in our makeshift movie theater. Tom's consistent companionship laid the groundwork for what would become a lifelong friendship.

Although most people in our neighborhood still had a single black and white television set, our family had two sets and one was a color console. Tom loved cartoons and he walked in the back door of our house at the crack of dawn every Saturday morning. On sunny days, mom would shoo the kids out of the house after a couple of hours, but Tom kept watching the cartoons. He was so engrossed he never even knew that we left! No matter how loud we yelled at him, he remained glued to the television set until dad turned it off one day in the middle of Top Cat.[116] My father glared at the stunned TV addict, until he came back down to earth and left the house. I'm not sure what goes on with girls, but when a boy reads about Robinson Crusoe[117] or watches The Swiss Family Robinson[118] he is absolutely compelled to build his own tree fort and the big elm tree in the center of our backyard was the perfect place for one. The only thing that had been missing was a companion to go along on the adventures. Tom became the boy who helped turn that dream into reality.

Tom and I asked dad if we could build a fort in the big elm tree. Dad thought it was a great idea, but questioned our architectural prowess. We were more than willing to learn and since dad had recently purchased The World Book Encyclopedia.[119] We looked up construction and began learning about: foundations, sills, studs, rafters, roofing, shingles, sheeting, wiring and even plumbing. Whew! We had no idea there was so much to it. Dad drove us down to Collins Hardware Store where we brought home some two-by-fours, a few sheets of plywood and a couple of bags of

---

[116] *Top Cat* - was a Hanna-Barbera cartoon that ran on ABC from 1961-1962. T.C. stood for Top Cat and he was the leader of a gang of New York City alley cats who had names like: Fancy-Fancy, Spook, Benny the Ball, The Brain & Choo Choo.
[117] *Robinson Crusoe* – is a novel by Daniel Defoe. First published in 1719, it is sometimes considered to be the first novel in English and is a fictional autobiography of the title character, a castaway who spends 28 years on a remote tropical island, encountering Native Americans, captives and mutineers, before being rescued.
[118] *Swiss Family Robinson* – was a 1960 film of a shipwrecked family building an island home. The screenplay by Lowell S. Hawley was loosely based upon the 1812 novel Der Schweizerische Robinson (literally, The Swiss Robinson) by Johann David Wyss. The film was directed by Ken Annakin and shot in Tobago
[119] *World Book Encyclopedia* - is published in the US and at the time was described as the "the #1 selling print encyclopedia in the world." It covered major areas of knowledge, but had a particular strength in the scientific, technical and medical fields.

nails. In order to keep things safe, dad worked together with us to build the base platform, which he attached to the trunk of the tree. After helping us lift a heavy sheet of plywood onto the frame, we pounded about four thousand nails, most of them bent, to secure our floor. Taking what we had learned from the encyclopedia, dad instructed us to come up with a set of drawings and then left us alone to build the fort with simple hand tools. We spent the next two weeks building our little fortress and used old paint from the garage to protect it from the elements. A few days after finishing, dad brought home a big old hunk of heavy green canvas, which we used to cover the roof.

In his comedy routine, Karate[120] Bill Cosby recalls, "When you have finally completed your training in Karate, you have not yet reached your ultimate goal, which is to wipe somebody out. So you walk down dark alleys, with ten-dollar bills hanging out of your pockets. And then it happens. "Give me your dough!" We had a solid fort with windows on two sides. What we really needed was an enemy to defend the fort against. It would not take us long to find one.

The following weekend, Tom Reeves and I went exploring down by the railroad tracks. We were looking in the sand for coins that we could place on the rails and then watch the train go by and flatten them. A somewhat stocky kid came over from the house on the corner of Chestnut Street and he introduced himself as Toby and asked us what we were doing. We told him we were looking for buried treasure and showed him a couple of the old broken bottles we had found. Toby Wilson was a big guy. He was roughly the same age as Tom and I, but he was a little bit taller and a whole lot bigger – as in heavier and stronger. Toby was also loud, very aggressive and filled with confidence. I wasn't sure what to make of him at first. He looked little bit like Fred Flintstone,

---

[120] *Karate* – is a classic comedy routine by comedian Bill Cosby, where he picks fun at the experiences of going to a Karate School & the secret motivations of those who attend them. The skit is captured on his 1970 Warner Bros. Record – *More of the Best of Bill Cosby*.

but I sure didn't want to tangle with the guy. I had seen him walking home from Church with his mother and sister, so I knew he was part of our parish, but I hadn't seen him at Saint Pete's because he attended Merchantville Public School. Word travels quickly in a small town and Toby already knew about our fort. He asked to see it and we were more than eager to show it off.

He told us that some kids in the neighborhood have apple fights and he thought we should gather up some ammo, just in case there was a war. Noticing a crabapple tree in back of Mrs. Martin's house, he led us over to it and shook the branches. Lots of apples fell and he gathered up a bucket full, but his lack of respect for the property of another seemed pretty bold. We told him we thought it was stealing, but he minimized our concerns by telling us, she would never even miss them. Still a bit uncomfortable, I knocked on the front door and asked Mrs. Martin if would be ok to pick her apples. She said she used to bake pies with them, but it was probably ok since she was getting older now and didn't do much baking any more. She said we could take all the apples we wanted, but asked us not to break any of the branches. We commandeered an old wooden milk box down by the railroad tracks, got a rusty metal bucket from the garage and borrowed mom's mop bucket. In no time at all we filled them all to the brim and hauled the apples back to our fort for some target practice. Almost anything became a target: a tree, a floating toy in the pool, or even a bird or a squirrel. Toby loved baseball and told us he was the pitcher for a little league team. Once he showed us how to pitch, we competed in both distance and accuracy. Although we kind of expected it, Toby beat us every time, however Tom and I secretly looked forward to the day when we could be just as accurate or even better than he was. We were confident it would simply be a matter of time.

On Sunday afternoons, dad worked as a flight instructor and by the time he returned home we had already finished dinner.

The blue laws[121] insured that the Good Humor truck would not be making its rounds so dad brought home a big bag of M&Ms. We crowded around him with cupped hands, but he refused our request. Instead he announced he was about to teach us arithmetic. Picking up a single piece of candy, he placed it in my hand. "One for you and one for me." Each time he handed one of his children an M&M, he popped another one in his mouth. We knew something was wrong, we just didn't know what. Like a deer in the headlights, we stood there staring at him and frozen in our confusion. After a couple of rounds I spoke up, "Hey, that's not fair!" To which he replied, "What's not fair? Here let me do it again." He proceeded to repeat the scenario, but I couldn't figure out the riddle. Although still feeling cheated I accepted the candy, but continued to watch him like a hawk. Every time one of us objected, dad would slow down the count insisting that he was being totally fair. Since each time he gave one of us a candy-coated piece of chocolate he only took one for himself and then ate the evidence, we couldn't catch him in the swindle. When I finally figured it out, he raised his index finger over his lips to let me know we now shared a very special relationship. Together we kept the secret so that the game could carry on. Dad continued to play the M&M Math game long after everyone understood what he was doing. He eventually swapped the M&Ms for Skittles, but still plays it with his grandchildren.

Sometimes dad took me with him to Aero Haven Airport.[122] I remained on the ground while he took his students up for their flying lessons, but in concert with the sons of the other pilots, we airport orphans made good use of our time. We

---

[121] *Blue Laws* – are designed to enforce the religious standards of a community, particularly the observance of Sunday, as a day of worship and rest. They often restrict Sunday shopping or the selling of liquor. Many of these laws have been repealed in recent years.
[122] *Aero Haven Airport* – was a private airport with a 2,780-foot bituminous runway, just south of Marlton, NJ. The owners had big plans for the airport, including several hangers, a bowling alley, indoor pool & a restaurant, as the clearing for the runway was roughly twice as long as the pavement and there were two additional clearings for what would have been crosswind runways. However due to the workings of an embezzler, other than a small coffee shop & a hanger, none of this presumed future expansion was ever realized.

drove Tonka trucks in the sand, built lean-to forts next to the runway and watched the older boys shoot off Estes Rockets.[123] As soon as dad finished with the lessons, he called me over to the office and gave me a dime to drop in the big red metal vending machine. I then struggled to pull down on the nickel-plated handle, until suddenly the leaver would give way and a deep-throated rattle would issue a thick green glass bottle, which abruptly ended its noisy journey with a thud at an opening in the bottom. A quick flick of the wrist on the mounted bottle opener removed the cap and my father and I split an ice cold ten-ounce Coke-A-Cola™. If he finished early enough, we went for a ride in his Piper Cub.[124]

Upon returning home, I got my weekly bath, put on pajamas and ran downstairs to watch The Wonderful World of Disney. While the rest of us were occupied in the family room, dad was in the den keeping up with the news. The cold war was heating up. There was a standoff between American and Soviet tanks in Germany because twelve East Germans had escaped communism by tunneling under the Berlin Wall. President Kennedy sent additional advisors to Viet Nam and committed U.S. ground troops, which included support from an aircraft carrier. Although Congress never declared war and officially it was considered a policing action, we were clearly at war in Southeast Asia. Meanwhile, The Soviet Union signed a trade pact with Cuba, claiming their newest Communist satellite country in our hemisphere. This prompted Pope John XXIII to excommunicate Fidel Castro and the U.S. announced an embargo.

---

[123] *Estes Industries* – was founded by Vernon Estes in 1958, after he created "Mabel", which was a machine designed to inexpensively manufacture model rocket engines for Model Missiles Inc.

[124] *Piper Cub* – was a small, simple, light aircraft that was built between 1937-1947 by Piper Aircraft. With tandem (fore & aft) seating, it was intended for flight training, but quickly became one of the most popular & best-known light aircraft of all time. The J-3 Cub's simplicity, affordability & popularity invokes comparisons to the Ford Model T.

After watching The Sign of Zorro,[125] we pulled wooden sticks out of the bottom of the window shades and began a big sword fight. It didn't take long before the noise level rose to a fevered pitch and one of the sticks broke, turning it into a lethal weapon. The ruckus prompted dad to turn off his television and end the sword fight by sending us all to our beds, which meant lights out and silence. The slightest violation brought a stern verbal warning, but anyone sneaking down the stairs risked the belt.

Thanks to my father's fascination with politics, it was quite natural for me to take an interest in History and Civics. In second grade we were studying The Declaration of Independence[126] and the Constitution.[127] We learned about the three branches of government, how a bill becomes a law and the importance of letting our congressmen know how we felt about things. Finally, we learned about our colonial beginnings, what led to our break with Great Britain and colonial history surrounding the Revolutionary War. Learning to participate in our government was part of that education and included an assignment to write to one of our representatives.

On February 10, 1962, I began the assignment by writing to State Congressman William T. Cahill, who represented the First Congressional District in New Jersey. My letter was a simple one, hand printed in pencil on loose-leaf paper, requesting that he come to my house so that I could meet him and introduce him to my parents. On Valentine's Day I

---

[125] *The Sign of Zorro* – was a half-hour Walt Disney TV series based on the well-known Zorro character, which ran from 1957-1961 on ABC. The series ran from the arrival of Zorro (Don Diego de la Vega) in America to the death of José Sebastian Varga, the leader of a conspiracy to take over California. The Wonderful World of Disney reran the series.

[126] *The Declaration of Independence* – is a statement adopted by the Continental Congress on July 4, 1776, which announced that the 13 American colonies were formally at war with Great Britain & were now independent states & thus no longer a part of the British Empire.

[127] *The Constitution of the United States of America* – is the supreme law of the U.S. It is the foundation & source of the legal authority underlying the existence of the USA & the federal government. It provides the framework for the organization of the government & for the relationship of the federal government to the states and to its people.

received a short reply from his secretary letting me know that he was out of the state on business, but that she would show him my letter as soon as he returned. On the 21st of the month he wrote back saying, "While I would very much like to stop and see you and your family, the pressure of business prevents me from making these personal visits. I hope your family will understand. Sincerely yours, William T. Cahill."

Although I was disappointed with his response, I was happy he had at least written back to me. Apparently, not everyone had taken the assignment as seriously as I did and I gained some more celebrity when I read the letter to our class. Republican Representative Cahill was a former FBI agent who would go on to become the 46th Governor of New Jersey a decade later. Actually my parents didn't need to meet him. He was an alumnus from Camden Catholic and they had graduated high school together. Like Cahill my parents were Conservative Republican patriots and therefore even though most Catholics supported Jack Kennedy for President, my parents didn't because they were aware of Jack's liberal bias and not happy about where he was taking the country.

When First Lady Jacqueline Kennedy took television viewers on a tour of the White House, the loyal opposition was quick to respond. Mom and dad purchased a Hi-fi record, spoofing Jackie's Whitehouse Tour. The impersonator playing the part of the president's wife carried off all the sophistry she was famous for, while repeatedly commenting on the gifts of dust left behind by Mrs. Eisenhower. Her caricatured imagery left us doubled over with laughter and began a tradition in our family of political discussion and satire.

Although family amusements like the Hi-fi records and Tom's afternoon visits mitigated some the loneliness of my being grounded, more and more I was living for the weekends. After watching cartoons on Saturday mornings, Tom and I got together with Toby to play war games. Toby took out his penknife and cut a thin branch from Mrs. Martin's apple tree. He stuck the sharpened end into an apple and whipped it off the branch like a missile. It arched all the way across the yard and into the driveway of our neighbors across the street. Wow! What a demonstration. If we ever mastered this technology, we could hit distant enemies before they ever had a chance to hit us. What a military advantage! We each tried the new technique and gradually got the hang of it. In time, we got so good at it that we ran out of room. So we loaded up buckets of apples and headed down to the railroad tracks, where we had unlimited range, for out practice shots.

I didn't like being grounded one bit. I worked hard all semester to improve my grades, but whenever I was given a quarterly report card, my grades had dropped even further. The look of disappointment on dad's face when I brought it home to him was devastating to me. Not only was I letting my father down, but the cascading grades meant I would be grounded for yet another marking period. Unfortunately, I had no clue Miss Looming was actually tinkering with my grades. I just thought I had to work harder and bringing up my grades became a top priority.

My babysitter's brother Vinny Riley was also our class clown. He was a very funny guy and his antics brought comic relief to the regimented assignments we were required to perform in total silence. He frequently said or did things that sent the entire class into hysterical laughter, but all the chaos abruptly ended as soon as the teacher flashed a shocked and disapproving glare. I'm not saying he didn't deserve it, but Vinny paid a steep price for his comedy routines. He got in more trouble than anyone.

During Advent and Lent the entire school attended daily Mass. One morning I was kneeling at the altar rail next to Vinny Riley, in preparation for receiving communion. It was taking Monsignor a long time to reach us and Riley was getting fidgety. Suddenly he looked over at me and for a split second I looked back. He bugged out his eyes and contorted his face and then just as quickly he turned back, faced forward and acted as if nothing had ever happened. I desperately tried to stifle my reaction, but burst out laughing anyway. Sister Mary Catherine immediately yanked me off the altar rail and angrily asked me what I thought I was doing. In a panic I stuttered, "But, but Vinny", and she interrupted my protest. "Vinny is being very reverent." I looked back and saw what looked like a saint. His hands were folded, his fingers pointed skyward and complete serenity washed over his angelic face. I had been had and there wasn't a single thing I could do about it.

Vinny wasn't a bad guy and he meant no real harm by the prank. When I confronted him in the schoolyard, he half apologized and half laughed. He also thought I was crazy when I suggested he tell Sister the truth, but even his answer wasn't mean spirited. The fact is he was downright friendly, but his answer was still an unequivocal "No!" Objectively, I had to concur with his logic and we ended up becoming friends for life.

Vinny lived in Pennsauken, on the far side of Merchantville, so it wasn't like I could just drop by his house after school, besides, I was still grounded. However, he drew me a map to his house and invited me to ride over on my bike as soon as school let out for summer vacation. He told me we could play army and I assumed it had something to do with apple fights, but I would soon learn about a very different kind of warfare; one that was not so much adventurous as it was cold, calculating and dark. In today's parlance, my introduction to playing army would be one of shock and awe.

For the time being, I had more pressing concerns. It was the end of the year and I was about to have a show down with Miss Looming. Not only did my final report card contain my lowest grades to date, but there on the back page was the designation 3-B. That meant I would be joining the slow kids in the third grade, instead of my peers. This humiliation was more than I could bear. By now it was obvious my teacher was deliberately falsifying my grades. Since I still believed in a just world and she was clearly in the wrong, I decided to confront her. I was convinced that once she was called to task on the matter, she would apologize and make it right. Deeply saddened by the betrayal, but resolved to stand up for myself, I summoned all my courage and approached Miss Looming's desk with my report card.

Standing beside her desk, she seemed preoccupied with some writing and I patiently waited. When she looked up I boldly challenged, "Why are you doing this to me?" "Doing what?" she said abruptly. "Giving me bad grades." I said with slightly glassy eyes. "I'm not giving you bad grades." she scoffed, "you're giving yourself bad grades." Now my eyes really filled up with tears of hurt and betrayal. This callous woman held all the power and was not about to let me force her confession. A quiet indignation rose up within me and I firmly stated, "No I'm not!" Seeing my resolve she ramped up her mocking ridicule, "Well, if you're so smart then after the first marking period your teacher will realize what a terrible mistake has been made and put you back in 3-A, now won't she?" I glared back at her from atop my moral precipice and almost inaudibly replied, "Yes. That's exactly what will happen." There was nothing left to say. I returned to my seat crying, having no idea why she was doing this. How could a teacher be so cold and manipulative?

When I arrived home with my report card, I showed it to mom and told her what had happened. She couldn't believe that a teacher would do such a thing, but she also saw how upset I was and gave me a big hug. Mom said she would go with me when it was time to show the report card to dad. After dinner I was uncharacteristically eager to help out with the dishes. Dad went into his den and Sarah enthusiastically handed him a straight "A" report card. He lavished his praise on her and then told her to come get me. Since I wasn't finished helping with the dishes, mom covered for my apprehensive foot dragging and vouched for me by saying that I would be in as soon as the dishes were done. In the mean time, dad adjusted the rabbit ears on his television set so he could watch the news. President Kennedy was giving a commencement address to Yale, the Telstar[128] satellite launch was announced and the Supreme Court banned prayer in public schools.[129] Despite his interest in all things newsworthy, none of that seemed to matter when I walked into the room.

Turning off the television set he said, "Let's see it." Trembling in fear, I handed him my report card and saw that old familiar disappointment come over his face. His head dropped and he placed his thumb on his right cheekbone while rubbing three forefingers across his forehead. Gradually his facial expression morphed into a look of his own personal failure. He continued looking over the grades a third and forth time, almost as if he were trying to find something he had missed. The silence was deafening. My father looked me over, glanced at mom and then stared up at the ceiling. Finally he spoke. "How do you think you did?" "Not very good", I answered with my head hanging down. Then with renewed energy in his voice he asked, "Did you do your best?" "Yes", I said resolutely. "Then that's all you can do. Go on out and play."

I was all set to tell him what happened with Miss Looming, but it never even came up. I couldn't believe my ears and wasn't sure what had just happened. I thought I was going to be grounded for the rest of the summer. Instead the entire

---

[128] *Telstar* – is the name given to communications satellites that relay television signals, pictures, telephone calls & fax images around the globe. Telstar 1 became the 1st communications satellite launched by the U.S. on July 10, 1962. Since then we have placed 18 in service. Most recently launching T-18 in 2004 and should orbit through 2017.

[129] *Engel v. Vitale* – was a landmark United States Supreme Court case in 1962 that determined that it is unconstitutional for state officials to compose an official school prayer and require its recitation in public schools.

weight was lifted off my shoulders and I was free to enjoy my vacation. I didn't know why or how, but I think mom and dad had somehow exchanged volumes between them during their muted eye contact. Whatever had transpired, it was over and I walked away feeling very much loved by both of my parents.

Summer Vacation had finally arrived. The next morning I jumped on my bike and raced across town to the Riley residence. The map Vinny gave me was crystal clear and when I arrived at his house, I found him cutting the grass in the backyard. Mrs. Riley, who was also our school nurse, showed me to the back door and said that as soon as Vinny was done his chores, he would be free to go out and play. When he finished he returned the mower to the garage, grabbed a canvas bag and led me down Rogers Avenue where we doglegged on Sherman to a place called Githens Field, which was just the gravel end of Githens Avenue. On one side of the dirt road were an old basketball court and a swing set, flanked by a neglected sandlot with a field that had long ago gone to seed. The backstop to the run down ballpark was a set of rails on a raised grade. We followed a clay foot path that cut through some overgrown bushes, as it snaked its way up the hill to the tracks.

From the vantage point on top of the rails we saw public school kids who had not yet been set free for the summer, running foot races on the oval and playing football in the valley below. Vinny ran down the other side of the grade and disappeared into a thick patch of woods. I followed quickly behind him and ducked under a mulberry bush that led to a hidden footpath. Vinny pointed out some poison ivy, which hungrily reached out to mess with us along the way. Eventually the trail opened up again and we saw several large yellowish-orange mounds of clay, which were almost twenty-feet tall. The hills were baked hard as a rock and were covered with a powdery dust from the searing summer sun. The second hill had a two-foot hole in the top of it and had the look of a volcano. Smiling back at me, Vinny raised his eyebrows twice in quick succession and then jumped into the hole. This was his secret hiding place. The tunnel went straight down for about eight feet and then took a sharp ninety-degree turn, but before I could see where he went, he popped out of a second hole on the side of the hill. Laughing out loud he said, "You try it!" I was scared about getting stuck in the tunnel and venturing into the unknown was not exactly my idea of having fun, so I just watched him play. After diving into the cave a few more times, he motioned for me to follow him over to the next mound for a different kind of adventure.

When I caught up with him, he opened up his canvas bag and showed me over a hundred green plastic army men. Vinny set them up in the dirt and began making noises that sounded like machine guns and bombs. He held onto one soldier and pretended it was firing its weapon at the other guy. Then he flicked the other soldier and sent it tumbling down the side of the hill. He explained that half of the army men were American G.I.s and the other half were either Germans or Japs. For the next hour, he developed strategies, executed battle plans and wiped out scores of enemy troops. After every major battle Vinny reached into his pocket and pulled out a Zippo lighter[130] and used it to melt the arms and legs off the enemy soldiers. It seemed pretty sadistic to me, but I was also fascinated by how much he was into it. When the five o'clock whistle blew, we both high tailed it back to his house and Vinny kept asking me if I would be back to play with him again some day. I assured him I would, but wondered why it was so important to him. He knew from my

---

[130] *Zippo Lighter* – is a refillable, metal lighter manufactured by Zippo Manufacturing Company of Bradford, PA. George G. Blaisdell founded the company in 1932 producing the first Zippo in 1933, which was based on an Austrian design. Blaisdell liked the sound of the word "zipper" & thought "zippo" sounded more modern. The lighters became popular with soldiers during World War II when the company dedicated all manufacturing resources to the military market." Originally made of brass, they used steel during the war years. Zippo never had a contract with the Army, but military personnel insisted that stores carry the lighter at the Base Exchange (BX), because unit crests & division insignia were popular among the American soldiers of WWII, Korea & Vietnam.

reaction, that torturing the toys had bothered me a bit and I think he truly wondered if he would ever see me again. Melting the soldiers did kind of creep me out, but I also had every intention of spending more time with my newfound friend.

I had a long way to go to get home in time for supper, so I grabbed my bike and sped off like a bat out of hell. Making my way up Rogers Avenue, I slowed down to cross Cove Road. Approaching the intersection I stood up on the pedals to look for traffic and then zipped through a break in the line of cars. When I cleared the curb, the chain jumped off its sprocket. I made it across the road, but I had neither the tools nor the know-how to fix it. I ended up walking the bike home and by the time I turned in our driveway I was twenty minutes late. I tried to explain what happened, but excuses didn't cut it in our house. I was sent to bed without my supper. I was hungry, but its not like I was starving or anything. After laying in bed for about an hour, mom came up and smuggled me a pickle. Although she told me not to tell my father, actually he was the one who sent her up with the contraband. The next day dad showed me how to realign my chain and where to tighten a nut on the back of the frame, so it wouldn't derail again. I had learned something about the mechanics of my bike, was insured against being late for dinner and was grateful to my father for his patient instruction.

Robert Gague was the kid who lived in the house behind ours and he often bragged about his father's model train set. After Mass one Sunday, his father invited me and dad over to see his Lionel layout. Descending a dark and narrow stairway from the kitchen only enhanced the mystery, as Robert's father led us to the edge of a very large table. He pulled on a string that was hanging down from the ceiling and the whole place lit up. It revealed a magnificent landscape encompassing half the basement.

Directly in front of us was a control panel. It included dozens of switches and on the edge of the table was a big, black, football shaped object with two handles that were used to control the speed of the train. There were villages, farms, mountains and forests. The Lionel steam engine even belched smoke from the stack and it whistled whenever Mr. Gage hit a red button. Freight trains disappeared into tunnels on one side of the mountain and reappeared a few seconds later on the other. Little men were busy loading and unloading lumber and woodsmen with axes hacked away at trees in the forest. A plane circled overhead on the end of a wire, which had a spinning propeller and an airport control tower with a rotating green and white beacon flashed at the far corner of the layout.

Mr. Gague was more than happy to have guests over to appreciate all of his hard work and Robert seemed especially proud of his father. And why not? What a set-up! Robert was a couple of years older than I was and his sister Alanna and brother Elliot were frequent guests in our pool. On rainy days Robert and I explored the crawl space under our kitchen, and we played with Tonka trucks in the sand under our front porch. He often joined us to watch cartoons on Saturday mornings and made plans with Tom and me to form a club, which excluded girls. One day we watched a World War I movie and many of the soldiers were fighting in fox holes that were surrounded with barbed wire. When the movie was over, Sean and I went out in back of the garage with Robert and dug foxholes of our own. Then we pretended to fight a war between the foxholes. Using sticks for guns, we popped our heads up just long enough to get off a shot, before ducking back into our sandy sanctuaries. When Tom Reeves came over to join us we dug a fourth hole, totally trashing the infamous asparagus patch. For days we reenacted World War I. Eventually we cut tunnels between the holes, so we could crawl from one hole to the next without getting shot. In our minds we had the same courage as the soldiers we saw in the movies.

Hanging out with Tom or the boy next door was carefree play, but it was different at the Riley residence. Vinny always had lots of chores to do, so he rarely visited me at my house. I didn't get to see him as much as Tom, but I rode my bike to his house whenever I could. We usually played army or one-on-one basketball, but the more I got to know him the more I began to see another side of the class clown. Vinny was not a very happy kid. He did his chores, played games with enthusiasm and seemed friendly enough, but he also emotionally left the planet from time to time and derived a bit too much pleasure from burning the limbs off those plastic soldiers. His sister Rachel was our babysitter and I really liked her, but she too was kind of hard to get to know. The entire family seemed to be under an enormous amount of stress, but it would be many years before I would find out why.

Rachel Riley was not just our baby-sitter. She was almost a member of our family and she was a big help to mom, but she was also still attending school. On August 17, 1962 my brother Shane was born, which increased mom's workload even more. Although we dearly loved Rachel, it was becoming increasingly difficult to take advantage of her services. We needed a full-time nanny and found one at a place called Europa.[131] Mom and dad filled out all their forms and the agency set about to find a match for our family. The first couple of women didn't work out, but mom and dad persevered and settled on Lisa Landers, a young woman from Wales and Rachel continued to help out until her arrival in January.

Before going back to school, mom and dad took us out to the drive-in to see the movie Big Red.[132] Dad liked the idea of

---

[131] *Europa* – was an Au Pair agency in Philadelphia that made arrangements for young girls in Europe, who were interested in coming to the U.S., to find work in the domestic field.

[132] *Big Red* – was a 1962 family-oriented adventure film from Disney Studios, starring Walter Pidgeon. Based on a 1945 novel by author Jim Kjelgaard & adapted to the screen by screenwriter Louis Pelletier. The story was about an Irish Setter who would rather run through the woods than be the perfectly trained and groomed show dog his sportsman

going to the drive-in, because he could pay for the movie by the carload, smuggle in popcorn and bring along a large thermos of Kool-Aid.[133] As usual, Rachel Riley came with us and everyone enjoyed the movie. By the time it was over Sarah and I were the only children still awake, which is another reason why dad loved going to the drive-in.

---

owner wanted. A ten-year-old orphan boy looks after the dog and rebels against his owner's strict discipline of "Big Red."

[133] *Kool-Aid* – was invented by Edwin Perkins in his mother's kitchen in Hastings, NE. Its predecessor was a liquid concentrate called Fruit Smack. In 1927 Ed discovered a way to reduce shipping costs, by removing the liquid & in 1931 they named the powder Kool-Aid, moving production facilities to Chicago & then selling the it to General Foods in 1953.

Chapter 5

Fighting Back

Miss Looming had not only done me dirty in the second grade, but she had handicapped me in the third. I entered 3-B on September 9, 1962 surrounded by the same morons that used to laugh at me on my way to the principal's office. I also had to explain to somewhat skeptical peers in the "A" class why I had been demoted to the "B" class. Embarrassed in front of my friends and needing to make dad proud of me again; I was determined to excel in my studies, so I could stick it to Miss Looming. I built up a good head of steam and entered the arena with fire in my belly, but it would not be a fair fight.

Over the summer Monsignor had dismissed the Franciscan Sisters and replaced them with the Religious Teachers Filipppini. The new order of sisters wore a much different style of habit than the stoic Franciscans. Sharply tailored black dresses with pleated trim adorning the front of their veils, replaced the drab loose fitting brown robes and large white bibs of the previous order. Most distinctive of all was the difference in their personalities. The Filipppinis were a kinder, gentler, more motherly sort and when they sang their voices fluttered at the end of every verse. Mother Cecilia Maria was especially nice, but as luck would have it, the sister I would have to contend with was the one bad apple in the convent.

I felt like a fish out of water among the ridiculing rabble in the "B" class. I didn't even try to make friends and was all business with my teacher Mrs. Fern. The goal was simple; excel academically and rejoin my classmates in 3-A as soon as possible. Coming to class with such a strong resolve, I aced every single subject and quickly demonstrated that I belonged back in the "A" class. My work was so exceptional that halfway through the first quarter Mrs. Fern also recognized the mismatch and transferred me back into the "A" class. I relished the victory and looked forward to rejoining my peers in the classroom across the hall.

As soon as my father pulled his car into the driveway, I ran up to him and shared the good news. I proudly presented him with the interim report that vindicated me. Carefully looking it over, he smiled, put his hand on my shoulder and said, "Good job!" His approving smile lifted all the stress from my shoulders and the reconciliation of our relationship warmed my heart. However, although the future looked full of promise, my return to the "A" class, like the pending game changer that was about to take place in Rome, would fail to bring forth the desired fruit.

In October, Pope John XXIII convened the Second Vatican Council. It would be the first ecumenical council in over ninety years.[134] The primary purpose of the council was to address a perceived weakness in the Church on matters of faith and obedience. A secondary objective was to find better ways to spread the gospel in a world that was now quite literally operating at the speed of light. On the surface, the spiritual life of the Catholic Church looked exemplary, but while most Catholics were devout, they had also become somewhat robotic in the practice of their religion. Intensity to spread the good news of salvation and do battle with evil, was on the wane. Many of the bishops attempted to address these issues, but post-counciliar machinations would send the Church into a tail spin. Lots of traditionalists thought the cure was worse than the disease, but the weaknesses would soon be exposed. In less than a generation, two millennia of Catholic Tradition began to unravel.

---

[134] *Vatican II* – addressed relations between the Roman Catholic Church and the modern world. It was the 21st Ecumenical Council of the Catholic Church with the largest gathering of bishops to date and the 2nd Council to be held at St. Peter's Basilica in the Vatican. Pope John XXIII opened the Council on 10/11/62 and Pope Paul VI closed it on 12/8/65.

Significant geopolitical events were simultaneously initiating nightmare scenarios. Kennedy and Khrushchev[135] played a high stakes game of chicken, as the two superpowers teetered on the verge of World War III in the Cuban Missile Crisis. Although technology was exciting it was also unsettling. Dad had grown up listening to the Lone Ranger on a large radio set in his living room and told stories of hanging out in rail yards filled with steam locomotives.[136] Now the trains were powered by either electric or diesel and thanks to transistors, the radios were portable. Kennedy had even promised to put a man on the moon. The scientific advances intrigued my father and he encouraged me to look for clues of future developments in magazines like Popular Electronics[137] and Popular Mechanics.[138] He even pointed out an article in the newspaper that mentioned the word personal computer for the very first time.[139]

I was excited about going back to third grade in the "A" class, but the transition would not be easy. Mrs. Fern had been very kind to me, but Sister Philip Maria might as well have been Attila the Nun.

Although a relatively new concept, universal equality is a widely held myth today. This egalitarian worldview is the bedrock of everything from welfare and corporate bailouts to education and foreign policy, but Catholic teaching has always rejected this argument as flawed theology. While the Church believes all people have value and are loved by God,

---

[135] *Nikita Khrushchev* – served as the 1st Secretary of the Communist Party of the U.S.S.R. from 1953-1964 and its Premier of the from 1958-1964 during the Cold War. (1894-1971)
[136] *Steam Trains* – 1960 is normally considered the last year for regular class 1 Main Line standard gauge steam operations in the United States.
[137] *Popular Electronics* – was an American magazine started by Ziff-Davis Publishing in 1954 for hobbyist & experimenters in electronics. It soon became the "World's Largest-Selling Electronics Magazine". The circulation was 240,151 in 1957 & 400,000 by 1963.
[138] *Popular Mechanics* – is an American magazine devoted to science & technology. It was first published in 1902 by H. H. Windsor & has been owned since 1958 by the Hearst Corporation. Today there are 9 international editions, including a Latin American version that has been published for decades & a newer South African edition.
[139] From the article *Pocket Computer May Replace Shopping List* in The New York Times, November 3, 1962.

She also teaches that in His Wisdom the Creator of the universe made each person unique. Some are rich, while others live in poverty. Many are weak and a few are incredibly strong. A fraction of the population is brilliant; most are average and a few are downright stupid. Based on this understanding, the good Sisters routinely separated out those students with an aptitude for college and placed them on a fast track in an "A Class". When carried out properly, it was a great way to produce happy and productive citizens, but Miss Looming had messed with that system.

The "A" class, spent first grade learning addition and second grade learning subtraction, so that by the time we all reached third grade, we would be ready for multiplication. The "B" class, on the other hand, was still learning addition in second grade and was just beginning to learn subtraction in the third. Placing me in 3-B was like having me repeat the second grade and it gave me a late start in my third grade subjects. I began my math classes learning the four times tables, with no real understanding of the concept of multiplication. Although my first semester report card redeemed my credibility with dad, there was no way I would be able to catch up with my new classmates and the next marking period ended with me being grounded again.

Sister Phillip was Sicilian and unlike the other warm Sisters in her order, she was absolutely task oriented and deeply prejudiced. There was no way she would slow her class down, just so that one struggling student could play catch-up; especially not if he was the son of an Irishman. Using flash cards, I drilled constantly and tried to keep up, but without an understanding of the concept of multiplication, I was always befuddled. I was convinced I could master the subject, but the results were proving otherwise. No matter how hard I tried, success eluded me.

The time I spent in the "B" class had stigmatized me and I frequently failed to give the correct answers in class.

Explaining my predicament to other students only seemed to make matters worse and I began looking like a pathetic wannabe. It was extremely embarrassing and my classmates began treating me like a leper. Not only had Miss Looming betrayed me, she had set me up for constant failure in a no-win spiral. Sister Drill Sergeant's callous attitude only added to my difficulties and left me feeling completely alone and frustrated at school.

Things were much better at home. Multiplication drills kept me busy at night, but at least I wasn't grounded – yet! Tom Reeves and I hung out so much we wore a path in the back yards that cut between our two homes. We rode bikes, gathered apples, practiced launching them from sticks and continued to work on our tree fort. One weekend, while our family was away on a camping trip, some kids jumped on top of the tunnels we had dug behind the garage. We returned to find every one of them caved in, but dad found a silver lining in the disaster. He suggested we start digging and turn our damaged foxholes into one big wide ditch. Tom and I feverishly dug in the dirt every day after school. We also enlisted the help of my brother Sean, Toby Wilson and Elliot Gague. Each night dad came by to inspect our work and told us he would have a surprise for us by the end of the week. Digging in the sand and clay soil was relatively easy and by Friday night we had a ten foot diameter hole in the ground, with equally deep trenches extending another ten feet both east and west.

On Friday, Cholly Monroe, the company truck driver, followed dad home and they unloaded a thick over-sized sheet of plywood, which was completely soaked in oil. Then they carried over a couple of four by eight sheets of plywood, three heavy timbers, some two-by-four studding and an old canvas tarp. Dad and Cholly placed the three long beams across the big hole, some two-by-fours across the trenches and the plywood on top of the lumber. After our ditch had a roof, we all pulled the heavy canvas tarp on top of the wood. Cholly lit up a big cigar and talked with dad, while the rest of us shoveled dirt on top of the canvas. The plan was so simple and yet so perfect. Attempting to enter the new underground fort, dad stopped us in our tracks and said, "I want all of you to jump on it first." When we knew the roof was solid we went inside, but it was really dark! So I got the kerosene lantern from the garage, while Sean ran into the house for some matches and Tom retrieved a can of kerosene. Dad watched us as we filled it up and lit the lantern. When we took it inside the fort, the whole place was bathed in long shadows and a dim light. To this day the smell of kerosene still evokes fond memories.

Our underground fort was now the talk of the town. What we did not know was that we had started an arms race. Eddie Bundy, the spoiled son of the doctor who lived on the corner, had a huge underground fort in the woods behind his house and Vern Gibson who lived a block away, made a fort out of screen doors. Toby introduced us to his friend Vern, but warned us about messing with evil Eddie. Toby Wilson told us that the Army held war games to practice for the real thing and suggested we engage in a mock siege of our fort. Toby, Elliot and Vern would try to take the tree fort from Sean, Tom and me. We decided on the following Saturday as a date for our skirmish, which gave us time to make preparations.

On Monday, I returned to the grueling work of getting through my multiplication tables. The fives weren't that bad, but the six times tables slowed me down and by the time I hit the sevens, I was befuddled all over again. I even drilled during recess with some flash cards, while sitting at the bottom of an old oak tree, but tiny red ants made their way up my pant leg and began biting me, so I had to quit for the day. Every time the teacher called on me, I was embarrassed by my ignorance and offered no response. By the time school let out at three thirty, I was mentally and emotionally wiped out and ready for a break.

Preparing to win a war seemed greatly preferable to loosing at school. Tom and I gathered hundreds of apples and cut down several green branches to use for launchers. Sean climbed Mrs. Martin's crabapple tree and shook off the fruit. We gathered them all up and used a plastic cooler for an ammo box. In addition to our buckets and boxes we doubled-up brown paper Acme bags and filled them to the brim with crabapples. Come Friday night, we were locked, loaded and ready for a war!

On Saturday morning, Toby and Vern wheeled a wagon load of ammo into our backyard. We climbed out of the tree fort to inspect their mobile munitions magazine and then went over the ground rules. The team still in possession of their fortress, by the time all the ammo runs out would be declared the winner. Also, no one would be allowed to pick up any ammo that was already on the ground. Other than that; there were no rules. Toby pulled his wagon behind the garage. Toby, Elliot and Vern would be defending the underground fort, while Tom, Sean and I would protect our tree fort. For the first few seconds, all one could hear were the chirping of the birds and the rustle of the wind blowing through the leaves of the massive elm tree. All was peaceful until Tom yelled out, "Let the games begin!"

Toby and Vern initiated the battle by circling the yard, while Elliot started pummeling the blind side of our fort. Each time we stuck our heads out the window; an apple would hit the side of the window and explode in our faces. Elliot kept us busy on one side, while Toby and Vern maneuvered to flank us. They began their assault through the front and side windows forcing us to drop to the floor to avoid being hit. The din from the apples smashing against the back wall sounded like kettle drums and bits of pulp ricocheted from almost every direction, but after each volley we jumped back up to fire and got walloped again.

Tom got off a few shots through the open door, but then Vern snuck up from behind the tree and using the trunk of the tree like a shield, fired through the open door at point blank range. Cowering on the floor in the corner of the tree fort, it looked as if we were about to be over run. But just when we thought all was lost, Tom gave out a blood curdling Indian war cry, hung out the front door and beaned Vern in the head.

Inspired by his bravado, I jumped up and spied Toby climbing up the front piers. I whipped his arm with the apple launcher and fired off three close range apples, hitting him dead center in the middle of his back. Stunned by the unexpected assault, he fell off the scaffolding and ran back toward the hedge. Taking advantage of the momentary retreat, Tom scrambled onto the roof and called for ammo. Sean handed him up a bag of apples and Tom started firing down at Elliot with abandon. While the three of them were reloading, I climbed up on the roof to join Tom and Sean gave me another bag of munitions. Tom was a darn good shot and he had lots of power, but the other team stayed out of range. Tom called for a couple of launchers and Sean handed them up to us. We feverishly began puncturing the apples and whipping them down at the enemy from the top of our elevated platform. All our practice paid off and we started hitting them again and again.

With every apple that met its mark, Toby began loosing his cool. Elliot even gave up and went home. Vern was badly bruised and also getting tired of the fight. He wanted to surrender, but his friend was seeing red. Firing as he made his advance, Toby grabbed the last bucket of apples and rushed the fort. When he got under it, he called on Vern to join him and they both made a last ditch effort to climb up the side. With all our might, Tom and I laid down a barrage of fire from the roof. The painful ordeal ended when they ran out of apples. Vern tried picking up ammo from the ground, but Sean called him on the rule violation and the three of us claimed victory. Defeated, hurting and out of answers, the two remaining warriors left the field of battle with their empty wagon wheels squeaking. Still smarting from their defeat, they began to cuss us out as they departed, complaining that we had turned a simple practice skirmish, into a full-blown war. What they said was absolutely correct and from that moment on, Vern and Toby became our sworn enemies.

Each day brought with it a similar routine that was repeated throughout the week. During the day I was a serious, hard working student desperately trying to catch up with my peers. The teacher offered little or no help and my classmates avoided me like the plague and had virtually no understanding or interest in what I was going through. Other than Rachael Riley, who helped me to study, I felt very much alone. In stark contrast to the school environment, I spent every afternoon and weekend living an adventurous life filled with excitement and success. Tom and I were building a strong personal relationship and he soon became my best friend. Most evenings were also spent alone going over multiplication tables, with mom testing me when I finished. In order to emotional survive; I compartmentalized these two very different worlds.

Winter brought with it outdoor play and I showed my younger brothers how to make snow angels, build snowmen and throw snowballs, but my mentoring would be short-lived. Tom and I began building snow forts, which provided a defense against the daily snowball fights with Toby and Vern. Sometimes they got home from school before we did and destroyed our forts, but our technology was about to improve. Dad filled up an empty trashcan with snow and dumped it upside down. His technique took a lot less time than rolling snow balls, but that was only the half of it. My father had a secret weapon. On a bitter cold night we hooked up the garden hose and sprayed water all over the snow fort. The next day it was frozen solid. Tom and I were winning every battle until Toby acquainted me with the ice ball. Vern mixed ice balls in with his regular snowballs and in the heat of battle, one hit me in the eye. It was like being hit with a rock. Blood gushed out of my head and I ran into the house to see mom for some first aid. While she was patching me up, Tom found the ice ball they had used and we wanted to make some of our own, but neither mom nor dad would allow it.

In school I was absolutely floundering in math and still deficient in spelling. My grades tanked and despite my best efforts, Sister Philip checked the same "uses time well" and "works to ability" boxes that Miss Looming had cited on the back of my report card. Nothing could have been further from the truth. While it was true that I was struggling academically, not only was I doing all of my homework in a timely manner, but mom and Rachael Riley were always drilling me on my multiplication tables. Sister was so unfair and never lifted finger to help.

Most Consecrated Virgins are warm, caring and holy women, but Sister Philip was sexually deviant, as well as verbally and physically abusive. While standing in line one day for a drink of water, I watched her grab a boy by his ear and drag him all the way down the hall like a rag doll, just for talking. Her evil ways were not confined to children either. Sister frequently flattened Monsignor's fedora with her fist and after teaching us Irish history on Saint Patrick's Day, the sleazy Sicilian Sister bowled oranges down the hallway, as the kindly old Irishman left her classroom. Her abuse of male students, hatred for the Irish and distain for all things holy continued to progress, until her selfish behavior eventually broke up a family. Following a New Year's Eve party, she seduced the inebriated father of a large family. The disgraced man's marriage tragically ended in divorce and although the scandal was quietly buried, Sister's transfer produced rumors of a pregnancy and her expulsion from the order.

Thanks to my latest report card, I was once again chained to my desk every afternoon, until all of my homework was finished. Tom came by every day, but I was not allowed to leave the property. Shunned at school and lonely at home, I began living for the weekends. One Saturday morning dad invited Robert Gague and his father to accompany us to the Philadelphia International Airport.[140] After sitting in the concourse to watch some planes take off, we climbed a narrow iron staircase up to the flight deck. From the eagle's nest, we observed planes taking off and landing through a big pair of coin-operated binoculars. After knocking on the control tower door, air traffic controllers invited us inside to watch them work and see their radar screens. Try pulling that stunt off today!

One of the upsides of being the first-born child was that I got to go on interesting daytrips like these with my father. I also went on camping trips with him on weekends. As the eldest, I was also duty bound to set a good example for my younger siblings, but had to learn through trial and error. By observing my behavior, Sarah and my brothers had the advantage of seeing which things brought praise and which ones resulted in punishment. Actually, I relished being at the top of the pecking order and considered the perks and the status worth the price I had to pay.

Lisa Landers finally arrived from Wales in January. Mother now had full-time help with babysitting and the housekeeping needs of our growing family. Miss Landers was given a bedroom in the attic, which included her own bathroom. Her enthusiasm and love of children endeared us to her. I occasionally gave her a hard time, but she stood up

---

[140] *Philadelphia International Airport* – is located in Philadelphia, PA & is the international hub of US Airways. In 1925, the PA National Guard used the site (historically known as Hog Island) as a training field for its airplane pilots. The site was dedicated by Charles Lindbergh in 1927, but there was no terminal until 1940, so airlines used the Camden airfield in NJ. Once the terminal was completed, American, Eastern, TWA & United regularly scheduled flights in & out of the facility.

to me and I respected her for it. Our new nanny was not a mere maid or babysitter, Lisa soon became an important member of our family and acted more like a playful Aunt than an Au Pare. In addition to waking us up in the morning and babysitting on Saturday nights, she also helped my mother with the groceries, assisted her with meal preparation, did the laundry and helped to clean the house. Lisa was paid a modest salary, had one day off a week and like Rachel Riley, came along with us on family camping trips. She ate with us, swam with us, played with us and taught us playful new songs she had learned back in Britain. Best of all she was a companion to my mother and the two of them got along like sisters.

Lisa was not the only British invasion in America that year. The Beatles released their first single Love Me Do[141] only a few months before her arrival. Having affection for all things British, she enjoyed watching the Fab Four rise to the top of the pop charts. This twenty-year-old beauty was drawn to good-looking men of integrity. So each week two television shows took precedence over any other shows we wanted to watch. One stared David Jansen in The Fugitive[142] and the other was Twelve O'clock High,[143] which was a story about a WWII bomber squadron flying out of England. Although we soon shared her enthusiasm for the TV dramas, I never warmed up to The Beatles.

---

[141] *Love Me Do* – is a Lennon/McCartney song, principally written by Paul McCartney in 1958–59 while playing truant from school. John Lennon wrote additional lines & the song was The Beatles' first single, backed by "P.S. I Love You" & released on 5 October 1962.

[142] *The Fugitive* – was a television series produced by QM Productions & United Artists Television that aired on ABC from 1963-1967. David Janssen starred as Richard Kimble, a doctor from the fictional town of Stafford, Indiana, who was falsely convicted of his wife's murder & given the death penalty. En route to death row, Kimble's train derails & crashes, allowing him to escape & begin a cross-country search for the real killer, a "one-armed man" (played by Bill Raisch). At the same time, Dr. Kimble is hounded by the authorities, most notably by Stafford Police Lieutenant Philip Gerard (Barry Morse).

[143] *12 O'Clock High* - was a TV drama series set in World War II. It aired on ABC for three seasons from 1964-1967 & was based on the 1949 motion picture of the same name. The series followed the missions of the US Army Air Force's 918th Bomb Group, equipped with the B-17 Flying Fortresses, stationed at [fictional] Archbury, England.

Lisa often helped me with my multiplication tables and mom schooled me in grammar. Between the two of them, I was beginning to catch on to the concept of multiplication and was doing exceptional work in English class where we were diagramming sentences. However, by the time I caught up to my classmates in math class, they had moved on to division. Without a proper foundation in one, it was impossible to comprehend the other. Dispirited at school, I longed for the weekends all the more.

One Saturday morning I wandered downstairs to find Tom Reeves engrossed in cartoons and watching Mr. Magoo[144] in the family room. I suggested we do some spring training out in the tree fort, but as usual Tom did not hear a word I said. I had to pry him away from the television set by turning it off. Once I got his attention we left the house, he rose to the challenge and by coming up with an exercise program, which included: running, calisthenics and rope climbing. Tom worked out a tough routine, with a swashbuckling finish that included an exhilarating jump off the roof of the tree fort and onto a stack of old mattresses.

After lunch, we walked the tracks for miles and tight roped the rails, until we came upon a bridge that crossed a six lane highway. Since the trestle had no floor to it, we stopped our high-wire act and settled for a safer method of travel; one railroad tie at a time. Full concentration was required on each railroad tie, which meant that we would not be able to see any trains coming. Anxious about our survival, every few seconds we stopped to look up for the train. In the hot noonday sun the tar on the ties stuck to the bottom of my Keds™ and looking up gave me a slight case of vertigo. After what seemed like an eternity, we made it to the

---

[144] *Mr. Magoo* – was a cartoon character created at the UPA animation studio in 1949. Voiced by Jim Backus, Quincy Magoo was a wealthy, short-statured retiree who gets into a series of sticky situations as a result of his nearsightedness, compounded by his stubborn refusal to admit to his problem. Affected people (or animals) consequently tend to think that he is a lunatic, rather than just being nearsighted.

opposite side of the bridge. There we found a small patch of woods and a marshy forest. It was a lot like the one back in Pennsauken. We named the place Pennypacker Woods, because of all the pennies we flattened on the railroad tracks. We buried our little treasures in a tin box on one of the many clay islands that dotted the marsh. Unfortunately, we could never build any forts there, because a bunch of older boys hung out in the woods and would chase us away. But whenever the hooligans were off somewhere else, we had a great time exploring the swamp. I pretended to be Huck Finn and Tom took up the last name of Sawyer, as we set out to navigate the forested everglade on rafts constructed of old oak skids.

Thanks to a lot of hard work and the help I was receiving at home, I managed to improve my performance at school just enough to advance to 4-A, but I still had no idea what I was doing in math class. Third grade had been a living hell and I couldn't wait for school to be over. Despite my best efforts, I was left with a weak foundation in mathematics and it would handicap academic pursuits for the rest of my life.

As summer approached, brochures were handed out at school with appealing sketches of boys in sharp blue uniforms who seemed to be having the time of their lives. Already excited about getting out of school, the invitation to join the Cub Scouts[145] multiplied my motivation to learn about life outside of the classroom. Older students spoke in glowing terms about their experiences with scouting and I ran home to ask my parents if I could join. It was an easy sell. Mom and dad thought it was a great idea and signed me up at the next Pack Meeting. Our first Den meeting was at Mr. & Mrs. Pine's house. There we assembled all sorts of arts and crafts

---

[145] *Cub Scouting* – is a program of the Boy Scouts of America. 1st year Cub Scouts (2nd grade) work toward the Wolf badge, then toward Arrow Points. 2nd year Cub Scouts (3rd grade) work toward the Bear badge & then earn additional Arrow Points. The Wolf badge has 12 requirements that empower basic life skills and the Bear requires completing several requirements within the areas of "God", "Country", "Family" & "Self".

on her dining room table. Betty Pine helped us to make pinwheels, taught us how to braid lanyard key chains and gave us all sorts of leather products to make, like wallets, link-belts and Indian moccasins. Mr. Pine taught us how to make birdhouses and wooden boats, which we sailed down the gutters immediately following afternoon thunderstorms. Barney Pine was also the Leader of the Pack and he made sure that we had fun whenever we pursued requirements for advancement. Dad picked me up on-time at the end of each meeting, but he spent so much time talking with Mr. Pine that I was almost always the last kid to leave.

Soon after joining the scouts, dad purchased a cabin on the Rancocas Creek in Mount Holly, New Jersey. The faded yellow clapboard retreat cabin was trimmed in a dark brown and was called Sleepy Hollow, which was the title of an old ghost story.[146] The road into the cabin was long, sandy and filled with potholes, which frequently filled up with rain water. One day I asked my father why there were so many puddles and he launched into a story about the galloping ghost. Apparently a powerful and mysterious horse left its hoof prints on the road, and when it rained, the huge footprints filled up with water. From then on, each time we bounced and splashed our way through the puddles on the road to the cabin, we all kept a lookout for the scary dark horse.

After awhile, dad worked out a barter agreement with Barney Pine. Barney maintained the cabin, in exchange for letting his family spend time there. The win-win agreement allowed both of our families to enjoy the benefits of swimming and canoeing in the rich brown cedar waters of the Rancocas Creek. Between the Den and Pack meetings at

---

[146] *The Legend of Sleepy Hollow* – is a short story by Washington Irving contained in his collection "The Sketch Book of Geoffrey Crayon, Gent." written while he was still living in Birmingham, England & first published in 1820, along with Irving's companion piece "Rip Van Winkle" & is among the earliest examples of American fiction still read today.

Saint Peter's, dad and I both became more and more involved in scouting.

One evening the entire Pack went out to see a new kind of movie called Cinerama.[147] How the West was Won[148] followed the lives of pioneers, as they pushed west, fulfilling the Manifest Destiny of our great nation. I thought it was a great way to learn history! And the movie made me proud to be an American. Although it was a fictional account, the film included many touch stones in history and captured the popular myth of our American heritage. The dramatic reenactment portrayed the many sacrifices that were made to tame a wilderness, which would eventually become the greatest civilization on earth that man had ever known. The story told of a diverse assortment of personalities that all came together to construct this great nation. Instead of dividing us, their individual struggles welded us together as one people. Mountain men, Indians, farmers, ranchers, politicians, preachers, gold seekers, railroad men, slaves and the sons of slave owners, all helped to shape America. This epoch flick made a deep impression on me and created an almost insatiable thirst to learn more about our history.

Using the scout handbook as a guide, dad and I worked together to build cool stuff like electromagnets, a telegraph set and a radio made from a cat's whisker. Dad drilled me on things like Morse code so I could earn arrow points and mom took me out shopping for a uniform. Steadily advancing in rank, I received my Wolfe[149] badge and went on to get more

---

[147] *Cinerama* – is the trademarked name for a widescreen process which works by simultaneously projecting images from three synchronized 35 mm projectors onto a huge, deeply-curved screen. It was the first of a number of such processes introduced during the 1950s, when the movie industry was reacting to competition from television.

[148] *How the West Was Won* – was a 1962 epic Western film that is set between 1839 & 1889. It follows 4 generations of the Prescott family, as they move ever westward, from New York state to the Pacific Ocean.

[149] *Wolf* – rank is earned by completing 75% of some basic tasks in a Cub Scout handbook.

Arrow Points and eventually rose to the ranks of Bear[150] and Webelos.[151]

Although I was learning a lot and having fun in scouts, dad always made me go way beyond the requirements of the book. After building a telegraph system from scratch, he brought home a real one, complete with an old-fashioned style key and a brass clicker. One week later he gave me a beeping oscillator on which to practice my Morse code. Pursuing the subject even further, he bought a used ham radio receiver, which we set up in the attic. Each night we listened to people from all over the world and dad suggested we get our own ham radio licenses. My father and I practiced Morse Code nightly, but when it came time to take the test, he passed and I failed. I only missed by one point and was still interested in radio, but I remember being pretty bummed out about not getting my license. Once he had his license, dad purchased a Heath Kit[152] transmitter. Every evening we assembled the radio in the unfinished portion of the attic. Our staging area for the building project was a sheet of plywood atop two sawhorses. I organized the small components by number and dad read the step-by-step instructions aloud. Calling out the part numbers, I organized dozens of color-banded resistors in tea cups. Then I handed him the item he needed and he soldered each one in place.

Building the transmitter was interesting enough, but standing around while dad used the radio soon grew boring. Noting my lack of interest, dad brought home another Heath Kit radio for me to build. The portable transmitter required no license and tapped into AM frequencies at close range. With

---

[150] *Bear* – to earn this badge, a Cub Scout must complete 12 of 24 achievements in 4 areas, God, Country, Family & Self.
[151] *Webelos Scout Badge* – is a transitional rank from Cub to Boy Scouts. It requires Scouts to earn 3 activity badges, demonstrating religiosity & knowing the basics about Boy Scouts, such as the Outdoor Code. Webelos is an acronym that stands for We Be Loyal Scouts.
[152] *Heathkits* – were products of the Heath Company, Benton Harbor, MI. Products included electronic test equipment, hi-fi home audio equipment, TV receivers & amateur radio equipment, which were sold in kit form for assembly by the purchaser.

some guidance from dad, in between playing with his own ham radio, I was able to put together my own transmitter. When the project was completed I sat down on the ground below Megan McGuire's open window, synchronize the frequency to the station her mother was listening to and began broadcasting. "We interrupt this program, to bring you an important announcement. The aliens have landed in Pennsauken and will soon be invading Merchantville. Lock your doors and windows and stay inside your houses."

It seemed like a harmless prank, but Mrs. McGuire looked out her window and started franticly yelling at me. I ran home laughing and told the story that night during dinner. Dad was not amused. He understood her anger and told us a story about the Orson Wells broadcast entitled War of the Worlds. Apparently, thousands of people who were listening to his show panicked, causing massive traffic jams and accidents, while they tried to escape from what they believed was a real invasion. Dad said that Mr. Wells had lost his broadcast license over the incident and my father instructed me to cease and desist. I refrained from similar pranks, but continued using the transmitter, as a walkie-talkie with my friends and family. Actually, this little boyhood prank was nothing, compared to what would later become known as the Radio Project.[153]

Sixty-one years after The War of the Worlds hit the airways, a documentary exposed the broadcast as a conspiracy between Edward Bernays of CBS and Ivy Lee of The

---

[153] *The Radio Project* – was a social research project funded by the Rockefeller Foundation, to look into the effects of mass media on society. In 1937, the foundation began funding research to discover the effects of new forms of mass media on society, especially radio. Several universities joined up & a headquarters was formed at the School of Public & International Affairs at Princeton University. One of their projects was the 1938 broadcast of *The War of the Worlds*. It found that of the estimated 6 million people who heard this broadcast, 25% thought it was real, but most people didn't think it was an invasion from Mars; they thought it was an invasion by German soldiers. Actually, the radio broadcast was a psychological warfare experiment & in the 1999 documentary, "Masters of the Universe: The Secret Birth of the Federal Reserve", writer Daniel Hopsicker claims that the Rockefeller Foundation funded the broadcast, studied the panic & compiled a report, for their small group of social engineers.

Rockefeller Foundation. These two leading crowd psychology researchers, colluded with Orson Welles and Frank Stanton, the president of CBS, to first create, and then study the ensuing panic. Of particular note was the fact that the Mercury Theatre had no advertising during its Halloween broadcast. Many a truth is said in jest and when confronted with the oddity, Orsen Welles mocked his critics, by saying that the program time was paid for by "secret sponsors". His partner in crime, Frank Stanton went on to become chairman of the RAND Corporation[154] and a later BBC documentary[155] confirmed the entire conspiracy as factual.

While social engineers were busy playing with people's heads, dad and I were engaged in a radio project of our own. Each night would start out the same. "CQ – CQ – CQ", which meant, Is there anyone out there in radio land that wants to talk?" "CQ – CQ – CQ, this is WN2MOR, CQ – CQ – CQ." After a few tries we would get some scratchy response back on the receiver and meet someone from West Virginia, North Carolina or Michigan. On clear nights, we could even contact people from the other side of the planet, in places like Japan, Poland or Egypt. The radio was fun for a while, but to be honest, dad was more interested in it than me. When he sensed my discontent he redirected the time we spent together into an alternate hobby. I had been raving about the massive train layout in Mr. Gague's basement and bugging him to let me build one in our cellar. The only problem was that our basement had become a virtual Indy 500 for tricycles on rainy days. There was no way dad was going to fill up our basement with trains, but he did do the next best thing. Dad took me to the hobby shop and bought me an "HO" gage train set and we set it up on the plywood table in the radio room. The tiny trains were about half the

---

[154] *RAND Corporation* – is a non-profit think tank developing policy & decision making through objective research & analysis. RAND stands for Research ANd Development.
[155] *The Century of the Self* – is a British TV documentary film that focuses its attention on Sigmund Freud's family, especially his daughter & nephew, who exerted a surprising amount of influence on the way corporations & governments throughout the 20th century have thought about & dealt with people. The Radio Project was just one of their examples.

size of a Lionel and so it was hard to line the wheels up on the ribbons of brass track, but I was thrilled to have my own train set.

Each week dad and I went to the hobby shop and bought a single item for the train. It might be some fake grass to glue onto the plywood, a railroad car, a trestle bridge or a crossing barricade complete with flashing lights and bells. Dad taught me how to hook up the electric wires, set limit switches and build papier-mâché mountains. While my father conversed on the ham radio set, I worked on my trains. We weren't exactly working together and didn't even talk all that much, but somehow just hanging out together in the same room was building a very close relationship.

Family tradition dictated that we reenact the revolutionary war every Fourth of July. However this year was a bit uncomfortable due to the presence of our British nanny. So I asked Lisa if she minded watching us glorify the victory over her king. She just laughed and said, "No. We got over that a long time ago." She even helped us to decorate our bikes and cheered for us in the parade. Later on we took turns reciting Patrick Henry's speech[156] and competed with each other to see who could memorize the most lines. That evening we ran around with sparklers and set off dozens of penny firecrackers. During dinner, I asked Lisa if there was a 4th of July in England, prompting her tongue-in-cheek response, "Of course we do silly, what do you think comes after the third?"

The next day we helped Miss Landers celebrate her own independence. It was her twenty-first birthday. Gathering

---

[156] *Patrick Henry* – is best known for the speech he made in the House of Burgesses on March 23, 1775, in Saint John's Church in Richmond, VA. The House was undecided on whether to mobilize for military action against the encroaching British military force & Henry argued in favor of mobilization. 42 years later, William Wirt, reconstructed his speech, which ended with words that have become immortalized: *"Is life so dear, or peace so sweet, as to be purchased at the price of chains & slavery? Forbid it, Almighty God! I know not what course others may take; but as for me, Give me Liberty, or give me Death!"*

around the kitchen table after dinner, mom brought out a cake and each of us gave her hand made presents and a birthday card signed by all of us. Apparently she was not expecting it and started to cry. We assumed we had somehow offended her, but she reassured us that her tears were tears of joy. Seems her biggest fear was that she wouldn't know anyone in America and would find it difficult to fit in. The party, the card and the gifts all demonstrated to her that she was not only welcomed, but profoundly loved.

The following day, Tom Reeves and I ventured a bit farther from home. While tight roping the rails we came across a couple of grain elevators by the side of the track. The two concrete silos had been abandoned for years. The bottoms were filled with sand and an old rusty cable hung down from the top of one of them. Tom grabbed hold of it and swung to the other side. We took turns rappelling off the sides and pretending we were swash-buckling pirates, but as the sun rose directly overhead even the shade inside the tower was not enough to keep two active privateers from fading in the heat. Tom and I followed the tracks back home and wasted no time before jumping into the pool. Like spacemen in The Twilight Zone,[157] we were so overheated that for the first couple of minutes, we floated face down and motionless in the water. Refreshed, we dove for coins and waterlogged toys until it was time for lunch. Our fingers looked like raisins, as we dried off and headed for the house where we helped ourselves to peanut butter and apple butter sandwiches.

Although I had never been inside his house, Tom practically lived at mine. I had not yet met his family, but after lunch he invited me over for his sister's birthday party. While cutting through the yards we came across an old rusty chain link fence. Since it was only about three feet high, we just

---

[157] *The Twilight Zone* – was a TV anthology series created by Rod Serling. Each episode was a mixture of self-contained fantasy, science fiction, suspense, or horror, often concluding with a macabre or unexpected twist.

jumped over it. On the opposite side was a three-car garage, a paved driveway and an enormous Victorian mansion. Everything was beautifully accented. The doors and the windows of the house and even the garage were all painted with jet-black trim and all the windows had green awnings with a white and gold family crest. Even the blacktop had a freshly painted white curb. The grass was recently cut and there was a large tree with low hanging branches, just begging to be climbed. In the center of the fine trimmed lawn was an in-ground trampoline, framed with green and white safety pads. The only item out of place in the entire property was a green tarp that had been pulled off to one side.

Cars parked in front of the garage made it obvious someone was home. Although we knew it wasn't our property and were quite sure we weren't supposed to be cutting through the yard, the opportunity was simply to irresistible to ignore. Our only hesitation was a split-second sideways glance at each other, followed by a mad dash for the trampoline. We jumped up and down for about ten minutes and occasionally bumped into each other, as we discovered how to use this acrobatic dream machine. Once we got the hang of it, we alternately launched each other like rockets into the stratosphere. Caught up in the moment we forgot where we were, until we heard a terrifying sound. Two ferocious barking dogs came running out the front door and made a beeline for us. Terrified, Tom and I froze in our tracks. The duo of large black poodles, each weighing in at about a hundred pounds a piece, stopped just short of the trampoline and continued barking, until their master called them off.

I had never seen poodles this big and we only later learned that kings often used them for guard dogs. Mr. Ellerman, the owner of the property, walked over to us yelling, "What are you doing here? Get off of there. Look what you've done." When we looked back we saw muddy foot prints all over the black mesh. In all the excitement, we hadn't even noticed.

We offered to clean it off, but he snarled back, "It's not the dirt that's the problem. You shouldn't even be jumping with shoes on. It could tear the trampoline." He demanded we leave his property and never return. Although we never did jump on his trampoline with our shoes on again, the temptation to return was just too great. Our frequent return visits eventually morphed into an exciting game of cat and mouse with him, while always remaining vigilant for the sound of barking of dogs.

Walking in the back door of Tom's house, I was greeted by the din of a noisy mad house of fun and excitement. His mother was a stunning long-haired blond and she was the most beautiful woman I had ever seen. Mrs. Olivia Reeves warmly welcomed me and sat us down at an already crowded table. I couldn't take my eyes off her, as she lit the candles on the cake. Leaning over to Tom I said, "Your mom is beautiful!" He matter-of-factly acknowledged the compliment saying, "Yeah, I guess she is." Something was downright exceptional about Mrs. Reeves and I knew it was more than just her beauty and charm. There was something especially familiar about her. And then it dawned on me. Mrs. Olivia Reeves was as Irish as a shamrock, but she looked Swedish. Katy Holstrum was the name of the governess on a new sitcom called The Farmer's Daughter.[158] The show would not air until next September, but ABC was already running commercials for their new comedy show. Since we now had a nanny who was an important part of our family, we quickly identified with the cheerful farm girl and looked forward the weekly sitcom. Tom's mother looked exactly like Inger Stevens, the woman who played Katy Holstrum. Meeting Mrs. Reeves was like getting a back-stage pass to meet a movie star. Olivia had made quite an

---

[158] *The Farmer's Daughter* – was a situation comedy TV series produced by Screen Gems Television & aired on ABC from 1963-1966. The series starred Inger Stevens as Katy Holstrum, a young Minnesota woman who becomes the governess for widowed Congressman Glen Morley & his two sons. Katy was played by Inger Stevens (1934–1970).

impression on me and was the warmest woman I had ever met.

Chapter 6

Soldier Of Christ

In grade school students remained in the same classroom for the entire day, with the exception of lunch and a couple of bathroom breaks. Sister Augustine switched classrooms with my teacher Miss Judith, every afternoon to teach us religion. In the fourth grade we were being prepared to receive the Sacrament of Confirmation. Already an important year for catechesis, a combination of outside influences converged that would mold me into a patriot, a righter of wrongs and a dedicated soldier of Christ. In 1963 our president was shot, the bishop smacked me in the face and I was introduced to a Scarecrow. These three seemingly disconnected events coalesced to lend added meaning to my life and helped to develop passion as a halmark of my personality. At about the same time that I was aquiring that fire in my belly, there sat within the eye of that huricane a good, holy and peaceful religious teacher who would help me to handle the pain of loss and begin to understand the nature my calling. Sister Augustine knew her theology well and was an excellent educator. She had a warm way about her that convinced our class that she cared about us and that she was deeply in love with Jesus. Following each lesson she carefully answered every one of our questions.

The first thing we went over were the three parts of the Church: The Church Militant, The Church Suffering and The Church Triumphant. Sister Augustine explained in detail each of the three classifications. Those of us here on earth made up The Church Militant, because we were still fighting the battle of temptations. The souls in Purgatory are refered to as The Church Suffering, because they are still being purged of their imperfections, so that they can one day commune with our Triune God. Finally, those enjoying the

Beatific Vision were the ones who had made it to heaven. They are known as the Church Triumphant, because they are finally living with God and rejoicing in His victory over Satan.

Sister Augustine covered some pretty complex theological concepts, yet she also helped us to clearly understand them by painting word pictures that made sense to us. She explained that as members of The Church Militant, we were still fighting in a war with evil and that we were part of God's army. In Baptism we were equipped with the weapons we needed for battle. Confession was like a hospital emergency room and Eucharist was nourishment for the journey. The Sacrament of Confirmation would teach us how to use our wepons and would give us the ammunition. In this way, Sister taught us that we were all destined to be warriors in Christ's Army. She even impressed on us that we must be willing to die for Christ our King and for His Holy Church. To encourage us along the way as we marched into battle were even given a triumphant battle hymn to sing.[159]

An Army of Youth
Flying the standard of truth.
We are fighting for Christ the Lord.
Heads lifted high
Catholic Action our cry,
And the cross our only sword...

Almost as powerful an influence in my life was the Disney miniseries The Scarecrow of Romney Marsh.[160] The Scarecrow in this tall tale was a righter of wrongs by night and a valiant Vicar by day. So, compared to watching

---

[159] *For Christ the King* – is a triumphant hymn that also goes by the title "An Army of Youth" with lyrics by Daniel Lord S.J. & published by The Queens Work, St. Louis, MO.

[160] *The Scarecrow of Romney Marsh* – was a 3-part TV miniseries produced by Walt Disney in 1963. Patrick McGoohan played the part of Dr Syn, a clergyman by day & the dreaded Scarecrow by night. He was a righter of wrongs in a time of oppressive governmental tyranny in England.

goofball shows like Petticoat Junction[161] or Fireball XL5;[162] the Scarecrow of Romney Marsh was both patriotic and high adventure, but the political reality of the story[163] was about to hit me square in the face.

On November twenty-second our classwork was interrupted by our pastor somberly requesting prayers for our President John F. Kennedy. Within days of the newscasters announcment about the shooting and Kennedy's subsequent death, there were troubling questions surrounding the assassination. Those questions still persist to this day and bring home the realization that evil really does exist in this world and it requires our confrontation. I so identified with the character of the Scarecrow that I virtually became him. The man was smart; he was hard working and he was just. He was a good role model and a man's man. Those who trusted in him were never betrayed, but he cleverly outwitted evil bureaucratic tyrants who lived off the sweat of others. Although the Disney story took place in England, the similarities to our own American Revolution and now the assassination of of our President, bore a striking resemblance to reality.

The following week in our religion class we learned about the power of The Holy Spirit and about the gifts that He wanted to give to us.[164] So I studied hard and looked forward

---

[161] *Petticoat Junction* – is an American situation comedy produced by Filmways, which originally aired on the CBS television network from 1963-1970.
[162] *Fireball XL5* – was a science fiction-themed child TV show aired by ITC Entertainment in 1962. It introduced Supermarionation marionettes, a new form of puppetry.
[163] *Content* – the fictional character of the Scarecrow faced the same deadly realities that JFK would face, after giving a speech to the Economic Club of New York on 12/14/62 in which he said, "The final and best means of strengthening demand among consumers and business is to reduce the burden on private income and the deterrents to private initiative which are imposed by our present tax system and this administration pledged itself last summer to an across-the-board, top-to-bottom cut in personal and corporate income taxes to be enacted and become effective in 1963." For this offense he would pay the ultimate price.
[164] *CCC 1831* – "The seven gifts of the Holy Spirit are wisdom, understanding, counsel, fortitude, knowledge, piety, and fear of the Lord. They belong in their fullness to Christ, Son of David. They complete and perfect the virtues of those who receive them. They make the faithful docile in readily obeying divine inspirations."

to one gift in particular; the gift of fortitude.[165] The Scarecrow was the embodiment of what sister called intestinal fortitude or guts. He lived an adventurous life filled with risk, outsmarted tyrants and all their bureaucratic minions and he did so in order to protect the good citizens of his parish. I prayed that I would one day do likewise. In time that simple prayer would be answered.

Scarecrow! Scarecrow!
The soldiers of the king feared his name.
Scarecrow! Scarecrow!
The country folk all loved him just the same.
Scarecrow[166]

In the Man of Lamancha,[167] Miguel de Cervantes explains to his fellow inmates that it is not enough for a knight to right all wrongs; every knight must also have a lady. And my Lady Dulcinea[168] was Annabel Logan. She was a delicate flower with a pleasant smile and she had long brunette hair. I took a liking to her and could not think of anyone my age who was nearly as beautiful. One day I decided to do something about it and went down to the jewelry store to buy her a friendship ring.

It took me a few days to get up the courage to give her the ring and she wasn't quite sure whether or not to accept it. When I assured her it was just a friendship ring, she thanked me for the gift and put it on her finger. The gentle smile on her face made it all worthwhile. During recess she showed it to a couple of her friends and word of the gift soon spread

---

[165] *Fortitude* – causes a man to be brave, when he would otherwise shrink, contrary to reason, from dangers or difficulties.
[166] *Refrain* – from the theme song of "The Scarecrow of Romney Marsh".
[167] *Man of La Mancha* – was a Broadway musical adapted from a 1959 non-musical teleplay by Dale Wasserman, lyrics by Joe Darion & music by Mitch Leigh. It was in turn inspired by Miguel de Cervantes's seventeenth century masterpiece "Don Quixote".
[168] *Dulcinea* – refers to a man's sweetheart. It is taken from the name of Don Quixote's mistress Dulcinea del Toboso in Cervantes' novel. It is derived from the Spanish word dulce, which means sweet. In the movie *Man of La Mancha*, Aldonza the whore is transformed into the lady Dulcinea through the unconditional love of Don Quixote.

across the schoolyard like wildfire. All our classmates began teasing us. Annabel and I tried avoiding the croud by walking to the other side of the parking lot, but the rabid rabble followed us wherever we went. We even tried taking refuge inside the school, but the doors were locked. At that point we just wanted the whole thing to go away, but we were stuck at the top of the concrete stairs with half the student body chanting, "Patrick and Annabel sitting in a tree, K—I—S—S—I—N—G, first comes love, then comes marriage, then comes baby in the baby carriage." Annabel was mortified and thankfully Mother Cecilia Maria came out to rescue her. Our normally quiet principal was indignant with the mocking crowd and her stern voice was so loud it sent the abusive students fleeing like rats. Putting a comforting arm around the poor crying little girl, she pulled her inside the building. I stood there dumfounded at the top of the stairs, trying to make sense of what had just happened.

As sweet as the term sounds, puppy love can be downright painful. I pined over Annabel for the rest of the year, but she never responded to any of my affectionate gestures. Every now and then I would drive over to her house on my bicycle, hoping to see her. I even stalked her through the backyards on foot, but never once caught so much as a glimpse of her. I longed for the day when we could be reunited.

In April I turned ten and all the focus of the Confirmandes[169] turned toward preparation for the day of our Confirmation. We learned volumes about the tenents of our faith and had lively discussions with Sister Augustine about why the Catholic Church believed what She did. I chose Christopher[170] as my Confirmation name, because I had a strong sense that I would always be traveling. In addition to learning about the faith, our classroom conversations helped us form friendships and our discussions even spilled over

---

[169] *Confirmandes* – is the name given to candidates for the Sacrament of Confirmation.
[170] *St. Christopher* – is the patron saint of travelers.

into the schoolyard during recess. I loved discussing religious concepts with my classmates, sharing our struggles with sin and talking about how best to live out our Christian callings. My dad said that his friend Harry Steel was a good holy man and would make a great Confirmation Sponsor. He had attended Camden Catholic High School with my parents and he turned out to be an excellent choice.

On the day of our Confirmation, we wore white shirts and royal red robes with matching neckties. The bishop quizzed each of us from the Catechism and it was obvious to all present that our class had been well prepared. After laying his hands on my head, Archbishop Celestine J. Damiano asked me, "Are you ready to die for Christ?" To which I confidently answered "yes" and he promptly slapped me in the face! The symbolic gesture was meant to be a foretaste of my call to martyrdom.

After we left Church, Harry and my parents took me out to Kenny's Suburban House for dinner. I had never been in a restaurant that posh before and felt as though I had passed through some sort of portal. Suddenly, I was being treated with a lot more respect. For the rest of the year, I wore my little red tie to school, as a symbol of my willingness to shed blood for Christ, if I was ever called upon to do so. The tie became an outward sign of what had taken place in my heart. I took my faith dead seriously and loved Jesus more than ever, but the battle for the Kingdom began much sooner than I had anticipated. Similar to the night of our Savior's arrest, every one of my friends would abandon me.

As Confirmandes we supported one another in our spiritual journey, but once confirmed all that fellowship and comraderie evaporated. There were no more discussions in class and no one seemed willing to talk about God any more. It reminded me of kids who study hard for a test and then once the test is over, forget everything they had learned. I rarely approached learning that way and was quite sure I didn't want to end my relationship with Christ, especially after just being confirmed. The reality saddened me. Although I was deeply hurt and utterly confused, I moved on alone; still loving Jesus and wanting to serve Him more than ever.

Academically, I still had many of the same difficulties, but none of my struggles seemed to bother me anymore. I worked hard in class, did my homework and drilled with my flashcards. Eventually, I caught up with the rest of the class and was able to successfully complete my Math and English requirements. While I never quite excelled in either subject, I was able to improve my grades enough to have my grounding lifted, which meant that I could play outside after school again.

Riding my old bike after school or on the weekends was a special treat for me, but I became disenchanted with it after seeing an ad in the newspaper for a ten-speed bicycle at E.J. Korvets.[171] I asked dad if he would help me to buy it and he responded by saying that he would give me one dollar for every dollar I earned on my own. The bike sold for $32.50. Saving my meager allowance of (40 cents/week) and getting paid for doing odd jobs around town gave me the money I needed in just six weeks. Once I purchased the new bicycle, my new transportation went into high-gear and I was able to visit Vinny Riley a lot more often.

Just prior to school letting out, the Cub Scout Pack held its annual Pinewood Derby.[172] Dad took me to the store to buy a kit, which contained the balsa wood block, black wheels and

---

[171] *E. J. Korvette* – was an American chain of discount department stores, founded in 1948 in NYC. It is notable as one of the first department stores to challenge the suggested retail price provisions of anti-discounting statutes. Unfortunately it failed to manage its success & declared bankruptcy in 1980. Founded by World War II veteran Eugene Ferkauf & his friend, Joe Zwillenberg, it did much to define the idea of the discount department store, by displacing earlier 5 & 10 retailers & preceded discount stores, like Wal-Mart.

[172] *Pinewood Derby* – is a racing event for Cub Scouts in the Boy Scouts of America. Cub Scouts, with the help of parents, build their own cars from wood, usually from kits containing a block of pine, plastic wheels & metal axles made from nails.

four blue nails, which doubled for axles. I carved the aerodynamic shape of the car with my official Cub Scout penknife and dad helped me drill holes in the bottom, which we filled with hot lead. He said the lead added weight for speed and ballast for stability. Although I was not privy to the full extent of his plan, dad instructed me to refrain from putting the wheels on until the very end, because he said he had a secret strategy for winning the race.

Many years prior, my father had learned a valuable lesson about lubrication. One of the first jobs he was given in my grandfather's machine shop was to place twenty-four lag bolts in a heavy piece of lumber, which would then be used to hang a crane on from the ceiling of the shop. His Uncle attempted to show him an easy way to accomplish the task, but because of his know-it-all youthful disposition he rejected the advice. The wise old Uncle left him alone to struggle with twenty-three of the twenty-four bolts, before stopping him. It had taken my dad almost four hours to complete the task. His Uncle told him to take a break. He handed him a bar of soap and told him to scrape it across the threads of the last lag bolt. When my father returned to his job, the bolt went into the wood like a hot knife through butter. The young apprentice was mad as hell, but he had learned a valuable lesson.

In light of that experience, my father put together a high-tech racing team. Dad called in one of the sales representatives from a lubricant manufacturer. After discussing their normal business, he asked him which of his products would work best on the axels of my model race car. The man looked into the matter and put his company scientists to work determining the best possible lubricant. Dad brought home one of their latest products and after placing a couple of drops on each axle he carefully hammered the nails into place, with all the perfection of a tool and die maker. Dad let me know that with all the research that went into this project, there was no way we could lose. I finished up the paint job and looked forward to the race on Saturday night.

Almost 200 kids showed up for the Pack Meeting that night, making the place even more noisy than usual. The impressive track ran the entire width of our school cafeteria. Heats within each den progressed, amidst the roar of excited cubs until my car earned the right to represent my den. The decibels in the room increased with each successive heat and every time my car rolled down the track, it came in first. After several attempts to quiet everyone down, Barney Pine called the Pack to complete silence. As the gate lifted up, everyone held their collective breath. The race was neck-a-neck all the way down the wooden track until the final section, but then one of the other cars shot out ahead of mine. I was thrilled to have placed second, but my father was not. He thought he saw my car hit a crack in the segmented track and demanded a rematch. Being a shy kid, I didn't want to push the issue, but my father sure did. He argued with Mr. Pine and the fathers of the other finalists. The debate raged on for about ten minutes. Mr. Pine reluctantly agreed to reverse the cars on the tracks and re-run the race. There were boos, confusion and murmuring, but the rematch took place anyway and still the other car came out in front of mine. Most of the people thought that justice had been served, but dad was still shaking his head in disbelief. It didn't take me long to get over the loss of the race, but I was thoroughly embarrassed by the big stink dad had made over loosing. I was happy we left early that night and thought it would all blow over, but the loss stuck in dad's craw.

When I was eleven I became a Boy Scout. I naturally assumed I would be entering Troop 139 with the rest of my buddies, but dad had other plans. He had burned plenty of bridges back at Saint Peter's and was looking for a fresh new start. I entered the Boy Scouts of America, at the Temple Lutheran Church on the other side of town. At first I was upset and angry with my father, for not letting me stay with my friends, but the Scout activities were lots of fun and I resigned myself to the fact that there was nothing I could do about it anyway. I relished playing with the boys I met in the troop and in particular liked playing handball with them in the parking lot before meetings. In the Cub Scouts, we followed the instructions of adult leaders who had planned out every activity, but the Boy Scouts did things differently. Scouts in each patrol held their own elections for Patrol Leader and planned out every aspect of the activities they decided to pursue. The only reason the adults were even around was to answer our questions and handle any emergencies that might crop up. I really enjoyed reading the Boy Scout Handbook and the drawings in it wet my appetite for wilderness camping.

At my first patrol meeting we made plans to take a hike along the Delaware River. I volunteered to make baloney sandwiches for our journey and on a cold, clear, Saturday morning we all met at the Patrol Leader's house in Delair, New Jersey. There I was introduced to topographical maps,[173] over a cup of hot chocolate and we put all of our gear in a single backpack, which we each took turns carrying. Although it was fun to go on the hike together, this was not just a stroll along the edge of a river. We were there to learn about navigation, the wildlife along the riverbank and to fulfill requirements to advance us in rank. We all kept a vigilant eye on our U.S. Geological Survey chart and frequently huddled together to block off the wind and take compass readings of landmarks on the Philadelphia side of the river. The more experienced Scouts showed us how to read the signs of nature including: birds nests, animal scat and a myriad of tracks left on the beach. The older scouts also pointed out rare birds like blue herons and cranes, which

---

[173] *Topographic Map* – is a type of map characterized by large-scale detail & quantitative representation of relief, usually using contour lines in modern mapping, but historically using a variety of methods. Traditional definitions require a U.S. Geological Survey chart to show both natural & man-made features.

were wading among the reeds at the edge of the river and in small tidal pools.

Troop meetings were more formal than patrol meetings. They followed a strict agenda with very specifically allotted time slots for reporting on patrol activities, participating in ceremonial rituals and performing Scout Spirit skits. Each boy was required to grow in both knowledge and wisdom. We had to memorize things like: the Scout Oath, the Scout Law, the Scout Motto and the Scout Slogan. We practiced principles of conservation and each scout took the initiative to pull his own weight.

I soon became fascinated with Merit Badge booklets and took a particular interest in the one on Raising Pigeons. After reading through the book, dad took me to a county fair to buy some birds, but the only pigeons we could find were fully-grown. I asked the guy selling the pigeons, "Don't you have to raise them from babies?" It was a good question, but the shifty little conman reassured me that, "All you have to do is feed them for three months and then they will fly back to the place were they were last fed." Dad was pretty skeptical, but I was so excited to get started, he let me buy them in spite of his doubts. I kept the thirty pigeons in the backyard for four months, just to make extra sure they knew it was their home, but when I released them they flew away and never returned. Obviously the had guy had lied, but to his credit, my father never said those dreaded words, "I told you so."

Summer was the time when troops went on camping trips together. The Lutheran church had a storeroom that was filled with all kinds of equipment including heavy canvas wall tents and wooden poles. We stowed them away in pick-up trucks and after a long drive arrived at the edge of the forest. From there we carried the heavy equipment up long gravel trails to the place where we set up camp. The first order of business was pitching the tents together as a troop.

Later on, each patrol gathered its own firewood, built their own fires and prepared their own meals. Everyone complained about doing KP or kitchen patrol, but it was also how we learned the importance of using scalding hot water to wash dishes, so that it would kill bacteria and prevent Montezuma's Revenge.

Although I enjoyed camping, the entire weekend involved lots of grunt work and not very much adventure. Troop trips were not nearly as Spartan as the high adventure excursions I was used to going on with my father. Whenever I went camping with dad we traveled light, cut down trees and built our own lean-tos. Even day-trips included a stop at a tavern that had a pool table, trophy deer and bear heads mounted on the walls and served thick ham sandwiches with juicy butter pickles. Camping with dad was just a whole lot more fun, when I could do cool stuff like carving my initials on a tree, something that was forbidden in the Boy Scouts. I loved bragging to my friends about my weekend trips to the wilderness and all the time I got to spend with my father.

Unlike the Boy Scout camping trips or even the one-on-one weekend expeditions with my father, camping in our pop-up tent trailer was a family affair. The station wagon transported the entire family and included Lisa and Rachel. While traveling, the inside of the Nimrod trailer became a storage bin for our food and gear. We ventured as far away as the Blue Ridge Mountains of West Virginia, attended a Nimrod Jamboree in Ohio and explored the Finger Lakes region of New York.[174]

While touring on Skyline Drive[175] dad developed blisters on his hands from turning the wheel back and forth on the many

---

[174] *Finger Lakes* – are a chain of lakes in the west-central section of Upstate New York & are a popular tourist destination. The lakes are linear in shape, each lake oriented on a north-south axis. Collectively the lakes reminded early mapmakers of the fingers of a hand.
[175] *Skyline Drive* – is a 105-mile serpentine road that runs along the top of the Blue Ridge Mountains in Virginia. The scenic drive through Shenandoah National Park is particularly popular in the fall when the leaves are changing colors.

switchbacks of the scenic road. Then suddenly the axle on the trailer locked up and the hitch popped off. Luckily the safety chain caught hold of it, but there we were stranded on the side of the road with a car full of road weary passengers. Decades prior to the invention of the cell phone, we had little choice but to sit on the shoulder of the road and wait for help to arrive. That assistance finally came in the form of a park ranger several hours later. It took another couple of hours for a tow truck to arrive and fix the wheel. So, after being stuck in the car for the long drive from Jersey, waiting for help in the hot sun and carefully navigating the remainder of the road to the campground, the exit from our vehicle looked like jail break at recess.

At the Nimrod Jamboree in Ohio, we set up camp in the middle of an open field. Without a forest to explore, we wandered over to a pasture filled with Holstein cows. We had never seen cattle up close and Murray climbed a fence post to get a closer look. Frequently accident prone, the poor little fellow soon toppled off the fence post and fell smack into a liquefied cow pie. My brother was thoroughly embarrassed, but it was just too funny and we rolled in the grass laughing until our sides ached.

There were inevitable mishaps on almost every trip, but our trip to Rickets Glenn[176] was the worst. Mom wanted some creature comforts, so dad purchased a heater, a canvas porch and a portable toilet. As soon as we opened up the tent trailer it started to rain. Our new heater helped take the chill off the damp night air, but the heavy rain made a mess of everything. In the morning the sides of our brand new light green canvas porch was splattered with red mud. It was even worse in the afternoon, when all the kids tracked mud in on the bottom of their sneakers. Although the floor of the trailer

---

[176] *Ricketts Glen* – is a 13,050 acre Pennsylvania State Park, located near Benton & offers hiking, camping, horseback riding, hunting, swimming, fishing, canoeing & kayaking on the 245-acre Lake Jean, as well as cross-country skiing & ice fishing in winter. The Falls Trail passes 22 waterfalls on Kitchen Creek, with Ganoga Falls being the highest at 94 feet.

looked like a construction site, the worst was yet to come. In order to keep us from wandering around in the dark, dad set up the commode inside the trailer. The portable toilet had a disposable plastic bag tied to the bottom of the seat and it was held on by a drawstring. The bag was supposed to be changed after each use, but in our ignorance, we used the same bag for the entire weekend. Sometime during the night, the bag broke loose and raw sewage splashed all over the walls and the toxic tsunami was absorbed by our sleeping bags.

Every camping trip seemed to include at least one of these pathetic problems, yet every horrible hassle was also transformed into a hilarious memory. Somewhere in the telling and the retelling of all those comedic catastrophes the healing salve of laughter bound us together as a family. After returning home the whole family went to the drive-in to watch Mary Poppins[177] and we fantasized about Lisa Lander having the same magical powers as the delightful British nanny on the silver screen. We memorized the lyrics of the songs and practiced the tongue twisting supercalifragilisticexpialidocious to perfection. The following morning Tom and I rode our bikes over to Vinny Riley's house and played our last pickup game of baseball at Githens Field. On the ride home, we lamented the loss of our unbridled freedom and contemplated the return to school.

Dad noticed acceleration in our country's slide toward world socialism. To educate themselves about the dangers of communism, my parents became members of the John Birch Society.[178] Soon they were hosting presentations in our living room for concerned citizens. Each week they ran a movie that documented the expansion of satellite

---

[177] *Mary Poppins* – is a 1964 Walt Disney musical film, based on the similarly-titled series of children's books by P. L. Travers.

[178] *John Birch Society* – was founded in 1958 to promote the ideals of Americanism in order to battle an overwhelming wave of communism, which was taking over many countries at the time & having a prominent influence in America. It was named after John Birch, who was the first American killed by Chinese Comunists. www.jbs.org

governments around the globe, which were controlled by the Soviet Union and China. During the movie a world map quickly turned red, as country after country fell to totalitarian regimes. The film concluded by quoting Nikita Khrushchev who threatened to conquer America boasting, "We will bury you without firing a shot."[179] Dad even set up a table on our front porch to sell books and None Dare Call it Treason[180] was our best seller. In 1964 Barry Goldwater[181] became the Republican nominee for president. Along with Kenny Buchanan, he promoted Mr. Conservative and the two patriots registered the largest number of Republican voters in the entire history of Merchantville politics. I would soon follow in his footsteps.

The day I entered the fifth grade it was raining. Sister Marie LaGatta assigned me a seat in the middle of the room and put me in charge of collecting and hanging up all the wet rain coats. I began my political activism shortly thereafter when the passionate political wrangling on the national stage played out in our schoolyard. Alma Buchanan was a classmate of mine and the daughter of dad's friend Kenny. Since we both knew about the integrity of Barry Goldwater and had knowledge of the traitorous leanings of Linden B. Johnson, we brought Goldwater posters into school with us. It looked like an easy sell. All I really needed to do to get this stand-up guy elected was to let people know who he was and answer any of their questions. I was confident of my

---

[179] *Nikita Khrushchev* – in 1953 the Soviet leader predicted how communists planned on taking over America when he said, "We will bury you without firing a shot." Khrushchev has to be looking up through the smoke & flames & smiling. What he wasn't able to accomplish as Commander & Chief of a military complex that rivaled the world's most powerful nation, is now being accomplished just as he predicted, without firing a shot! As Norman Mattoon Thomas, presidential candidate for the Socialist Party said in 1984, "the American people will never knowingly adopt socialism, but under the name of "liberalism," they will adopt every fragment of the socialist program, until one day America will be a socialist nation, without knowing how it happened."

[180] *None Dare Call It Treason* – in the 1950s, John Stormer became disillusioned with the political candidates & philosophies corrupted by Communist infiltrators. In 1962, he left his career as editor & general manager of a leading electrical magazine to begin an intensive study of communism after which he wrote this book, which has sold 7 million copies.

[181] *Barry Morris Goldwater* – was a 5-term U.S Senator from Arizona & the Republican Party's nominee for President in 1964. He was known as "Mr. Conservative".(1909–1998)

facts and thought selling the kids at school would be a cakewalk.

Boy was I wrong. John F. Kennedy was the first Irish Catholic President. When he was shot, Vice President Linden Banes Johnson took his place and grieving Catholics in America assumed that Johnson was his hand picked successor. Actually the truth was that Kennedy and Johnson couldn't stand each other, but most people didn't know about their rift. To oppose Johnson was not only seen as disloyal to Kennedy's legacy, it was tantamount to being treasonous toward both God and Country. At first Alma Buchanan and I were just a curiosity. Puzzled classmates came up to us in the schoolyard wanting to know why we were carrying signs. But as the questions began to multiply, our answers were countered with vitriolic slurs. I enthusiastically answered each one of their objections, but as the crowd grew bigger I sensed heat in all of their questions. I was sure that as soon as they understood what I was saying, they would all join me and support this patriotic man of integrity, but my arrogant assumptions were quickly proved inaccurate. The din of the mob rose in sync with the size of the gathering herd. Out of the blue someone yelled, "Get the signs!" The entire student body moved toward us in unison. Standing our ground we lifted the signs high above our heads, but the posters were ripped from our hands and torn to pieces. In a mad frenzy they all pounced on us at once; punching and kicking us till we fell to the ground. Although saved by the school bell, we were both left battered, bruised and prostrate on the ground in pools of our own blood. Barely able to move myself, I helped Alma to her feet and asked if she was ok. She just burst into tears and ran away in the direction of her home. Trying not to cry myself, I slowly made my way to the edge of the schoolyard. While the rest of the student body was lining up to enter the building, I took advantage of the distraction and slipped through a break in the hedge to go home myself. I was physically hurt, intellectually confused and felt betrayed by my friends. Choking back tears, I cut through the yards and made my way home. When I got there I collapsed in a pile of leaves and let loose with uncontrollable sobbing. Mom heard the crying and came out to investigate. She wrapped her arms around me and asked me what had happened, but I was inconsolable.

The following day I reluctantly returned to school, but I kept to myself. No one ever apologized. No one even asked me a single question. In fact, no one spoke to me at all that day. No children were ever punished and the only one that ever said anything to me was Mother Cecilia Maria. She already knew what had happened and empathetically asked me if I was all right, but even this gentle religious refused to address the beating. Although I commiserated with Alma Buchanan for a time; neither one of us had the stomach to push the issue further.

Empty cartridges from fountain pens make great spitball guns and I had no problem joining in on school pranks. So along with everyone else in class I too wrote one thousand times, "I will not throw spitballs in class." I was not a recluse, but the beating I took in the schoolyard once again shattered my trust. I shied away from close relationships with the kids at school and the only friendships I pursued were outside the classroom.

I pretty much kept to myself and did my work, but I daydreamed a lot. One afternoon, while practicing penmanship, the continuous drawing of circles and slanted lines bored me into a stupor. Somewhere in the middle of my task, I mentally drifted off and stopped writing. I was off in never-never-land when someone dropped a book. The loud noise startled me and I jerked my hand. My pen flew across the room, squirting its dark blue ink on everyone and everything in its path, before finally slamming into the window.

Sister wheeled around and shouted, "Who did that?" Although a few kids looked my way, no one said a word. Sister slowly walked down the aisle, rhythmically slapping a ruler against her left hand. She threatened to punish the whole class if the perpetrator did not reveal himself. I knew the code of silence would protect my identity, but I also knew the fury that might await me in the schoolyard, if I didn't own up to the accident. My face turned beet red, as I sheepishly raised my hand and said, "I did it, Sister." I offered an explanation, but the account was not believed and I had to put my hand out for the discipline of the ruler. Although it smarted, it was hardly injurious and had I been at fault, the correction would have been totally appropriate. What else was she supposed to do? My story wasn't exactly plausible, so I was sent to the principal's office.

Thankfully, Mother Cecilia Maria was nothing like the former Franciscan Principal. She listened closely to what I had to say and actually believed me, but she also said that just because I hadn't deliberately thrown the pen across the room, didn't mean I was off the hook. Mother Superior pulled out her Bible and read a passage from Deuteronomy.[182] She explained that the man in the story, who accidentally hit another man with his axe, would not be put to death, because he meant the man no harm, but he was still responsible for the other man's death. Sister said the man had a responsibility to make sure his tool was in good working order. Mother showed me that my daydreaming was the root cause of the accident. It was my responsibility to be more diligent about my studies, even if they were boring. Her lesson had been clearly communicated and was presented in such a gentle way that I willingly received it.

---

[182] *Deuteronomy 19:4-5* – "This shall be the law of the slayer that fleeth, whose life is to be saved: He that killeth his neighbour ignorantly & who is proved to have had no hatred against him yesterday & the day before: But to have gone with him to the wood to hew wood & in cutting down the tree the axe slipped out of his hand & the iron slipping from the handle struck his friend & killed him: he shall flee to one of the cities aforesaid & live."

What Mother Superior did not see was that the pen incident was just the tip of an iceberg. The real damage had already taken place below deck. My spiritual ship was taking on water and some of my religious fervor was beginning to wane. The day dreaming was a way to escape the pain I was feeling. Although I still had a close relationship with Jesus, bolstered by weekly absolution, frequent Communion and religion classes, it was not all clear sailing. My classmates had ridiculed my relationship with Annabel, beat me up for supporting Goldwater and would have given me another beating, if I had not owned up to the pen accident. Worse than any physical pain; there was a gnawing sense of emptiness in my heart. After our class was Confirmed, no one ever talked about God. I felt spiritually alone and the lack of fellowship was weakening my relationship with God. The spiritual isolation was taking its toll.

Instead of seeking out new friends, admitting my fears or mourning my losses; I became a castaway on Gilligan's Island.[183] Playing outside gave way to a daily ritual of immersing myself in alternate realities like: Bewitched,[184] The Adams Family[185] and Flipper.[186] These distractions, although they provided temporary relief, didn't solve any problems. As soon as show ended that empty feeling returned. Everything and everyone began to annoy me and I let people feel my displeasure.

---

[183] *Gilligan's Island* – was a television situation comedy originally produced by United Artists. It aired for 3 seasons on the CBS, from 1964-1967. The show followed the comic adventures of seven castaways as they attempted to survive & ultimately escape from the island, where they were shipwrecked.

[184] *Bewitched* – was a situation comedy originally broadcast for 8 seasons on ABC from 1964-1972. The show was about a witch who marries a mortal & tries to lead the life of a typical suburban housewife.

[185] *The Adams Family* - was a group of fictional characters created by American cartoonist Charles Addams. They are a satirical inversion of the ideal American family; an eccentric, wealthy clan who delight in the macabre & are unaware that people find them bizarre or frightening. ABC created a television series based on Addams' cartoon characters, which was shot in black-and-white & aired from 1964-1966.

[186] *Flipper* – was a television series from Ivan Tors Films & MGM Television broadcast on NBC from 1964-1967. Flipper was the Bottlenose Dolphin companion animal of Porter Ricks, the Chief Warden at the fictional Coral Key Park & Marine Preserve in southern Florida, along with his two young sons Sandy & Bud.

Whenever Tommy came over to visit me, Sean wanted to tag along. I told my brother to get lost, but whenever he chose not to get the message I chased him through the house at a break-neck speed and tackled him at the end of the hallway. Then I pounded away on his back, knocking the wind out of him with every punch. If he persisted in shadowing of us, as he often did, I would grab a hatchet and chased him through the house yelling, "I'm gonna kill you!" Mom got hysterical screaming, "Stop!" at the top of her lungs, but I defiantly ignored her. The disrespect I was developing for my mother was not confined to these fits of rage either.

Whenever she smacked my backside, I laughed at her and said, "Ha, ha, didn't hurt!" Although I took my lumps from dad, by the time he arrived home from work, mom's recollection of events minimized the severity of what had actually taken place, but I was forming a contemptuous habit. One evening, while dad was reading the paper, Mom corrected me for some minor infraction and I reflexively told her to shut up. Dad quickly folded the Courier Post and smacked me across the face with it. He hit me so hard I flew off my feet, hit the wall and slid down the dark wood paneling. Half-dazed, I shook my head and looked up to see him standing over top of me thundering, "Don't you ever talk back to your Mother!" Although I never dared to tell her to "shut up" again; old habits die hard and I continued to argue with her whenever my father was not around. It didn't take long for me to get into another spat with her. While I was arguing with her one day, Father Justinian came riding by on his ten-speed bike. He quietly coasted up behind me and said "Do you always talk to your mother like that?" I was startled to hear the authoritative voice behind me and sheepishly whispered, "No Father." Much to my mother's delight he proceeded to give me a lengthily lecture on the Fourth Commandment.

In addition to being a welcome distraction, television shows provided me with a plethora of fresh new ideas. In the premier episode of the series Daniel Boone,[187] Indians used flaming arrows to attack Boonesboro. Inspired by this story; Tom and I borrowed dad's bow the following afternoon and shot a flaming arrow over the rooftops of the houses across the street. We were attempting to hit Vern's fort, but we missed it and never did find the arrow. When Toby and Vern discovered we had tried to burn down their fort, they threatened to destroy ours. I never told dad the real reason they planned to attack, but I did advised him of their threat and begged him to let Tom and I sleep out in the tree fort to defend it. After persistently pleading with him, he reluctantly agreed to the vigilant adventure, but specifically warned us not to leave the property. Tom and I took turns guarding the fort, but neither one of us could get much sleep. We jumped up at the sound of every leaf that rustled or twig that snapped. The suspense was killing us since we didn't really know if our enemies were coming or not.

Curious as cats we ran across the street and cut through the yards till we could see Vern's hideaway. No one was there, so I found a pair of hedge clippers and began slicing up every one the screen doors that made up the walls to his ground level fort. Suddenly a yellow porch light came on and someone opened the back door. They were probably just letting the cat out, but we thought they saw us! Hightailing it over the fence, Tom ran ahead of me and ducked under badminton net. I never saw the netting and was close-lined by the mesh. My feet flew straight out in front of me and I landed flat on my back. Tom heard the thud when I hit the ground and wheeled around to whisper, "Are you alright?" With the wind knocked out of me I was barely able to answer. He helped me to my feet and we hobbled back to my place, where I laid down on the picnic table behind the house in pain. The skin on my neck was ripped raw, my back ached

---

[187] *Daniel Boone* – was an action/adventure TV series that followed the exploration & settlement of America during the period leading up the the Revolutionary War. It aired from 1964-1970 on NBC & was produced by 20th Century Fox Television. Daniel was played by Fess Parker & Ed Ames co-starred as Mingo, his American Indian friend.

and my neck was beginning to spasm. We both knew I needed first aid, yet we debated for over an hour about whether or not to go inside for help. Eventually the pain overcame any fear of getting into trouble and we went in the house. Mom gave me a couple of aspirin and spread some Vaseline on my neck. Dad put a frozen orange juice can on the back of my neck to bring down the swelling and wanted to know how it all happened, but he never mentioned anything about punishment. Figuring we had learned our lesson the hard way he just smiled.

Although Toby and Vern quickly deduced that we were the culprits who ruined their fort, it was difficult for them to prove and while they promised revenge, it would never materialize. These boyhood skirmishes gradually lost their luster and would soon give way to weightier battles, but for now we were still children. Hidden behind a door in our dining room was a secret stairway. It spiraled up to the right leading to the second floor, but the top of the stairway had been closed off creating two storage closets. Just inside the door of the first floor was a window that overlooked the driveway. Lisa sat each of us down on the steps and had us to pretend we were sitting in a bus. Occupying the lowest step Lisa faced out the window and pretended to be the bus driver. Holding an imaginary steering wheel and occasionally glancing over her shoulder, she led us in a rip-roaring rendition of The Wheels of the Bus.[188]

The wheels of the bus go round and round
Round and round
Round and round
The wheels of the bus go round and round
All around the town

---

[188] *The Wheels on the Bus* – is a popular children's song in the US, Canada & the United Kingdom. It is often utilized on journeys to keep children amused & has a very repetitive rhythm. In particular it is popularly sung by pre-teens on bus journeys.

Lisa was a delightful nanny. We all loved her and the woman's joy and playfulness was infectious. Still clinging to the innocence of my childhood I relished our daily bus trips and gleefully sang my heart out in a daily celebration of life, but that carefree lifestyle was literally about to go up in smoke.

Chapter 7

Blackout Drill

On November 9, 1965, almost the entire East Coast experienced a blackout.[189] Thirty million people lost their electric for about twelve hours. Houses were dark and there was no opportunity to watch TV. Millions of Americans went to bed early that night and nine months later there would be a mini baby boom. The electric starter on our oil burner shut down and the house was getting cold. For several years a propane fireplace[190] had been used to take the chill off the family room, but tonight it would be given the Herculean task of heating our entire house.

Come morning our house was toasty warm. The electric power had been restored and all of us were sitting around the dining room table eating our oatmeal. Brennan said he heard a dripping noise coming from the family room, so I called for silence and went in to investigate. I slowly walked around the room listening for tattle tale tones. The investigation quickly led me to a small closet beside the fireplace. Opening the door I noticed some water pouring down the back wall. Thinking it came from the upstairs bathtub, I ran up to the second floor to turn off the water, but the bathroom was bone dry. The hall closet contained an access panel behind the shower, so I opened the door to find

---

[189] *Northeast Blackout of 1965* – was the result of a significant disruption in the supply of electricity on November 9th. It affected Ontario in Canada & Connecticut, Massachusetts, New Hampshire, Rhode Island, Vermont, New York & New Jersey in the United States. Over 30 million people and 80,000 square miles were left without electricity for up to 12 hours. The failure was caused by an incorrectly set relay on a transmission line connecting the U.S. & Canada. The safety relay is supposed to trip if the current exceeds the capacity of the transmission line, but it was set way too low.

[190] *Fireplace* – the Fire Marshal determined that the cause of the fire was an improperly installed gas fireplace. Although the fireplace was installed up against the chimney used for the oil burner, its flu was never vented into the chimney and the escaping heat ignited the timbers inside the wall. The tell tale dripping noise came from melted copper pipes.

the source of the leak. A billowing cloud of gray smoke poured out from behind the door and it forced me to retreat into the hallway.

I yelled out, "Fire!" prompting Lisa to come running up the stairs. Bright orange and yellow flames were leaping from the floorboards; so I grabbed a fire extinguisher from a hook in the hall and began dousing the fire with a powdery white chemical retardant. Lisa ran back down the stairs and led the rest of the family out of the house and across the street. Meanwhile mom phoned the fire company and pleaded with me to leave, but I felt duty bound to put out the fire. When help arrived the fireman was in no mood to argue with me. Picking me up by the waist under one arm he carried me out to the safety of the sidewalk. Soon a whole slew of additional fire engines arrived together with the rest of the neighborhood. All of us watched with fascination, as dozens of firemen efficiently hooked up their hoses and let loose with thousands of gallons of water from a hose the on top of a ladder truck.

Despite a chorus of whining, mom made us leave for school. Upon seeing so few students lined up for class; Mother Vivian wondered aloud where all the children were. Although I told her they were watching our house burn, she didn't believe me. Sean and Sarah confirmed my story, but the principal still refused to believe it. Even though half the student body and even a few teachers watched the spectacle; not one of the Callahan children was able to witness the burning of their own house.

Although the fire was under control within the hour, the entire attic was gutted and the rest of the house sustained major smoke and water damage. I spent my first night at Tom's house and Sarah stayed overnight with her friend Alanna. The rest of our family took up residence at the

Hillside Motor Lodge.[191] After about a week, dad rented a split-level house on Drexel Avenue in Pennsauken, which brought us all back together again. It took the better part of a year to fix up the old homestead, but other than having a few of our neighbors ferry us around in cars, life moved on relatively undisturbed. Since the Reeves residence was located directly across the street from Saint Peter's, I spent a lot of time at Tom's house and quickly became a member of their extended family. Tom and I converted his cellar into a man cave and like the ebb and flow of the tides; we vacillated between the innocent adventures of being little boys and the first tentative missteps of adolescence. One day we would be crawling around in the coal bin, pretending to be miners and the next day we were rigging up stereo equipment in preparation for a dance party.

In January a new student joined our class and his name was Chris Lang. I introduced him to Tom and the three of us started palling around in Tom's party room after school. We painted walls, brought in furniture we had trash picked and even stocked our own liquor cabinet, which we hid behind a panel near the record player. Whenever Tom's parents went out for the evening, we pinched another bottle of his father's stock and threw an impromptu party. We invited some of our classmates and kids from the neighborhood. Although we often sampled the booze, so we would look cool; we never consumed enough alcohol to get buzzed. We were much more interested in meeting the girls. We listened to music, awkwardly conversed with them and pretended to enjoy their company.

Whenever the phone rang, Tom answered by saying, "Hold on a minute." He raised his hand for silence, turned off the stereo and the room fell silent. If the caller asked about the noise Tom reassured them that he had been listening to some

---

[191] *Hill Side Inn* – is a 2-story motel located on Route 38. Its main clientele frequented the Garden State Park, which was a harness & thoroughbred racetrack in Cherry Hill, NJ.

loud music. Whenever his parents called, he told them the babysitting was going smoothly and convinced them that all was ok. If a call was for someone at the party, he motioned them to the phone. Once he hung up we all had a big laugh, the music was turned on and the party resumed. It was a matter of pride with us that none of the adults ever caught on. It was pretty easy, because they all seemed to be preoccupied with entertainments of their own.

My mother's favorite movie was The Sound of Music[192] and it was the last movie we ever saw together as a family at the drive-in theater. One month later the drive-in closed and the owners turned the entire parking lot into a flea market. Our family tradition had ended. Movies were replaced by TV programs and our family was soon engrossed in a virtual world of fantasy, watching weekly shows like: I Dream of Jeanie,[193] Green Acres,[194] Lost in Space,[195] The FBI[196] and Hogan's Heroes.[197]

---

[192] *The Sound of Music* – is a 1965 musical film directed by Robert Wise & starring Julie Andrews & Christopher Plummer. The film is based on the Broadway musical The Sound of Music, with songs written by Richard Rodgers & Oscar Hammerstein. The musical book was written by Howard Lindsay & Russel Crouse, with the screenplay written by Ernest Lehman. It is based on the memoir of Maria von Trapp, The Story of the Trapp Family Singers, who escaped from Austria when the Nazis took over their country.

[193] *I Dream of Jeannie* – was a sitcom with a fantasy premise. The show starred Barbara Eden as a 2000-year-old female genie & Larry Hagman as an astronaut who becomes her master & with whom she falls in love & eventually marries. Produced by Screen Gems, the show originally aired from 1965-1970.

[194] *Green Acres* – was a TV series starring Eddie Albert & Eva Gabor as a couple who move from NYC to a country farm. Produced by Filmways, Inc., as a sister show to Petticoat Junction, the series was broadcast on CBS from 1965-1971.

[195] *Lost in Space* – was a science fiction TV program created & produced by Irwin Allen, produced by 20th Century Fox Television & broadcast on CBS from 1965-1968. The first season was shot with black & white film, the rest in color. The show focused primarily on Jonathan Harris as Dr. Zachary Smith, originally an utterly evil would-be killer who as the first season progressed became a sympathetic anti-hero, providing comic relief to the show & causing most of the problems.

[196] *The F.B.I.* – was a TV series that was broadcast on ABC from 1965-1974. Produced by Quinn Martin & based in part on concepts from the 1959 WB film The FBI Story, the series was an authentic telling of or fictionalized accounts of actual F.B.I. cases. Efrem Zimbalist, Jr. played Inspector Lewis Erskine, while Philip Abbott played Arthur Ward, assistant director to F.B.I. chief J. Edgar Hoover. Although Hoover served as series consultant until his death in 1972, he was never seen in the series.

[197] *Hogan's Heroes* – was a TV sitcom produced by Bing Crosby & Desilu that ran from 1965-1971 on CBS. Set in a German POW camp during WWII, Bob Crane played Colonel

Dealing with fire insurance issues cut down on the time dad was able to spend watching the news on television; but on September 21, 1965, KYW 1060, began broadcasting "All News – All the Time" on the Radio! Each day, on his way to and from work, dad listened to these broadcasts in his car. Dad heard the first reports on the radio regarding our combat troops being deployed in Vietnam. He learned about the racial tensions building in the south, which confirmed his decision to move Callahan Machine Company out of the city. Philadelphia was beginning to look like a powder keg. A single spark might ignite chaos in the streets and a move to the country seemed more prudent than ever.

While dad was trying to understand the future, by analyzing current events, I sought inspiration and guidance from the heroes in our past. Although an exceptionally skilled hunter, the Daniel Boone of history actually failed miserably as a family man, but the Daniel Boone show,[198] which I watched regularly, sanitized his legacy and presented a role model endowed with courage and integrity making him worthy of being an icon of American folk lore. Fess Parker portrayed the tall pioneer with the coonskin cap as a paragon of virtue, a devoted husband and loving father. The series highlighted his legendary bravery, leadership and wilderness survival skills. His family, his neighbors and even the Indian tribes he fought, all had great respect for him. Daniel Boone was my hero. Inspired by this man of action, I could often be found singing the catchy theme song from the weekly show. At the opening of each episode, Daniel Boone threw a tomahawk at a tree and split the trunk down the middle. I longed for the day when I could acquire the same level of skill. In the back

---

Hogan, who coordinated an international crew of Allied prisoners running Special Ops from the camp. The program also featured Werner Klemperer as Colonel Wilhelm Klink, the commandant of the camp & John Banner as the inept sergeant-of-the-guard, Schultz Both Klemperer & Banner were Jewish & relished making the Nazis look like inept idiots.

[198] *Daniel Boone* – was an action/adventure TV series that aired from 1964-1970 on NBC & was made by 20th Century Fox Television. The title role was played by Fess Parker, with Ed Ames co-starring as Mingo his American Indian friend. The lyrics from the theme song were written by Vera Matson with music by Lionel Newman & published by 20th Century Music Corporation, New York, NY. ©1964,1966.

corner of our yard was a cedar tree. Every day I threw my hatchet or knife into its trunk. Unfortunately, dad didn't share my enthusiasm when he saw the damage I had done to his tree. He was outraged and befuddled by my lack of respect for his property. The truth was I had no idea I was hurting anything. When he realized I was clueless, he lowered his voice and sat me down to explain how sap is the lifeblood of a tree and that the bark protects a tree's arteries. Once I understood I was killing the tree, I promised not to do it again. I continued to practice my throwing skills on an old plank of wood, but it wasn't the same and I soon lost interest.

One Saturday Tom came over to play and we spent the morning jumping out of the tree fort onto a pile of mattresses. After lunch, mom told me to go upstairs and see my father. Tom started to come with me, but mom stopped him by saying that dad wanted to see me alone. She assured us it would not take long and that Tom could play outside until I was finished. When I reached the top of the stairs I could see my father sitting on the edge of his bed with a pen and a spiral notebook. Motioning with his hand he said, "Come on in." I sat down on the bed and watched him, as he continued to draw a picture in silence. "What's that," I naively asked, "a cannon?" "No!" came his sharp rebuke. He was apparently frustrated with his lack of artistic ability and irritated by my caviler attitude over what he saw as a momentous occasion. I had no idea what was coming and even less interest in the subject at hand. He was a nervous father, fulfilling a very serious responsibility and my innocence was about to get flanked by the birds and the bees.

He started off by asking me if I knew where babies came from. I said, "Sure! Mom's stomach." He gently responded by saying, "Well, sort of... When a man and a woman love each other, they get married and promise to love each other for the rest of their lives. When they love one another," he continued, "it makes a baby." I still didn't understand what he was getting at, but I was starting get the idea he wasn't going to send me to the garage for a wrench. I looked back down at the strange drawing on the paper, as he asked, "Do you know how?" Now I felt the full weight of the conversation. I answered in the negative and was apprehensive about the answer. Locking eyes with mine, he dove into the meat of the subject. "Only married people are allowed to make babies and it is something they can only do with God's help." The explanation went on for about a half-an-hour and I eventually learned that what I thought was a cannon was in reality, a drawing of the male anatomy. He used the illustration several times to explain the process, but the information conveyed was anything but a straightforward biology lesson.

God's creative power, the depth of love between a man and a woman, the permanence of marriage and the grievous nature of participating in sex outside of marital bonds, were all lovingly and clearly communicated. He concluded by advising me that some fathers wait until later to tell their sons about the birds and the bees, but that he had chosen to tell me early, so that I would not learn about it on the street. I was strictly warned not to talk to my friends about it, because it was up to each father to decide when the best time was to tell their sons and that mothers would explain these things to their daughters. I think he was expecting a whole bunch of questions, but I had none. It was way too much information for me to digest on the spot and besides he had pretty much covered it all.

While dad and I were talking, Chris Lang rode over on his bicycle. I found my two friends spinning on the Whirly Bird[199] at a break-neck speed and laughing their heads off. I wandered around the yard to ponder the sex talk. In light of

---

[199] *Whirly Bird* – was a 4-seat metal spinning toy manufactured by Hedstrom that seated 4 kids facing each other. The kids pumped it with their hands & feet causing it to spin faster & faster. The lawn toy was about 8 foot across with a hand & footrest that moved back & forth. The seats were shaped like an hourglass & it was like a backyard merry-go-round.

the life changing information, there was no way I could keep silent. As soon as Tom and Chris finished their ride, I motioned them over to the fort and whispered, "Meet me in the garage. I have something to tell you guys." Finding an old extension chord, I held it up in front of them and inserted the plug into the socket. In one of the most abbreviated instructions ever given; I told them this was how our parents created us. It sounded really gross to them and neither one could believe their parents would do such a thing. But I convinced them otherwise and the knowledge of this secret seemed to bond the three of us together. From that moment on, we became The Terrible Triangle.

The following week I felt feverish and was allowed to stay home from school, but was not permitted to watch any television. Since reading was my only form of legitimate entertainment and Daniel Boone had inspired me with an interest in the wilderness, I read a book called Summer of Little Rain.[200] I also looked up the white tailed deer and American Indians in the World Book Encyclopedia. I learned about the Indian way of life, the names of all the different tribes in America and how they used sign language to overcome tribal language barriers. The more I read about deer, the more fascinated I became with my father's eight-point trophy buck hanging on the wall of our living room.

When dad returned home from work, he took down the deer head. He let me feel its fur and look at it up close. Dad also showed me a tanned deerskin and let me use it to make some frontier style clothing. Puzzled over the holes in the hide, my father told a glorious tale about jumping out of a tree to stab his first deer with a buck knife. He did so because his arrow had failed to kill the animal right away, but he warned me that it was a dangerous move and that things could have

---

[200] *Summer of Little Rain* – parallels the lives of a squirrel & a beaver family, describing their respective instinctive roles in the balance of nature & conservation of the environment, as they face the dangers of a season of drought. The book was written by Aileen Lucia Fisher, with illustrations by Gloria Stevens & published by Nelson, NYC, NY ©1961

ended tragically. He said a deer can kill a man with its hooves. I took him up on his offer to use the hide, making mittens and a pair of moccasins out of the buckskin.

On her day off, Lisa Lander often took a bus trip into Philadelphia to go shopping with her girlfriend Julie MacDonald. The two British nannies had much in common. Julie worked for my godparents and was a governess to twelve of my cousins. On one of these outings the two budding beauties met up with a couple of sailors on shore leave. The swabbies offered to give them a personally guided tour of their ship. Graciously accepting their invitation, they toured the Navy ship and then went out to see Doctor Zhivago.[201] Lisa was positively giddy when she returned home and gleefully told my parents all about the wonderful man she just met. Mom and dad were dumbstruck! Lisa was admittedly an adult, but they still felt responsible. Miss Lander seemed recklessly naïve and was obviously unaware that sailors had a horrible reputation.

When they pointed out her naiveté and listed all the dangerous things that could have happened, Lisa was deeply hurt and befuddled. She had come to share her joy, but they were treating her like a two-year-old. Actually the service men had acted like perfect gentlemen. Lisa also vehemently disagreed with their assessment of the danger and indignantly objected to their Naval prejudice, "I don't know what you think of sailors here in America, but in Great Britain they are honorable men with high moral values." Our nanny was twenty-one, so it was a sticky situation for mom and dad. Although they were responsible for her physical and spiritual wellbeing, like most teenage parents, they had little controlling authority. Fortunately, Lisa had read the situation accurately. Simon the sailor was an honorable

---

[201] *Doctor Zhivago* – is an epic 1965 drama-romance-war film directed by David Lean & loosely based on a 1957 novel, Boris Pasternak which bears the same name. The novel is named after its protagonist, Yuri Zhivago, a physician & poet. It tells the story of how his life was affected by the Russian Revolution of 1917 & the subsequent Russian Civil War.

Southern Gentleman and he fell head-over-heels in love with Lisa. It was a case of love at first sight for both of them. After dating for a time and then corresponding by mail and telephone; they eventually married and our nanny would become Mrs. Simon Moore.

Unlike Lisa, my perceptions were not nearly as error free. The brevity of the explanation I had given my friends regarding the birds and the bees, apparently left out a few details, which led to a few misunderstandings. In my crude example of sexual coupling, Chris thought I was referring to a woman's derriere. The next time he went grocery shopping with his mom, he stared at the women pushing their carts and tried to figure out how or why, someone would want to do that. When he finally asked Tom and me about it, we rolled on the floor laughing at the comedic error. He was pretty embarrassed, but as was his nature, he took it all in stride and joined in on the laughter, with some self-deprecating humor of his own.

Since Sleepy Hollow was only a half-hour from home, the old Nimrod trailer sat in dry-dock under the shade of the old Elm tree. We spent most of our Saturday afternoons paddling up and down the slow moving cedar waters of the Rancocas Creek. The cabin was so close to our home that dad occasionally took us over in the evenings to build a fire, cook some hot dogs for dinner and roast a few marshmallows.

As soon as school let out, dad took me up to uncle Hans's Farm and dropped me off for the summer. Uncle Hans Schmidt was not really my uncle, but he supervised the night shift at Callahan Machine Company and had become a good family friend. Uncle Hans had a 100-acre farm up in Hereford, Pennsylvania. His wife, Aunt Dorothy was a kind, energetic woman, but that in no way diminished her strict German ways. The couple's son Jerry was my age and their daughter Mary Ann was a strikingly beautiful young woman and just a few years older than me. Jerry and I rode horses, explored the old mill, fed the chickens and jumped in big piles of hay. During the day we swam in the pond and at night we sat on the porch sucking on cream cycles. I thoroughly enjoyed my stay at the farm and participated in all of the action. It's not like they planned anything in particular, there were just lots of chores to do, places to explore, horses to ride and a pond to swim in when it got too hot. After bailing hay one day, which was hot sweaty work, I got a bath and joined the family for dinner. Later on in the evening we were all sitting on the porch with our cream cycles when Mary Ann came running up from the barn franticly calling for her dad. That night we all got to witness the birth of a colt. It was an awesome experience and it blew me away when the newborn pranced around the stall less than an hour after it was born.

Lightning, the sire of the colt was a massively muscular stud horse. The strapping stallion was so powerful and fast that I refused to ride him. However, near the end of the summer I had become a pretty fair rider and thought I would give him a try. Firmly gripping the reins, I gave him a swift kick in the sides and he took off! The quick quarter horse skipped the canter completely and went straight to a galloping gate. It was everything I could do to hold on. Riding like the wind, we circled round a ten-acre field and flew back to the house in no time flat. This was raw power and while terrifying, it was also downright exhilarating!

Mary Ann Schmidt was drop dead gorgeous. She was always nice to me and I couldn't help dreaming about her, but she was almost four years older than me, so I wasn't even on her radar screen. Still, I pined for the day when this long lean beauty with the flowing brunette hair would look my way. Unfortunately, reality hit me one day when I walked around the side of the barn and saw her kissing a stranger. My grand fantasy died a painful death, but it was time for me to end my vacation anyway and return to the stability of Merchantville; or so I thought.

Racial trouble was brewing all over the country. The peaceful marches of Dr. Martin Luther King, Jr. and his eloquent I Have a Dream speech[202] were juxtaposed the radical calls of the Black Panther Party[203] whose mantra was "Burn Baby Burn!"[204] This rising tide of racial unrest convinced my father and his partners that sooner or later there would be riots in Philadelphia. Besides, Callahan Machine Company was growing and needed larger accommodations. Twenty-miles north of the city they found an old knitting mill by a little railroad stop in North Wales, PA. The new factory would now have a great location and room to expand. The only downside was that dad would have a much longer commute.

The first thing that rattled my cage after summer vacation was my sixth grade teacher. Not that I had a problem with him, but Mr. Nardo was my first male teacher. The change threw me off my game. The man knew his stuff, expected us to study hard and didn't cut anyone any slack. The upside was that his no nonsense style created a great environment for learning. I especially enjoyed his class on History. The Roman Empire fascinated me and I listened with particular interest, as Mr. Nardo described how this once great civilization came to power, built roads and nearly conquered the world. I relished my reading assignments and made a clay model of Roman roads for extra credit. Unfortunately,

---

[202] *I Have a Dream* – is the famous 16-minute public speech given on August 28, 1963, by Dr. Martin Luther King, Jr., in which he called for racial equality & an end to discrimination. Delivered on the steps of the Lincoln Memorial during the March on Washington for Jobs & Freedom, it was a defining moment of the Civil Rights Movement.

[203] *Black Panther Party* – was an African-American revolutionary left-wing organization working for the self-defense of black people. Active in the US from the mid-1960s into the 1970s, they were known for their provocative rhetoric & militant posture.

[204] *Burn, Baby, Burn* – was a phrase adopted by the Black Power movement & attributed to William Leo "Bill" Epton Jr. (1932-2002) who was a Maoist African-American communist activist. He was Vice Chairman of the Progressive Labor Party until 1970 & chairman of its Harlem branch until he was incarcerated for incitement to violence in 1964. Epton was the first person convicted of criminal anarchy since the Red Scare of 1919.

when it came time for the test, I flunked! The exam was all about the dates. There were no questions about the story and it floored me. How could I enjoy a subject so much, relish every bit of my homework, participate in class discussions and then fail? I was beside myself. I thought this way of studying history was stupid, but Mr. Nardo was not going to let me slide just because I couldn't remember dates. I would have to get cracking, because with an "F" on my report card, I was sure to get grounded again.

The way in which history was taught was not the only thing I began to question. Sister Raymond Maria taught us religion and was nothing like my beloved Sister Augustine. One day while we were going over the Ten Commandments, she zeroed in on the Fifth Commandment. After writing "Thou Shalt Not Kill" on the black board she added, "Except in: war, self-defense and capital punishment." Wondering about these reservations, I raised my hand. "Where does it say except?" Although she repeated the list, she never answered the real question. "I understand what the exceptions are, but where does it say except?" Thinking I was trying to steer her off topic, she bellowed, "Sit down Mr. Callahan." I persisted, "But Sister you still didn't answer my question." Clearly perturbed she raised her voice and said, "I answered your question. Now sit down!" I remained standing, which prompted her to repeat the command, "Sit down now Mr. Callahan!" I was confused by her response and was sincerely interested in getting an answer. So I stood my ground and said, "As soon as you answer my question." Her face got bright red and the entire class braced themselves for what was about to happen. Compassionate classmates urgently whispered their warnings. "Sit down. You'll get in big trouble." Sister walked down the aisle with a her pointer. Even though I was shaking all over, I stayed on my feet. "Sit down now! I'm not going to tell you again!" Albeit with a quivering in my voice I responded by saying, "I'll be glad to sit down, as soon as you answer my question." Crack! Her hardwood hickory stick whipped across the back of my shoulders. "Sit down in that chair!" Now steeled with almost stoic resolve, I still stood tall and she went ballistic, beating me till I collapsed in the chair sobbing. She had crushed her defiant student and could return to the front of the classroom. She was so wrong. I called out to her one last time, "You still didn't answer my question." Unlike Sister Augustine, who prepared me for Confirmation, understood her theology and was always open to questions, Sister Raymond had no idea why the Church had exceptions. Actually the Magisterium[205] does have a highly developed and well founded basis for Her teachings on life issues, but decades would pass before those questions would be satisfactorily answered for me.

Not all my dealings with Sister Raymond were quite so honorable. I had a habit of sitting sideways in my chair and leaning my elbow on the desk behind me. My friend Chris Lang happened to sit in that chair. He liked a cute girl in our class and she had been responding to his eye contact. In spite of an outright ban on passing notes in class, Chris passed one to Francine Simmons indicating that he liked her. Fran stealthily passed it back, acknowledging his attention and letting him know that she liked him too. Sister Raymond knew something was up and was watching the room like a hawk. When she turned around to write on the blackboard, Chris folded up one of the love notes, placed it under my elbow and started pounding on my arm with his fist to flatten it. Sister wheeled around just in time, to see me turn around and punch him in the chest.

That little exchange landed both of us in detention and our parents were called in for a conference. Nervous about the possibility of being suspended, we anxiously waited for our parents outside the principal's office. Suddenly we heard a cheerful commotion down the hall. "Oh hi Theresa." "Hi

---

[205] *The Magisterium* – is the "teaching authority of the Catholic Church". It teaches & interprets the truths of the Faith, including the authentic interpretation of the Word of God, both from Sacred Scripture and from Tradition. The Magisterium of the Church, includes: the Pope & the bishops in communion with him."

Bernadette. What brings you here?" Listening to the impromptu reunion, it soon became apparent that our parents knew each other from high school. Chris looked over at me with a great big smile on his face, raised his thumb and whispered, "We're in!" To our surprise, Sister's main concern was that we had been in a fight and she wanted us to remain friends. In truth, Chris and I were just fine about the incident, but we instinctively feigned irritation with one another, before gradually agreeing to shake hands. It worked! All this reconciliation stuff seemed to be making our parents happy, so I decided to seal the victory by asking if Chris could stay over night at our house. After a slight pause, the proposal was accepted and no further punishment came our way.

In February 1966 my brother Neil became the eighth child in our family to be baptized. Counting mom, dad and Lisa, there were now eleven of us. During the christening party, I had the distinct honor of changing his diaper. In the middle of my chore Neil spouted a two-foot fountain of pee. Dad doubled over laughing when I reached for a clean diaper to wipe my face. I asked him what was so funny, but he was laughing so hard he was unable to answer. Lisa and mom placed their hands over their mouths, torn between empathy and the hilarity of the situation. Soon the whole family was joining in on the roast. When things settled down dad explained that I had done the same thing to him when I first came home from the hospital. Although I didn't think it was so funny, dad started laughing again and said, "There is justice in this world!"

On the feast of the Immaculate Conception,[206] the 2nd Vatican Council came to a close and Pope Paul IV signed off on the final documents. Gradually what took place in Rome,

---

[206] *The Immaculate Conception* – is a dogma of the Catholic Church, which states that from the first moment of her conception, Mary was granted a singular Grace by God preserving her from the stain of original sin & filling her with Divine Grace, so that she lived her entire life free from all sin. December 8th is the Feast Day of the Immaculate Conception.

worked its way down into the basement of St. Peter's Church. Although I longed to become an altar boy, I was not yet old enough. That privilege was reserved for seventh and eighth graders. Dad let Monsignor know of my desire to serve at the altar and asked if he would be willing to make an exception. Looking my way he said, "There is a lot for an altar boy to learn, before he can serve at the altar. Are you willing to work hard?" When I assured him that I would, he put his hand on his chin and searched my eyes for clues indicating the depth of my sincerity. Turning back toward my father he offered, "I am not sure he can handle the Latin, but soon the Mass will be said in English. If he can memorize the responses on the altar card, I will let him serve." Then he sent one of the altar boys up to the sacristy, to fetch me an altar card. I studied that card every chance I had and soon passed the verbal quiz and learned what to do on the altar. Wearing the traditional white lace surplice over a black cassock, I served my first Mass in March of 1966. For the next three months I took advantage of every opportunity to faithfully serve at the altar. Were it not for the Vatican II directives in Sacrosanctum Concilium,[207] I might never have become an altar boy. Unfortunately, the Church would also experience tremendous upheaval and confusion from the dissenters of Church teaching in the decades that followed the Council.

The religious revolution began on October 10, 1962 at the Notre Dame Conferences.[208] It was a series of seminars, which brought together hundreds of influential leaders. The entire forum was financially underwritten by the Rockefeller Foundation. The symposium laid out an elaborate plan to hijack the proceedings of the Vatican II Council. The

---

[207] *Sacrosanctum Concilium* – is the Constitution on the Sacred Liturgy, which is one of the documents of the 2nd Vatican Council. Approved on December 4, 1963, the main purpose of the constitution was to achieve greater lay participation in the Catholic Church's liturgy. To that end, parts of the Mass could be said in the native language instead of Latin.
[208] *Notre Dame Conferences* – information derived from the article "Heart Attack: Catholic Academe Meets Ex-Corde Ecclesiae", by Michael J. Mazza, in the February 1995 issue of "Fidelity" Magazine", 206 Marquette Avenue, South Bend, IN 46617.

objectives were to democratize the Church and fundamentally change the Mass and Catholic moral teaching. At the top of their agenda was an effort to force the Church to accept birth control.[209] Conference attendees included: bishops, priests and religious, as well as lay people and even non-Catholics. Many of them actively participated in the proceedings of the Vatican II Council. While it is true these dissenters were successful in bringing many of their proposals to the table, most of their initiatives ultimately failed to make it into the final documents.

Stunned by their losses, the liberal reformers left Rome depressed and angry, but they had not given up. They wrote over thirty books about the council. Their accounts made it sound like everything had gone their way. Faithful Catholics unknowingly purchased the propaganda and came to believe that their ancient religion had been completely changed. Nothing could have been further from the truth, but by the time the Church issued her official account; most of the parishioners in the pew assumed they already knew all about it and never read the official Documents of Vatican II.[210]

Over the next forty years, the Church in America fell flat on Her face. Convents emptied out, two generations of children went un-catechized and the ad-libbed liturgical changes in the Mass made it virtually unrecognizable. Catholic Seminaries[211] began accepting fags and turning away candidates with true vocations. A vile homosexual scandal invaded the Church and even some bishops became complicit by moving the perverted priests around to avoid legal liabilities. Although he never breathed a word about it to anyone until 2002; Elliot Gague, the boy who lived in the

---

[209] From *Intended Consequences: Birth Control, Abortion and the Federal Government*, by By Donald T. Critchlow, published by Oxford University Press, 198 Madison Avenue, New York, NY. ©1999, pg. 64.
[210] *Vatican II Documents* – vatican.va/archive/hist_councils/ii_vatican_council/index.htm
[211] *Catholic Seminaries* – this information comes from the book "Goodbye, Good Men: How Liberals Brought Corruption into the Catholic Church", by Michael S. Rose, published by Regnery Publishing, Washington, DC ©2002

house behind us, went to school with us and swam in our pool; was one of the victims being abused by one of those renegade priests. The barrage of buggery tore away the innocence of young boys like Elliot, who tragically suffered in silence.

When the weather warmed, Tom, Chris and I headed over to Githin's Field to played baseball with Vinny Riley and his new friend Bob Wallace. Bob was a big guy with an even bigger heart, but he was no push-over. Whenever it was too cold or rainy to play outside, we hung out in his attic lifting weights. Our inspiration was a large poster of Jimmy Hendrix with a caption that read, "I chew aluminum foil." Bob lived with his mother Helen, who was a widow and Bob was her only child. Helen was a kind woman who had lost her husband in the Korean Conflict. Her thick black hair was pulled back in that gorgeous style of the forties. She often served us milk and cookies along with her warm smile. I think our presence took away some of her loneliness, yet a sadness remained and we all felt empathy for her ever present grieving.

The late John F. Kennedy had founded The President's Council on Physical Fitness and in his honor Mr. Nardo started our school's first track and field team. Every afternoon a group of us met him in the field behind the rectory. Mr. Nardo filled a couple of pits with sawdust for the High Jump and the Pole Vault. I frequently came home from practice with an aching back and although I enjoyed it and persevered to the end of the year, I looked forward to a summer vacation free of back pain. Unlike the surprise move from Pennsauken; dad let me in on his plans to move the family to Pennsylvania. I knew how tired he was from his daily commute, so I offered no objection to the relocation, but I also had no idea how traumatic it would be or how much I would miss my friends.

Before we left for Pennsylvania, dad took Tom and I on a survival trip. He had to do some work on the cabin so he took us with him to Sleepy Hollow. Convinced we knew all about the forest, we were sure we could forage around in the woods and find plenty of food. After all; we were Scouts, we read books on the subject and were veteran campers. Tom walked up river while I headed down stream along the Rancocas Creek. We agreed to meet back in the middle within the hour for breakfast. I found nothing and the only thing Tom found was a powder blue robin egg that fell from a nest. We hid the egg and tried going after some ducks on the creek. We lashed a penknife to the end of a long stick, but before we even got to use it, the lashing came loose and the knife fell off. So we retooled by carving a point on the end of each spear and returned to stalking the ducks. Each time we got within striking distance the flock would fly a couple of hundred yards down stream. We attempted to move slower and quieter, but every time they saw us coming our dinner flew away. In a last ditch effort we rushed them, only to watch the Mallards double back upstream and land next to our dock. Convinced they were laughing at us, Tom tried a Hail Mary pass, but to no avail. The ducks just sat there floating in the water and quacking at us.

At this rate we were going to starve to death. Dad came out to see how we were doing and was not all that surprised at our lack of success. "Its not as easy as it looks; is it?" he said with some level of understanding. He watched us for a while, as I knelt down beside our unused cooking fire and Tom tried candling the egg. Our heads hung low and our bellies were actively growling. Suddenly dad said, "I've got an idea. What if we go out to the Acme,[212] buy some chicken and pretend you caught those ducks?" It sounded like cheating, but we were too hungry to worry about such ethics. We all

---

[212] *Acme Markets* – is a Philadelphia-based supermarket chain owned by Eden Prairie, Minnesota-based Corporation Supervalue. Acme was founded in 1891 by Samuel Robinson & Robert Crawford in South Philadelphia & now operates about 130 supermarkets in Delaware, Maryland, New Jersey & Pennsylvania, still under the Acme name.

drove in to Mount Holly and bought a whole chicken. Returning home to cook our meal, we built the fire back up and placed it on the spit. Oh how we relished that wilderness feast!

Sleepy Hollow was a great place to spend leisure time. It was rustic, had a shallow creek for swimming and canoeing, not to mention it was very close to our home; but as soon as we moved to Pennsylvania the close factor would disappear. School was almost over and I had failed Geography in the third quarter. Dad was sure I could do better, so he took me on a ride up to Hickory Run[213] for a "Study Trip". The weekend would be a win-win for my father, since he could also use the time to hunt around for a new cabin in the Poconos, but it was a pressure cooker for me. I had looked forward to camping with my father and working on my scout craft, but this trip was strictly designed to "motivate" me to study. There were plenty of reading assignments and not much time in which to do them. Using shear grit and determination, I might have been able to pull it off, were it not for him calling me Cholly the whole time. Cholly meant I was a no good lazy bum. The derogatory nickname was supposed to "motivate" me, but all it ever did was to shame me about my work habits. I'm sure my father meant well, but the name calling just shut me down emotionally. Although I tried my best and studied hard, in the end it was never quite good enough.

School let out for summer vacation on June 17, 1966. I managed to pass all of my subjects and was easily promoted to the seventh grade, but the right side of my report card was still littered with check marks. Sticking out like a sore thumb was "Works and Plays Well with Others". I could hardly disagree with my teacher's assessment, since I had pretty

---

[213] *Hickory Run* – is a State Park with 15,990-acres, in Carbon County, Pennsylvania. The park is spread across the Pocono Mountains of Northeastern Pennsylvania & is easily accessible from I-476 & I-80. The most notable feature is the huge Boulder Field located in the northeast corner of the park.

much withdrawn from all my classmates in deference to those outside of school. Tom and Chris were my best friends and the three of us hung out together, but the kids at school were another matter. I was doing quite well with my outside relationships. Even though I had started out at the top of my class in the first grade, I left Saint Pete's with a mediocre record. I had found virtually no loyalty among my peers at school and routinely avoided most of my classmates. Were it not for my friends in the neighborhood, I would not have had any friends at all. Even my spiritual life was on the skids. Once ecstatic about being a soldier for Christ; I now found myself struggling to even remember when the last time was that I talked with Jesus.

I had very little fellowship and my spiritual well was running dry.

Chapter 8

Life On The Farm

Thanks to my uncle Hans, I had some pretty pleasant images of agricultural life. So I talked it up with Tom and Chris who were looking forward to visiting me in the country. My two best friends helped the family to pack for the move. Our friends joined us on the 4th of July weekend, to make the move up to Pennsylvania.

It was oppressively hot and humid in the back of the rented U-Haul truck. The trip was long and we all got fidgety. Tom pulled a straw from his soda and started shooting spitballs out a crack in the back door. It didn't take long for the rest of us to join in on the fun. Tom hit the window of the car beside us and Chris yelled, "Nice shot!" The next thing you know, we were all in on the game. When we stopped at a diner for lunch Tom couldn't resist firing one last spitball at the head of a bald guy who had just exited his Cadillac. It was a direct hit! The angry man wheeled around to see who hit him just as my father was rounding the back corner of the truck. Tom hurriedly retreated from the door and the rest of us covered our mouths to keep from snickering. Once dad understood what had happened he profusely apologized to the gentleman for our rudeness. Tom owned up to his offense, but my father was disappointed in all of us.

Driving up the Northeast extension of the Pennsylvania Turnpike, in what seemed like the inside of an oven, we took the Lansdale Exit and drove north on Sumneytown Pike. Within a half-hour we arrived at the Vernfield General Store. A small bell tinkled as we opened the door to an ancient four-story brick building. It was like we were stepping back in time. Crossing a well-worn wooden planked floor, we carefully navigated narrow aisles in between hand-made wooden shelves painted with layers of cracked white enamel paint. I slid open the glass door on the top of a freezer filled with ice cream and glanced back at dad. He nodded approvingly and like a bunch of starving wolves attacking the carcass of a caribou, we dove into the chilly chest to retrieve ice cream sandwiches. Dad directed us out onto the front porch to eat them, but the sun was so hot we soon moved to a bench in the shade on the side of the building. Within minutes our ice cream turned into a sticky mess that covered our hands and faces. Returning inside we found an old-fashioned water closet with an elevated wooden cistern. In the boys room we crisscrossed our streams of pee into the toilet, before inquisitively pulling the iron ring on the end of a long chain. Apparently we didn't do a very good job of cleaning our faces. Dad wrapped a handkerchief around his index finger, wet it on our tongues and wiped the melted ice cream and chocolate off. Still overheated and thirsty, dad led us to a big red metal Coca-Cola[214] chest for some soda. I slid back the condensation covered glass door on the top of it and saw a strange new brand of A-Treat[215] soft drinks, in a rainbow of colors. Still overheated, our hands lingered in the icy waters before we made our selections. Dad told us to get back in the truck and take the sodas with us, as he opened his three-sectioned billfold to pay the tab. By the time he finally exited the quaint Vernfield General Store, we had all piled back into the truck for the final leg of our journey.

With only one mile to go, we peeked out the crack in the back door and looked over lush green corn fields, big red barns and pastures dotted with grazing black cows. Turning off the blacktop, dad slowed down the pace on a dusty gravel road that seemed better suited for a tractor than a truck full of furniture. Ruth Road was pocked with potholes, forcing

---

[214] *Coca-Cola*™ – was invented by pharmacist John Pemberton in 1886. It is the flagship product of the Coca-Cola Company, which is a beverage company, manufacturer, distributor & marketer of non-alcoholic beverage concentrates & syrups. The formula & brand was purchased in 1889 by Asa Candler, who incorporated the company in 1892.

[215] *A-Treat*™ – is a regionally popular brand of carbonated soft drinks, manufactured & distributed by the A-Treat Bottling Company in Allentown, PA.

the load to precariously pitch back and forth. Low hanging branches snapped and squealed, as they brushed past the side of the vehicle. Finally we turned onto a circular driveway that cut through a small grove of cedar trees. The brakes squealed and the truck came to a grinding stop on the stones. Red dust billowed in the back door and an almost reverent silence came over us, as we shielded our mouths with our t-shirts. As soon as we heard dad exit the cab, we jumped up with anticipation and waited for him at the back door. When the door swung open fresh air flooded in and we were blinded by the sunlight. My little gang from the city quickly jumped out. Squinting our eyes we beheld a strange new world of silent beauty, but it would not last long. Sounding like a train pulling into Thirtieth Street Station, Tom and I pulled out the ramp from a slot below the deck of the truck. The clickety-clack of the rails came to a grinding halt in the middle of the loose red stone in the driveway. Then the rest of our crew scurried down the gangplank and ran into the side yard. Looking up we took in a picturesque view of the old two-story farmhouse set against a clear blue sky.

We couldn't wait to start exploring. Murray ran over to an old wooden pole with a green dinner bell on top of it and he began ringing it. Others chimed in until mom called for a moratorium on the bell. Stepping inside the back door, the only thing missing from the décor of the ancient kitchen was a wood stove. Handcrafted cabinets lined the walls from floor to ceiling; the windowsills were over a foot deep and anything made of wood was painted a dull shade of yellow including the cabinets. The dining room floor was made up of wide planks that were painted jet black and the living room had a small fireplace. The front door led out to a covered porch, which had a steep concrete stairway that led down to the road. The back of the living room had a stairway that led to a large bathroom on the second floor. It had an old porcelain bathtub with cast iron feet, but there was no shower! There were also no hallways. Instead handcrafted wooden doors with black wrought iron latches separated each of the rooms. I feared we would be living in a colonial museum, until I discovered a second bathroom with a stall shower outside the master bedroom. The basement was at ground level so it had a door that led outside to a concrete porch, with a cast iron hand pump. We took turns pumping the black handle and cooling our heads under a waterfall from the cold well. Sitting on a bench swing, we could look out over a sloping field with small stream near the bottom. Just beyond the creek was an overgrown pasture, a weatherworn chicken coop and an old white barn. Behind the house was an old garage, which doubled as a workshop. The place had three bays, sliding doors and an extra long workbench. Above each bench was a row of coffee cans. They were filled with rusty nails and sat atop dusty pine shelving. Old baby food jar lids were attached to the underside of them and the tiny glass jars were filled up with thousands of screws, nuts, washers and bolts. My buddies and I were fascinated with the creative way the former residents had utilized the things we referred to as trash. Sean tagged along as usual, but he asked fewer questions and eagerly worked the hand pump for us, so we didn't mind having him around. Suddenly dad bellowed out like John Wayne, "Let's go! We're burnin' daylight!" The four of us grunted our way up the stairs with the furniture, while Sarah and the younger kids helped mom and Lisa with clothing, toys and boxes. Within a couple of hours we unloaded the truck and piled back in the truck for another trip.

Amelia Jones, dropped by with her kids Matt and Julia, to help out with the move. Amelia was my dad's secretary. She helped mom and Lisa baby-sit the little kids back at the farmhouse, while the older children rode back and forth to Jersey. Julia Jones brought along her best friend Mandy. Mandy Grassley introduced us to a new game called Spin-the-Bottle. It was innocent enough, watching the empty A-Treat bottle point to one nervous victim after another, as our preteen moving crew attempted to traverse the gender divide for the first time. With each trip to Jersey, dad pushed us hard to: load, unload and get back on the road. We labored like slaves at either end, but while the truck was in motion we collapsed on the mattresses and slept for most of the journey before playing another round of spin-the-bottle. We made five trips over the course of the next two days and by the end of the weekend we felt like professional movers.

After waiting in line for showers and finally getting a good night's sleep, we attended Mass at St. Maria Goretti, our new parish in Hatfield, PA. Pastor Father O'Malley celebrated the Mass and we gave thanks for a safe and successful move. Having a Catholic Church to go to was a comfort to me, but the building looked much different than St. Pete's. Although the Mass was still the same, the brick architecture looked nothing like the granite cathedral I was used to. The interior was a simple wooden structure and during the week the place doubled as a basketball court and social hall. After Mass, Lisa took us out to the parking lot, and despite the noonday sun, we all joined in an action packed game of Jail Break. Meanwhile, mom and dad walked back to the Rectory with Father to register our family in the parish. Then an Immaculate Heart of Mary[216] Sister gave my parents a tour of the facilities and registered four of us for school. Sarah and I peered through the windows in the classroom and Sister Mary Magdalene[217] gave us a tour of the classrooms. The tall and stately woman demonstrated a confident and friendly manner. She would soon become my seventh grade teacher. My school and even the order of sisters that would teach me were changing again. This made the move a bit unsettling, but at least I could still attend a Catholic School.

On the way home from Church dad stopped off to see our new landlord Mr. Fischer. While the adults were settling

---

[216] *Immaculate Heart of Mary* – the IHM teaching order of Sisters began in the frontier settlement of Monroe, MI, in 1845. Two visionary & action-oriented personalities, Father Louis Gillet & Sister Theresa Maxis, began by taking the initiative to educate young girls & established the IHM community.

[217] *Sister Mary Magdeline* – was an excellent teacher & went on to become a successful IHM principle of Villa Maria Academy, a prestigious academy for girls in Malvern, PA.

affairs, we explored the dam, the race[218] and the water wheel attached to the old mill. Behind the man's house was a four-foot high milldam with a pond the size of a football field. The water was covered with islands of green algae and the humid, malodorous air and hot sun made it difficult to breathe. Once we explored beyond the waterfall of the spillway, the woods became incredibly quiet. There were no ripples on the pond, save those made by a couple of ducks. The only sound that could be heard, came from a lone bull frog on the far side a marsh below the mill. The Fischer place, as well as our ten-acre farm, both bordered the East Branch of the Perkiomen Creek. We rented an old horse farm, which included: the house, a barn, the garage, a chicken coop and a springhouse. The whole estate rented for the modest fee of two hundred dollars a month. By the time we returned home, we were famished. As was his custom on Sundays, dad made us breakfast, with scrambled eggs and one new item: Scrapple![219] We had never heard of the stuff, but it sure tasted good.

After breakfast, we fanned out on the farm to explore the property. The house stood atop a small hill, overlooking a valley filled with weeds and raspberry bushes. Jumping over a small stream that cut through the field, we slowly pushed through weeds above our heads on our way to an old wooden chicken coop. The front door hung precariously from a single rusty hinge and the exterior of the shed was covered with flaking chips of whitewash and torn pieces of black tarpaper. The inside was littered with shattered glass, rusty old feeding troughs and crumpled up beer cans. Four chicken ladders, covered in gray excrement, ascended from the floor to rows of brown wooden nests that were mounted on the

---

[218] *Race* – is a channel, usually made of wood or stone that carries water & runs from the pond behind a dam to the top of a spillway that pours over the water wheel of a mill.
[219] *Scrapple* – is a mush of pork scraps & trimmings combined with spices, cornmeal & buckwheat flour. The mush is formed into a semi-solid congealed loaf & slices are then pan-fried before serving. Scraps of meat left over from butchering were traditionally made into scrapple by the Pennsylvania Dutch to avoid waste & it is best known as a regional American food of the Mid-Atlantic States.

walls and covered over with spider webs. The corral behind the barn was a muddy mess of dried up manure and a cornucopia of thistles. On the front of the whitewashed stonewalls of the barn were Dutch doors leading to horse stalls made of ironwood and an earthen floor that was carpeted with a mixture of loose straw and equine droppings, which were covered with horse flies. The rough-cut lumber of the second floor was blanketed with bone dry dust, except for one large black oil spot, where a tractor had been parked. Climbing up on some bales of golden straw in the attic, we took turns jumping into a pile of loose hay on the floor below. This was more fun than a trampoline.

Bushwhacking my way through the overgrown fields our pant legs became covered in burrs.[220] It was a pain picking them all off of our jeans, so we headed back to the house along the red gravel road. Still hungry to explore, we headed down a well-worn path along the side of a hill behind the house. The end of the trail descended down a treacherously steep path to the Perkiomen Creek, but as soon as we began looking over the banks of the creek, we heard the dinner bell ringing. We raced each other up the steep hill, back down the path and up the grassy knoll, to the kitchen. Playtime was over and there would be no dinner. We had to get the U-Haul back to the dealer in Jersey before they closed, or dad would be charged for an additional day.

Somewhere during that final trip to Jersey, joy turned into sadness. The reality of the impending separation was beginning to hit me. We all sat in the front of the cab on the way back to Merchantville and we looked forward to weeklong visits. We tried planning our schedules, but things were not working out. Chris and Tom were both going to

---

[220] *Velcro* – is the brand name of fabric hook-and-loop fasteners, which was invented in 1941 by Swiss engineer, George de Mestral. The idea came to him one day after returning from a hunting trip in the Alps. He took a close look at the burrs (seeds) of burdock that kept sticking to his clothes & his dog's fur. He examined them under a microscope & noted hundreds of "hooks" that caught on anything with a loop. By duplicating the hooks & loops, he invented a new kind of fastener, which we refer to today as Velcro.

Pine Hill with the Boy Scouts. Mr. Reeves had recently purchased a building. He planned on expanding The Sonata School of Music and Tom had promised to help his dad to renovate the new home/office combination. There was also the pesky little problem of transportation.

The reality of the move was beginning to set in. The unspoken pain and frustration of trying to maintain a distant relationship and my inability to control my own destiny became painfully clear and our conversation changed course. We started reminiscing about things like apple fights, getting chased off the trampoline or shooting Larry Ferrari with hard candy in Wellwood Park. Following our last supper at the McDonald's on Route 70, we dropped off the U-Haul and took Chris Lang back to his home in Pennsauken. Chris, as always was upbeat and he enthusiastically reassured me that he and Tom would be back at the farm in no time. Tom tried to be just as cheery, but experience had given him a different perspective. He knew all too well from his own moving experiences that the adjustments necessary for relocation would not be easily overcome. When we arrived at his house I got out to say good-bye. We stared at each other through glassy eyes and then broke the uncomfortable moment with a handshake and a bear hug. Getting back in the station wagon I choked back tears, as dad and I drove away in silence. The reality finally hit me while we were crossing the Ben Franklin Bridge. Like a dam bursting, I started crying inconsolably and didn't stop until we reached the Schuylkill Expressway. I was so upset, my chest was heaving and hyperventilation sent my whole body into a nitrogen-induced stupor. I knew in my heart of hearts that life as I had known it was over.

Although he wanted to comfort me, there wasn't much my father could say or do. He turned on the radio to the familiar sound of the teletype machines and the signature jingle, "KYW, Newsradio – ten – sixty!" Jack O'Rourke began his report at the top of the hour. In Haiphong Harbor, forty-six planes from the aircraft carrier Ranger just upped the ante in the Viet Nam war. In a single raid, fighter jets had destroyed eighty percent of the Viet Cong's oil supply. Meanwhile down South in the land of the free, Julian Bond, a duly elected black man, was refused his legislative seat in congress, because he had spoken out against the war. The decision would later be reversed by the U.S. Supreme Court in Bond vs. Floyd.[221]

Thanks in large part to the war in Vietnam, youth were challenging authority, questioning established values and numbing out on drugs. The country was convulsing and so was I. The deracination[222] of the move to Pennsylvania was life shattering. Leaving the predictability of a small town, so we could live on a farm in the middle of nowhere was culturally shocking. But for all its negatives, the country also provided a place of solitude, where I could reflect on the upheaval that had just befallen me. The weather was hot, humid and filled with the pungent odor of sumac, which came from the trees in the wind breaks between the corn fields. Every morning around ten the fog lifted. By noon the dew on the grass was gone and the brown blades were so baked it crunched beneath my feet like potato chips. The setting was peaceful enough, but never quiet. A never-ending symphony of ten thousand crickets and a couple of croaking bull frogs were always performing for us.

Although it was hot and uncomfortable, there was plenty of work to be done. The first priority was to set up our pool. I spent hours pushing through the tall weeds with the Gravely mower[223] on an overgrown pasture at the bottom of the hill.

---

[221] *Bond vs. Floyd* – in disqualifying Bond because of his statements, the State violated the First Amendment, made applicable to the States by the Fourteenth Amendment. 385 U.S. 116 Appeal from the U.S District Court for the Northern District of GA, No. 87, which was eventually decided on December 5, 1966.
[222] *Deracination* – to isolate or alienate a person from his native culture or environment.
[223] *Gravely Mower* – the Gravely line of mowers was established in 1916 by Benjamin Franklin Gravely. Gravely was a man of inventive & creative genius with a vision to produce a tractor, which would revolutionize gardening & lawn maintenance. Working

Then Sean and I took turns chopping the ground into a fine powder with an old roto-tiller so we could protect the liner of the pool. The rest of the afternoon we put together a tubular metal framework. When dad got home the entire family helped to put up the metal siding and open up the plastic liner. Although the hot sun was now setting, the evening brought forth a different set of discomforts. Swarms of mosquitoes feasted on our flesh as we stood for hours, in the frigid ankle deep well water, holding up the liner. By the time darkness settled in, the pool liner was able to stand on its own. We all retreated to the safety and comfort of the house for dinner and retired early. The hose ran at full blast filling the pool all night long, but in the wee hours of the morning the pump started making an awful noise. Dad walked down to investigate only to discover that our well had run dry. It would need to be recharged, which meant we would have no water and no ice tea. The next day we resumed filling the pool, albeit with an intermittent schedule of water use and by the end of the week the pool was filled to the top. The pool provided a respite from the heat, but the days were so hot the icy well water in the pool felt like a warm bath by the third day.

Our new residence was not exactly a working farm. Dad turned the place into a virtual petting zoo. It had been awhile since I rode horses at Uncle Hans' farm, but dad said I would soon have a horse of my own. So Sean and I energetically mucked out the fly infested stalls in preparation. Meanwhile Murray and Brennan swept out the chicken coop and made room for some two-dozen peepers dad purchased from the local hatchery. Sarah was given a nanny goat, which she named Annie and it came with a kid she called Amy Lou. Sean received a pregnant cat and Brennan, still pretty young, patiently waited for his promised puppy.

---

together with his engineering partner Eustance Rose, they created Gravely Tractors, which had an exceptional reputation for quality, strength & reliability.

The nanny goat was tethered to a stake in the middle of a field behind the chicken coop and wherever Annie went Amy Lou was sure to follow. Sarah moved the stake every few days using the goats to knock down the weeds with her chain and it ate just about everything else in sight, including sticker bushes. Within a few weeks the entire overgrown field was completely cleared and the pasture looked like a lush Irish meadow. My chestnut brown Quarter horse was a mature mare with a white marking down the front of her face, so I named my new horse Blaze. Dad took me to a tack shop where we picked up a bridle, a blanket and a saddle. Stopping by the Agway[224] on the way home, we ordered 250 bales of alfalfa hay, 100 bales of golden yellow straw for bedding and took home two 50-pound sacks of oats. The following Saturday we began installing an electric fence, which kept me busy for weeks. Life on the farm was kind of lonely, but taking care of the horse was similar to building a relationship with a friend. Murray and I used black and white spray paint and some cardboard stencils to make up signs on pieces of old plywood. Over the Dutch door leading into the stall my sign read, "Use Horse Sense" and on top of the chicken coop my younger brother advertised his new business, "Murray's Eggs".

Absent my friends from Jersey, I felt cut off and alone, but Blaze changed all that. She was much gentler than Lightening. At 10.2 hands,[225] she was almost two hands shorter than the scary stallion back at Uncle Hans' farm. Traveling on horseback in the country is akin to riding a bike

---

[224] *Agway* - was an agricultural business that offers feed for livestock & poultry, as well as seed, fertilizers & herbicides. Agway was formed on July 25, 1964 in Dewitt, NY from a merger between Grange League Federation & Eastern States Farmers' Exchange. In 1965 the Pennsylvania Farm Bureau Cooperative also joined Agway. But in 1999 Agway sold or closed all its retail outlets & sold their warehouse system to Southern States Cooperative. It was the victim of a "corporate culture" that relied on huge inventories financed by debt & in October of 2002 Agway filed for bankruptcy.

[225] *Hands High* – is the measurement used to convey the height of horses. It is measured from the ground to the highest point of the withers, where the neck meets the back. The English-speaking world measures the height of horses in hands (abbreviated "h" or "hh", for "hands high") & inches. One hand equals 4 in. Therefore, the height is expressed as the number of full hands, followed by a decimal point, or the number of additional inches.

in the city. I could go anywhere! Blaze and I walked along old tractor paths, galloped on the edges of cornfields, ducked under branches in the partially wooded pastures and meandered along stony creek beds. I knew Quarter horses could do the quarter mile in less time than any other breed. So I wanted to find out just how fast and far my horse could run. I would arrive at that answer the hard way. One very hot afternoon, Unfortunately, I decided to run my horse on the blacktop at a full gallop all the way down to the Vernfield General Store. Blaze ran the mile with all the gusto of a Thoroughbred,[226] but when we arrived at our destination, the poor thing was panting and sweating like it was dying of emphysema. Thinking I had pushed her too far, I ran inside the store and asked to borrow the garden hose. I filled an old tin trough and Blaze began gulping down the water. She was drinking too fast so I had to forcefully pull her away. After several unsuccessful attempts at restraining her, I yanked on the reins and tied her to a tree, while I took off her saddle and blanket. The air was smelled a putrid mix of sweat, leather and wet wool. Foam dripped from her mouth and detracted from her beautiful chestnut coat. The blanket was completely drenched in sweat. Panicked, I promised God that if He let my horse live, I would never again mistreat her, just to satisfy some curiosity of mine.

I used to think of dogs as boys and cats as girls. I knew it wasn't true; it's just how I looked at things sometimes. Even though my horse was female, to me horses were also masculine animals. I saw Blaze that way and he soon became the best buddy I had in Pennsylvania. Caring for a horse is a lot of work, but it has its rewards and mine was hanging out with my new friend. Every morning I fed him a quarter bale of alfalfa and a coffee can full of oats. In the afternoons, I mucked out the stalls, laid down some fresh straw and used a curry brush to comb his soft coat. The treat came when all

---

[226] *Thoroughbred* – is a horse breed best known for its use in horse racing. Although used to refer to any purebred horse, it technically refers only to the Thoroughbred breed. These "hot-blooded" horses are known for their agility, speed and spirit.

the chores were finished. Laying on his bareback while he walked through the pasture eating grass was like getting a massage. I would often talk with him and those inaudible conversations did much to diminish my depression. The intimacy we shared was similar to the camaraderie between a boy and his dog. I started to wonder if cowboys had the same relationship with their horses.

Horses drink lots of water. The biggest chore I had was carrying buckets of water from a small stream in the pasture over to the stall in the barn. The little tributary, which ran the length of the pasture, was not deep enough for a horse to drink from, but dad had a creative solution. His company produced Base Plugs, which were primers on the back of Navy cannon shells. Although Callahan Machine Company lost money on the deal, the government contract provided much needed cash flow, when other projects were not yet completed. Base Plugs were a little over an inch thick and cut from five inch diameter steel bar stock. The out-of-spec pieces of scrap wound up in a big wooden box. We used stacks of the scrap iron to block the flow of the small stream and called our project the Base Plug Dam. The water that built up behind it gave Blaze a place to drink. It took me a few hours to finish the project and I was hungry, tired and not paying attention. So I began climbing up the hill next to the stream to return to the house. Still standing in the water behind the dam, I reached for a handhold and grabbed the electric fence! Bam! I was thrown back in the water. My heart was racing, my butt smarted and despite an entire afternoon of hard labor, I was wide awake.

While thumbing through a Boy's Life magazine; I came across a story about Lone Scouts. The feature article was about boys that were not affiliated with any particular troop. They worked independently on their requirements for advancement in rank. I identified with these boys, because I too felt like I was living in the middle of nowhere. I sent away for a Lone Scout application and with only three items left to go on my Second Class rank, I set out to fulfill my lashing requirement. At the top of our driveway was a grove of cedar and sumac trees. The ground was carpeted with a thick layer of pine needles and it seemed like the perfect place to set up a camp and build a lean-to. I used my hatchet to cut down several cedar saplings and retrieved a bunch of old baling twine from the barn to use for lashing them together. Everything was going fine till I ran out of twine. With vines growing everywhere, I began pulling them off the trees, ripping them out of the ground and stripping away their shiny green leaves. The vines worked just fine and I was able to finished lashing the shelter together before mom rang the dinner bell. Sometime during supper I began itching and by bedtime my arms were covered with the leprosy of poison ivy. Mom applied copious quantities of calamine lotion to the oozing sores, but she used up her entire supply and had to run out to the general store for some more. She purchased two large bottles of the pink stuff and a bars of Fels-Naptha[227] soap. A few days later my whole body blew up like a balloon and I looked like a fat kid. Dad took me to see a doctor and the doc gave me a prescription, but the little blue pills had almost no effect. My face was so large it looked as though I had been attacked by a nest of hornets. Since we had no air conditioning, I spent the rest of the summer sitting on a folding chair in the middle of the springhouse. Although mosquitoes took their turns at torturing me, the building was the most comfortable place on the farm.

Tom and Chris finally came up for a couple of weeks, but my terminal case of poison ivy threw a monkey wrench into the vacation. They rode my horse Blaze, camped down by the creek and went swimming in the mill pond. They even

---

[227] *Fels-Naptha* – the original soap product was developed by Philadelphia manufacturer Joseph Fels around 1893 & was historically used as a home remedy in the treatment of contact dermatitis caused by exposure to poison ivy, poison oak and other oil-transmitted organic skin-irritants. Washing the skin directly with the soap helps break up the oils that carry the toxin even though in its own caution use sheet, from Dial Corp. states that Fels-Naptha is a skin irritant and should not be used directly on skin.

took the B-B gun along with them on a canoe trip. There wasn't much we could do together and even when we could, I had almost no energy to join in on the activities. Before long it was time for them to head back to Jersey. I felt that gut wrenching feeling again. I had missed another opportunity to spend time with my friends and their leaving was more than I could bear. Depressed and alone, I returned to the solitude of the beach chair in the springhouse.

Chapter 9

An Angry Young Man

Come September I entered the seventh grade at Saint Maria Goretti. Sister Mary Magdeline was my teacher and Mother Mary Olivia was an absolutely ancient principal. I carried a "B" average with moderate effort, but my anger over the move showed up on the left side of the report card. If Character and Citizenship received letter grades, I would have flunked. I didn't want to be there and was letting everyone around me know it.

When dad started talking about putting us in the public school the move to Pennsylvania suddenly felt like a betrayal. If my father was willing to put our family into a pagan school, what else was he capable of doing? Although I did my chores, participated in class and completed my homework assignments, I wanted nothing to do with making new friends. Schoolmates back in Jersey had brought me nothing but pain and embarrassment. The only real friends I ever had came from the neighborhood and no kids lived this far out in the country. My parents tried to get me to join the local Boy Scout Troop, but I was perfectly content being a Lone Scout. In addition to being mad as hell about the move, I saw making new friends as being disloyal to my buddies back in Jersey. I wanted nothing to do with the kids at school and resisted mom and dad's attempts to hook me up with other groups like the 4-H Club.[228] I even avoided contact with my own sister and brothers. I lived a lonely life of solitary activities exploring the creek or riding my horse.

---

[228] *4-H Clubs* – began around the start of the 20th century in different parts of the United States. The focal point of the clubs was the idea of blending practical & hands-on learning, with a public school education to make it more connected to rural life. Early programs tied both public & private resources together to benefit the rural youth.

The East Branch of the Perkiomen Creek, which bordered our property, was a bit too shallow for navigation. Even so, I was able to canoe upstream as far as Mr. Shepherd's dairy farm and downstream all the way to Mr. Fischer's dam. I built rafts, went fishing, built camp fires on the banks of the creek and even lay naked in the tall grass, to experiment with getting an over all tan. I joined my sister and brothers, when it was really hot out, to swing on the rope behind the dam and go swimming. In the summertime the flow of the creek was low and slow. It was also heavy with the smell of algae. In most places the water was only about a foot deep. However after a heavy downpour, the creek swelled and turned muddy. Following the spring thaw, she overflowed her banks and deposited copious amounts of a reddish brown silt. The spring floods littered the flatlands with scores of uprooted trees and piled up lots of bleached firewood for our impromptu campfires. Carefully hidden on the ground in these silt laden grasslands were the nests of the ring-necked pheasants and each one contained one to two dozen olive green eggs.

Dad gave me a brand new 20-gage shotgun for my birthday. The ring-necked pheasants were everywhere! Trudging through the grasslands, cornfields and windbreaks, I was hunting long before I had a license. Although rarely close enough to hit one, the colorful males were the real prize and usually the first to fly, but hens evoked the most excitement. The female birds were extremely well camouflaged. They hid in thick matted grass and under the laurel in the windbreaks. Hens were absolutely quiet until you almost stepped on them. Startled by the loud clucking and frantic flapping of their wings, these panicked birds were often long gone, by the time I realized they were only hens.

Sarah loved her goats and went down into the pasture every morning and evening to milk the floppy-eared Nubian. She used the milk to feed Sean's cats, which were becoming more and more numerous with every litter. Once the kittens found the rich creamy treats, they regularly attended the milking sessions. Sarah entertained us by squirting the kittens in the face and we were delighted to watch them gleefully lick themselves clean. There was almost no traffic on Ruth Road, so Sean's cats would often spread out in the middle of the gravel road for a siesta. Every few weeks a car would came by and flattened one. No matter how often it happened, Sean came in shocked and angry. Fortunately, the birth rate outpaced the mortality rate and Sean eventually had over forty cats.

Within a few months Murray's egg business became a profitable operation. Every morning Murray walked down to the chicken coop, reached under the hens in their nest boxes and filled up recycled egg cartons. Since chickens lay about an egg a day, we had plenty of them for the family and Murray sold the surplus at school. Still waiting patiently, Brennan looked forward to the day when he would have his own dog. Mom never really wanted any animals and was absolutely overwhelmed with our growing animal farm. Raised in the city of Camden, she was not exactly enchanted with country life. Having just learned how to drive back in Jersey, she wondered where all the streetlights went. However, overcoming all obstacles, the Lord took pity on Brennan and touched his mother's heart. Mom drove down to the Vernfield General Store, at night no less, to purchase a bag of potatoes. Placing the bag on the counter she wandered around the small country store, looking for any other items she might need. In the far corner of the store was a cardboard box filled with newborn puppies and she picked one up to pet it. The sign on the box caught her eye and read *Free To A Good Home!* The cuddly little bundle of joy cooed helplessly when his dark brown eyes met hers, in what can only be described as love at first sight. Surprising everyone in our family she brought the pup home and named it Spud, after those little eyes on the potatoes. Mom gave it to her son to take care of, but we all knew it was as much mom's dog as it ever was Brennan's.

In the fall dad took Chris and I deer hunting at Hickey's Hut.[229] Along the way we stopped off in Lock Haven,[230] to buy groceries and supplies at the local IGA.[231] We also stopped in at a hunting and sporting goods shop to pick up ammo, a hot seat and the scent of a doe in heat. Dad lent me his double-barreled 12-gage Parker[232] to use with a box of pumpkin balls.[233] Each night we spotted deer in fields that were punctuated with crab apple trees across from the Little Pine State Park.[234] I spent the following day sitting at the foot of a tall pine tree, patiently anticipating my prey. I was trying to remain quiet, but a pesky little squirrel harvesting acorns was deliberately throwing them at me. Since I did not want to make any noise that would scare the deer, I put up with the arrogant little rodent until dusk and then took my revenge by blowing him away with a single shot.

Miss Hickey was the original owner of the cabin we were staying at and had never married. She was buried a mere stone's throw away from where I was hunting. This mysterious spinster lady had been a God fearing Catholic woman from West Chester, PA. In her youth, she belonged

---

[229] *Hickey's Hut* – was a small cabin located on 30 acres along the Little Pine Creek, in Waterville, Pennsylvania, just south of the Little Pine State Park.
[230] *Lock Haven* – is the county seat of Clinton County, PA. Located near the confluence of the West Branch of the Susquehanna River & Bald Eagle Creek. In the 20th century, a light-aircraft factory, a college & a paper mill, along with many smaller enterprises, drove the economy. In 1937, William T. Piper, Sr., built the Piper Aircraft Corporation factory in a building that once housed a silk mill, after the company's Taylor Aircraft manufacturing plant in Bradford, PA, was destroyed by fire.
[231] *IGA* - the Independent Grocers Association was founded in 1926, bringing together independent grocers across the U.S. to ensure that the trusted, family-owned local grocery store remained strong in the face of growing chain competition.
[232] *Parker Shotguns* – have been highly desired since 1868, cherished by their owners & often passed down as priceless heirlooms from one generation to another. The craftsmanship found in a Parker was not surpassed in the years the company produced what has become known as the finest American made shotguns of the 19th & 20th century.
[233] *Pumpkin Balls* – the earliest shotgun slugs were just lead spheres slightly smaller than the bore diameter. These slugs had very poor accuracy & were only effective at close range, where they could be relied upon to hit the target in a vital area. The Brenneke & Foster slugs came later & used a weight-based design & rifling-like fins to provide stability.
[234] *Little Pine State Park* – is a 2,158 acre state park in Lycoming County, PA. It is situated along 4.2 miles of the Little Pine Creek & includes a dam with a 94 acres lake. The Little Pine Creek is a tributary of Pine Creek, which is located in Tiadaghton State Forest. The park is just north of Waterville, Pennsylvania.

to the Singles Group at Saint Agnes parish and she generously offered to share her place on the weekends and during the summer time, for retreats and relaxation. Along with her friends they built a small cabin on thirty acres of forested land, which she had purchased along the Little Pine Creek. They pieced the cabin together with plywood, chewing gum and bailing wire. Later on in life she met and befriended my Uncle Leon Kowalski. When she died, the place was willed to my Uncle who had helped her to maintain the cabin. Uncle Leon was married to my father's sister Mary, which is how we came to be invited there. The only thing Miss Hickey asked in return for her hospitality was that the guests fill out a logbook. The tradition she started allowed others the privilege of reading past entries and sharing in the other guest's adventures and musings. Now stored in a firebox, the journal continues to provide incredible insights into the past.

Each night we poured over topographical maps, making plans for the next day's hunt. We ate hearty meals cooked in the cabin and occasionally ventured out to the Waterville Hotel, where we learned how to play pool. We also listened to the tall tales of all the other hunters. After lunch we went to a trading post called Fin, Fur and Feather. The unique little tourist trap featured caged wildlife in the back and many keepsakes; an antler handled knife, a lamp with a deer on its base or a sweatshirt with a picture of a Pennsylvania black bear. Hanging on the varnished pinewood walls of the Waterville Diner were fine samples of the work of a local taxidermist. The waitress had missing teeth and she looked like a hillbilly. The entire trip was surreal. Hunting was never so much about getting the deer, as it was about doing lots of fun things together with dad. The sizzle was always better than the steak.

If heat, humidity and bugs were the discomforts of summer, drifting snow was the wicked witch of the winter. When we returned from our hunting trip, men in township trucks were hard at work putting up rolls of red picket fencing. The fences ran parallel to the road and were set back almost twenty feet from the edge. I had never seen fences like this before and did not understand their purpose, but the Blizzard of 1966 would soon satisfy my curiosity.[235]

During Advent we peered out the windows of our farmhouse to watch the falling snow create four-foot high snowdrifts, but that was just the beginning. The temperature plummeted into the teens and forty-five mile an hour winds emptied open fields and piled up the accumulated dry snow into fifteen foot drifts. The next evening even more snow blanketed the farm and by Christmas day only the top foot of our front door was even visible. I had heard of storms like this, but had never really seen one. We were snowed in! So in order to get out, dad opened up the second floor window and I slid down the porch roof into a snowdrift. Tunneling my way back to the porch by hand, I found a shovel by the door and cleared a path to it. There was no way we were getting out. For the first time in our family's history, we would not be attending Mass on Christmas morning. The blizzard prevented so many people from going to Church on Christmas it was rumored that the Diocese of Philadelphia endured a serious financial crisis that lasted straight through to Easter.

When the roads were finally plowed, we made our way out to the store. I now knew why snow fences had been erected. Wherever there was a fence, there was a ten to twenty foot mountain of snow, but the leeward side of the drifts sloped almost all the way down to the ground, leaving the road virtually cleared. As soon as we were able to get out of the driveway, we took a trip over to New Jersey to visit our Grandparents for Christmas. Although we enjoyed visiting

---

[235] *Blizzard* – on Christmas Eve in 1966, a snowstorm accompanied by thunder & lightning swept through Abington in suburban Philadelphia. A strong high pressure system over Canada was delivering a massive Arctic flow into the Northeast, causing frigid temperatures, as a huge Nor'easter developed & moved up the coast.

our relatives, the real treat came on the way back. Dad surprised me by picking up Chris Lang and Tom Reeves. They were coming home with us for the holidays. It was a long drive to Pennsylvania and by the time we arrived home it was pretty late.

During the day the sun was beginning to melt some of the snow. Come nightfall, the top layer had frozen into a solid crust of ice capable of supporting our weight. We slid across the crystalline surface on our boots in a moonlit winter wonderland. The sky was clear and the full moon shone through a royal blue canopy. Another thousand brightly lit pinholes illuminated the Milky Way in a clarity we had never before witnessed. The celestial floodlight reflected off the snow like a sandy white beach. The snow lit up the hill behind the house like it was daytime and all of the trees, in the partially wooded field down in the valley, were covered in a veil of silvery luminescence. And the silence was deafening as we stood there reverently soaking in the magical moment.

Although it was almost midnight, we ran to the back of the garage to retrieve our sleds. Lined up on outside wall was a standard sled with runners, a wooden toboggan, an aluminum saucer and a snow wing. Tom tried using the sled, but the runners dug through the crusty ice. We needed something with a little more surface to it. I jumped on the toboggan and went slowly down the hill, curving gently in an "S" pattern until I slid under the electric fence. Chris sat on the aluminum saucer and having absolutely no control, went careening off the hill and into the bushes. Tom sat on the snow wing, grabbed the plastic handles and sailed down the hill. Luckily he turned just in time to avoid falling into the small stream that ran through the pasture.

Dad emptied some kerosene out of a tank used for heating the kitchen and applied a generous amount of the thin coal oil to the bottom of the saucer. Chris went zooming down the icy surface at twice his original speed. Providentially, he crashed into a drift and stood up laughing and covered in snow. Excited by his impressive run, Tom called out, "Hey Mr. Callahan, put some of that on mine!" My father applied the kerosene and Tom strapped himself into the snow wing. Chris and I gave him a running start and he rocketed down the hill. The aluminum cutting across the ice gave off a thunderously shrill din like the sound of a fighter jet. It seemed to echo with intermittent patterns like Morse code, as the sled hopped over crusty moguls. Then all of a sudden there was silence! Less than a second had passed, but it seemed a lot longer and then CRACK! Tom had launched himself past the fence, through the air and into the icy stream buried in the pasture. The frigid runoff water flowing beneath the ice drenched his clothes. He scrambled out of the ditch in a panic. His back was hurt and the single digit temperatures made his breathing labored, but he knew he had to move and move fast! Running up the hill he ran into the kitchen and stripped off his wet clothes. Dad sat him down in front of the kerosene heater and put a wool blanket over him. Tom shivered uncontrollably, as the rest of us looked on in fearful silence. Meanwhile mom made some hot chocolate for all of us, but Tom was given first dibs and the lion's share of the hot drink. Little by little Tom began to warm up until we finally felt free to speak to him. Chris was the first one to break the silence saying, "That was one fast run man!" His shivering eventually subsided and because it was almost two o'clock in the morning, we were all sent up to bed. Adventure, crisis, resolution; it was like old times again!

Early the next morning the plow came by and piled up a huge mountain of snow in front of the house. Using garden shovels and buckets, Shane and Art cut a long tunnel that paralleled the road. The two children worked all morning long and were tired and cold, but they continued to load buckets of snow onto a sled and pull them down the long corridor they had created under the ice-cold mound.

Suddenly a low rumbling sound captured Shane's attention and he wondered aloud, "What's that?" "What's what?" said Art. "Shhh" Shane whispered, as they both looked at each other with a sense of foreboding. The grinding noise grew from a dull distant rumble to a thunderous tumult. "A Plow!" Art screamed, as he scrambled toward the exit. Shane, who was located too far down the tunnel to escape, watched in horror as the collapsing passageway revealed the ruthless edge of a snowplow. Catching hold of his boot it dragged him down the street and left him trapped under a pile of ice and snow. Art called out to him franticly following Shane's cries for help, but was unable to find him. Finally Shane freed one of his hands and punched his fist through the snow. Art grabbed hold of his hand and pulled. Adventure, crisis, resolution; the family tradition continued.

Chris and Tom returned to Jersey, which once again left me alone in a foreign land. Following each Siberian squall very little snow melted away and the drifts kept piling up, one layer upon the other. The temperatures regularly plummeted into the teens during at night, which turned any snow that did manage to melt during the day into a solid block of ice. When spring arrived, the accumulated snow was everywhere and then came the rain. For three days during February the skies opened up and a torrential downpour swelled the creeks. Rising water levels busted up the frozen waterways, sending icebergs sailing through the heavily silted Perkiomen creek, like torpedoes. The reddish brown floodwaters rose to colossal crests, as winter liquefied into turbulent waters, worthy of kayaking. It was all pretty exhilarating.

So it was with adventure in mind that dad drove Sarah and I a couple of miles up the river to Branchwood Park. The local picnic grounds were already flooded, so we launched our aluminum canoe from along side one of the wooden tables. Dad sat in the back to steer, Sarah seated herself in the middle and I manned a paddle in the front of the canoe.

Asleep In The Light

Since the air was freezing cold and it was still raining, we all kept our winter coats and boots on. The plan was to take a short daring ride down the muddy rapids back to the farm. With the exception of a narrow spillway over a small dam, the trip down the swollen creek was uneventful. It was so boring I started looking for opportunities to spice things up a bit. I spotted what looked like the rock of Gibraltar with whitewater swirling violently around the outcropping. Although paddling over to it seemed like a harmless little thrill, the canoe flipped over. Dad quickly stabilized our flooded canoe, but Sarah panicked and stood up capsizing the canoe again. Dad and I tried to convince her to sit down, but she was so paralyzed with fear she couldn't hear us. After the third roll, I abandoned ship and swam for the safety of the shore. Dad continued to steady the canoe, but Sarah fell out and began floating down the river. Although he tried to rescue her, a rope on the floor of the canoe wrapped around his legs and pulled him under water. Grabbing a low hanging branch he tried to break free from the rope. Meanwhile Sarah was bobbing up and down in the swiftly flowing current of the icy waters. I ran down the wooded bank to get ahead of her and picked up a small sapling to rescue her, but she reached out and missed. On my second try she grabbed hold of the branch and I was able to pull her to safety. Meanwhile dad's life was flashing before him. Eventually he broke free of the rope and climbed up the snowy bank to join us. The three of us sat down on the top of the hill to rest and catch our breath watching our partially submerged canoe float down away and out of sight. Shivering and weighed down by wet heavy clothing, we followed Ruth Road past Mr. Shepherd's barn and on to the safety of our home. Freezing temperatures turned the steady rain into a blizzard. Mom had been anxiously watching for us at the window. She greeted us with clothing and blankets, as soon as we walked through the front door. Dad was obviously suffering from the ill effects of hypothermia and quickly jumped into the stall shower. Sarah was the girl, so she got first dibs on the bathtub. That left me sitting on the hallway floor along with my guilty conscience and chattering teeth.

Dad had almost drowned. Sarah was nearly swept away in the frigid waters. We all had mild cases of hypothermia and the canoe had been lost. For what? An adventure? A cheap thrill? Dad considered it the stupidest decision he had ever made and anguished for years with "what if" scenarios. He could always buy another boat, but what if his children had died? My guilt feelings were much more criminal. I saw no problem with shooting the rapids; it seemed relatively safe and even a bit boring. I knew that what had created the disaster was my secret desire to head for those rushing waters around the big rock. I had nearly caused the deaths of Sarah and my father, but was too embarrassed to own up to the deed. When I finally got my turn at the shower; I felt justly punished for my depraved indifference and was simply thankful we had all survived.

I was still angry about the move to Pennsylvania, but the incident left me feeling much closer to my family. Dad became increasingly irritated with my lack of cooperation and initiative. I did what I had to do at school to maintain my grades, but remained thoroughly resistant to forming any new friendships. The bad attitude I maintained at school also followed me home. I generally practiced the letter of the law, but never went the extra mile on anything. I took care of Blaze, burned the trash regularly and grudgingly did the dishes when it was my turn to do them, but I never helped out with anything else. I took my good old time doing mediocre work and complained about almost everything. I often disappeared without a word. I would frequently hang out by the creek or wander around aimlessly with Blaze. While the solitude did nothing to improve my behavior, it gave me time to step back and reflect on things.

One thing I noticed was that my relationship with Sean had changed. Back in Merchantville we fought all the time and his very presence irritated me, but ever since the move we were getting along just fine. I started to wonder why. One thing I noticed was that every time I asked him to do something, he cheerfully agreed. If I asked him to clean something up, he returned a couple of hours later to let me know it was all done. Believing there was no way he could have accomplished the task so quickly, I went over to inspect the quality of his work. Each and every time the task was not only accomplished, it was done much better than I even thought possible. I was so impressed, I had to restrain my facial reactions and find something small to complain about, but even then, he cheerfully and quickly made it right. How could anyone be upset with this guy? I still wondered what his angle was, but every time I tried to find an evil intent, he came up smelling like a rose.

In math, when things don't add up, you're probably missing some of the information. What I wasn't seeing at the time was that Sean had created a subterranean dictatorship for himself. Unfortunately, he had learned how to survive by duplicating my own brutality. He forced all the younger boys, to do his work for him and then threatened to beat them up, if they told on him. In this way he was able to take credit for their work and that allowed him to keep me happy and quite literally off his back. Although the practice was a bit dark, it also demonstrated creative political genius.

My father developed a friendship with a man named Bernie Downey. Bernie was a Christian evangelist and he also ran Heston S. Swartly, a local gas station. The tall trapper with the booming voice, who pumped my father's gas, wore a coonskin cap and reminded me of Daniel Boone. Mr. Downey was charitable to a fault and he trusted in his heavenly Father's providence without any reservations. He would help anyone in need, even if he knew it would cost him dearly. When dad told him about my interest in pigeons, Bernie dropped by to give me six baby pigeons and a coop made out of two old wooden barrels.

The pigeons were called Tipplers,[236] a name that had more to do with their flight maneuvers than it did with their markings. When I first let them out of the cage, they flew a few hundred feet up in the air, tipped a wing and free fell almost two hundred feet, before spreading their wings in a spectacularly swooping recovery. For about two hours they repeated their acrobatics before returning to the perch and waddling into the barrel. After about a week dad and I released them at the end of Ruth Road and watched them fly home. The following week we took them to the Vernfield General Store, then to the Swartly station in Harleysville and finally dad took them into to work with him and let them go in North Wales. Each time without fail, they returned home to the coop.

Unlike my previous experience with pigeons, this time it was working! The next time dad drove me over to Jersey to see my friends, I brought along my pigeons. When it was time to go back to Pennsylvania, my friends and I let the birds go. Although dad and I thought the pigeons would beat us home, the coop was empty. A storm had passed through the area and dad thought the birds might have been blown off course. On the second day direr possibilities began coming to mind. Maybe they got hit by lightning or were eaten by hawks. For three days I waited and worried. On the fourth day Shane came running in with the good news, "I see Tom's pigeons!" We all ran outside to see the tipplers soaring high in the sky, tipping their wings, diving and then swooping back up again. Around sunset, they fluttered down on to the garage roof and then made their way back into the coop. Two weeks later I

---

[236] *Tippler* – is a breed of domestic pigeon, bred to participate in endurance competitions & are noted for soaring to tremendous heights, tipping one wing & then free-falling before recovering from the stall. Pigeons have been selectively bred to be able to find their way home over extremely long distances & will generally return to their own nest or mate. Flights as long as 1,118 miles have been recorded by birds in competition & their average flying speed, over moderate distances, is around 30 mph. They are called carrier pigeons when they are used to carry messages written on thin light paper & rolled into a small tube called pigeon post, which is attached to the bird's leg. Homing pigeons can only go back to one "mentally marked" point that they have identified as home. So "pigeon mail" can only work when the sender is actually holding the receiver's pigeons.

convinced my father to go back to Jersey again. I put the pigeons in shoeboxes and gave them to my friends. Then I showed them how to attach little notes to their legs and then returned home to wait for the airmail to arrive.

The dove is often used as a symbol to designate the presence of the Holy Spirit. While I was playing around with live pigeons, the Catholic Charismatic Movement was being born.[237] The spiritual revival began in 1967 when some inspired students[238] at DuQuesne University in Pittsburgh prayed for the Holy Spirit to renew the Church in our time. God answered their request and prayer groups began springing up all across the country. Although it was still a long way off, one of those prayer communities would eventually grow into a spiritual home for me.

On April 1, 1967, I officially became a teenager. The move last summer had only served to amplify any normal rebellious attitudes. Being born on the first of April, I saw it as my mischievous duty to be the prankster for April Fools Day. I brought a reel of very thin copper wire to school with me and wired up the entire classroom. I was smart enough not to pull anything on Sister Mary Magdeline, but drove our principal Mother Mary Olivia absolutely bonkers. Mother Superior came over to our seventh grade classroom to teach English. I happily evaded detection for a while, but eventually got caught. Instead of standing down, I became stubbornly defiant and that smoldering angry attitude followed me for the rest of the year. Although my academics qualified me for promotion, the hardness of my heart and my constant resistance to norms of behavior prompted both Sister Mary Magdeline and my parents, to label me incorrigible. My belligerent attitude forced my parents to

---

[237] *Catholic Charismatic Renewal* – was a movement of faithful Catholics, worshiping through vibrant prayer meetings & centered on the gifts of the Holy Spirit.
[238] *Inspired students* – these college students were inspired by Pope John XXIII's prayer at the Vatican II Council, "O Holy Spirit... pour forth the fullness of your gifts... Renew your wonders in this day, as by a new Pentecost."

start looking for a more disciplined school environment for me.

As soon as school let out for summer, Chris and Tom came up to the farm to visit. We rode my horse, swam in the creek and shot bats with shotguns. Even though they both loved riding Blaze, only one of them could ride at a time, so they took turns riding and helping me with my chores. The novelty wore off quickly and my friends ended up pulling guard duty at the pool. Soon even that became a bore, so we headed down to the rope swing next to the swimming hole. On the way down to the creek, Chris stumbled upon a most curious site. Mr. and Mrs. Fischer, who must have been in their eighties, were skinny dipping near our rope swing. Not only did we find it extremely odd that anyone would be swimming naked, but these people were older than our grandparents and we were absolutely scandalized. In our nervousness, we hid behind some trees, making catcalls before returning to the house to watch some afternoon TV.

Our favorite new cartoon hero was Speed Racer.[239] Since the road in front of our house was fairly steep and we were inspired by our new hero, the need for speed was satisfied by building a couple of scooters out of wood scraps and a couple of old metal roller skates. The trouble was that it didn't work very well on gravel. The following day my father brought home a sheet of plywood, some half-inch bar stock and four brand new wheels. We built a go-cart out of the materials and although we were covered from head to toe with red dust from the road, we relished the thrill of victory in every run. Using a close line rope for a steering mechanism, the skills we acquired at the end of that rope laid

---

[239] *Speed Racer* – was an English adaptation of the Japanese cartoon Manga & Anime, Mach Go Go Go, which centered on automobile racing. Beyond Speed Racer's appeal as an early animation series it was generally for family entertainment & did not contain the deep intellectual conflicts or controversies of today's cartoons. It can be argued that the plots in Speed Racer were more complicated than conventional American cartoons of the 1960s, but the overall purpose was to please a growing fan base worldwide with exciting stories that involved facing adversity on the race track & beyond.

the groundwork for motorized go-carts later on. Even though there were accidents and we occasionally experienced the agony of defeat, we had a lot of fun racing that cart, but our fun would be short-lived. The real agony came when my Chris and Tom left early, to attend summer camp with the Boy Scouts, at the Pine Hill Scout Reservation.[240] Once again I found myself all alone. Although the Summer was not yet over, my vacation had come to an end. Life would become much more serious.

---

[240] *Pine Hill Scout Reservation* – is located in Pine Hill, New Jersey. For decades it has been the preferred location for Boy Scouts from Merchantville, NJ to attend summer camp.

Chapter 10

Summer Camp

Summer vacation goes by fast when you are a kid, but this year it seemed to be over before it started. Mom and dad had done everything in their power to try and help me adjust to the move and make new friends, but I was constantly thwarting their efforts with my defiant resistance. It was time for dad to take the bull by the horns and knock some sense into me. My father had never served in the military, but even as a kid he secretly wanted to go away to military school. He convinced my mother that the relentless discipline of the corps, would force me to conform to societal norms and build up in me, the character I so desperately needed.

Mom and dad decided to enroll me in a boarding school, just outside of Trenton, NJ called Bordentown Military Institute. In order to ease the transition into military life, they signed me up for a summer camp at Valley Forge Military Academy. The reality of what was about to happen to me first hit home when I was presented with a brochure for the camp. On the front cover were the words, "From the embattled fields of Valley Forge, went men who built America. From the training fields of Valley Forge, go men who will preserve America."

I had been offered all sorts of help in order to adjust to living in Pennsylvania and to make new friends. I had also received all sorts of warnings about adjusting my piss poor attitude. Parents, friends and teachers alike had all advised me of the consequences of my actions and now it was time to pay the piper. This was actually happening. I would be living away from home for the first time in my life. Complete strangers would be teaching me an entirely new way of being. This time I could not get out of being punished for my obstinacy.

Life... as I had known it, was about to change... again!

Mom and dad drove me to camp and signed me in at the front desk. There I received an orientation folder, was shown to the barracks and told to report on the front steps of the dormitory within the hour. After the cadets were assembled, we were formed into a platoon, given a schedule and sent back to our rooms to unpack and dress for dinner.

We all marched over to the mess hall in crooked lines, but that sloppiness would not be the case for long. We marched everywhere! The platoon leader was constantly calling a cadence of singsong rhymes, which fit the meter of our marching and always ended on the down stroke of the foot that was supposed to be hitting the ground at the time.

Your mother was there when you left
Your right
Your father was there when you left
Your right
Sound off, one, two
Sound it again, three, four
Turn it around and rack it on down
Four, three, two, one
One, two...THREE FOUR!

We marched straight into the mess hall and were led to predetermined seating. There we stood behind our chairs and waited stoically at attention. After grace was said and the order given, we all sat down in unison. Cadets were then instructed to take our napkins and place them just so in our laps, tucking the corner in just behind our brass buckles. Each tidbit of etiquette was clearly instructed and accomplished simultaneously. Any infractions were quickly corrected. Meanwhile, back at the dorm, we were given specific instructions on how to arrange our clothing on olive green shelves. The rooms were inspected each morning and all of our neatly folded laundry could be observed at a glance. If so much as a single pair of sox were not matched, folded and stacked in a neat pile we received demerits. Too many bad marks and we had to march additional hours in what were called penalty tours.[241] Each day we received assignments to read books, pamphlets or mimeographed handouts. After reading the material, we were then tested on that information or had to use the knowledge to perform specific maneuvers. They ranged from simple techniques of marching or swimming to more precision training for our participation in complex strategic war games. In addition to learning how to swim or clean weapons, we also learned military history and were drilled on military etiquette and protocol.

General Von Steuben[242] was the hero of our academy and the namesake of our dorm. The General's drill manual was used to train us up in the arts of war. We were being formed by the same training program he used to defeat the British during the Revolutionary War and the General's Blue Book is still used today by the U.S. Army. Everywhere we went, we marched and we marched in step. We learned to follow orders without question, which meant that we were to do what we were told, when we were told, for as long as we were told to do it. Each cadet became thoroughly familiar with all the commands: right face, left face, forward march, about face, column right, column left, halt and a plethora of other precision directives and combinations. I think the General would have been proud to watch us instantly respond to the precision commands.

---

[241] *Penalty Tours* – consisted of 1 hour of marching, as a penalty for not complying with a rule. The forced marching took place during free time & the severity of the infractions dictated the number of hours required for the disciplinary action. For instance, if one was marching out of step, one might receive a single hour tour, but for insubordination one might receive 5 hours. All infractions were posted on a bulletin board that had to be checked each morning & appeals could be made to the camp commandant.

[242] *General Von Steuben* – Friedrich Wilhelm Ludolf Gerhard Augustin Von Steuben served in the Prussian army as an inspector general & later as a Major general in the Continental Army. While stationed in Valley Forge under General George Washington, he penned a drill manual & used it to whip a gaggle of farmers into effective citizen soldiers, who defeated the most powerful force on the planet. Later editions of this manual evolved into the *U.S. Army Blue Book*, which is still used to train soldiers today.

There was plenty to be proud of, but I was terribly home sick and could frequently be found crying on my bunk. Mail Call was the highlight of my day and I spent most of my free time reading letters from home and writing responses back. One day I caught my roommate reading one of my letters and something in me snapped. I grabbed a wire hanger, raised it above my head and yelled, "I told you to leave my stuff alone" and I began whipping him with the hanger and chasing him down the hallway. His back was covered with welts and we were both called into the Commandant's office. When I was threatened with expulsion I responded by saying, "Good! I didn't want to be here anyway." However, upon learning that my roommate had provoked the incident, the officer believed I had received sufficient punishment and the matter was dropped. We were each given stern warnings and our room assignments were changed. I generally saw myself as a shy and likable fellow, but similar to that boulder incident with Richard Rubin back in Pennsauken, the run-in with my roommate demonstrated that I had a trip-hammer response towards people who crossed the line.

I had dodged the bullet this time, but soon I would be on the receiving end of someone else's anger. Whenever we went swimming, we kept our clothes in locked wire baskets. I was goofing around in the locker room and kicked a basket across the tiled floor, hitting some big guy in his toe with the high-speed projectile. Although I immediately apologized, he would hear none of it. Running across the room, he jacked me up against the locker and punched me in the face. One of the other boys grabbed a bleached white towel and placed it over the cut above my profusely bleeding eye. The drenching promptly turned the towel bright red and I was rushed to the infirmary. Although butterfly stitches were quickly applied, I still have a scar above my left eyebrow.

Every Saturday evening in the mess hall, we had something we called mystery meat. Actually it was only meatloaf, but invariably someone found something vile in the meat, like a band-aide or a toenail. We were all grossed out by the weekly scuttlebutt, but we also looked forward to teasing the unfortunate cadet who happened to win the crackerjack prize.

On Sundays mom and dad came by to visit. They took me into town to attend Mass at Saint Katharine of Siena[243] parish in Wayne, PA. After Mass we had breakfast, at Minella's Diner.[244] These visits were bitter sweet. While they provided me an opportunity to reconnect with my family, the very presence of my parents made me all the more homesick. One upside to these visits was Parent's Day. My mother and father were given the opportunity to watch me compete with the other cadets and I could show off the skills I had been learning. I raced around a track in a go-cart, won an Equitation[245] ribbon on a beautiful black stallion named Eldorado and earned my Pro-Marksmanship Certificate at the rifle range.

Summer Camp cadets were called Rangers. Each week we went out on bivouac and were divided into red and blue teams. Our group goal was to capture the enemy flag, but it was much more complicated than a simple pick-up game. We used maps and a compass to plan out sophisticated military strategies. It wasn't long before we learned that almost anything can happen in war. In addition to military history and tactics, Rangers were also required to learn American history and Indian lore. When not in our summer dress uniforms, we donned an eagle-feathered headdress. I

---

[243] *St. Catherine of Siena* – was a tertiary Dominican, a scholastic philosopher & theologian. She worked to restore the Papacy in Rome, after its displacement in France & established peace among the Italian city-states. She was proclaimed a Doctor of the Church in 1970. She lived from 1347–1380 & a parish which bears her name is located on Lancaster Avenue in Wayne, PA.

[244] *Minella's Diner* – is a 24/7 Greek diner, serving breakfast, lunch & dinner. They continue to serve the patrons of the Main Line on Lancaster Avenue in Wayne, PA.

[245] *Equitation* – refers to a rider's position while mounted & encompasses his ability to ride correctly with effective signals. The rider, rather than the horse, is evaluated. Judging criteria covers the rider's performance & control of the horse, use of cues, proper attire, correct form including: rider poise & the cleanliness & polish of horse, rider & equipment.

worked hard on every lesson and competed vigorously with the other cadets. In general I enjoyed my summer at camp. The training I received at Valley Forge Military Academy brought out the best in me and I look back on the experience as a very positive influence in my life.

Meanwhile back on the farm things were changing. Sean took care of Blaze in my absence and Sarah acquired a horse of her own, which she named Flossy. Murray was continuing to grow his egg business and Brennan cherished his new little dog, surprising almost everyone by taking very good care of Spud. Concerned about the complex world his children would have to compete in, dad brought home an entire set of educational filmstrips for the kids. Art and Shane learned lots of little facts by watching the slides and were inspired to perform scientific experiments. The two young scientists were pretty excited and they pestered the other family members with a constant barrage of stories about their latest experiments and discoveries. Irritated and annoyed, Sarah, Sean and Murray began referring to their complex conclusions as Scientific Duh. Blissfully unaware of these changing dynamics was my youngest brother Neil. This happy little kid in diapers spent each day jumping up and down in his playpen and thoroughly enjoying his life.

When camp was finally over, Chris and Tom came up for another visit, but this time they could only stay for a week. We spent our time reminiscing about our respective camps. I told them war stories about life as a Ranger at Valley Forge and they related many funny tales from their scouting experiences at Pine Hill, but the most exciting event of our summer vacation involved an air ship. Older cadets at Valley Forge had built a hot air balloon out of a cleaner bag, some straws and a bunch of birthday candles. So we constructed one of our own. According to plan, the airship ascended a few hundred feet into the air, but then the candles burned out. The hot air in the bag began to cool and our adrenalin started pumping. We helplessly watched the airship come fluttering back down to earth engulfed in bright orange flames. We were all grateful that our worst fears were never realized and no hayfields were ever set on fire.

I had been pushed hard to work, grow and develop self-discipline, but I was also well protected by loving parents and a time-tested curriculum at a traditional academy. I matured a lot that summer and thrived in the structured military environment. However, the societal walls of safety my parents had come to rely on and I had taken for granted; were about to come crashing down on me.

Chapter 11

Boarding School

On Wednesday, September 13, 1967, I entered the eighth grade at Bordentown Military Institute in Bordentown, NJ. My summer vacation had been cut short and I was not at all thrilled about getting back to school. However, I knew dad had paid over three thousand dollars to send me there and I felt duty bound to make his investment pay off. Ernest Rollo III was assigned to be my roommate. He seemed like a nice enough fellow, but he was a bit stuffy and like a lot of other cadets he came from a family with incredible wealth.

Although the dorm accommodations were a bit Spartan, after my stint at Valley Forge Military Academy, the soldier like routine was quite familiar to me. Knowing I would be homesick, dad made it a point to visit me every couple of weeks and would often take me home for the weekend. On one visit he surprised me by bringing along my friend Chris Lang. Dad and I proudly showed him around the campus and I introduced him to my roommate. Feelings of loneliness were minimized with so many tasks to perform and books to read. Daily room inspections required the waxing the wooden floors, cleaning of windows and making up our beds so tightly that one could bounce a quarter off the blanket.

At dawn we were jolted to life by the bellowing of a bugle, but unlike the reveille of Valley Forge, the disheartening din emanated from a record played over some loud speakers. We quickly dressed and within minutes were assembled on the parade ground. Once attendance was taken, all of the cadets marched to the mess hall, where we followed the exact same procedures for meals that I had learned in summer camp. We filed in quietly and stood behind our chairs until grace was said and then strictly followed every single rule of proper etiquette.

With only sixteen pupils per class there was plenty of individualized attention. I had easy access to having my questions answered, but the smaller class size also meant there was no place to hide. The result was that I was called upon more frequently and had to study harder in order to be prepared for the next day in class. On the plus side, the school also opened up a large lecture hall and forced us to spend a full four hours on our homework every night. Large mahogany tables provided plenty of room for us to spread out our work. The mandatory study time insured that all of our homework assignments would be completed thoroughly and on time.

The slightest infraction of the rules resulted in a penalty tour.[246] Marching was conducted during our free time, so there was a powerful incentive to follow the rules. Even so, by the end of the school year I had worn out three pair of patent leather shoes. My free time was generally spent down at the "Y" hut, which was a log cabin hang out in the woods at the bottom of a steep hill. One could buy snacks, play pinball and watch the older cadets occasionally lock horns. It was a great place to hang out and just have fun.

Bordentown Military Institute had a trick drill team they called the Landon Rifles. Although it was only for upper classmen, they also had a Junior Rifle team for younger cadets. I joined the precision team and worked hard to perfect the coordinated movements of the drills. I especially liked performing for my parents, when they came to visit on the weekends. Unfortunately there was a klutz in our outfit.

---

[246] *Penalty Tours* – consisted of 1 hour of marching, as a punishment for not complying with a rule. The forced marching took place during free time & the severity of the infractions dictated the number of hours required for the disciplinary action. For instance, if one was marching out of step, one might receive a single hour tour, but for insubordination one might receive 5 hours. All infractions were posted on a bulletin board that had to be checked each morning & appeals could be made to the camp commandant.

One night the uncoordinated kid sliced my back open while practicing a maneuver called a blackout. When my shirt ripped I flipped out and screamed, "That's it! This guy is dangerous! I want him off the team!" To my utter surprise he was immediately kicked off the squad. Wow! Righteous anger seemed to be a powerful tool that got things done.

Not every difficulty I encountered would be so easily handled. Much of our time was centered on dorm life, but there was a serous problem in my particular building. The house parents were pot smoking, LSD tripping, swingers who generally had no idea what we were doing and didn't seem to care either. For starters, upper classmen regularly bought booze and drugs from them. The two adults often got high with the students and the Resident Assistant's wife was prostituted out to the older boys. It did not take long for their perverted lifestyle to spill over into my own life.

One Friday afternoon I went to flush the toilet in the bathroom and the handle would not go down. I removed the lid from the reservoir to see what was wrong. There in the frigid water were four brown quart bottles of Colt 45.[247] Checking the other stalls I discovered additional bottles. Although I was curious, I said nothing about it and returned to my room to write a letter. As was their custom, the uniformed cadets trickled in from school and changed into more comfortable clothing for the weekend. Within the hour our recreation room at the end of the hall was filled with raucous laughter. I ventured out to see what was going on and found a smoky room filled with cadets who were drinking beer, smoking cigars and telling vile jokes. Never before in my life had I seen or heard anything so profane. I wanted to object, but was afraid of being ridiculed.

---

[247] *Colt 45* – was a relatively strong (6.2% by volume) beer introduced in 1963 by the National Brewing Company. The label was designed with a kicking horse & horseshoe, a subtle reference to its "extra kick" compared to other brands. Though many believed the beer was named after the Colt 45 revolver, it was actually a reference to running back #45 Jerry Hill of the 1963 Baltimore Colts & not the gun.

Returning to my room I continued writing a letter to my folks back home. It was hard concentrating with all that noise coming down the narrow hallway, but I soon became engrossed in my writing and tuned it all out.

Later on that evening, an upperclassman quietly knocked on my door. I responded by saying, "It's unlocked." Looking up from my paper was Herman Wickerman, the sergeant who inspected my room each morning. Clad only in his underwear, he poked his head through the door and motioned for me to follow him. "Come here; I have something to show you." Putting down my pen, I complied with the directive. He led me into his bedroom, which was barely lit from the light in the hallway. Pointing to a spot next to him on the bed he said, "Have a seat."

Now for the record, guys walked around in their skivvies all the time and it wasn't all that unusual for cadets to go into each other's rooms either. Every one of us used our beds for chairs, but the darkness bothered me. So I asked him if he wanted me to turn on the light. Sergeant Wickerman responded by saying, "No. I don't want anyone to know I'm talking to you." Although that too seemed a bit odd, I sat down on the bed anyway. "Give me your hand," he commanded. When I apprehensively stretched out my hand, he quickly pulled it down towards his crotch and wrapped my fingers around his dick. Reflexively I pulled back, but he held my hand tightly and I froze. "I don't want to" I pleaded, but he glared at me and said, "If you yell I'll tell all the guys you're a queer." I had no idea what the word meant, but I knew that if the other guys started ridiculing me about something creepy, the harassment would never end. I was horrified by my situation. The threat was absolutely real, but my predicament was even worse. Jumping up from the bed, I ran back into my room and shut the door. As it turned out, he never said a word to anyone, but from that moment on, my door remained locked. The experience left me filled with shame. It amplified my feelings of abandonment and left me even more reticent about building close personal relationships with other guys. I felt extremely vulnerable and the lack of supervision by our house parents provided none of the guardianship that was intended by their position and rightfully expected by my parents.

A similar scandal was also afflicting altar boys. Less than a year after I escaped the predatory intentions of the queer kid at Bordentown, an obscure perverted priest left his native Belgium to become a papal diplomat. By 1973 Archbishop Jean Jadot[248] had become the papal nuncio to the Diocese of the United States. On his recommendation Pope Paul VI began elevating liberal priests to the office of bishop. They were known more for their advocacy of gay rights, the protection of pederasts and a commitment to modernism, than they were for promoting and defending Catholic doctrine. Once elected their dissent was not limited to heretical homilies. As soon as they gained control over the seminaries the belligerent bishops opened up the priesthood to homosexuals and purged the applications of men with true vocations.[249] Promoting their "new religion" they conducted reeducation retreats for priests and nuns. The result was that the religious sisters left the convents, churches emptied out and innocent boys became the victims of predatory priests.

Very early on, my father had taught me about the beauty and sacredness of sexuality. His teachings protected me from becoming the next victim of rape at my boarding school, but that little pervert had still destroyed my innocence. Shocked and embarrassed, I started second guessing my response. I was afraid to speak with anyone about what had transpired, including my own parents. Another twenty years would pass before I said anything about it to anyone. Although I was

---

[248] *Jean Jadot* – referenced from *The Rite of Sodomy*, by Randy Engle, published by New Engle Publishing, P.O. Box 356, Export, PA ©2006, pg. 895.

[249] *Vocational Inquisition* – from the book Goodbye, Good Men: How liberals brought corruption into the Catholic Church, by Michael S. Rose, Regnery Publishing, Inc, An Eagle Publishing Company, 1 Massachusetts Avenue, Washington DC 2002. Pg. 145.

unable to tell mom what had happened, just being with her was a comforting salve for the emotional pain I was feeling.

Mom had recently purchased a new book called Chariots of the Gods.[250] We took turns reading the sensational pop treatise, while traveling on the train from North Wales to Philadelphia. I was on a weekend leave and mom needed to purchase some Christmas gifts at Gimbles.[251] I needed a new pair of patent leather shoes, so we went shopping together. Her new book raised several questions concerning what the bible had to say about sightings of aliens from outer space and many other unexplained items. The topic was admittedly far fetched, but it was interesting reading. Together we shared a universe of speculation, which was far removed from the harsh realities of life. But while mom and I were enjoying our escape together; Art and Shane were about to walk into a trap. It was Fire Prevention Week at school. The children received fire safety instruction and were given little red plastic fireman hats. Of course all of this training only served to ignite their curiosity.

As soon as Art arrived home, he swiped a box of matches from the kitchen. He and Shane proudly wore their hats while they rode their tricycles down the dusty road in front of our home. Dropping their bikes in the weeds by the side of the road, they ran into the barn and closed a Dutch door behind them. Art pulled out a single wooden match to show Shane the proper way to strike it. Soon sulfur filled their nostrils, as the fiery tip hissed and flared. Art shoved the kitchen match in Shane's face so he could get a closer look, but he reflexively slapped it out of Art's hand. The match flew through the air and ignited a small pile of loose hay.

---

[250] *Chariots of the Gods?* – which is subtitled *Unsolved Mysteries of the Past* is a book written in 1968 by Erich von Däniken. It involves the hypothesis that the technologies & religions of many ancient civilizations were given to them by space travelers who were welcomed as gods. These ideas have been largely rejected by historians & scientists.
[251] *Gimbel Brothers* – was an iconic American department store from 1887-1987. The store is famous for the *Gimbels Thanksgiving Day Parade*, the oldest parade in the country. In its day it was the largest department store chain in the country with 36 stores in the U.S.

Running over to put out the fire, Art kicked it away with his boot, but it lit even more hay. Like a flaming version of The Sorcerer's Apprentice,[252] the more the two boys tried to subdue the fire the bigger the inferno grew. Panicked, Art grabbed Shane by the back of his shirt and shouted, "We gotta get out of here!" They ran away and hid in the garage, while the barn went up in flames. When Lisa saw the fire out the window, she immediately called the fire company. The rest of the kids ran down the hill to rescue the animals. By the time the fire trucks arrived, there was not much they could do except to keep the fire from spreading into the woods. My father arrived home from the Agway to find his barn burning, some firemen mopping up and Lisa sitting on a rock wall with Sarah and the baby helplessly watching the smoldering spectacle. Beside their older sister sat five young boys, all wearing their little red plastic fireman hats.

Meanwhile back in Philadelphia, mom and I finished up our shopping and had lunch at Horn & Hardart.[253] On the trainride back, we boarded at Reading Terminal and took turns reading her facinating book again. When we finally arrived at the North Wales train station, we debarked and loaded all the packages into our Ford Fairlane Station Wagon.[254]

On our drive home we questioned the credibility of what was written in Chariots of the Gods. Even though we had our doubts we were still filled with images of strange visitors from far away planets. We began to speculate about the possibility of invaders from outer space, as we drove down

---

[252] *The Sorcerer's Apprentice* – is one of the best-known Mickey Mouse shorts. It was adapted from Goethe's poem "Der Zauberlehrling" & is a story of a wizard's ambitious, but lazy, assistant who attempts to perform his master's magical feats, before knowing how to properly control them.
[253] *Horn & Hardart* – was a food services company noted for operating the first automats in Philadelphia & New York City.
[254] *Ford Fairlane* – was an automobile model sold between 1955-1971 by the Ford Motor Company. The name was taken from Henry Ford's estate, Fair Lane, near Dearborn, MI. The station wagon was a passenger car body style that incorporated a full-size back cargo compartment, often including a 3rd passenger row accessible by a back door.

the dark country roads. The overcast night made it pitch black, as we made our final turn down the dry and dusty gravel of Ruth Road. Suddenly our headlights illuminated something off to the side of the road. "What's that?" I asked, half afraid of the answer. Mom slammed on her brakes and the tires ground to a halt. She apprehensively whispered, "I don't know." The indistinct almost humanoid looking figure started moving toward us amidst the dust cloud that migrated forward in the headlights of our car. We were both petrified! We each held our breath and pressed our bodies into the backs of the seats. A deafening silence enveloped us, as the ominous figure approached. It was Dad! "Oh Tom, its just you" she said as we both breathed a sigh of relief, "we thought you were an alien." Having no clue what we were talking about, a look of pained confusion poured over his face. Then mom said, "What are you doing out here?" Ironically, dad explained that he wanted to catch us before we got home, so we wouldn't be frightened when we saw the fire.

First it was the house in Jersey. Now he lost a barn in Pennsylvania. Lightening had indeed struck twice and dad was worried about the cost. As it turned out, the fire was actually a win-win for almost everyone involved except my father. Mr. Fischer was happy to collect on the insurance. Township officials were happy, because they had wanted to straighten out the road, which curved around the barn. Finally the kids were safe and they had learned a valuable lesson. Although there were no serious consequences to the fire it still dramatically changed things at home. The loss of the barn meant that there was nowhere to put the animals. Since I was away at school anyway, dad saw no point in keeping horses around. Sarah and Murray did get to keep the goats and the chickens for a while, but eventually they too went as well. My father's dream for the farm had gone up in smoke, along with the barn.

Now that our family lived in Pennsylvania, the cabin at Sleepy Hollow was a long way from home. Therefore dad began looking for a cabin much closer to where we lived. In order to find a new place we started roaming around the Pocono Mountains, instead of going home during my weekend leaves. Lincoln Log style kit cabins were all the rage and we looked at several of the model homes. Although we never found a cabin, we saw lots of deer and stayed in several rustic motels. I treasured those trips especially because I could spend time hanging out with my father.

Over the Christmas holiday, Sean and I went on our first bear-hunting trip with dad to a place called White Deer Lake near Schiola, PA. Sean was a welcome addition to our party, thanks to a novel he read, which was called My Side of the Mountain.[255] The storyline of the paperback followed a kid who ran away from home to the wilderness and survived in a hollowed out tree. Sean picked up a lot of woodsman skills from the book and developed a particular interest in edible plants. He could identify almost all the trees and his fascination with nature added to the excitement of our trip. We both enjoyed hunting and camping with our father and the aroma of Canadian bacon still evokes pleasant memories.

On the way back to school, dad stopped for gas at the Heston S. Swartley gas station on Sumneytown Pike in Harleysville, PA. His friend Bernie Downey cheerfully greeted us with his booming voice as he started to pump our gas. Replacing the cap he said, "Come over here Patrick. I have something I want to show you." I jumped out of the pickup and followed him. Besides being an itinerant preacher, Bernie was also an accomplished trapper. He led me around behind the station to a cage he had made out of chicken wire. Inside was a red

---

[255] *My Side of the Mountain* – is a 1959 fictional book by Jean Craighead George, about a boy who learns about nature & himself. The book won the Newbery Honor Award & was loosely adapted into a movie in 1969. Set in the Catskill Mountains near Delhi, NY, the story is an account of how Sam Gribley survives in the wilderness of upstate New York. George's descriptions of the flora, fauna & how he uses them, not only to survive, but to live quite comfortably.

fox he had named Herod.[256] Bernie explained how the fox is the smartest, most cautious and most cunning of all the furbearing creatures in Pennsylvania. The bottom of the cage had a sheet metal pan that collected urine and he used it to lure other foxes into his traps. His wife Abigail came out the cellar door of his home and he raved about her collection of African Violets. Taking me down into the basement she showed me dozens of beautiful flowers growing on long wooden tables under purple florescent lights. The man in the coonskin cap joyfully introduced me to his five children and then led me back outside. There he showed me how he prepared his traps. His rustic little factory included a fire pit and a huge iron pot suspended from a wooden tripod. There were wooden barrels for soaking, special rubberized clothing and hooks to hang up the traps. Bernie invited me to go muskrat trapping with him, up on Thousand Acre Road in West Rockhill Township. He also invited dad and I on a trip he was planning up north to trap beaver. Dad thought it was a great idea, but hurried us along so we could get home in time for dinner.

The following week dad stopped in to fill up his VW Bus. Bernie told him about a man who had come in earlier that morning and said that his car died. The man was terribly upset and wondered how he was going to get to work. Bernie prayed for the man and told dad he was confident that his Father in heaven would provide for the guy's needs. Dad also prayed for the man and stopped back a week later, to see how the man made out. Bernie beamed from ear to ear telling dad, "My Father in heaven provided him with a car!" Puzzled by the statement dad asked, "What do you mean he provided him with a car?" Bernie smiled and said, "I mean the man now has a car." Still a bit confused, dad pushed for a more detailed explanation, "I heard you say God gave the

---

[256] *Luke 13:32* – At that time some Pharisees came to him and said, "Go away, leave this area because Herod wants to kill you." He replied, "Go and tell that fox, 'Behold, I cast out demons and I perform healings today and tomorrow, and on the third day I accomplish my purpose.'"

man a car; but how?" With a gentle smile Bernie said, "The Father put it on my heart to give him mine." Dad's eyes bugged out with a glaring combination of surprise and anger. At this point he was sure he was dealing with a crazy man. "Are you nuts? You have your own family to take care of. How are you going to get groceries home from the store?" Bernie looked gently into dad's fiery eyes and compassion poured across his face. "Tom, I told you my Father would provide for my friend. He will provide for me too." Dad shook his head in disbelief and drove away, but the man's faith impressed him and he wished he had a tenth of this man's trust in God.

The next time I came home from Bordentown, Bernie Downey dropped by and pulled a fifty-five gallon drum out of his recently acquired vehicle. This time the Father had provided for Bernie by putting it on father's heart to give his new friend our Volkswagen Bus. The tall trapper with the coonskin cap, filled up the barrel with water, horse corn, honey still on the comb and small bricks of paraffin. I helped him to put the barrel up on a couple of cinder blocks and we built a wood fire beneath it. For the next three hours the mixture boiled away, as he directed my brothers to gather up the blackened walnuts in the side yard and throw them into the sweet smelling brew. We hammered a line of nails onto the side of the garage and used rubber gloves to dip a dozen shiny new steel traps, into the boiling potpourri and then hung them up to dry. The next day he returned before daybreak to show me how to set the blackened traps. We laid them out all up and down the banks of the Perkiomen creek and checked them the following morning. We snagged two muskrats in the conibear traps and a raccoon and a possum in the leg hold traps. Before removing them from the traps, he showed me how to dispatch the animals with a nightstick. Subsequent trapping expeditions with Sean and dad only yielded possums, prompting Mr. Downey to howl with laughter and call dad The Great American Possum Hunter of Montgomery County. And so it went, day after day, baiting traps and selling the furs to a dealer, who stopped in twice a week at the Vernfield General Store.

On New Year's Day we took a trip up to Bushkill Falls to set some beaver traps. It was freezing cold and we slept in the back of dad's pickup truck, which had a cap on it. Sean and I had our own sleeping bags, but for extra warmth, we covered them with a big old army surplus down bag. Bernie brought along a real buffalo hide, which was so large it covered him and my father. The next day we woke to the bugling voice of Mr. Downey, echoing off the mountain.

Rise and shine and give God your glory, glory...
Rise and shine and give God your glory, glory...
Rise and shine and give God your glory, glory,
Children of the Lord!

Dad gave Bernie a cup of hot chocolate and said, "Boy were you right! That buffalo skin sure was warm!" Mr. Downey quickly thundered back, "What buffalo skin?" Seems that while dad was toasty warm, he had pulled the buffalo skin on top of himself, leaving Bernie half frozen.

Dad and Bernie had a special relationship that would continue for years. He tried to take me under his wing from time to time. However, as nice as he was, I always kept him at arm's length. In addition to pumping gas, trapping and raising his family Bernie belonged to The Church of the Brethren and eventually became its pastor. I guess you could call him a born again Christian, but his beliefs would more accurately be described as Dispensationalist.[257] Despite his

---

[257] *Dispensationalism* – is a Protestant evangelical theology, based on a series of chronologically successive "dispensations" whereby God relates to human beings in different ways under different Biblical covenants. First developed by John Nelson Darby & the Brethren Movement, it consists of a distinctive eschatological "end times" perspective. They believe that the nation of Israel is distinct from the Church & that God will fulfill His promises to Israel including the land promises, resulting in a millennial kingdom where Christ, upon His return, will rule the world from Jerusalem for 1,000 years. The theology of The Rapture. is less than 200 years old. Catholics believe that Jesus already established his earthly rule when He said, "Thou art Peter, and upon this rock I will build my Church and

incredible faith and trust in the Father's Providence, which was absolutely admirable, he had rejected the Catholicism of his youth. And he made it his life's work, to rescue those he saw as the poor souls being seduced by the Whore of Babylon.[258]

Bernie was a great storyteller and he used real-life parables to set his sheep stealing snares. The same cunning and skill used to capture the beaver and the fox were used to capture souls. For him, every encounter was an opportunity to spread the Good News and rescue the lost sheep. Inevitably, somewhere during the conversation, he would pull out a miniature green copy of The New Testament and Psalms, relate the Scriptures to his story and call for an on-the-spot conversion. Now was always the acceptable time to reject religion and submit to the Father. Total trust in Divine Providence was his constant witness and his arguments were so compelling that Sean wanted Mr. Downey to be his Confirmation sponsor. Mom gently explained to him that he could not be his sponsor, because he was not a Catholic, but that only served to puzzle Sean and he asked, "Do Christians love God more than Catholics?" Bernie's faith was irresistible. Several times, he had me close to rejecting the one true faith, in favor of what seemed to be a more faithful following of Jesus Christ, but deep in my heart I sensed something was off.

While it's true that my own selfishness often kept me from turning my life over to Christ, there was more to it than that.

---

the gates of the netherworld shall not prevail against it."(Matthew 16:18) Catholics further believe that the second coming will involve the final judgment, not a second chance. The false comfort of "The Rapture" is therefore a diabolical deception.

[258] *The Whore of Babylon* – is a Christian allegorical figure of evil mentioned in the bible. Protestant fundamentalists, who misunderstand the scriptures, use it as a slur to refer to the Catholic Church. *Apocalypse 17:3-5* "And he took me away in spirit into the desert I saw a woman sitting upon a scarlet coloured beast, full of names of blasphemy, having seven heads and ten horns. And the woman was clothed round about with purple and scarlet, and gilt with gold, and precious stones and pearls, having a golden cup in her hand, full of the abomination and filthiness of her fornication. And on her forehead a name was written: A mystery; Babylon the great, the mother of the fornications, and the abominations of the earth."

The truth is I already had a personal relationship with Jesus. Early on I had the simple faith of a child. In school I gained a deeper understanding of just who God is and strengthened that relationship with the sacraments of Confession, Eucharist and Confirmation. It was not just ritual to me, I knew the voice of my Savior and what I was hearing from Bernie was not the same voice![259] Unfortunately, I was not a very obedient subject. Along with an increase in age came greater temptations and one of those snares would be alcohol.

Our nanny Lisa maintained a letter writing relationship with her sailor friend Simon Moore. After he left the Navy he returned to his home in Tennessee. Simon made several trips up to our farm in Pennsylvania to visit her and it was not long before he bought her an engagement ring and asked for her hand in marriage. Father O'Malley agreed to marry the young couple and mom and dad threw a party for them at our farmhouse, the night before the wedding. Although we were all sad to loose our nanny, we were also very happy for her. It was time...

In preparation for the party, dad purchased a portable bar and we all had fun taking turns spinning on the bar stools. There were plenty of chips, dip and hot cider for the kids. Dad showed me how to make highballs and then made me the official bartender, which freed him up to circulate among the guests. The more people drank the more they seemed to be having fun, which made me curious. When the room was buzzing with conversation; I poured a drink of my own and was sneaking my third alcoholic beverage when dad caught me and sent me to my room. Upstairs I lay down to go to sleep and the room started spinning. Like the merry-go-round back in Wellwood Park, it started slowly and gradually picked up speed. I was dizzy and felt sick to my stomach, so I sat up and the spinning stopped. I thought I

---

[259] *John 10:14* – "I am the good shepherd, and I know mine and mine know me,"

was ok until I lay back down and the room started spinning again. Scared and out of control, I sat up a dozen or more times before I finally fell asleep. I swore off alcohol, but like many my vow would have the permanence of a New Year's resolution.

In our house Jesus was always the reason for the Christmas season. We opened little cardboard windows on an Advent Calendar, which hung on our kitchen wall. Walking with Mary and Joseph, we took turns moving two little statues of the saints around the perimeter of our living room. They journeyed toward Bethlehem and the stable that sat on the mantle above our fireplace. Christmas Day was a joyful family affair that culminated with Mass at St. Maria Goretti. After Church dad treated us to a scrambled egg breakfast with bacon and some thick rich store-bought eggnog with nutmeg.

Returning to Bordentown, I stuck to myself and hit the books. I spent so much time shining shoes, cleaning my room and studying to avoid marching penalty tours that I didn't have much time to hang out at the "Y". Providentially, that little pervert Herman Wickerman mysteriously disappeared and no one seemed to know what had happened to him. My suspicion was that he probably tried to assault another cadet and got expelled, but I had no way of knowing what had really happened. God seemed to be taking care of the situation and that enabled me to continue my schooling in relative safety.[260]

Every year Bordentown Military Institute held a formal military ball. Our gymnasium was transformed into a ballroom that looked like a winter wonderland. Cadets had to find their own escorts and I saw in the dance an opportunity to finally take Annabel Logan out on a date. I had not seen

---

[260] *Romans 12:19* – "Revenge not yourselves, my dearly beloved; but give place unto wrath, for it is written: Revenge is mine, I will repay, saith the Lord."

her in years, but I was proud of my school and thought she might be impressed by my uniform. Pushing through paralyzing fear, I dialed the phone. To my absolute delight she readily accepted my invitation but said her dad wanted to meet me first. Now all I had to do was arrange transportation. There was just one small problem; I didn't know how to dance. Sarah came to my rescue and all of a sudden my creepy, competitive, distant sister, became a close personal friend and confidant. Never having been out on a date before, I asked my father how I should go about kissing her at the end of the night. He suggested I ask for her permission. It sounded kind of awkward and risky, but what did I know?

On the night of the formal, I put on my Class A blue uniform. Dad drove me over to meet his friend and my Confirmation Sponsor, Harry Steel. Mr. Steel had a yellow Cadillac and the two chauffeurs reminisced about the good old days back at Camden Catholic, while Annabel and I sat nervously in the back seat. I made vain attempts at inane conversation until we arrived at the school. Once I was on my own turf a sense of confidence returned and I introduced her to the other cadets. At the same time I was showing her off I was also warding off the well-polished comments of the suave upper class wolves. We ate our dinner, carried on conversations with the other couples and I did my best to dance with her. She was much more comfortable fast dancing than I was and it looked as if she had been dancing for years. But thanks to my sister Sarah, I held my own, but was also relieved when the music slowed down.

On the way home I held her hand in silence, waiting for that magic moment. But the moment never came. In a burst of bravado I asked, "Would it be ok if I kissed you?" Her answer was whispered yet firm, "No." That was not exactly the answer I was looking for nor the one I had expected. Confused and embarrassed the two of us sat in the back of the car staring straight ahead, like two subjects in a Norman

Rockwell portrait. I think we were both relieved when I finally walked her to her front door and we stoically shook hands to say good bye.

I wanted to cry. It had not worked out in the fourth grade and nothing had come to fruition as a teenager. She was a cute girl and I had many fine memories of what might have been. But the reality was that it had never been more than a fantasy and now even that had evaporated.

Chapter 12

Anything Goes

On September 25, 1888, after praying the morning Mass, Pope Leo XIII heard something so traumatizing that it made him collapse and those with him thought he was dead. While genuflecting in front of the tabernacle the Pope overheard a conversation between Jesus and the Devil. Satan was bragging that if given 100 years and "a greater influence over those who will give themselves to my service," he could destroy the Catholic Church. Our Lord gave him permission to *try* by saying, "you will be given the time and the power." Shaken to his core by what the Pope overheard, he composed the Prayer to St. Michael.[261] The Pontiff subsequently ordered that his short exorcism be recited worldwide following every Low Mass, as a protection against these pending attacks.

Almost immediately demonic characters like Jack the Ripper,[262] began surfacing globally. Here in America a powerful new novel entitled Looking Backward[263] excited the intelligencia with visions of a godless socialist utopia. For a hundred years the Church was indeed attacked in a variety of ways. In 1968 Humanae Vitae[264] was pronounced

---

[261] *Prayer to St. Michael* – "Saint Michael the Archangel, defend us in battle; be our protection against the wickedness & snares of the devil. May God rebuke him, we humbly pray: & do thou, O Prince of the heavenly host, by the power of God, thrust into hell Satan & all the evil spirits who prowl about the world seeking the ruin of souls. Amen."

[262] *Jack the Ripper* – was the name given to an unidentified serial killer who was active in the largely impoverished areas in and around the White Chapel district of London in 1888.

[263] *Looking Backward: 2000-1887* – is a utopian novel by Edward Bellamy first published in 1888. It was the 3rd largest bestseller of its time, after Uncle Tom's Cabin & Ben-Hur: A Tale of the Christ. It influenced many intellectuals who coalesced in "Bellamy Clubs" to discuss forming a utopian society. The book tells the story of a young American who falls asleep in 1887 & when he wakes up in Boston it is the year 2000 & the U.S. has been transformed into a socialist utopia.

[264] *Humanae Vitae* – meaning "Of Human Life" is a papal encyclical promulgated on July 25, 1968. Subtitled "On the Regulation of Birth". It re-affirmed the traditional teaching of the Catholic Church regarding abortion, contraception & other human life issues.

dead on arrival. The following year the ancient Tridentine Mass was replaced by the spiritually weakened Novus Ordo.[265] Although the big guns were reserved for the Catholic Church, many other strategic targets here in the United States were laid waste. The effects were both devastating and widespread.

The MPAA[266] supplanted the Hays Code[267] and soon after that, the Seal of Good Practice[268] was abandoned on TV. This virtually eliminated all moral censorship of the entertainment industry. The Graduate[269] led a shameless stampeed of movies at theaters and Playboy After Dark[270] aired on television the following year. Plays and musicals pushed the envelope even further with profligate productions like Anything Goes.[271]

Federal dollars poured into childhood education programs, providing the public schools with better lab equipment than their counterparts in the parochial schools. This prompted my father to begin wondering whether the Catholic school system would be able to provide his children with the science and technology background he knew they would

---

[265] *Novus Ordo* – also called the Mass of Pope Paul VI it is the liturgy of the Catholic Mass of the Roman Rite promulgated by Paul VI in 1969 following Vatican II. In practice, the Novus Ordo Mass virtually supplanted the ancient Tridentine Roman Rite of the Mass.

[266] *MPAA* – the Motion Picture Association of America replaced the Hays Code, which was a much stricter movie rating system of censorship guidelines in the United States.

[267] *Hays Code* – was a set of industry censorship guidelines, which governed the production of the vast majority of U.S. motion pictures released by major studios from 1930-1968. It grew out of the Catholic Legion of Decency & was named after William H. Hays.

[268] *Seal of Good Practice* – was a commitment to quality by the National Association of Broadcasters, which also included a list of standards similar to the Hayes Code.

[269] *The Graduate* – was a 1967 film directed by Mike Nichols & based on the 1963 novel by Charles Webb, who wrote it shortly after graduating from Williams College. Calder Willingham & Buck Henry composed the screenplay, while Embassy pictures & UA distributed the movie. The story is about a recent university graduate with no well-defined aim in life, who is seduced by an older woman & then falls in love with her daughter.

[270] *Playboy After Dark* – was a TV show hosted by Hugh Hefner, which ran in syndication from 1969-1970. The format of the show featured Hugh Hefner chatting with celebrities & Playboy Playmates, who would then perform in a laid-back party atmosphere.

[271] *Anything Goes* – was a musical with music & lyrics by Cole Porter. The book was the collaborative effort of Guy Bolton & P.G. Wodehouse. The story concerns madcap antics aboard an ocean liner bound from New York to London. Highly sexualized, the lyrics promoted a world, where all morality is disposed of in favor of one where anything goes.

need to compete in an increasingly high-tech world. So Sarah became the first person in our family to attend a public school. She entered the seventh grade at Indian Valley Junior High School in the Souderton School District.

Sarah's English teacher quickly deduced my sister's people skills and put her in charge of tryouts for the drama club's musical Anything Goes. Sarah picked her recently acquired friend Rebecca Collins, to play the part of Reno Sweeney, a sexy and charismatic forty-year-old nightclub singer in love with the leading man. Every evening for the next several months, Rebecca practiced lines that would make a prostitute blush. The musical trashed almost all of our social mores and the constant repetition burned the promiscuous propaganda into the hearts and minds of the impressionable cast. Although Rebecca entered Indian Valley as an innocent, bubbly, energetic teenybopper; she soon internalized the earthy role of Reno. I first met Rebecca while I was home for Christmas break. Miss Collins carried the conversation well, which made it very easy for me to talk with her and I soon acquiesced to her attention and affection.

I wanted to ask her out on a date, but I had no money. The latest issue of Boy's Life[272] had an ad for Superior Match Company. They were looking for representatives to sell their advertising book matches. Lots of people smoked cigarettes and those who didn't often carried book matches in their pockets. Before the invention of Bic butane lighters, Zippos were common and free books of matches were available on every checkout counter. So becoming a salesman for Superior Match Company seemed like a profitable venture and I sent away for a sales kit.

The only problem I had with a career in sales is that I was terminally shy. It was almost impossible for me to walk up to

---

[272] *Boys' Life* – is the monthly magazine of the Boy Scouts of America (BSA) & is targeted toward readership of young boys between the ages of 6 & 18.

total strangers and then make a presentation, let alone ask them for an order. I started out by getting my own matchbooks to use for business cards. My first order came from Callahan Machine Company, but then my sales career was virtually over. So dad introduced me to the owner of a deli where he and his partners frequently ate their lunch. Sitting down with the proprietor, I gave him my pitch and signed a second order for twenty dollars. I kept a five-dollar commission and mailed the remaining fifteen dollars in with his order. As luck would have it, when the matches arrived in the mail a couple of weeks later, the picture on the back displayed a chef winking with text that read, "Pizzas Made to Order". Unfortunately, the sandwich shop didn't sell pizzas.

Obviously I had to refund the man's money or re-order for him; but I was too embarrassed to face the guy. Besides I had already spent my commission and could not ask the company to make good on my mistake. Dad took me back to the deli, so I could rectify the situation. Although I tried to get up the courage to talk with him I was too ashamed to face the guy. Dad even offered to give me the money, but I remained intimidated. The owner lingered by the table after bringing us our sandwiches, but I was frozen with fear. Dad was embarrassed that I did not own up to my responsibilities. He even tried to grease the rails by offering to throw in an extra twenty bucks to sweeten the deal for me. I felt the pressure, but he confused me when he upped the pot to sixty dollars. I started to wonder what was really going on. When he brought the enticement up to eighty dollars I felt cheap and when he made it a hundred I was convinced I was being bribed. The situation turned into a personal sovereignty issue for me and I dug in my heels. Embarrassed in front of his friend and unable to figure out my behavior, dad took the bull by the horns and gave the owner his money back. Dad had saved face, but the event also initiated a power struggle between the two of us.

While I was locking horns with my father, the government was dealing with an international power struggle of its own. President Johnson ordered an additional Ten-thousand Five-hundred troops to Vietnam for the Tet Offensive[273] and when about Four-hundred and Fifty innocent men, women and children were murdered in the My Lai Massacre[274] many young people demanded a quick end to the war. It didn't take long for the national debate to hit home and show up on my own doorstep.

Peter Callahan came to the farm and we raced around on a small Harley and an old BMW motorcycle. We both enjoyed a lighthearted fun-filled day, but in the evening things turned deadly serious. My cousin and I sat down on the porch swing that overlooked the pasture and the ruins of our burned out barn. After lighting up a cigarette Peter broke the silence. He said he was opposed to the Vietnam War and was seriously considering running away to Canada, in order to avoid the draft. At age fourteen, he already felt forced to mull over a monumental decisions regarding life and death. Having attended a military school, I was solidly in the hawk column of the debate and reflexively spoke to him about duty, honor and the obligation we all have to defend our country. Although deeply troubled by the morality of killing in any war, he also had serious doubts about the justification of this war in particular. I had all the canned responses at the ready. It was our duty to defend the country. Running away to Canada would be an act of cowardice. Hippies who advocated such nonsense were all screwed up on drugs and were being manipulated by Communists. It all made perfect sense to me, until he began to break down crying. Looking up at me with tears streaming down his face he confided, "I don't want to die." I was dumbfounded. We sat there in

---

[273] *Tet Offensive* – was a military failure for North Vietnam, but it was a political & psychological victory for them, because it dramatically contradicted optimistic claims by the United States that the war was all but over.
[274] *My Lai Massacre* – was the murder by U.S. Army troops, of between 347 & 504 unarmed citizens in South Vietnam, all the victims were civilians & the majority were women, children (including babies) & elderly people. Event took place on March 16, 1968.

limbo, listening to a symphony of crickets and tree frogs. Peter looked off in the distance chain-smoking his Marlboro cigarettes. I believed everything I had told him, but was apparently detached from the realities of war. I was also embarrassed at having spoken to him so dogmatically.

An equally frightening situation concerned my own survival. Nightly I watched civil rights and peace demonstrations turn violent on the news. Riot police beat up on hippies with nightsticks and dragged them away by their long hair. Black men were being chased by German Shepherd dogs and water cannons tossed young peaceful protestors around like rag dolls. These marchers were well within their Constitutional rights[275] and while it was true that agitators were exploiting the unrest, it was equally true that the cops and the politicians were routinely violating the rights of peaceful American citizens. All my life I had been taught to respect the police and to see them as the good guys, but these heavy-handed tactics and the flagrant disregard for individual liberty made me question whether they disserved my support. Buffalo Springfield also captured this sentiment with his hit single, For What It's Worth.[276]

To address racism in the country, Martin Luther King Jr. advocated peaceful, nonviolent change in the way blacks were treated. Juxtaposed his movement were the Black Panthers who were calling for violent insurrection. Bobby Kennedy joined King in calling for peaceful agitation, as a way to end discrimination, poverty and war, but the energy of their gentle prodding was redirected by anarchists like

---

[275] *1st Amendment* – states that, "Congress shall make no law respecting an establishment of religion, or prohibiting the free exercise thereof; or abridging the freedom of speech, or of the press; or the right of the people peaceably to assemble, and to petition the Government for a redress of grievances."

[276] *For What It's Worth* – is a song written by Stephen Stills & performed by Buffalo Springfield. Released as a single in January 1967; it was later added to the re-release of their 1st album, Buffalo Springfield. It peaked at #7 on the Hot 100 chart & holds #63 on the 500 Greatest Songs of All Time. Their cautionary lyrics gave people pause.

Abbie Hoffman.[277] Steady progress was being made until James Earl Ray shot Dr. King[278] and then the Black Panthers let out their venomous war cry, "Burn Baby Burn!"

I tried understanding the anger of the black man when the riots broke out, but the only colored person I ever really knew was Mimi. She had been the exceptionally kind and humble woman that did our ironing back in Merchantville. Other than some characters on TV, I had never even seen a black man and felt no animosity toward the Negro race. American history books had documented the evils of slavery, but that seemed like a long time ago and I had no experience or even knowledge of modern day prejudice. None of the explanations I heard from others made any sense to me, until one day a member of the Black Panther Party was being interviewed on TV. He said his group would overthrow our government and make all the white people their slaves. Pundants opined it could never happen, but it was still a scary thought. If what I was seeing on television was true, the danger was not only real, but real close.

Bordentown Military Institute was located on a hill above the New Jersey capital of Trenton. After watching coverage of the riots on TV, I went out to our football field to verify what I was seeing on television. Trenton was clearly a city in flames. Orange embers eerily glowed against the backdrop of a pitch black sky. This was a real war! It would just be a matter of time, before the insurrectionists reached the Bordentown campus and marched us away in chains. It May have been a paranoid conclusion, but I believed it and so did many other adults.

---

[277] *Abbie Hoffman* – was a social & political activist who co-founded the Youth International Party or "Yippies". He was convicted for conspiring to incite a riot during the 1968 Democratic National Convention.

[278] *Assasination* – Martin Luther King, Jr. was booked in room 306 at the Lorraine Motel, in Memphis, TN. On April 3, 1968, King gave his *I've Been to the Mountaintop* sermon. At 6:01 p.m. the next evening, as he stood on the motel's second floor balcony, a shot rang out. He was rushed to St. Joseph's Hospital & pronounced dead at 7:05 p.m.

Paranoia strikes deep;
Into your life it will creep.
It starts when you're always afraid;
You step out of line, the man come and take you away.
I think it's time we stop, children, what's that sound?
Everybody look what's going down.[279]

With the fear of being taken prisoner at any given moment, letters from home took on a whole new level of significance. I had always written to mom and dad, but now I was also corresponding with Chris and Tom. I even started writing love letters to Rebecca. Every letter I received back was precious to me. Sarah made arrangements for Rebecca to see me on weekend visits. Its not like we were ever left alone or anything, but her hugs were a comfort to me at a time when I was feeling very much alone.

Thankfully, the violence in Trenton never did spread to our school, but every night on the six o'clock news, the reporters gave us a play-by-play description of the race riots. One word that kept being repeated was Molotov cocktail.[280] I asked my father what the reporters were talking about and instead of answering me verbally he showed me. We kept several cases of empty beer and soda bottles in our garage and would return them to the distributor for refunds. Dad filled one of the bottles with gasoline and stuffed a rag into its neck. Walking down to a cliff by the creek, he turned the bottle upside down, lit the rag on fire and threw the bottle up against the cliff. A large fireball exploded, just like on TV!

---

[279] *For What It's Worth* – lyrics were written by Stephen Stills & the song was performed by Buffalo Springfield. The hit single was released in January 1967.
[280] *Molotov Cocktail* – is a generic name used for a variety of improvised incendiary weapons. Due to the relative ease of production, they are frequently used by non-professionally equipped fighters & those who cannot afford, manufacture, or obtain professional-grade grenades. They are primarily intended to set targets ablaze rather than instantly destroy them. The bombs were derisively named after the then Foreign Minister of the Soviet Union, Vyacheslav Molotov, by the Finns during the Winter War.

The next day, while my father was at work, I took an entire case of empty beer bottles down to the creek, along with a can of gasoline. I filled them all up and ripped up an old bed sheet to use for fuses. The rest of the afternoon was spent breaking the bottles on the rock wall of the cliff. Living so far out in the country, no one even noticed the huge black plumes of billowing smoke. But when dad pulled in the driveway he noticed Indian smoke signals coming from the far end of the hay field. Walking over to investigate, he peered over the cliff just in time to see me getting ready to throw another Molotov cocktail. There could be no good answer to his angry question, "What the hell are you doing?"

My father was the third child in a relatively happy family that was born in the beginning of The Great Depression.[281] His parents had many friends and they were very active in their parish. The youngest brother in the family was unfortunately born with a severe illness. The infant died despite medical attention and his mother's indefatigable efforts. Although Amanda Callahan had done all that she could for the child, she blamed herself for its death. This led to a severe postpartum depression, which landed her in the Friends Hospital in Northeast Philly. Misdiagnosed as schizophrenic, she soon became the latest Ginny pig for a new experimental treatment known as Shock Therapy.[282]

Tragically, the doctors scrambled her brain with this relatively new therapy, leaving my father to grow up with a

---

[281] *The Great Depression* – was a severe worldwide economic depression in the decade preceding World War II. It began with the stock market crash on October 29, 1929. Banking panics started one year later, when conglomerates in New York & Los Angeles failed, in prominently-covered scandals. Although it began in America, the world-wide depression lasted until 1940 & was the longest, most widespread & deepest depression of the 20th century. It is used, as an example of just how far the world's economy can decline.

[282] *Shock Therapy* – is the collective term to describe Insulin coma therapy & the convulsive therapies (electro & cardiazol/metrazol). Insulin shock therapy or insulin coma therapy was a form of psychiatric treatment in which patients were repeatedly injected with large doses of insulin in order to produce daily comas over several weeks. It was introduced in 1933 by Polish-Austrian-American psychiatrist Manfred Sakel & used extensively to treat schizophrenia throughout the 1940s & 50s, before falling out of favour & being replaced by neuroleptic drugs. In recent years the controvercial therapy has been making a come back.

mother who rarely even recognized her own son. To compensate for the loss of his mother, my grandfather asked the good sisters at Our Lady of Perpetual Help to look after young Tommy. Although the religious sisters did their best to provide oversight, their constant hovering was perceived as smothering. The ongoing psychological and emotional injuries took its toll on him as well as on his mother. After the death of my grandfather, his children took the troubled woman into their homes on a rotating basis.

Whenever it was our family's turn to take care of grandmom, she slept on the bottom bunk in Sarah's room. Dad's mom pretty much kept to herself, chain-smoking her Chesterfield cigarettes, keeping up with her soap operas and watching her favorite sitcom, the I Love Lucy show.[283] My grandmother virtually ignored us. She thought nothing of walking into a room full of children watching cartoons and changing the channel. Whenever she did this we ran in to my mother to object, but she always sided with our grandmother and told us to go out and play. Mom knew she was being unfair, but out of compassion for her mother-in-law's mental illness, she felt we should leave her the few pleasures she had left.

On June 3, 1968 my father walked in to Sarah's bedroom to wake his mother and noticed her body was lying in a contorted position. Avoiding the obvious conclusion, he gently nudged her shoulder and whispered, "Mom?" Tears welled up in his eyes, as he listened for an answer that would never come. The emptiness squeezed his heart like a vice as he choked back his tears. Waking Sarah, he quietly told her what had happened. Helping his young daughter out of the top bunk, she asked about her grandmother's twisted figure. Dad speculated that she probably struggled near the end and cautioned Sarah not to say anything to the other children

---

[283] *I Love Lucy* - was a comedic television sitcom, starring Lucille Ball, Desi Arnaz, Vivian Vance & William Frawley. The black-&-white series ran from 1951-1960 on CBS & reached the status of the most-watched show in America for 4 of its 6 seasons. I Love Lucy reruns are still syndicated & running in dozens of languages around the world.

about it. The two of them walked down to the kitchen together where mom was making breakfast. Sarah sat down at the table and whimpered, while dad told mom the news. He speculated that she probably died from a diabetic coma. Mom looked up into his glassy eyes and leaned forward to hug him, but the teapot whistled and the crackling of the neglected bacon demanded her immediate attention.

When my father walked outside to be alone, Sarah burst into tears and my mother explained to us that our grandmother had died during the night. None of us had ever seen a dead body before and there was a certain kind of morbid curiosity about it, but dad returned to the kitchen just in time to stop us from going up the stairs to investigate. Although we never saw him cry we intuitively knew he was hurting and instinctively hugged him. Truth be told, I didn't much like my grandmother and there was a certain relief about her death. She was the grouchy old woman who always changed the channel on our TV. I'm not saying I was gleeful or anything, but the most important thing on my mind was figuring out how to hide my true feelings of apathy from dad.

Actually, I was not the only one conflicted about her death. Mom felt for her husband and wanted to comfort him, but she too had a sense of relief about his mother's death. No longer would she have to referee the use of the TV or crush up insulin tablets for her mother-in-law's diabetes and then hide them in her coffee. Caring for her had not been easy and my mother looked forward to a more peaceful home life. Dad was in shock and he felt numb, but his mother's death would have a huge impact on his life. The upheaval following her passing would also wreak havoc on our entire family. Little things began to change within days.

Dad attended Cursillio.[284] While attending the retreat weekend he met Eduardo Arizmendi, an impoverished Puerto Rican who lived in the ghetto of Philadelphia. Ed introduced my father to his wife Maria and invited him to bring our entire family to his home in Northeast Philly. The dinner invitation jolted us our of a quiet isolated life in the country. The two families shared an ethnic meal, inside the safety of their row house. But the home was located in a neighborhood that looked like a war zone. A few weeks later the Arizmendi family came up to visit us at the farm. Eduardo longed to have a pig roast, just like the ones back home in Puerto Rico. Dad purchased a piglet from a farmer over on Long Mill Road and we slaughtered it in the back yard. After digging a pit we filled it with bags of charcoal and constructed a spit. The pig took the rest of the afternoon to cook. Maria directed the final preparations in our kitchen with the speed and efficiency of an Army nurse in a MASH unit.[285] Eventually an elaborate feast was set out before us on picnic tables covered with plaid plastic table cloths of red and white squares.

All afternoon dad wanted me to make their eldest son Bernardo feel welcome, but he was a pretty cocky guy and I found it hard to fulfill his request. When I refused to eat pork dad felt I was being deliberately insulting our guests. Actually, my reticence stemmed from the fact that I had

---

[284] *Cursillos Movement* – is a conversion ministry that began in the Roman Catholic Church & has since spread to other Christian denominations. It was founded in Majorca, Spain by a group of laymen in 1944, while they were refining a technique to train pilgrimage leaders. It has since been adapted by numerous other Christian denominations, some of which have retained the name "cursillo" while others have given the program a different name. The cursillo method focuses on training lay people to become effective leaders over the course of a 3-day weekend. The weekend includes 15 talks, some given by priests & some by lay people. One emphasis of the weekend is on preparing those undergoing it, to take the movement's methods back into the world, on what they call the "4th day".

[285] *MASH* – the Mobile Army Surgical Hospital refers to a United States Army medical unit serving as a fully functional hospital in a combat area of operations. The units were first established in August 1945 & were deployed during the Korean War & subsequent conflicts. The U.S. Army deactivated the last MASH unit on February 16, 2006.

recently learned about a disease called Trichinosis.[286] The entire pig roast celebration seemed overly important to my father and I wondered why. Soon after the Arizmendi family departed I discovered the answer. Dad gathered the family together and asked us how we would feel about letting Bernardo come to live with us for a few years. He wanted to give the boy the advantages of a better school and take some of the financial strain off of his family. We were dumbfounded. After the uncomfortable seconds that followed, the younger children thought it would be a nice thing to do. The older kids stammered, trying to come up with an acceptable response and I withdrew in silence. What would life be like with another person in our home? More importantly, what would a boy who was a full two years older than me do to the pecking order?

When I finally spoke my retort was swift, loud and definitive. "No way! What were you thinking? There's no way this is happening! If you bring him here, I'm leaving! It's either him or me, so forget it!" My do-gooder parents were just trying to put their faith into action, but between the move to Pennsylvania, summer camp and boarding school, I was tired of just going along with everyone else's agenda. I put my foot down and took back control of my life. Boldly risking what they would do with the ultimatum, I was ready to put it all on the line. The commanding tone I took and my apparent lack of charity stunned my father, but it also served as a wake up call that challenged his priorities. A Catholic Utopia here on earth is a heresy and the dizzying heights of my parent's spiritual fantasy had just run smack into the concrete wall of the family and its primacy of place in decision-making. They must have seen some truth in the explosive confrontation, because I never saw nor heard of the Arizmendi family again. Charity begins at home and while it may have been a charitable thing to help out a poor

---

[286] *Trichinosis* – is a parasitic disease caused by eating raw or undercooked pork or wild game infected with the larvae of a species of roundworm called Trichinella spiralis, commonly called the trichina worm.

man, from my perspective taking care of our own family was much more important.

My adolescence was beginning to flower. I was nurturing the first reciprocal relationship I had ever had with a girl. In contrast to Annabel, my sentiments toward Rebecca were happily being returned. Through the vehicle of weekly letter writing with my sweetheart, we were getting to know each other and falling in love. After much pleading, dad brought Rebecca along for the ride on my last trip back to Bordentown. Making a pit stop along the way at the Dairy Queen in Harleysville, we ate ice cream and played a leisurely round of miniature golf together. Rebecca was a spirited young woman and my father enjoyed a lively conversation with us. Once we arrived at the school, I showed her around the campus and gave her a big hug and a kiss good-bye.

My final week of military education was filled with preparation for the commencement exercises. The prestige of the school demanded a fabulous show for the guests, demonstrating all the pride, dignity and exactitude that the institute had inculcated within the character of each cadet. The education had been first rate. I had improved my academic performance, met the challenges and graduated with honors. Even more important, I had adjusted my attitude. Mom, Dad, Sarah, Rebecca, Chris Lang and Tom Reeves had all come up to attend my graduation. I marched proudly in my spiffy dress blue uniform, which included my third pair of patent leather shoes. We later celebrated at a local diner and returned to the farm in our Ford Fairlane wagon. Dad had also installed a special new gadget in the car; an air conditioner!

After arriving back home, mom make an announcement, "Ever since the barn burned down, your father and I have been looking for another place to live. Well we finally found it!" All of the children were shocked and we paused to consider the implications of the move. Sarah was the first to speak up, "Where is it?" Dad told us where it was located, but our lack of knowledge regarding the local geography made his answer unintelligible. Then we hit our parents up with a series of follow-up questions. Sarah wanted to know what school she would be attending. Sean asked if he could bring all of his cats. Murray wanted to know if he could still see his friend from school. I sat there silent, lost in my thoughts.

Although I looked back at my recent history: the pain of the move from Jersey, transition to an unfamiliar school and feelings of abandonment at the military academies, none of it seemed to matter. The only thing I really cared about was Rebecca. We were already pen pals and rarely saw one another. The only thing a move would do is bring us geographically closer together. Disturbing me from the deliberating daydream, mom pulled me aside to ask me if I remembered how hard it was to leave my friends in Jersey. Then she solicited my help in smoothing the way for the rest of the children in the upcoming move. Her request gave me a renewed feeling of purpose and I proudly accepted the task. Reestablished in my role as the firstborn son, I took back the mantle of trailblazer and set out to grease the way for my siblings.

In the meantime there were trail bikes to ride, rope swings to jump from and guns to shoot. My friends from Jersey came up we took advantage of the limited time we still had left to play around the farm. Dad drove us over to the new place, which seemed to hold out a lot of promise and if nothing else, it would be another great place to explore. The only downside to me was that I would now have to go to a public school.

Robert F. Kennedy was assassinated on June 6, 1968, at the Ambassador Hotel in Los Angeles, by a Jordanian named

Sirhan Sirhan.[287] Death seemed to be in the air and the passing of my grandmother launched my father on a quest to find himself. Once a total stickler for rules, dad began to see every ordinance as if it were a shackle. He said as much when he ran into a renegade bishop who granted our family a dispensation from going to Mass on Sunday. Worship prompted by desire alone seemed like a good thing, but within a few months our family pretty much stopped going to Mass altogether and even when we went to Church it was not the same. The Latin Mass had been reconstituted in English. Altars were turned around and sacred music was reduced to campfire sing-alongs. Liturgists began removing the sacred art of statues and replacing them with banal burlap banners covered in abstract images of pastel felt.

When the Food and Drug Administration approved The Pill,[288] Rome was deluged with questions about the Church's position on artificial birth control. So on July 25, 1968 Pope Paul IV signed off on an encyclical entitled Humanae Vitae,[289] which was penned by a relatively unknown Polish Cardinal named Karol Józef Wojtyła.[290] Tragically, many dissenting bishops rebelled against the clear teaching of the Church. In the wake of this scandalous rebellion; married

---

[287] *Sirhan Sirhan* – was the man convicted in the assassination of Robert F. Kennedy in 1968. His attorney Lawrence Teeter believed that Sirhan was under the influence of hypnosis when he fired his weapon & linked the CIA's MKUltra program to mind control techniques used to control his client. Project MKUltra was the code name for an illegal, covert research operation conducted by the CIA beginning in the early 1950s.

[288] *The Pill* – is a birth control method that includes a combination of estrogen & progestin. The chemicals inhibit female fertility & were developed to prevent ovulation by suppressing the release of gonadotropins. The primary mechanism of action inhibited follicular development thus preventing ovulation. A 2nd mechanism, called the endometrial effect, prevented implantation of an embryo to the uterus, thereby killing the child, making it an abortifacient, rather than a contraceptive. The FDA approved it in 1960, but the pill was not available in all states until *Griswold v. Connecticut* legalized it nationwide for married women in 1965 & *Eisenstadt v. Baird* made it available for unmarried women in 1972.

[289] *Humanae Vitae* – which in Latin means "Of Human Life" is an encyclical written by Pope Paul VI & promulgated on July 25, 1968. Subtitled "On the Regulation of Birth", it reaffirmed the traditional teaching of the Church regarding abortion, contraception & other issues pertaining to human life. Some believe it was actually penned by Karol Wojtyła.

[290] *Karol Józef Wojtyła* – was a bishop in Kraków, Poland who went on to become a cardinal from Poland & participat in the Vatican II Council. He also became the 1st Polish Pope, taking the name John Paul II & he served from 1978-2005, making his the 2nd longest reigning pontificate. (1920-2005)

couples were misled about the Church's position and parents attempting to teach sexual morality to their children during the sexual revolution were virtually abandoned.

Law and order was being trampled everywhere and it seemed as if our whole culture was Born to be Wild.[291] Race riots broke out in one-hundred and twenty-five cities and every night, on the evening news we watched images of jets laying down napalm in Vietnam along with wounded soldiers grimacing in anguish on stretchers. Americans witnessed unprecedented police brutality at the Democratic National Convention. From the bishops on down people were questioning, not only established authority, but every belief, policy and norm of our society. The country was polarized over the war, race relations, drugs and the immoral behavior of the youth. And it was not just the young. Middle-aged swingers swapped wives. Materialism was on steroids and the military industrial complex had become institutionalized.

The deaths of Martin Luther King, Jr. and Bobby Kennedy left a vacuum of competing political ideologies, cultural upheaval and violence. When the dust settled a three-way race for the presidency emerged. Republican Richard Nixon and Democrat Hubert Humphrey both claimed their party stood for law, order and prosperity, while the Independent candidate George Wallace pushed for a return to state sovereignty and opposed federal troops being used to enforce federal civil rights laws.

America was cascading toward an uncertain future and so was my family. We reassembled the original moving crew and loaded up another U-Haul truck with furniture and lots of labeled boxes. Our veteran crew was bound on a much

---

[291] *Born to be Wild* – is a rock song written by Mars Bonfire & made famous by the Canadian rock band Steppenwolf. Often used in popular culture to denote a biker appearance or attitude, it is sometimes described as the first heavy metal song & the 2nd verse lyric "heavy metal thunder," marks the first use of this term in rock music. The song was eventually used in the soundtrack for the movie *Easy Rider* in 1969.

shorter voyage to yet another farm in Souderton, just a few miles away. Having been through this before, the trip seemed like a piece of cake. From our vantage point the future looked bright and the uncertainty only served to pump up the pleasing possibilities.

Chapter 13

A New Beginning

On the surface the move didn't change all that much. Our family simply relocated from a rented horse farm in Telford, to an old dairy farm near the Lansdale exit of the turnpike. However, like the culture around us, much was boiling just below the surface. Bishops were defying the Vatican, Negroes were at war with the police and the anti-war movement was polarizing the entire nation. Hippies refused to trust anyone over thirty; flower children were growing up high on drugs and the social and sexual mores were breaking down at an alarming rate. The foundational Christian values of our country were being questioned and my own family would question them as well.

Our rag-tag moving company was an experienced crew. We energetically swung into action, loading and unloading all the furniture and boxes in short order. Then we returned to the U-Haul dealership to drop off the truck. On the way home we stopped off at a beverage warehouse in Telford to pick up twenty cases of A-Treat soda and several bags of ice. Returning to our new home we filled up coolers with as much soda and ice as they could handle and stacked the remaining cases in the garage.

The eight-bedroom farmhouse was a three-story structure made up of fieldstone covered over with white plaster and the stately home was accented with black shutters on every one of the windows. The main entrance faced a blacktopped Wambold Road and a skinny little concrete sidewalk led from the macadam parking lot to a mudroom on the side of the house. The back door opened onto a concrete porch, which overlooked the back hill and at the bottom was a rain creek[292] with fields of hay and corn on the opposite side of the creek. On the left side of the porch was a black handled pump and half-way down the hill was an old chicken coop. A four-story barn made of rough-cut lumber with a fieldstone foundation sat on the other side of the parking lot. The basement of the barn had a smooth concrete floor and was formerly used for milking cows. An earthen ramp ran from the front door of the barn down to Wambold Road. The upper floors were designed for chickens and an attached low barn with four bays adjoined a two-car garage with a workshop.

While the girls were busy nesting, the boys went outside to explore; but our playtime was cut short when my friends had to go back to Jersey. After they left, my thoughts returned to Rebecca. I wanted to take her out to the movies or something, but I was still broke. I knew I was too shy for sales, so I decided to interview for a job with Jim Cleaver, the plant manager at Callahan Machine Company. When dad found out I wanted a job at the shop he offered to drive me in, but instructed his foreman to make it clear to me that I would not be treated differently just because I was the son of the boss. Mr. Cleaver knew just how to handle it.

Jim was a rough looking character who rode a Harley Hog, chain-smoked Pel Mel cigarettes and towered over me. Some scaring on his face gave it a ruddy complexion and betrayed the fact that he had never recovered from a teenage case of terminal acne. He loved to tell war stories and spoke in glowing tones as about drag racing on city streets, tangling with MPs in the Army and his adventures installing natural gas lines in Philadelphia. The man ran with greasers and had apparently been the leader of the pack. I thought I was familiar with the machine shop and knew some of the men,

---

[292] *Rain Creek* – during the summer the flow of water was almost non-existent. The creek had a putrid smell to it & was covered in white fur. We would later learn that the fur was from *The Smiling Porker*, at the *Hatfield Packing* slaughterhouse, just a few miles upstream. A few years after we moved in, they installed a sewer line to solve the problem.

but Jim still escorted me through the factory and introduced me to all the other workers. With a cigarette in one hand and a cup of coffee in the other, he pointed out machines, material and staging areas, while explaining how each operation came together to produce the final products.

Jim said that the job he had for me would involve sweeping the floor, shoveling metal chips into dumpsters and assembling mechanical parts. It would be a forty-hour a week job involving heavy-duty physical labor. I was young and determined, so I felt confident I could handle the work. The hardest part of the interview came when he asked me how much money I wanted. The question threw me since I thought every job had its own hourly rate. Minimum wage at the time was $1.60 an hour, but I would be working under the table, so I only asked for a dollar. Although I thought I was being reasonable he said, "That's a lot of money. Do you have any experience?" The question seemed ridiculous to me and I responded by saying, "I've been sweeping our kitchen floor for most of my life." A condescending frown cascaded down his face and he replied, "That's great that you've helped your mother around the house, but sweeping a shop floor is very different. Do you have any experience in sweeping factory floors?" His question seemed downright demeaning and I thought he was playing with me, but what could I do? I wanted to be paid adequately for my labor and shoveling chips was going to be back breaking work. I contemptuously fired back, "I can handle it." His eyes almost twinkled like he knew the strength of his bargaining position and he confidently closed the deal. "Since you have no experience, I'll start you out at fifty cents an hour. After you gain some experience, maybe I'll give you a raise. How does that sound?" I felt humiliated but also powerless to do anything about it. Since I needed the job I accepted his terms. Mr. Cleaver told me I could start on Monday morning and he introduced me to Paul Schultz, who offered to give me a ride on his way in to work each morning. Jim led me back to dad's office and cheerfully told my father I had been hired. Dad and Jim both seemed pretty happy about it, but I felt like I had been suckered into the abusive world of child labor, I even envisioned mental pictures of black faced Irish kids in coalmines. Was this just the way of the world? Was my father and his foreman no better than Henry Frick[293] or a task master in the Deep South? Only time would tell. Not wanting to appear ungrateful, I swallowed my pride and feigned a smile.

Dad purchased an alarm clock for me and told me how important it was for me to take responsibility for getting myself up in the morning. He also said I should make sure to be waiting by the side of the road when Paul Schultz drove up and that I should offer him some money for gas. On Monday morning I rose early, dressed quickly and ate my breakfast. When Mr. Schultz came by to pick me up, I was waiting by our mailbox on Wambold Road. We spent the first couple of days getting to know each other and I learned volumes about the work ethic of a tradesman. Paul rarely looked me in the eye, but he politely answered all of my questions. Mr. Schultz did accept my offer to chip in for gas, but not before I had a couple of paychecks under my belt. Once we got to know each other, I found out that he had escaped from behind the Iron Curtain[294] in East Germany. Although this middle-aged man had a heavy German accent, he also spoke with good diction and had a better understanding of grammar than me. The German gentleman was grateful for his opportunity to live free in America and yet he was somewhat homesick for his own culture. He told me about his seven-year apprenticeship and how it was

---

[293] *Henry Clay Frick* – was an American industrialist, financier & art patron. He founded the H. C. Frick & Company & was chairman of the Carnegie Steel Company. He was such a ruthless task master that on July 23, 1892, Alexander Berkman attempted to murder Frick in revenge for 9 steelworkers who were killed when they were attacked by the Pinkerton detectives hired by Frick to disperse locked-out workers during a strike. (1849-1919)

[294] *The Iron Curtain* – symbolized the political divide & physical boundary that broke Europe into two separate areas when World War II ended in 1945 & persisted until the end of the Cold War in 1991. On both sides of the line, states developed their own international economic & military alliances with the Soviet Union & the Warsaw Pact on the east side & Europe & NATO on the west. The Berlin Wall was a longtime symbol of the Iron Curtain.

something akin to an army boot camp. Proud of having run this gauntlet, he shared that he spent the totality of his first year, filing the burr off the edge of a single piece of bar stock. As a young apprentice he was only allowed to stroke the file in one direction and he said that the purpose of the exercise was to form good habits and to develop pride in workmanship. Mr. Schultz was a first class machinist and whenever I had a question, he had an accurate answer. I found his example of pride in workmanship admirable and worthy of emulation.

On Friday I was sweeping the floor over by the vending machines when Mr. Cleaver bought himself a coffee and then offered me a carton of chocolate milk. Thanking him for the much appreciated cold drink, I wiped the dripping perspiration from my forehead with my sleeve and guzzled down the drink. After lighting up a cigarette my boss asked, "How's it going?" Filling dozens of dumpsters daily with heavy metal chips and sweeping a thirty thousand square-foot facility was hard work, but it was also satisfying. I let him know I was enjoying the use of my newfound physical strength and that I also had a sense of accomplishment at the end of each workday. Jim Cleaver listened intently and then offered his own positive observations of my work ethic and performance. Acknowledging my recent experience, he gave me a fifty-cent raise. I guess Jim Cleaver wasn't exactly Simon Legree.[295]

On Saturday dad had us clean out some old wooden doors, a few pieces of furniture and timbers that were cluttering up one of the rooms in the barn. We burned the items on an old concrete foundation in back of the garage, which soon became the place where we burned all of our trash. The fire burned all afternoon and while dad stood guard over it, Sean and I used some of the doors to build a dam across the creek.

---

[295] *Simon Legree* – is the main villain of the classic anti-slavery propaganda novel Uncle Tom's Cabin by Harriet Beecher Stowe. The iconic name refers to a brutal task master.

In the evening we roasted hot dogs and gathered up green sticks to toast marshmallows. Sean and I then sat down on the back hill to eat our meal. It was a great vantage point to admire our amateur feat of engineering, but it would take a thunderstorm and a flash flood to really test the barrier.

The Kildare family was our closest neighbor. They lived about a quarter mile down the road from us. We met them one Sunday after Mass and they invited our family to come over and go swimming. Peter Kildare was an extrovert and he had a booming voice that was so loud it scared us, but he also had an Irish heart of gold. Peter was a family man who worked in construction. He was as strong as an ox physically and would stand up to anyone or anything that tried to hurt his family or his friends. In his younger years he had even been a contender for the Golden Gloves tournament in Philadelphia. His wife Monica was a sweet woman; she was generous, funny and full of life. Together they had five children, many of whom we knew from school. Melissa was the eldest, followed by Enya, Matt, Maggie, Abby and Darren.

Our otherwise isolated families hit it off right away, enjoying the hospitality of an impromptu barbeque with hot dogs and hamburgers. After eating we had to observe a mandatory waiting period before entering the pool. In the interim our newfound friends showed us a small barn behind the house and a Shetland pony they had named Footloose.[296] We took turns grooming the pony and I helped Melissa to muck out the stall. I knew this task would be something she could appreciate and besides it brought back fond memories of taking care of Blaze. While my parents got to know each other over a few drinks on their screened in porch, we played Marco Polo in the pool. When the sun set Mr. Kildair built a

---

[296] *Shetland* – is a breed of pony originating in the Shetland Isles. Shetlands range in height from 28 inches to 11.2 hands for an American Shetland. They have heavy coats, short legs & are considered quite intelligent. A very strong breed, these ponies are used for riding, driving & pack purposes.

fire using cut-off pieces of pine he had brought home from work. Meanwhile Monica brought out long wire forks for the marshmallows.

Melissa and Enya sat with me and my sister in the dining room beside the adults, while the younger kids were relegated to the kitchen table for dinner. Melissa was a year older than me. At fifteen she was already a voluptuous young woman with a vivacious personality. Enya was thirteen and comparatively homely, but she was also very attentive, incredibly witty and had a beautiful singing voice. After dinner Maggie played the piano and Enya accompanied her, as they sang a repertoire of old Irish tunes. Mr. Kildare loved to brag about his talented children, especially after he had a few beers. Their heavenly harmonic hymns developed into a tradition whenever our two families came together.

In Jersey we saw our neighbors on a daily basis, but it was different out here in the country. An unspoken protocol stated that the best neighbor you could ever have was the one you never saw. There was a much stronger sense of individuality in the farming community than there was back in the city. Farmers generally left each other alone to go about their business in their own way and expected their neighbors to do the same. Yet, if you were ever truly in need, the neighbor you never spoke with would bend over backwards to lend you a hand. It was like that with the Kildare family. The time we spent together was relatively limited. Other than a handful of family events we rarely played together, yet the bond between our families was as solid as the Rock of Gibraltar. We always knew that we would be there for each other whenever it really mattered.

All summer long I worked my butt off, sweeping floors, shoveling chips and assembling flagpole trucks.[297] Even

---

[297] *Trucks* – are pulley mechanisms that went on the tops of *Lingo* flag polls. Jack Lingo was not only a customer, but had been my father's flight instructor back in New Jersey.

though my hourly rate was well below minimum wage, it was under the table and earned me forty dollars a week, which was a lot of money for an eighth grader. When school resumed I continued to work Saturdays and was moved into the Shipping and Receiving department, where I built crates. I maintained a good work ethic, had money in my pocket and was feeling good about myself.

Dad had a multicolored rooster painted on a sign next to our driveway. He named our new home the De Colores Farm.[298] Cursillo had been a powerful turning point in my father's life and the colorful bird was their cherished logo. Dad formed friendships with some of the men who had been on the retreat with him including George Rosellini who opened up his home for follow-up group meetings. The sign hung beside our driveway for many years. Except for one of his friends who died, my dad continues to meet with that same group of men on a regular basis.

As the summer came to a close the morning sky took on a reddish hue. By mid morning it was raining and in the afternoon a deluge began that continued non-stop for three days. The creek swelled and our wooden dam was finally tested. When the clouds eventually cleared, the structure remained and the water had filled up behind it. The baked mud of the creek bed was gone and the little puddles had been transformed into an elongated lake. Within days the water was teaming with minnows and tadpoles. The brown scrub brush that lined the edge of the creek turned a deep dark green and the stench of pig fur was replaced with the fragrance of honeysuckle. In reality the dam probably had little to do with the transformation. The water would probably have risen with or without our little dam. Even so Sean and I relished our apparent success and basked in the glory of having beaten back the powerful forces of nature.

---

[298] *De Colores Farm* – in the context of the *Cursillo* movement the name came from the oft-repeated greeting "De Colores," which meant *The Colors of Love are Many*.

In September of 1968, I entered the ninth grade at Pennfield Junior High School in Hatfield, Pennsylvania. Entering the Public School System for the very first time was a cultural shock! Absent were the jackets, the neckties and the uniforms. The silence of the classroom was gone and chaos supplanted the orderly flow of students. Respect for authority was virtually non-existent and every teacher had their own subjective ideas about discipline. Some educators had wooden paddles hanging beside the classroom door, while others refused to so much as raise their voices. The resultant confusion was pure unadulterated pandemonium.

In Science my classmate Dylan Harris threw a piece of chalk at the black board while Mr. Watson was writing down an outline. The teacher ignored his belligerent act and after a short pause, continued writing. Emboldened by the lack of response, Dylan picked up a felt eraser and nailed the back of Mr. Watson's jacket. I had never seen anything like it. The teacher wheeled around and asked, "Who threw that?" The pernicious punk proudly raised his hand and barked, "I did! What are you gonna do about it?" The whole class held its collective breath, as the teacher ordered him to the front of the room. Dylan sported an ear-to-ear grin all the way up to the side of the teacher's desk without an ounce of repentance. Mr. Watson sat down at his desk and filled out a hall pass to the principal's office. Without warning, Dylan grabbed Mr. Watson's necktie and slammed his jaw on the desk. One girl screamed and a teacher ran across the hall and dragged Dylan out. He repeatedly threw him up against the lockers, until the defiant hoodlum finally submitted. Mr. Watson's jaw was shattered and our substitute teacher gave us daily updates about his recovery, but we heard nothing about Dylan Harris. After only a three-day suspension, Dylan returned to school mocking his light sentence and declaring it an example of the faculty's impotence.

If there was a dress code there was little evidence of it and with the exception of one teacher, discipline of the students was virtually nonexistent. Even the expectation to learn had evaporated. The only anomaly was Mr. Thackeray. This exceptional educator taught American History, advised our Student Council and served as my homeroom teacher. Mr. Thackeray ran a tight ship and he did so without ever raising his voice. This man obviously cared about us and we responded in kind, by doing our very best to please him. Although I learned a lot from him about American history, politics and how our government functions, my grades in other subjects were slipping. I soon found myself looking outside the classroom again, for a path to some semblance of success.

As the leaves started falling, dad took me up to Quinby's Gun & Sport Shop in Dublin to get a hunting license. He lent me his double-barreled 12-gage Parker and I headed to the field across the street to hunt doves. The freshly harvested field of faded yellow cornstalks provided camouflage for the birds that hid in between the dried clay ridges and the muddy valleys of the reddish brown soil. After crossing half-a-dozen rows, one flew up in front of me. Bam! Bam! My first shot missed, but the second found its mark. I ran over to pick up my trophy, but the poor thing was bleeding, limping and obviously in pain. Seeing no rocks big enough to dispatch the bird, I raised my foot and crushed its head with my boot. Deeply saddened by the experience, I ended my hunt early, fed the dove to the cat and swore off dove hunting forever. The overreaction gave me pause. Why was I so gun shy with these birds when I had no such problem killing the animals in my traps?

Like the poor bleeding bird on the ground, the loss of innocence I had experienced back in boarding school, left me spiritually and emotionally crippled. Public school was devoid of discipline and hostile toward any kind of firm moral code. The resulting chaos made social navigation at school confusing at best. As challenging as all these things were, the most painful blows would come from my own family. No longer strengthened by sacramental life, the breath of the Spirit disappeared from beneath my wings and no longer held me aloft. I was left crawling in the dirt; just like that helpless little dove.

Ironically, my spiritual demise coincided with the death of Padre Pio, who for over fifty years had endured the pains and savored the blessings of the Stigmata.[299] Born on May 25, 1887, Francesco Forgione was given the name Pio when he entered the monastery of the Capuchins. Early on the morning of September 23, 1968, that good and holy priest made his last confession, renewed his Franciscan vows and fingered the beads of his Rosary, before breathing his last word "Maria! Thirty-two years later, Pope John Paul II would canonize him a saint.

Saint Pio's passing marked the end of an era for me. The wild pigeons had been rescued from the lethal force of my shotgun. The Tippler pigeons were now safe from harm in a brand new coop I had constructed for them up in the barn. I felt safe and secure in our new family home, but the apparent safety and security of my family life was a mirage. Everything was about to change and the coming cultural tsunami would prove unstoppable.

---

[299] *Stigmata* – are the bodily marks, sores, or sensations of pain corresponding in location to the crucifixion wounds of Jesus, usually occurring during states of religious ecstasy.

Chapter 14

Cultural Convergence

Most of the land owners in early American history were British, Pan-European and Protestant. So despite the Revolution, the aristocracy still owned most of the land and often stood in the way of socio-economic mobility. The Potato Famine[300] brought peasants from Ireland to work in the fields and the coal mines of landed gentry. The Industrial Revolution required an ever-increasing labor pool to run machinery in their factories. Immigrants from Italy, Poland and other Western European countries provided a cheap labor source and packed the cities. Following World War II the populations of these predominately Catholic immigrants and their descendants were exploding. Along with the population increase there was a steady rise in educational opportunities offered by local parish parochial schools. Add to that the training offered to veterans through the GI Bill and Catholics were seeing a dramatic increase in both their economic and political power. This ascendancy translated Catholic morality into law. Laborers began forming unions and many mackerel snappers[301] moved up the ladder to become mayors of many American cities. The phenomenon eventually reached its zenith in 1960 with the election of

---

[300] *Irish Potato Famine* – between 1845 & 1852 there was a period of mass starvation & disease in Ireland. A potato blight began the Great Hunger, but huge quantities of food were also exported from Ireland to England while the people of Ireland were dying of starvation. During the famine approximately 1 million people died & a million more emigrated from Ireland, many to the United States.

[301] *Mackerel Snapper* – was a sectarian slur that began in the 1850s & was put upon Roman Catholics. It referred to their discipline of Friday abstinence from red meat and poultry, for which fish was substituted. The practice distinguished Catholics from other Christians, especially in North America, where Protestant churches prevailed and Catholics tended to be poor immigrants from Italy, Poland, and Ireland.

John F. Kennedy, but displaced politicians, progressive elites and especially the Masons[302] were not at all happy about it.

Like their champion the Marquis de Sade,[303] progressives continuously pushed for greater freedom of sexual expression and experimentation. Radicals made some headway during the roaring twenties, but hard times in the thirties and forties convinced Americans to return to their faith in earnest. Catholic religious fervor thwarted the influence of these liberals, but the affluence of the sixties brought it all back again with a vengeance. For centuries a perverted underground found sanctuary in Masonic halls and speakeasies, but in 1969 thousands of demonic degenerates burst forth from their shadowy lairs like cobras. The innocence of Camelot may have been lost the day a magic bullet killed a Catholic President, but it took decades for Americans to shake off the horror of the assassination and to realize the magnitude of the evil they were up against.[304]

Lonely, confused and unable to relate to their parents; kids escaped into an anarchistic world of Sex, Drugs and Rock & Roll. The disillusioned youth rejected the materialism of their parents and vowed not to trust anyone over thirty. Liberal college professors fanned the fires of their youthful

---

[302] *Masonry* – teaches a naturalistic deistic religion which is in conflict with Christian doctrine. The papal declaration *Quaesitum est* forbids Catholics from joining Masonic organizations & asserts that those who join are in a state of grave sin & may not receive Holy Communion. Joseph Cardinal Ratzinger who later became Pope Benedict XVI issued the declaration in 1983. Contrary to Masonic propaganda, *Quaesitum est* is still in effect.
[303] *Marquis de Sade* – is best known for his erotic novels, which combined philosophical discourse with pornography, depicting bizarre sexual fantasies with an emphasis on violence, criminality & blasphemy against the Catholic Church. *Donatien Alphonse François, Marquis de Sade* was a proponent of extreme freedom, unrestrained by morality, religion or law. Sade was a homosexual pedophile who was incarcerated in various prisons & in an insane asylum for 32 years. The term *sadism* is derived from his name. (1740-1814)
[304] *Warren Commission* – was established by Lyndon B. Johnson to investigate the assassination of President John F. Kennedy. It concluded that Lee Harvey Oswald acted alone in the killing of Kennedy & that Jack Ruby acted alone in the murder of Oswald. The Commission's findings were challenged by later studies & remain controversial. A November 1963 Gallup poll found that 52 % of Americans believed there was a conspiracy to kill Kennedy & today 70 % know in their hearts it was a conspiracy.

student's passions and misdirected their genuine quest for answers toward an amoral Brave New World.[305]

Teachers slam-dunked the values of parents, characterizing them as repressive and advocated replacing their values with more progressive ideas, like free love and communal living. In response, hippies began moving into cheap row houses in the cities, so they could live together in a less materialistic society. The only problem was that their migration gobbled up the limited supply of housing and drove up the price of rental agreements. The sudden surge in population, made possible by the influx of spoiled little white kids from the suburbs, was not well received by poor blacks already struggling to survive in the ghetto. The only economic plus to the whole migration was that the progeny of the affluent were also looking to buy drugs. Local pushers were all too happy to accommodate them, but turf wars broke out among suppliers and turned the once quiet neighborhoods into life threatening danger zones. In addition, naive suburbanites became easy prey for muggers. In order to protect themselves, some of the formerly peace-loving hippies began packing heat.

The utopian society spoken of by their college professors was not exactly coming to fruition, but the hippies were not ready to give up the dream. Figuring their failure in urban communities had more to do with the metropolitan nature of the environment than it did with the concept; they left the cities almost as quickly as they had arrived. The reformers decided it was time to go up to the country[306] and begin again. The term utopia actually comes from a mythical society that Sir Thomas More wrote about in his book <u>Of the</u>

---

[305] *Brave New World* – is a novel by Aldous Huxley, which anticipated developments in reproductive technology & other radical changes in a futuristic society devoid of morals.
[306] *Going Up the Country* – is a song that was written by Alan Wilson, performed by Canned Heat & released on 10/28/67. It captured the mood of the hippies quick exodus from the cities & included such lyrics as: *I'm going where the water tastes like wine, I'm gonna leave this city, got to get away* & *All this fussing & fighting, man, you know I sure can't stay.*

Best State of a Republic, and of the New Island Utopia. However, in 1516 More was writing an allegory and like his beloved Catholic Church, he did not believe a state of perfection was possible here on earth. Yet, college professors continued to push utopian societies as plausible and the disoriented, idealistic youth persisted in trying to build them.

Two of the most powerful groups dominating the music scene were The Beatles and The Rolling Stones. In 1967, shortly after the British invasion landed in America with Sergeant Pepper's Lonely Hearts Club Band,[307] the Stones presented Their Satanic Majesties Request album.[308] By 1968, the messages of the dynamic duo moved even further into the occult. Influenced by Maharishi Mahesh Yogi,[309] the Beatles got cracking with their White Album,[310] while the Stones promoted some Sympathy for the Devil.[311] Along with the rest of the British Music Invasion,[312] came boatloads of bohemian fashions. Throughout the sixties, nearly every stylish young woman in the western world wore a mini-skirt and by the end of the decade the androgynous look was everywhere. Frayed bell-bottomed jeans, tie-dye shirts and headbands, became a kind of uniform, as shoes gave way to sandals and dark suits were replaced with buckskin vests and paisley shirts. Some women went braless

---

[307] *Sergeant Pepper's Lonely Hearts Club Band* - is the 8th studio album by The Beatles, which was released in June 1967.

[308] *Their Satanic Majesties Request* – is the 6th studio album produced by The Rolling Stones & was released in the U.S. on December 9,1967 by London Records. Its title is a play on the words "Her Britannic Majesty requests & requires..." this text appears on the inside cover of a British passport.

[309] *Maharishi Mahesh Yogi* – was the guru of TM or the Transcendental Meditation movement in the 1960s & was known for influencing celebrities. He also became known as the "Beatles guru". (1917-2008)

[310] *White Album* – sometimes called their "tension album" it reflected the first cracks in the unity of the Beatles & included the wildly frenetic "Helter Skelter," which approached heavy metal & became infamous, as one of serial killer Charles Manson's favorite songs.

[311] *Sympathy for the Devil* – is a song performed by The Rolling Stones, written by Mick Jagger & Keith Richards, which first appeared on the band's 1968 album *Beggars Banquet*. Rolling Stone magazine placed it at #32 in their list of the 500 Greatest Songs of All Time.

[312] *British Music Invasion* – described a large number of rock & roll, beat & pop performers from the UK, who became popular in the US, from 1964-1966.

and sex appeal was used to market everything from Mustangs to Pepsi.

I was neither immune to the call of the wild, nor prepared to deal effectively with its temptations. While visiting my friends in Jersey, we stopped in at Blankenbush's Drug Store to buy our first pack of cigarettes and our first Playboy magazine. A few weeks later I attended the Junior High School Dance. It took half the evening, to get up enough courage to ask a girl to dance, but somewhere in the middle of our third slow dance Kate Taylor, introduced me to the French Kiss. Kate was a voluptuous young woman and her full body hug, disguised as a Waltz, lit a fire in me that blazed throughout my high school years and beyond. Prior to the dance I had never even seen Kate, yet we were acting as if we had known each other for years. That miniscule taste of honey made me wonder what it would be like to kiss Rebecca in the same way. It would not be long before I would get the opportunity to find out.

Sarah told me about a semi-formal Christmas Ball at the Indian Valley Junior High School. She asked if I wanted to take Rebecca and I readily agreed. Sarah made arrangements for her girlfriend to stay overnight and we attended the Winter Wonderland dance with my sister and some guy named Freddy. The four of us enjoyed the evening together and continued our foursome after returning home. Rebecca and I sat together in an overstuffed chair in the living room holding on to one another and kidding around with Sarah and her date, while he waited for his ride. When he left Sarah felt like a fifth wheel. Knowing the two of us wanted to be alone; she suggested we take our cuddling out to the cabin.[313]

Although we wore heavy winter coats, in the dead of the night the cabin felt like an icebox, but it was better than

---

[313] *Cabin* – the building was actually a chicken coop, located behind the house & had been converted into a small cabin. It had a picture window that looked out over the creek. The place was paneled on the inside & it heated by a Franklin stove.

hanging out with my sister in the brightly lit living room. French kisses served to distract us from the frigid air, while we impatiently waited for the flames in the Franklin stove to warm our little snuggery. Sensual desire kindled quickly and kept pace with the blazing fire and the steadily rising temperature of the room. At long last the cabin was comfortable enough for me to shed my parka. Peeling back the fur collar of her coat I gently kissed the side of Rebecca's neck and she gasped! We both paused for a moment and then I backed away to look into her eyes. Ever so slowly she guided my hand to the outside of her thick woolen sweater and enveloped my fingers around one of her voluptuous breasts. For a split second we pondered the unfamiliar territory we were about to explore. Except for the crackling of the fire; the room was absolutely silent. As I tenderly squeezed her bosom she let go with a deep tranquil sigh. The ecstatic cooing repeated itself following every tender stroke. Suddenly without warning, she pressed her whole body up against mine. She began drinking in my kisses with the inhalation of someone who had just found an oasis in the Sahara desert. Seconds later our legs were intertwined, my hands migrated up under her sweater and my fingers roamed freely across the warm surface of her soft supple skin. Following the initial befuddlement of a novice, I managed to unhook her bra and began to familiarize myself with every beautiful contour of her bountiful breasts. Our passionate frenzy eventually gave way to a gentler style of kissing. Like the glowing orange embers beneath the iron grate, our satiated appetites cooled in tandem with the flames in the Franklin stove. Reluctantly, we retrieved our coats and returned to the house.

Sarah met us in the kitchen angrily whispering, "Where have you been?" Actually she knew exactly were we were and had a pretty good idea about the seriousness of the sin we had just engaged in; but she was also relieved to see us back in the house again. One last kiss good night and Rebecca disappeared up the stairs following my sister into her bedroom.

I never knew what Sarah said to Rebecca that night in her bedroom, but I have my suspicions. Phone calls to Becky were not returned and my letters went unanswered. My sister had a much more objective vantage point than I did. Sarah could see where this was headed and at the cost of the relationship with her girlfriend, she had put the kibosh on our budding romance. Unfortunately, my sister's costly gesture would not be enough to stem the tide of promiscuity for either of us. The forces arrayed against our generation were just too numerous, disguised and powerful. A few weeks later, I heard it through the grapevine[314] that Rebecca was going out with some older guy, over at Souderton High School. Sadly, I never saw my sweetheart again.

My first sexual encounter could hardly be called love; but it sure felt like it. Rebecca was no stranger. We had been pen pals for over a year and my feelings for her were genuine. Technically I guess you could say it was lust, but not in the full sense of the word. Although the encounter was decidedly pleasurable, my only intention throughout the entire evening was simply to please Rebecca. Her affectionate gestures seemed equally magnanimous. So what was driving this sexual blitzkrieg?

The hormonal arousal of sexual desire during the teenage years is pretty normal. After all this attraction is what keeps the human race going. A God given longing to love and be loved, helps us to break down the long established natural barriers between younger boys and girls, but this natural courtship is supposed to happen ever so gradually. As a rule, our moral training, natural inhibitions and even our insecurities, assist in guiding us gently through the mate

---

[314] *I Heard It Through The Grapevine* – written by Norman Whitfield & Barrett Strong, performed by Marvin Gaye, Tamla Records 10/30/68.

selection process, as we develop into adults and form families of our own. Unfortunately, that's not what was going on here. Thanks to the sexually permissive drilling Rebecca received while practicing lines for her sensual part in Anything Goes and my equally damaging experience back at boarding school, both of us had experienced a violation of the Latency Period.[315] Tragically, we were not alone in this premature exposure to sexuality. The constant drumbeat of the lyrics in music, illicit imaging on TV and the pictures in magazines, as well as the fashions, all militated against normal sexual development.

In his inaugural address, Nixon pledged Peace with Honor in Vietnam. The Age of Aquarius[316] seemed like it had finally arrived. Although Tricky Dick was re-elected in 1972, the defeat in Vietnam and the scandal of Watergate would lead to his resignation on August 9, 1974.[317] Unfortunately, the Plumbers[318] were not the only mischief-makers. Ever since their protest of the Miss America Pageant, feminists and a plethora of political activists began tying their causes together under the single banner of freedom.[319] Women, blacks, queers, the poor and the anti-war crowd, all saw the established order as oppressive. Progressives sought to break loose from their oppressors by completing their take-over of the entertainment industry. Raquel Welch pined away for her black lover in the movie 100 Rifles,[320] tying feminism and

---

[315] Latency Period – is that period of time between childhood & puberty, when sexual development remains dormant.
[316] *Aquarius/Let the Sunshine In* – was a single released in 1969, by The 5th Dimension, on Soul City Records. It was a medley of two songs from the musical *Hair*. The song, written by James Rado, Gerome Ragni & Galt MacDermot was based on the astrological belief that the world would be entering the *Age of Aquarius*, an age of love, light & humanity. It held the #1 position on Billboard for six weeks & went Platinum.
[317] *Watergate* – was a political scandal resulting from the burglary of the Democratic National Committee headquarters at the Watergate hotel & led to Nixon's resignation.
[318] *The Plumbers* – were members of a covert Special Investigations Unit who got caught burglarizing the Democratic National Committee headquarters at the Watergate hotel.
[319] *Miss America Protest* – While it came to be known as the "bra burning protest", no bra was burned that day, although a bra was thrown into a trash can, along with other feminine products, symbolizing male oppression. The story was later linked to draft card burning.
[320] *100 Rifles* – was a 1969 romantic western directed by Tom Gries with music composed by Jerry Goldsmith, staring: Jim Brown, Burt Reynolds, Raquel Welch & Fernando Lamas.

the civil rights movement to the sexual revolution. Midnight Cowboy[321] attempted to normalized homosexuality and I am Curious Yellow[322] sought to legitimize graphic sexual scenes in movies. This legitimacy was highlighted when Jackie Onassis publicly attended the premier opening and the Supreme Court declared that pornography was free speech.[323] Following their lead in the cinema Broadway's opening salvo was Oh! Calcutta![324] This outrageous assault on moral sensibilities included a virtual orgy on stage. Yet even this depravity was just the beginning. On June 28, 1969, New York's finest raided a queer speak-easy in Greenwich Village called The Stonewall Inn.[325] When the gay community resisted the arrests, police called for backup and a four-day riot ensued. Activists for all of these groups published newspapers and called for confrontational tactics to meet their objectives. One month later Charles Manson, using the same idea, attempted to start a race war on the West Coast.[326]

All this upheaval created an intense longing for peace. Nowhere would that hunger for peace and freedom be more

---

[321] *Midnight Cowboy* – is a 1969 dramatic film based on the 1965 novel by James Leo Herlihy. It was written by Waldo Salt & directed by John Schlesinger. The film was the first X-rated movie to win the Oscar.
[322] *I Am Curious Yellow* – was a 1967 Swedish film directed by Vilgot Sjöman & starring Lena Nyman. Nudity, explicit sex & controversial politics kept this film from being shown in the United States, while its seizure by Customs was appealed.
[323] *Byrne v. Karalexis* –Supreme Court of the U.S., 396 U.S. 976, 1969.
[324] *Oh! Calcutta!* – was an avant-garde theatrical revue, created by British drama critic Kenneth Tynan. The show, consisting of sketches on sex-related topics, debuted Off-Broadway in 1969 & then in London in 1970. It was the longest-running revue in Broadway history. The show sparked considerable controversy at the time, because it featured extended scenes of total nudity, both male & female. The title is taken from a painting by Clovis Trouille, itself a pun on "O quel cul t'as!" French for "What an arse you have!"
[325] *The Stonewall Inn* – is a bar located at 53 Christopher St., between West 4th St. & Waverly Place, in Greenwich Village, NYC. The Stonewall riots were a series of spontaneous, violent demonstrations against a police raid on the gay bar, which began on June 28, 1969. Gay Pride day commemorates this date & place, which are widely considered to be the starting point of the modern gay liberation movement.
[326] *Charles Manson* – a white supremacist sociopath, inspired by *The Beatles* song *Helter Skelter*, along with groupies from his commune, began a reign of terror, by conspiring & carrying out the Tate/LaBianca murders. Charles intended to make it look like blacks did the gruesome murders, in order to start a race war in Los Angeles.

evident than at the Woodstock Music & Art Fair.[327] Originally marketed as an outdoor concert for one-hundred and fifty to two-hundred thousand people, it wound up being a free concert that drew over a half a million young people from all over the country. Using sex, drugs and Rock & Roll, progressive reformers arrayed their forces against the establishment. Throngs of young people clogged the highways on their way to the concert, which made the event a top news story. Prior to the first note being played, reporters interviewed hippie-hating hard liners who mocked the youthful utopian dreams and predicted a self-destructive riot. Many feared the worst. Some Americans prayed, while others licked their chops and looked forward to the demise of the idealistic malcontents. Like the calm before a storm, Americans watched and waited; holding their breath and tuning in to see what would happen.

On Friday the fifteenth day of August in 1969, Richie Havens[328] opened the pivotal concert with Motherless Child.[329] He continued to play for three hours straight, because none of the other bands had showed up yet. They were all stuck in traffic. Finally thirty-two bands arrived to entertain a mass of humanity for three days in relative peace and harmony. Thousands of scantily clad kids demonstrated by their actions that the culture war was well underway and virtually unstoppable. Music fans alternately braved rain, mud and the hot summer sun. There was limited access to food, water and medical services. Sanitation facilities were completely overwhelmed and promoters lost money, but the

---

[327] *Woodstock Music & Art Fair* – was a music festival, billed as "An Aquarian Exposition: 3 Days of Peace & Music", which was held at Max Yasgur's 600-acre dairy farm near Bethel, NY, from August 15-18 in the summer of 1969. During the sometimes-rainy weekend, 32 acts performed outdoors in front of 500,000 fans. It is widely regarded as one of the greatest & most pivotal moments in popular music history & was listed among Rolling Stone's 50 Moments That Changed the History of Rock & Roll.

[328] *Richie Havens* – is an American folk singer & guitarist who is best known for his intense rhythmic guitar style, soulful pop & folk songs & his opening performance at the 1969 Woodstock Festival. (1941-Present)

[329] *Motherless Child* – is a traditional Negro spiritual, which dates back to the era of slavery in the United States when it was a common practice to sell children of slaves & take them away from their parents.

youth of the nation had peacefully and successfully stormed the Bastille.[330]

Woodstock shocked the nation, but it also impressed them. In spite of over five-hundred thousand people, limited provisions and highly charged emotions, the police reported only a few minor arrests. In a country where the world's largest superpower could not end a war, hippies had demonstrated the ability to live in harmony. And in a country where materialism was seen as an ideal, the children of wealth had illustrated how much fun it was to live with less. On the surface all looked well, but beneath the celebratory mood, the tectonic plates of time-tested traditions were being violently tilted away from Christianity. Hidden in plain sight was a spiritual invasion of epic proportions. Swami Satchidananda was choosen to give the opening invocation for the festival. Most of the attendees were high on grass and pharmaceuticals were in plentiful supply. Thousands tripped on LSD for the entire weekend, leading many to later remark, "If you remember the sixties, you probably weren't there." Wholesale promiscuity reigned. There was an orgy of nude bathing, provocative dancing and copulating couples in pup tents. The bathhouses of Rome couldn't hold a candle to this crowd.

I had no special attraction to the hippy culture of the Woodstock Festival, until I happened upon a copy of Life magazine and a feature article about communes caught my eye.[331] Although still on my summer vacation, I decided to make up my own report on the subject. Admittedly the picture of a naked woman bathing her child in a creek drew my attention, but as I read the article and assembled my project, I became more and more curious about alternative

---

[330] *The Storming of the Bastille* – occurred in Paris on the 14th of July in 1789. The medieval fortress & prison in Paris known as the Bastille represented royal authority & while the prison only contained 7 prisoners at the time its fall became the flashpoint of the French Revolution. In like manner, Woodstock became the iconic flashpoint of the Sexual Revolution in America.

[331] *The Commune Comes To America*, Life magazine, July 18, 1969.

religions and a simpler way of life. Further research led me to another article on premarital sex.[332] Already traveling on the road to perdition, this liberal propaganda encouraged me to question the moral teachings of my youth.[333] I still wanted to save myself for marriage, but was redefining what "save myself" actually meant.

The convenient interpretation I came up with to justify my recent dating activity moved the line back from avoiding all impure thoughts, to not engaging in sexual intercourse. Then on August 25, 1969, in the midst of my crisis of faith; I was asked to be Godfather to my baby cousin Rose Thornton. I guess from God's perspective it was timely, but I felt like my Uncle Tom and Aunt Katie had picked the wrong man. Even so, I felt honored to have been chosen and did my best, to answer the questions for my little cousin and try to reaffirm my own faith.

It could have been a turning point for me, but the moral underpinnings of family life were being challenged across the country. Sex and drug education classes were being taught in the public high schools and no-fault divorce became the law in California.[334] Soon hundreds of men started trading in their wives for new ones like cars. Drugs were everywhere and recreational sex seemed to be a normal part of every dating situation.

The same bus that transported us to Pennfield Junior High also took us to the high school at North Penn. Since the rough boys generally sat in the back of the bus and the girls sat in the front, I picked a seat in the middle. That left me out of the range of the bullies and close enough to the front to talk with the girls. Sarah introduced me to her new friend

---

[332] *But Mom We're In Love*, Woman's Day magazine, 1969.
[333] *CCC 2396* – Among the sins gravely contrary to chastity are masturbation, fornication, pornography & homosexual practices.
[334] *Family Law Act of 1969* – California law that made "No-fault" divorce easier to obtain. Gov. Ronald Regan signed the No Fault bill into law on September 4, 1969.

Lesley Wright. Although I often dreamed of dating her she never really saw me in that light, but we did become very good friends. I also met Jon Baker and Jessie Allen. Jon was a tough hombre from Texas. He smoked cigarettes and could beat the crap out of anyone, but I never saw him pick a fight. He did finish quite a few fights though, skillfully using a pair of black army boots and a spring-loaded stiletto. I didn't like the guy at first because he had a thing for my sister, but he grew on me and proved to be a loyal friend. Jessie on the other hand was a clown. Although he sat in the back of the bus with the tough guys, his bark was much worse than his bite and he really was a funny guy. Quite often he drew cartoon caricatures of our bus driver. His illustrations, along with their comical captions, created the impression that quiet Mrs. Ashley, who was already in her sixties, raced a supercharged funny car version of our school bus at the Atco Speedway over in Jersey on the weekends. I spent endless hours after school with these two motor heads, but my weekends were still reserved for my friends in the Garden State.[335] Morally, my life was torn between my strict Catholic upbringing and the secular society that surrounded me, which was hell-bent on destroying Christianity. Socially, I was lost between two shores.[336]

---

[335] *Garden State* – is the official nickname of New Jersey, so named because of her bountiful truck farming agribusiness, especially with regard to Campbell Soup Company.
[336] *I Am...I Said* – is a song written & sung by Neil Diamond & released as a single in March 1971. One of his most intensely personal efforts, it depicts the singer lost between two worlds: "*Well, I'm New York City born and raised, but nowadays, I'm lost between two shores, L.A.'s fine, but it ain't home* — New York's home but it ain't mine no more..."

Chapter 15

Meltdown

Serious difficulties were on the horizon for my father. Economic instability at work and issues surrounding the death of my grandmother were bubbling to the surface for the Leader of the Band.[337] Dad started getting into psychology and wanted me to partake of the popular pseudoscience. He sent me to the Penn Foundation for Mental Health. I saw no need for the counseling sessions and resented being looked upon as some kind of mental midget. Despite my misgivings, I agreed to go anyway out of a sense of wanting to please my father and also to find out for myself what this therapy thing was all about.

The aroma of cherry tobacco filled the air in the room, as I answered the doctor's questions. He puffed away on a mahogany pipe that protruded from his black wooly beard. But he seemed more fixated on cleaning out his pipe every few minutes, than he did about addressing any of my concerns. Most of his questions seemed inane to me. The entire field of psychology was a relatively new profession. The medical community openly attacked their competition and questioned whether psychology was even a real science. Insurance companies refused to cover their services and most doctors referred to psychologists as quacks. These therapists saw guilt as the source of almost every psychological problem. Although pretty close to the mark, they had no authority to forgive sins, so they attempted to unburden their patients by telling them that there was no such thing as sin and didn't have to feel guilty about anything. These new age advisors were actively usurping the role of the priest in the

---

[337] *Leader of the Band* – is a song written by Dan Fogelberg from his 1981 album The Innocent Age. The song was written as a tribute to his father Lawrence Fogelberg, a musician & the leader of a band. Lawrence was still alive at the time the song was released.

confessional. Unlike parish priests, they charged big bucks for their services and had a powerful financial incentive to keep their patients coming back. I stopped going to see the shrink after only a few visits, because I though he and his profession were pathetically fraudulent.

Dad was also worried about work. Westinghouse was his primary customer and they kept reducing the size and quantity of their orders. It looked as if Callahan Machine Company would soon go out of business. He not only anguished over taking care of his family, but was equally tormented by the forthcoming fate of his employees and their families. Scrambling to find a solution, he decided to attend a business leadership-training seminar at Princeton University.[338] The three-day curriculum was taught by the likes of Abraham Maslow,[339] Fritz Perls[340] and a team of trainers from the Esalen Institute.[341] Under the guise of introducing business improvement techniques, the avantguard gurus agressivly utilized an unorthodox teaching technique known as Gestalt Therapy. Esalen Institute was on the leading edge of the counterculture movement of the sixties. Their novel programs included an admix of social experiments involving: alternative forms of psychology, sociology and religion. Most of their sessions were sexually based and since resident teaching positions were readily

---

[338] *Princeton University* – is a private research university located in Princeton, NJ. The school is one of the 8 universities of the Ivy League & is 1 of the 9 Colonial Colleges founded before the American Revolution. Princeton provides undergraduate & graduate instruction in the humanities, social sciences, natural sciences & engineering.

[339] *Abraham Maslow* – was an American psychologist noted for his conceptualization of a "hierarchy of human needs". He is considered the founder of humanistic psychology, but Conservative social critic Christina Hoff Sommers has asserted that Maslow is no longer taken seriously in the world of academic psychology. (1908-1970)

[340] *Fritz Perls* – was a noted German-born psychiatrist & psychotherapist of Jewish descent. Friedrich Salomon Perls coined the term "Gestalt Therapy" to identify a form of psychotherapy, which he & his wife Laura developed in the 40s & 50s. He became associated with the Esalen Institute in 1964 & he lived there until 1969. (1893-1970)

[341] *Esalen Institute* – is a retreat center in Big Sur, CA, which describes itself as being devoted to multidisciplinary studies ordinarily neglected or unfavored by traditional academia in subjects ranging from meditation to massage, Gestalt, yoga, psychology, ecology, spirituality, art & music. Michael Murphy founded the institute with Dick Price in 1962, with the goal of exploring work in the humanities & sciences that would advance the full realization of what Aldous Huxley called the Human Potential.

available, it soon became the Mecca for experiential workshops. The most notorious leader at the Institute was a college professor by the name of Timothy Leary.[342] This Berkeley graduate opined that everyone in the country should trip on LSD in order to reach their fullest potential. He also thought that the use of the drug would finally produce the ever illusive utopian society.

As the year approached its conclusion, so did the reality of closing the shop. Other than a few part-time jobs as a kid and his life guard experience at the shore; my father had never been employed outside of the family business. If Callahan Machine Company closed its doors; how would he support his wife and eight children? The question dogged him and he was running out of answers. Trying to picture what loosing his business would look like; he began to worry about what the neighbors would think of him. The idea of becoming destitute overwhelmed him. He found it almost impossible to sleep, so he walked down stairs to the kitchen. Pulling out a bottle from the cabinet, he began pouring himself shots of Southern Comfort.[343] With each successive drink, he tried to picture what living without an income would look like. The frightening images that he conjured up only increased his pain and made his predicament seem all the more dire. Eventually he by-passed the glass and drank straight from the bottle.

Throwing on a winter coat, he walked outside in the cold to clear his head. Traversing two-inches of tundra, which crunched beneath his shoes; he walked across the driveway to the field on the other side of the barn. Despite the frigid wind that burned his face and the exposure of his frozen red

---

[342] *Dr. Timothy Francis Leary* – was an American writer, psychologist, futurist & advocate of psychedelic drug research. An icon of 1960s counterculture, Leary is most famous as a proponent of the therapeutic, spiritual & emotional benefits of LSD. He coined & popularized the catch phrase "Turn on, tune in, drop out." (1920–1996)
[343] *Southern Comfort* – is a fruit, spice & whiskey flavored American liqueur made from neutral spirits & was first produced in 1874. The brand was created by bartender Martin Wilkes Heron in New Orleans, when he wanted to make a better tasting whiskey.

fist; he desperately clung to his half-empty bottle of booze. My father looked out over the field and down the hill to the creek. The full moon reflected off the ice and the trees along the windbreak cast their shadows across the banks of the small stream. Tilting his head back to take another swig, he marveled at the contrasting clarity of a navy blue sky that was speckled with the bright white stars of the Milky Way.

"Why?" he shouted, "Why me?... Why now?... What about Theresa and the kids... Don't you give a shit?" The only audible response was a sudden gust of wind, which blew some light powdery snow off the barn roof. Inebriated and assaulted by polar winds his entire face was numb. Once again he raised a chapped frozen fist to his lips and took another sip. Looking across the street toward the newlywed's ranch house, he wondered what his neighbors would think of him if he failed to support his family. The humiliating conclusion prompted him to upend the bottle.

Cornered, alone and fighting back tears; he threw the bottle into a galvanized trashcan on the side of the barn and went back into the house. Even an entire bottle of whiskey had not been enough of a sedative to lessen the pain he was feeling. Walking into the living room, he threw down his overcoat on the sofa. Quietly he opened the gun cabinet and removed a .45 caliber pistol. To a man who had won dozens of ribbons and trophies target shooting, the grip fit comfortably in his hand. Picking up a box of shells he loaded the clip, as he had done over a thousand times before. He slid the magazine into the handle with the heel of his hand. Click! He paused for a second to see if anyone upstairs heard the noise. Hearing nothing, he pulled back the slide, bringing the bullet up into the chamber. Having found no way out of his dilemma; he placed the muzzle against his temple and felt the cold hard steel press against his flesh. Gritting his teeth and bracing for the end, he paused to reflect on his pending demise. "If I commit suicide;" he wondered, "will people think I was a coward?" How ironic; here he was about to kill himself and the man was still worried about what the neighbors would think. Suddenly he laughed out loud and said, "I don't give a shit what the neighbors think! Come to think of it; I'm never gonna care what anyone thinks about me ever again." Lowering the weapon, he popped out the clip, unloaded the chamber and put his pistol back in the cabinet. Lying down on the sofa, he pulled his winter coat up over his shoulders and drifted off to sleep.

By the time dad woke up from his terrible nightmare we had already left for school. He got a shower while mom made him some soft-boiled eggs. Then his wife asked him why he was sleeping on the couch, but the only thing he owned up to was that he was having some trouble getting to sleep last night. He cheerfully kissed her before running off to work, as if it were just another day; but everything had changed. As soon as he arrived at work, he asked Amelia Jones to get him the file from the business leadership seminar he had attended at Princeton University. When she brought it into the office, he pulled out a catalog for the Esalen retreat seminars in Big Sur, California. Then he instructed Amelia to cancel all his appointments, sign him up for a two-month retreat and make all the travel arrangements. Come January my flattop, crew cut, conservative, businessman father, with the dark rimmed glasses; boarded a TWA jet in Philadelphia bound for California. Although I hardly even noticed his departure, the father I had grown up with and had learned to love was gone and would never return again.

A couple of months later mom summoned the courage to brave the highways and drove down to Philadelphia to pick my father up at the airport. Waiting by the gate she perused the parade of passengers and looked for her husband. When he finally emerged from the gangway she didn't even recognize him. Figuring he must have missed the flight, she looked over the crowd one last time and then noticed a strange man off in the corner. He wore a straw hat and was playing a bamboo flute. The nonconformist looked like a beatnik from Borneo. He had a full head of dark wavy hair, a jet black beard, flowered pants and love beads dangling from his neck. A pendant also hung from a rawhide shoestring and was draped over an Hawaiian shirt. Although she didn't know any hippies, something about this odd man looked vaguely familiar. Squinting her eyes, she hesitantly inquired in a soft voice, "Tom? Is that you?" Looking up sideways from his bowed head, he flashed a mischievous grin. Refocusing his eyes on the flute, he waved it back and forth like a snake charmer and slowly made his way over to the curious but apprehensive young woman. "Hi Theresa" he said prompting her hand to reflexively cover her mouth. She didn't know whether to laugh or cry. Was he just playing around or had he gone stark raving mad? Who was this strange character? She had no idea what to make of this man that was obviously flirting with her.

The rest of our family was no better at handling dad's transformation than mom was and in the weeks that followed many more things would change. One statement of his would rock the very foundation of everything we had ever been taught. Dad announced that, "If you want to tell a lie, its ok." We had always been taught that honesty was the best policy. In fact, the worst infraction anyone could ever make was to tell a lie. The policy was so engrained in me that I would rather tell on myself, than risk getting caught deceiving my father. Dad often related a story to us about how the Indians cut out the tongues of liars; and now it was suddenly ok? Not only were the rules being changed, but so was our physical environment. Dad had us clean out the living room, ripping up our wall-to-wall carpet and replacing it with a drab green and white shag carpet. He hung ruby and gold love beads in the doorway, placed a black light on the mantle, wallpapered zodiac posters on the ceiling and overstuffed pillows replaced our sofa and chairs. When the project was finished I walked into the kitchen and asked my mother, "What's up with Dad?" With a pained, tearful and whining voice she said, "I don't know."

In an attempt to explain his behavior, my father shared the story of his attempted suicide with me as well as his struggles growing up. He said he often lied to the nuns and his neighbors, who had been requested by his father to keep an eye on him when he was starting the machine business. Dad told me how guilty he felt when he attempted to get out from under their scrutiny by lying. He told me he didn't want his children to experience the same type of guilty feelings and besides, he no longer considered it a sin. Dad went back to the Esalen Institute a few months later to experience another set of workshops and when he returned he signed up for local encounter groups, gestalt therapy sessions and sensitivity seminars almost every other weekend. Each new forum taught him another set of psychological techniques, which he gleefully tried out on the rest of our family.

Wanting to please their daddy, most of my siblings went along with the exercises, but I stubbornly refused to be manipulated. One of the most potent demands he made was his requirement that we use the words, "I want..." at the beginning of every request. The phraseology allowed him to either grant the boon or not without the pressure of feeling guilty for not rescuing us. It was a clear form of communication that worked well for him, but it was also devoid of any decorum. These strait-jacketed phrases made me feel like I had to jump through his hoops in order to get what I needed. It was a burdensome game and I had no intensions of playing along. Instead I made it a point to be direct in all my requests, demonstrating a clear understanding of the concept, but at the same time I religiously avoided the rigid phraseology.

Although my friends thought it was cool to have a hippy for a father, his abrupt change in direction apeared to threaten the stability of our family. Following each weekend seminar, our house rules became more and more relaxed. In my mind, dad was abdicating his responsibility and someone had to take charge. Since I was the eldest, I felt it was incumbent upon me to take the reins. Although I knew it was a usurpation of authority, it seemed necessary until some sense of sanity resurfaced. This immediately set up a power struggle and dad confronted me about commandeering his rightful command. I told him I would stop calling the shots when he started acting like an adult again. Naturally, my "grow up" speech didn't go over very well and dad countered by telling all the other kids they didn't have to do anything I told them to.

Dad egalitarian ideas destroyed the pecking order of our family. He instructed each child that they were all equal and that the only authority they ever had to listen to was him or my mom. I ignored his directive and whenever any of the kids defied me, I thundered back at them until they complied. The sofa soon became my throne and the symbol of my authority. I threw anyone off the couch who did not relinquish their seat the minute I entered the living room. Although my brothers hated me for it, after a few aggressive take-downs, I reestablished the pecking order.

Ever since my father told me about his suicide attempt, I thought he might try it again. With little understanding about financial instruments like life insurance, I thought that in the event of his death, the entire responsibility of taking care of our family would fall to me. I wanted to go out looking for a job, but the first thing I needed was some wheels. On April 22, 1970, I passed the written portion of my driving test and secured a Junior Learners Permit. Early the following month, I also passed the driving test and was issued a Junior Operators License.

Although I still felt responsible for the leadership role in our family and hadn't backed off my original confrontational stance with my father, the balance of power was about to shift. Whenever I asked to borrow the family car to get to work or go out on a date, dad would say "We'll see." After a couple of days I asked again and he would say, "Want a quick answer?" which of course meant no. It soon became aparent that without my own car, I could never maintain a steady job. I would have to get a different job; one that was within walking distance.

Our seven acre farm was smack in the middle of an industrial park, so I went door to door looking for employment. The first job I landed was with the Nice Ball Bearing Company. It was less than a mile from our house. I began working as a laborer in their inspection department. Men generally ran the machines that made the ball bearings and the women subsequently inspected the component parts. My task was to cart barrels of finished products over to a small elevator, which lifted the barrel up and poured the parts onto a table for inspection. I got along well with both my boss and the ladies. Each day a loud buzzer would sound to announce the beginning and end of shifts, breaks and our lunch hour. The work was physically exhausting and during the breaks I found some stacks of cardboard boxes in a back room to lay down on and take a nap.

An old fat guy with a big cigar, often walked around the plant and I never saw him do a lick of work, but for some reason he never got into any trouble. One day he walked over to our department and all the women started fussing over him, like he was some kind of rock star or something. He was short of stature and one of the women put her arm around him, pasted a great big smile on her face and said, "What do you think of our new union president?" Glancing up from my work I said, "I think he's a bum." The next day while washing up for lunch at a big round sink in the men's room, two goons started crowding me. At first I thought it was an accident, but they continued to squeeze in closer and elbowed me while they washed their hands. Finally, I pushed them both away and thought I was about to get my ass kicked. To my surprise they just laughed, dried off their hands and walked away. I figured it was some kind of a test of my metal, but I would soon find out differently.

Later that afternoon the boss said that he would have to let me go. I was slack-jawed! Assuming the layoff had something to do with the economy I asked him why. He simply repeated that he had to let me go. Puzzled by the response, I asked if he was happy with my work, to which he replied, "Oh sure. It has nothing to do with your work." A pained look covered his face and I decided to ask him point blank, "Am I being fired?" Although he was silent, the answer was obviously yes. Suspecting some foul play I blurted out, "On what grounds?" He looked down at the floor and said, "Sleeping on the job." When I asked him what he was talking about, he said that someone had complained they saw me sleeping on cardboard boxes. "Oh, is that all it is?" I told him I was sleeping on my break. "The guys do not get breaks" he said, "Only the women do." I told him I didn't know that and promised not to do it again. Frustrated, he raised his voice and said, "Look, I just have to let you go. The union wants you out and they're threatening to walk out, if I don't fire you. We can't afford to deal with a wildcat strike right now. I'm Sorry."

There was an absence of malice in his eyes and it was obvious he felt real bad about it, but short of being fired himself there wasn't a whole lot he could do. The owners of the company were in a tough spot too, but I still saw them as cowards. On my way out I had to run the gauntlet past the union president and his two goons, who were standing by the back door and laughing at me. All I could do was glare back at them with disgust and walk out. Coming from an ethical business family, where workers were treated fairly, I never saw the need for unions. It may be snobish, but I knew I was better than these lazy union workers, the pathetic potentate and his low-life henchmen. I held my head high and left with my dignity intact, but the crushing reality was that two weeks into my first minimum wage job, I had been fired. I didn't feel like a very good provider. Still determined to make my own money I looked in the want ads of the newspaper, but there were no jobs for a kid my age.

Dad had always taught me, "Don't get a job. Make a job." Businesses are organized around three things: land, labor and capital. Since I had very little money, but lived on a farm and was physically able to work, I began by digging a large garden in the field next to our barn. While slaving away in the hot summer sun a local farmer drove by on his tractor and stopped to ask me how I was doing. Happy for the break I bagan chewing the fat with him. When he was about to leave I asked him how much it would cost for him to plow my field. He offered to do the job for five bucks. I thought it was a steal and gave him ten. He not only plowed up the sod, but disked and cultivated the dirt into a fine powder. I drove to The Store[344] and purchased seeds for several assorted vegetables and bought seventy-two tomato plants. I was officially in business, but plants take time to grow and it would be awhile before I could reap rewards.

Dad bought me a 100cc Yamaha motorcycle, for use when other family vehicles were not available. That let me get around town and even drive as far away as New Jersey. The combination street/trail bike could only go forty-five miles-per-hour and was a mess to drive when it rained. Still it was much faster than the train for my weekly trips to Jersey. Once in Merchantville I would meet Chris at Tom's place and the three of us would go over to Vinny Riley's house together. Vinny was responsible for cutting the grass, straighten his room and cleaning out the garage. Before we could do anything with him, his chores had to be done so we all pitched in to help move things along. After several visits we started to notice that Mr. Riley was always sitting in the living room, drinking a beer and watching college ball, while Mrs. Riley was either cleaning the house, making dinner or supervising the chores of their five children.

---

[344] *The Store* – although not nearly as large, this discount retail store was the equivalent to today's Walmart. The sole proprietorship was located in an old stone warehouse at the intersection of Forty Foot Road & Allentown Road in Towamencin.

Since none of us ever saw Mr. Riley without a beer in his hand, we assumed Vinny's dad was an alcoholic, but we never actually saw him drunk and there was a lot more to the story. Richard Riley had a high level position at RCA.[345] He worked extensively with the CIA[346] in conjunction with the armed forces in Vietnam. The Notre Dame graduate had a brilliant mind and was a dedicated patriot. He became an integral player in the development of battle field communications and of the infrastructure for satellite assisted assets. Unfortunately, what he saw on his frequent trips to Vietnam made him absolutely furious. He discovered that there a deliberate effort on the part of our government to keep the war going, without actually winning it. Although he felt guilty about his participation in such a traitorous enterprise, he also felt compelled to stay in the war effort to do what he could to minimize the carnage of our young men at arms. In spite of his best efforts, he witnessed the needless killing of American boys by the thousands. What we had observed was a moral man taking the edge off of a very stressful job, which never departed his mind and left his conscience constantly conflicted.

Vinny Riley converted the basement of his split level home into a crash pad. The walls were lined with shelves containing empty beer cans of every brand and were punctuated with posters of rock stars. The ceiling was illuminated with colored lights, black lights and florescent posters, which picked up the reflective lime green and pink psychedelic colors of the posters or anything else that was white. The perimeter of the room was lined with old couches making it the ultimate party palace and his stereo system was top drawer. Vinny endured all kinds of stress in his family life, but there was also an unspoken rule about the basement.

---

[345] *RCA* – was founded as the Radio Corporation of America & was an electronics company in existence from 1919-1986. It became one of the largest companies in the world & diversified its interests far beyond the original focus on electronics & communications.
[346] *CIA* – the Central Intelligence Agency is a civilian intelligence agency responsible for providing national security intelligence to policymakers. It has also engaged in covert activities at the request of the President.

It was his own private sanctuary. Most of my friends were more extraverted than I was and Vinny was the most outgoing of them all. He invited half the neighborhood over for his parties and filled the place on Saturday nights. We drank like fish, danced to loud music and before each night concluded, we would invariably be coupled off on couches with the girls. Despite much drinking, Vinny had some hard and fast rules, which he vigorously enforced. No one was ever allowed to smoke in the house and the use of drugs were never tolerated anywhere on the property.

At the end of every party we all headed home bombed out of our sculls. Often we played a dangerous game of cat and mouse on neighborhood streets. Sparks flew from the undercarriages of our cars, as we traversed the dips that punctuated every intersection at unbelievably high speeds. Drinking and driving, although illegal, was considered normal and did not have the taboos attached to it that it does today. I often spent the night at Tom's place, which was only a few blocks away. Tom lived at the Sonata School of Music, which was a one-story building, so we frequently climbed through his bedroom window after curfew. On nights that we had some extra money, we rented rooms at the Hillside Motor Lodge.[347] Although we occasionally brought girls back to the motel for some intimate necking, technically I managed to remained a virgin.

On Sunday afternoons we went over to Bob Wallace's attic to lift weights. His beautiful mother was still serving us milk and cookies, which we gratefully accepted along with her standard peanut butter and jelly sandwiches for lunch. Bob was a real motorhead and he had a jet black Pontiac GTO[348] in his garage. Although few of us knew much about engines, we watched with interest as Bob and his mechanic friends

---

[347] *Hillside Motor Lodge* – was located at Rt. 38 & Cuthbert Road in Cherry Hill, NJ.
[348] *Pontiac GTO* – is an automobile built by the Pontiac Division of GM from 1964-1974. It is considered an innovative & now classic muscle car of the 1960s & 1970s. GTO is often said to refer to the copious amounts of gas, tires & oil that this powerful car consumed.

worked on the gas guzzling muscle car. Among other magic tricks these high-performance experts confidently tweaked their carburetor with a screw driver, as they adjusted the timing of the engine with a strobe light.

We thought they were the coolest kids on the block, when they did things like switching out standard wheels for chrome with the speed of an Indy racing team. However the most exhilarating experience of all was going for a ride in the GTO on Route 130. I was sitting in the back seat, when the light turned green. Bob made a right turn off Cove Road peelling wheels onto six lanes of highway. When he punched the gas pedal, the tires squealed, smoke poured out the tail pipes and we were all pressed into the backs of our seats like astronauts. The car danced all over the washboard surface of the road like a jumping bean. After several violent corrections, Bob regained control of the car, luckily without taking out any of the telephone poles or smashing into the concrete medial strip. The experience scared the crap out of me and from that day forward, I politely declined any rides from Bob in his GTO.

Drug free beer parties at Vinny's were a welcome alternative to the drug infested parties back at North Penn High School. Even though we were getting plastered, we felt we were somehow better and more responsible than the space cadets who smoked weed and lacked all ambition. Drinking was about being social and I almost never took so much as a sip of alcohol during the interludes between my trips to the Garden State.

The Terrible Triangle (Chris, Tom and Patrick) in conjunction with the Bud Brothers Association of America (Vinny and Bob) envisioned life-long friendships. We put together scrapbooks of our adventures and even drew up blueprints for a house we planned on sharing after our graduation, but problems were already brewing, which threatened to divide us. My father frequently spoke to my pals about his latest pop psychology stuff and initiated many adventurous outings for us. As a result, my friends all thought he was cool and compared his live and let live style, with the strict discipline of their own fathers. I was getting sick and tired of hearing about it. These guys had no idea what life was like living with dad, nor did they realize how much I wished I had a normal father. This intrusion eventually became so egregious that I sat down and wrote my father a letter about violating my boundries. I told him to, "Stop invading my culture and acting like a hippie."

Chapter 16

Sex, Drugs & Danger

In the aftermath of Woodstock, life was all about having a good time. The consequences of my actions and how they affected those around me were barely even a consideration. Fantastic dreams of wealth, power and fame, while utterly unrealistic, helped me to survive some pretty stressful times. Keeping me grounded in reality was an old carpenter by the name of Joe Birchman.

By the time Independence Day rolled around, my garden looked like a cornucopia. Although Mom was my biggest customer, I also sold crops to strangers that passed by our house in cars. I made enough of a profit to hire my younger brothers. They helped me harvest corn, tomatoes and assorted vegetables from the thirty by fifty foot garden. I took turns with them selling the produce from a long folding table, which sat un-shaded in the hot summer sun along the side of Wambold Road. Even though I was happy to be making a small profit and my brothers seemed content with their pay, I didn't make any real money until I started working as a carpenter's helper. Although Joe Birchman taught me a great deal about the trade of carpentry, the leather faced Korean veteran taught me even more about life in general. My boss worked hard and had little patience for slackers. Although he was a hard driving taskmaster and often pushed me to work harder, he never asked me to do anything beyond my ability.

Joe was a native Philadelphian and had been a painter for most of his life. He was adventurous in his youth and even tackled steeplejack work, while painting the Ben Franklin Bridge. Mr. Birchman was an excellent carpenter and was also a machinist in my father's shop. Since Callahan

Machine Company was a cyclical business, it could ill-afford to lose skilled labor during short downturns in the economy; so my father periodically brought men home from the shop, to do work around the house. I first met Joe when dad asked him to convert our chicken coop into a small cabin. Later on we paneled the living room and fixed up a room in the barn. Through these projects, Joseph Birchman gradually taught me the trade of carpentry. Once he felt confident in my basic skills, we tackled bigger projects together.

My first assignment as a paid worker was to carry two packs of shingles up a ladder to the roof of our house. Whenever I whined about the weight and how the shingle packs were cutting into my shoulder, he mimicked me and called me a baby. Joe was tough, but he also had a compassionate streak. The following day he rented a motorized lift to transport the rest of the building supplies to the roof. Over the course of the summer, Joe taught me how to shingle, frame, panel, and hang ceiling tiles. I also sanded floors, put in electrical wiring and installed fiberglass insulation.

While Joe and I were installing the roof, he told me tales about growing up in the city, his military service in Korea and a tragic story about being in a car accident, which resulted in the death of a child. After finishing the house we re-shingled the roofs of the barn and the garage. Finally we turned the second floor of the barn into a recreation room. We paneled walls, hung a ceiling and installed heating and air-conditioning. We had accomplished a lot, but the summer was over and so was my gravy train. I worked as hard as I could for this man whom I admired. I earned good money and walked away with a solid work ethic, a saleable skill and a new awareness of reality.

In September I entered the eleventh grade at North Penn High School.[349] My major switched from general to business, which put me in with the girls who were studying to become secretaries. Sitting across from me in my Bookkeeping class was the incredibly gorgeous Sandy Loren. Sandra had long brunette hair, a gorgeous face and a beautiful womanly figure. In an effort to avoid staring at this shapely senior, I started noticing some of the other young women in the class. Something had changed over the summer. Almost all of the girls were flowering and in no small measure. Paying attention in class was difficult and I felt like a kid in a candy store. Still, my eyes were inexorably drawn to The Impossible Dream.[350] One day I hoped I could ask the incomparable Sandy Loren out on a date.

My grades soon began to suffer. That prompted my father to introduce another one of his motivational programs called the Canada Ninety Trip. In order to go on the Maple Leaf vacation; every one of my grades had to be above ninety percent. Dad offered the same challenge to Sarah, Sean and my friends Chris and Tom. When the report cards were issued, I was the only one who didn't get straight A's. True to his word, my father left for Canada without me. Although his decision was disappointing and downright humiliating, there was nothing unfair about it. In addition to missing the mark for the contest, I was also failing in my typing class and spiraling downward in almost every other subject.

The economy was rebounding and things were steadily improving at the Callahan Machine Company. One sign of the recovery was that dad was now driving a company car.

---

[349] *North Penn High School* – the original North Penn High School occupied a building within the borough of Lansdale, PA. When the new high school opened, the old building was became Penndale Junior High School.
[350] *The Impossible Dream* – is a song composed by Mitch Leigh with lyrics by Joe Darion. It became the theme song for the 1965 musical Man of La Mancha. Also known as The Quest, it was sung by Don Quixote, as he stands vigil over his armor & answers a question posed by the kitchen wench Aldonza, whom he calls his highborn lady Dulcinea, to explain to her what he means when he says he must "follow the quest".

That gave me access to his pickup truck, which I started taking to school. Sarah drove with me and we often picked up Lesley along the way. Having my own wheels meant I could sleep later, get home earlier and proudly parade into the school parking lot. It was fun while it lasted, but on December 11, 1970 it all came to a screeching halt. I was making a left turn at the intersection of Valley Forge Road and Sumneytown Pike. All of a sudden a bright yellow Barracuda[351] with black racing stripes came roaring over the hill at seventy miles an hour. I never saw it coming and the flashy muscle car slammed into my dad's faded green pickup. Although no one was badly injured; Lesley banged her knee on the dashboard, I split my lip on the steering wheel and both vehicles were totaled. Traffic was tied up for hours. We dodged the bullet, but not every close call would be physical.

In her Grammy Award winning song Angles, Amy Grant sings about how actively our guardian angels work to protect us.[352]

Near misses all around me,
accidents unknown;
though I never see with human eyes
the hands that lead me home.
but I know they're all around me,
all day and through the night.
When the enemy is closing in,
I know sometimes they fight."

---

[351] *Barracuda* – the redesigned E-body Barracuda shook the stigma of the economy car & the high-performance models were marketed as "Cuda" a 1969 option, whose larger engine bay facilitated the release of Chrysler's 426 cu in Hemi for the regular retail market.

[352] *Angels* – is a song by Christian singer Amy Grant, from her album *Straight Ahead*. It won the 1985 Grammy Award for Best Gospel Vocal Performance, Female. The song begins with an account of Saint Peter's capture by Herod's guards in the Bible & goes on to describe how God has His angels watching over believers, to guide & protect them in times of fear, doubt, confusion, or temptation. The song is noted for its inspirational lyrics, especially the first verse, *Angels watching over me*.

We were incredibly naïve, which made us vulnerable to the voracious appetites of vultures. Although we considered ourselves invincible and sailed through life without a care, we often missed subtle clues that could have alerted us to impending danger. And no one took advantage of our inattentive gullibility like the homosexuals. Were it not for the protection and prayers of St. Peter Damian and our guardian angels, we might have been spiritually, psychologically and sexually twisted beyond recognition for life.

In 1049 A.D., St. Peter Damian wrote Letter 31, Book of Gomorrah – A Medieval Treatise on Sodomy. The document condemned the practices of homosexuality and the moral turpitude, within and without the church. After obtaining Papal authority, this holy and manly saint excommunicated priests, bishops, brothers and nuns. He closed down entire orders of convents and monasteries, because they had become virtual dens of iniquity. The sexual scandal he exposed and addressed in the Catholic Church rivaled that of simony[353] and was one of the hidden factors underlying the Protestant Reformation.[354]

Chris Lang got a job as a bus boy in the Starlight Room. Dennis Frank was his boss and the culinary artist of the kitchen. The man was well paid for producing tasty meals and for his imaginative ice carvings. Although the overweight chef was a jovial man, he liked to brag about his wealth. Fat Den told my buddy about his indoor pool and invited us over to go swimming. The chef told him he would have a fridge full of free beer waiting for us. We met up with Chris after he got off work and he led us over to the cook's palatial mansion. We downed pony bottles like they were

---

[353] *Simony* – is the crime of paying for sacraments, holy offices or positions in Church. The name comes from Simon Magus, in the Acts of the Apostles 8:18-24.
[354] *St. Peter Damian* – from the book *The Rite of Sodomy*, by Randy Engel, published by New Engel Publishing, Export, PA. ©2006, pg. 48.

water and in short order, the lot of us were all falling down drunk.

None of us knew the cook had an indoor heated swimming pool and since it was the middle of winter we brought no bathing suits. Dennis saw no problem with that and said, "We're all guys; just jump in naked." A couple of the boys stripped, but the rest of us kept our underwear on to play a game of water polo. There were about ten of us and we were all laughing and having a good time, but after a while something seemed off. Fat Den was quietly sitting on a chair by the diving board and ogling us. We started feeling creepy and one by one we began getting dressed. Despite his exhortations to stay, we quickly moved toward the door.

Chris and I were way too drunk to drive. Of the three of us, Tom Reeves was the most sober, so even though he didn't have a license, he became the designated driver for the night. The back door was locked when we arrived, so we climbed in through Tom's bedroom window. It must have been three in the morning; so in addition to being drunk I was also dead tired and fell fast asleep. I thought we had evaded detection, but Mr. Reeves woke up when we climbed through the first floor window. A short time later he entered the bedroom and walked me out to the kitchen. I didn't even remember getting out of bed. After handing me a cup of coffee, he began asking me a series of questions. I must have been pretty pliable, because I started telling him where we had been; what we were doing; and who had given us the beer. I even told him that his unlicensed son had driven us home. There was virtually no restraint on my answers until he asked, "How's your sex life?" The odd question startled me and it was only then that I realized how forthrightly I had been answering his other questions. When I opened my eyes I saw my best friend's father sitting on a stool in front of me with a half opened red velvet smoking jacket. I was petrified about the situation and kept wondering what I had told him. I dummied up and said I wanted to go back to sleep. I walked straight back to the bed, but had trouble going back to sleep. How much of the beans had I spilled? Would I get the other guys in trouble? More importantly, why was he asking me questions about my sex life? Would he do something weird like this again? Unfortunately, it would not be long before I would learn the answers to my questions.

Several weeks later there was another shindig over at Vinny's. Getting ready for the party at Tom's house, I went into the bathroom to take a shower. In the middle of washing my hair Mr. Reeves opened up the sliding glass door behind me and offered to wash my back. I was totally freaked out that he was even in the bathroom, let alone that he had just opened the door. Trying to be diplomatic I acted like it was no big deal and said, "No thanks. I'll take care of it." Undeterred, he grabbed the soap and proceeded to wash my back saying, "Oh don't be shy, we all need help sometimes." Now I was really mad! I swung around and shouted, "Get out!" He backed away muttering, "No need to get upset. I was just trying to help." Sliding the door closed, I finished rinsing the shampoo out of my hair.

The incident really creeped me out. Turning off the water, I felt like a scared rabbit hiding in Mr. McGregor's garden. Sliding open the glass door, I peeked through the crack to make sure he wasn't still around. After drying off, I looked out into the hallway and quickly ran across it to the safety of the bedroom. Tom was putting some clothing away in his dresser drawer and listening to a loud rendition of Won't Get Fooled Again.[355] He tried telling me that Vinny had called, but I placed my finger in front of my lips and motioned for him to be silent. With a towel still wrapped around my waist, I walked over to him and told him what had just happened. "I think your dad is a fag." He brushed away my comment like

---

[355] *Won't Get Fooled Again* – is a 1971 song by The Who & written by Pete Townshend. It speaks of an endless cycle of revolutions, where each successive new regime turns out to be just as oppressive as the old one. In the refrain, the author winds up by saying, *I'll get on my knees and pray we don't get fooled again.*

it was nothing and turned back to folding his clothes. "That's just his way of letting you know that he cares. I know its weird sometimes, but he's just a touchy feely kind of a guy." Standing there in utter disbelief I said, "Tom! It's way more than that!" I guess it was too hot a topic for him to handle, because no matter what I said, he just couldn't grasp what I was trying to tell him. The conversation was going nowhere. I wanted to cool down from my shower before getting dressed, so I laid face down on the bed with a towel draped over me.

Suddenly the door burst open. Mr. Reeves came strutting into the room. He asked Tom where we were going that night and then moved on to asking about school, our girlfriends and whether parents would be present at the party. Knowing how uncomfortable I felt, Tom tried to cut the conversation short, but the old man continued to quiz him. His father even sat down next to me on the bed. Panicked, I looked to Tom for help. Barely clothed himself the persistent little predator put his hands on my shoulders and said, "Here let me give you a back rub." Despite my refusal, he began rubbing my back. Meanwhile Tom silently stood by folding his clothes and placing them neatly in his dresser drawer, as if nothing was wrong. Suddenly the hoggish homo jumped up on the bed, straddled my legs and said, "Here let me give you a real backrub!" The rapacious maneuver startled Tom and he finally intervened, "Ok pop, that's enough." Unfortunately the obstinate bohemian defended his abusive behavior by enthusiastically responding, "Everyone loves a backrub." That was the last straw. I screamed at the top of my lungs, "Get the fuck off me!" Like a bucking bronco, I jumped off the bed and threw him to the floor. Tom knew I was ready to kill, so quickly rescued the stunned pervert. Leading the stupefied degenerate out the door, he whispered, "Come on pop. Leave him alone. He doesn't want a backrub."

Despite the close proximity to danger and my friend's denial of his father's obvious perversion, I remained friends with Tom for many years. Following that violent confrontation, Mr. Reeves never bothered me again; but sadly he was not the only sodomite venturing out of the closet. In the summer of 1970, New York City and Los Angeles became the first cities to hold Gay Pride Day, celebrating the riots at the Stonewall Inn. Long before those riots ever took place; I had already been solicited at boarding school and my best friend's father was quite literally on my back, with an equally perverted agenda. Although I was never actually raped or seduced, this firsthand experience left me hyper vigilant and certain about the aggressive nature of the homosexual agenda. I pick up on warning signs sooner than most and stand ready to defend my rights and the rights of others from their queer and often deceptive tactics.

America was in freefall. All In The Family[356] juxtaposed the rock solid values of those born before WWI with the irresponsibility of those born after WWII. Although this show was comedic in nature, the fictitious family directly dealt with some of the same serious issues we were all confronting in the midst of the Culture War. Although I had known Chris Lang for a long time I never actually met his father. When I finally did I was blown away by his personality. Mr. Carl Lang went on a tirade about blacks, which stunned me into silence. Soon after Chris and I left the house I remarked, "Your dad is just like Archie Bunker." Having grown up in a blue-collar world, it all seemed pretty natural to him. So he objected to my negative characterization of his father. Once I got to know him, Mr. Lang's dogmatic slurs seemed much more about comedy

---

[356] *All in the Family* – was an Emmy Award-winning sitcom, which aired on CBS from 1971-1979. It was notorious for language & epithets, previously absent from TV, such as fag, Hebe, spic, mick, dago, wop, polock, chink, Jap, gook & spade. It was also the first time a TV show used phrases like *god damn it* or featured the sound of a flushing toilet. The show was decidedly progressive, but while Archie's bigotry & short-sightedness were the focus of much of the humor, Mike Stivic's naive, liberal nature was also on the receiving end of occasional jabs.

than they were about hatred. Even so the caricatures he invented in his tall tales also seemed to reference an underlying and disturbing truth. There was a racial divide in our country and whites were not the only culprits.

While I thought nothing about drinking and driving, my friends all hated the druggies, who pretty much dominated the North Penn party scene. We wanted nothing to do with the lazy little space cadets. Although Jon Baker occasionally did shots and Jessie Allen drank beer, none of us were interested in going to any organized parties unless we threw them. Most high school parties provided candy dishes on coffee tables filled with pills and the atmosphere was always heavy with the smell of pot. Instead we held our own private dances up in the barn. Five of us from school formed a top Forties band called *The Eternal Flame*. We installed a fake fireplace on the floor behind our stage, which sent red, yellow and orange tongues of fire darting across the ceiling. We charged twenty-five cents for the guys and let the girls in for free. A couple of guys from the football team volunteered to be our bouncers and they gladly tossed out anyone who showed up uninvited or started causing trouble. Years before the advent of disco balls, we used an old crystal whiskey bottle filled with colored marbles, a turntable and a projector, to send lights darting around the room. Our dances were pretty popular and often filled to capacity. Our band never really went anywhere and our biggest gig was a birthday party. It paid us one-hundred dollars and we had to split it five ways. Still, we had a lot of fun and as the lead singer I put everything I had into belting out pop and embracing the emotions of the slow songs.

Life was pretty peaceful in Pennsylvania, but not so much in the rest of the world. On March 29, 1971 after a four-month-long trial, William Calley was convicted of premeditated murder for ordering the shootings of men, women and children, at the My Lai Massacre in Vietnam. The government sentenced him to life in prison, but President

Nixon released him, pending an appeal. When all was said and done, he only had to serve four-and-a-half months in the base prison at Fort Benning, Georgia. The ruling brought closure to a dark cloud that was hanging over our military, but there was a different kind of darkness forming stateside.

Thanks in part to the anti-nuclear protests, America had become severely underpowered. Electric companies were able to keep up with demand, so long as the oil kept flowing from the Middle East, but economic pressure from OPEC[357] including the threat of another embargo caused a shortfall in electric power generation. Since engineers had planned on a nuclear-based power grid and we had not built a coal-fired plant in over forty years, Westinghouse launched a slew of new building projects. Callahan Machine Company had seen this coming on the horizon and had retooled. They were well-positioned in the market and I became one of the first beneficiaries of my father's newfound wealth. Dad asked Joe Birchman to take me over to Ardes Buick-Pontiac in Phoenixville to pick out a car for my birthday. We came home with a 1965 Chevy Impala Super Sport. When I showed Jon and Jessie they immediately took me to the Watash Speed Shop in Lansdale. The present they bought for me was an ahooga horn, which we installed that very afternoon. What a birthday!

Callahan Machine Company hired me and since I had my own car I could get myself to work after school. Although I had to pay for things like insurance and auto repairs, I earned enough money to go to Jersey on the weekends. Tom was now seriously dating Kitty Carter. She was a very pretty girl with long straight brunette hair that was silky smooth and

---

[357] *OPEC* – the Organization of Petroleum Exporting Countries is an intergovernmental organization of 12 developing countries made up of Algeria, Angola, Ecuador, Iran, Iraq, Kuwait, Libya, Nigeria, Qatar, Saudi Arabia, the United Arab Emirates & Venezuela. Headquartered in Vienna since, it hosts regular meetings among the oil ministers of its Member Countries. The principal goal is to safeguard the individual & collective interests of the members. It pursues ways & means of ensuring the stabilization of prices in international oil markets.

shiny. Kitty was absolutely precious to Tom and it was no surprise to any of us that he wanted to go steady with her. The girl with the signature bangs worked behind the counter at the candy shop and she gave her best friends free samples whenever we stopped in to see her. Butter crunch was my favorite, so whenever I was in town I made sure to meet up with Tom at the candy shop. After she got off work, the three of us usually went to one of Vinny's, parties, where I met lots of other girls and got to hang out with my friends. The weekends were fabulous, but school was still a struggle.

From the time I was in grade school my father introduced me to dozens of self-made men who had built successful businesses of their own. Often these captains of industry had made good with less than an eighth grade education. So I learned early on that business was prized over labor and that the entrepreneurial initiative was much more valuable than an education. Therefore in our family, a college education was not exactly held out to me as a commodity worth pursuing. If I ever had any respect for higher education, it was totally obliterated the day dad brought home a couple of professorial pinheads. This duo of dimwits with doctorates was trying to convince my father to participate in controlled LSD experiments. Although I knew he had been under a lot of pressure lately, I found it difficult to believe he was seriously considering their offer.

I had recently witnessed the economy turn around and thanks to my father's business acumen; Callahan Machine Company was now doing better than ever. From my perch, the economy and the government did pretty much whatever it wanted to and there wasn't much anyone could do about it. The army could draft me at any moment. College, once the bastion of leadership training for the rich, was now nothing more than an expensive place for parties. I saw no real value in education and wondered why anyone would ever want to go out into that big bad world. Why should I leave home? Where was the cost benefit? At least at home I knew the ropes, had a roof over my head and could come and go as I pleased. After making my amateur analysis, I came up with what I thought was an ingenious plan. I would maintain the status quo, by deliberately flunking the eleventh grade. I did none of my homework, slept through classes and resisted any attempts by others to motivate me. For the first time in my life, I had a goal that was absolutely achievable. I could win on grades, enjoy a secure place to eat, sleep and avoid the draft. I didn't even have to feel guilty about spending gobs of dad's money on college. By the end of the second quarter I flunked most of my subjects, earned plenty of money at work and was having the time of my life. When not in Jersey, I played in the band, hung out with Lesley and danced the night away out in the barn. Soon after I acquired my first car; a movie and a new girlfriend would lure me to the shore like sirens.[358]

---

[358] *Sirens* – in Greek mythology these femmes fatales lured nearby sailors with their enchanting music & voices to shipwreck on the rocky coast of their island.

Chapter 17

The Summer of '42

Chris Lang often dated as many as three women at a time, but now he was going steady with the drop-dead gorgeous Sophia Romano. Whenever he went MIA all the guys busted his chops about being henpecked. Meanwhile Tom and Kitty Carter were also becoming pretty exclusive and the four of them began double dating. That left me out in the cold until one day when Chris introduced me to a statuesque young woman from Pennsauken high school. Mary Kate O'Neil was a foxy lady with a charming personality and she immediately swept me off my feet. As we drew near to the summer of 1972, the six of us went off to see a new coming of age movie called The Summer of '42.[359] After watching the classic film together, Tom drove all six of us to a shadowy street on the east side of Merchantville and quietly coasted to a stop. Magically transported to our own surreal beach in 1942, we began making out with our dates and attempting to relive the tender scenes in the movie.

Nothing could ever have prepared me for Mary Kate O'Neil. Physically she was a lovely creature with an ear-to-ear smile that lit up her face as well as my own. She had long silky brunette hair with natural red highlights that accented her glorious shoulder-length locks, which she wore up in a flip. The fetching, femme fatale had a sexy and sensual stride, as she confidently walked down the street and her hair was not the only thing that bounced. Best of all she was capable of carrying on intelligent conversations about topics other than school gossip and rock bands. We engaged in deep probing

---

[359] *The Summer of '42* – was a powerful coming of age story written by Herman Raucher & directed by Robert Mulligan. During his summer vacation in 1942, an innocent youth (Hermie played by Gary Grimes) falls in love with a young married woman, (Dorothy played by Jennifer O'Neill) who awaits the fate of her husband, a soldier killed in WWII.

discussions about real life issues and for the first time in my dating experience the dialogue was amazingly interactive. We enjoyed making out for hours on the side of the road that evening, but she never let me lay a finger on her enticing figure. Although Mary Kate was an exciting and playful young woman, I would later learn that she was also a very troubled teen. Subsequent conversations led us to ponder school, parents and the dreams we had for our future. While both of us dearly loved our parents, we often felt that they did things that made them more difficult to love. We often discussed the things we thought we could do about the situation. Her parents were full-blown alcoholics. Mr. O'Neil owned the Stardust Bar and Grill on Route 130 and Mrs. O'Neil was a stay-at-home lush, which is why whenever I dropped her off at her place, Mary Kate never even considered inviting me inside.

I made it a priority to take trips to Pennsauken every single weekend. We gradually got to know each other and went on several more triple dates. One night I dropped Chris and Sophia off before driving to Mary Kate's, but because Tom and Kitty were in no real hurry to get home, they sat in the car while I walked Mary Kate to the door. Neither of us wanted to say good-bye so we stood on the front step kissing for almost an hour. Eventually she had to go in so I leaned forward to give her one last kiss. To my utter surprise, she firmly squeezed my gonads, turned around and disappeared behind the front door. I stood there in shock. I had been hoping beyond all hope that she would allow me to see her again and was even afraid that I might have blown it, by trying to make a move on her earlier that evening. Apparently all those fears were without foundation. From that night forward we saw as much of each other as time would allow. Mary Kate and I attended parties, went bowling, watched movies and enjoyed picnics together. Although we rarely saw Chris and Sophia; we frequently double-dated with Kitty and Tom. I often borrowed dad's pickup with a cap telling him I needed it for a place to sleep.

Many an evening was spent making out with my new girlfriend on a mattress in the back of that wonderful truck. Although increasingly sexually active, technically we both remained virgins using my "anything but" strategy, but deep down I knew we were playing with fire.

I never did go steady with the incomparable, kissable Kate. In fact I often juxtaposed my apparent independence against what I jokingly referred to as the slavish lifestyle of my pussy whipped friend Chris. The truth was that I rarely dated any other girls in Jersey and neither did Chris or Tom, but when we were in Pennsylvania it was like living in another world and as long as we were there, we all considered ourselves confirmed bachelors. Lesley Wright and my sister knew plenty of girls and frequently set us up with their friends. Sarah introduced me to Natalie Larsen, a tall slender woman with long sandy blonde hair who had a bubbly and at times even zany personality. I took Natalie out to dinner at a restaurant she had suggested at the Peddler's Village in New Hope, PA. I liked the idea of getting all dressed up for supper and found the food to be excellent, but the place was a bit too hoity-toity for my tastes and way too expensive for my bank account. Our conversation led me to believe she expected to go out like this all the time, which for me was out of the question. Seeing her as one of those high maintenance girls with unrealistic expectations, I decided to stop seeing her after just one date.

I landed a steady job as a dishwasher at the Holiday Inn. The hotel chain offered more money than Callahan Machine Company and it was located closer to my home, but I needed working papers to secure employment. The bureaucratic rigmarole I had to go through to get them was both annoying and time consuming. In the name of protection, the child labor laws were also costing me money by limiting my freedom to work the hours I needed to survive. Who the hell was the government to decide these things for me? I secured the position and got along well with my boss Linda Mavin, as well as most of my coworkers. I derived great satisfaction from the production aspect of the job. According to Linda, I cleaned more dishes than any of my predecessors. I took great personal pride in my accomplishments each day and even worked a few weekends to build up my bank account. I wasn't exactly sure what it was I was saving up for, but the larger my savings account grew, the more secure and independent I felt. I was earning a good buck and spending only what I needed to spend for the necessities.

My father finally found his vacation property at Arrowhead Lake in the Poconos. He named the place Dad's Deer Stand and it was located on Tee Pee Circle, which backed up against the State Game Lands. The lot was located on an old bulldozed logging road in the middle of the forest. In a few months construction would begin on a charming Swiss Chalet, but for now we set up tents in what would soon become the front yard. As usual we gathered wood to cook hot dogs and roast marshmallows. Although memories of the boy scouts were rekindled, my friends were already anticipating ski trips and meeting snow bunnies on the slopes.

Each day after school my brothers and I attempted longer and longer jumps with our trail bikes. We also played an intense game of cat and mouse, racing all over our seven acre De Colores Farm. My favorite chore was cutting the grass. Sometimes I even fought with my younger brothers for the chance to ride our brand new lawn tractor. For several weeks running, I had been talking with a cute blonde on our bus named Molly. One afternoon I asked her if she would like to take a ride with me on my trail bike. She accepted the invitation and we set the date up for Friday afternoon. Like a deer in the rut, I mounted the tractor and began cutting a long circuitous trail through our neighbor's fields in preparation for our rendezvous. One of those unwritten understandings out here in the country is that private property rights are sacrosanct. To deliberately trespass or damage another man's property is an egregious transgression. So when the farmer caught me mowing down the hay in his field there was simply no excuse for what I had done. After yelling at me and chasing me off his land, he called my father. I knew that when I got home there would be hell to pay and I accepted my punishment, but there was no way I could tell my dad the real reason for what I had done.

On Friday afternoon, as if none of that had even taken place, I tied a blanket to the back of my trail bike and picked up sweet innocent Molly, to take her for a ride on the taboo trail. I drove slower than usual in order to keep her fears at a minimum. We crossed the creek, climbed a hill and made our way up through the serpentine paths. Cutting off onto one of the small cul-de-sacs I had constructed. We sat down on the blanket and talked for a while. Then I kissed her and lowered her tender frame to the ground. In silence we made out for a while and then I gently stroked her soft baby fine hair. I marveled at the way the sun brought out the golden highlights of the silky strands that framed her bright blue eyes and tender smile. It was all so perfect and yet something was terribly wrong. She was the girl next door. Although she offered no resistance to my advances, no passions were ever unleashed either. It had all been a mistake. Sure we liked each other and felt comfortable together, but we had crossed a line with this forbidden fling and there was a hidden cost. The budding friendship we had so carefully been developing on the bus gradually devolved into an exchange of greetings between acquaintances.

Finally the end of the school year arrived. I successfully fulfilled my ill-conceived mission of flunking my junior year. I now had a few more years of stability. I had avoided the draft and now had time to figure out how to deal with the rest of that big bad world out there. I was meeting plenty of girls, felt relatively productive at work and had more money in the bank than ever before. I felt successful and was looking forward to summer vacation when I got a call from

Chris Lang. The Janitor from Saint Pete's had died. Paul Campanella had fallen off a ladder while fixing roof of the Church. Paul was a humble man who spent his life serving the children and the parishioners of Saint Peter's parish. Almost everyone we knew attended the funeral. Although it was a very sad event, Chris reminded me that Paul would not want us to see his death as anything other than him going to his final reward. So we rejoiced with him, but his death also signaled the end of my childhood. It was the beginning of something else too, I just didn't know what that would be.

In May Chris invited Tom and I to spend the weekend with his family down in Ocean City, New Jersey. The extended Lang family rented the same wooden bungalow every summer; but for Tom and I it was the first inhalation of salt air we would know as teenagers. The first thing we did was to hit the boardwalk in search of babes. Although there were plenty of lovely ladies to choose from we were clueless as to how to meet them. Chris said he had a plan and bought a flip pack box of Marlboro cigarettes. He told us we could use them as an ice breaker by walking up to the girls and asking them for a light. Since it was his plan and Chris seemed absolutely fearless, we let him do all the talking. Although the practice led to a decade long smoking habit for Chris and I, his ruse never worked and we would have to find another way of meeting the girls.

The seashore was like a foreign country to me. The coastal communities had a unique culture with their own set of social protocols that operated entirely differently from the way they did back home. Yet the beaches, bays and boardwalks held out the promise of adventure. This newly discovered gold mine could be a bonanza for anyone willing to take a few risks and let go of conventional paradigms. Like the sand crabs grabbing blindly at tender toes, wanderlust captured my heart along with my imagination.

If ever I wanted to go steady with anyone, it would have been with the incomparable Mary Kate O'Neil. I liked everything about her, including the way her name rolled off my tongue. I cared for her, had a strong desire to protect her and thoroughly enjoyed her company. Although sex was a big part of our relationship, I never really felt like I was using her. However, it would not be long before that unspoken commitment would be put to the test. Chris, Tom and I decided to take Sophia, Kitty and Mary Kate on a picnic by the Wading River in the Wharton Tract.[360] After building a small fire, we ate some hot dogs and then went swimming in the deep swift running brown cedar water that snaked its way through the Pine Barrens. Later on we coupled off and found secluded places in the forest to make out on our beach towels.

After about an hour of cuddling and pleasuring each other, we had virtually removed all of our clothing. I felt privileged to know that Mary Kate felt comfortable enough with me to reveal her beautiful body so unashamedly in the bright sunshine, but we soon arrived at the point of no return. Although she made no aggressive moves, it was obvious I was being given the green light and she quietly waited for me to make my next move. As our eyes locked, I anguished over my inability to handle the responsibility of a child, which I realized was a very real possibility. Knowing I shouldn't be writing checks with my body that I couldn't cash with my life, I turned away in shame. After a long uncomfortable pause, we each got dressed and returned to join the others at the campfire.

I wanted to share what was going on in my heart, how much I loved her and why I thought we were way too young to be

---

[360] *Wharton Tract* – is the largest single tract of land in the New Jersey park system. It encompasses 115,000 acres of Pinelands & is named for Joseph Wharton, who purchased the property in the 19th Century in the hopes of providing a source of clean drinking water for Philadelphia; but New Jersey quashed the plan by passing a law that banned the export of water. New Jersey eventually bought the land from Wharton's heirs in the 1950s.

taking on commitments that would last a lifetime. In the past it had been easy to have those kinds of conversations, but now it seemed almost impossible. What I was clear about was that I was in no way prepared for marriage. Hell... I couldn't even support myself, let alone a wife and kids. True love does not lead someone on. How could I make love to Mary Kate and still call it love?

Not making love to her was the right moral choice, but it was hardly an honorable decision. For months now I had implied by my actions that the two of us were destined for a lifelong relationship. Although she only had eyes for me, I was still dating other women on the side. In less than a month I would be living at the Jersey shore and I wanted to feel free to date whomever I pleased. That one-sided attitude made me oblivious to her pain and unwilling to back up my sexual overtures with the commitment she wanted, needed and deserved.

Tragically, that clueless arrogance continued to grow in me and followed me down to Long Beach Island where I puffed up like a peacock.

Chapter 18

Mr. Big Stuff

In the summer of 1971 our family rented a small cottage on 10th Street in Surf City, New Jersey. The small rancher was less than a block from a custard stand and a couple of blocks from the beach. The short two-week vacation instilled an attraction within me toward the sand and surf that would endure for many years. Despite some recent dating successes, I was still basically a shy kid and lacked the social skill of initial contact. My fledgling confidence was nearly destroyed by that bashfulness on the very first day, but my sister came to the rescue. Sarah met a young man at the custard stand and set me up on a date with his sister. To my surprise the evening turned out rather well and by the end of the summer my ego was in bloom. To combat my meteoric rise in self-confidence my friends often teased me with the lyrics from the song: You're So Vain[361] and gave me the nickname Mr. Big Stuff.[362]

Long Beach Island is primarily a family resort. Most of the shoreline was punctuated with umbrellas, blankets and young married couples smearing Coppertone[363] on small children. After our family arrived in town we got a sneak preview of the ocean and returned to the rented house to

---

[361] *You're So Vain* – is a song written & performed by Carly Simon. The song is a critical profile of a self-absorbed lover. It is ranked #72 on Billboard's Greatest Songs of All-Time.

[362] *Mr. Big Stuff* – is a song by R&B singer Jean Knight & became a huge crossover hit. The song spent 5 weeks at #1 on the Billboard Hot 100 Singles chart. Her signature lines *Who do you think you are?* & *Your never gonna get my love*, made it one of Stax Records's most popular & recognizable hits.

[363] *Coppertone* – was a brand name owned by Schering-Plough, for an American sunscreen. It dated back to 1944, when pharmacist Benjamin Green invented a lotion to darken tans. The company became famous in 1953 when it introduced the Coppertone girl, which was an advertisement showing a young blond girl in pigtails staring in surprise as a Cocker Spaniel snuck up behind her & pulled down her blue swimsuit bottoms, exposing her pale white buttocks in stark contrast with her tanned body. The caption of the ad read, "Don't be a paleface!" Merck & Co., Inc. now owns & produces the Coppertone brand.

unpack. As soon as we were finished I walked down to the boulevard to get a feel for the holiday haunt. A hopeful sign in front of a large brick building read, "Teen Dances Every Wednesday Night". The Surf City 5 & 10, took up the entire next block and they sold everything from T-shirts and post cards to plumbing supplies and crab traps. I purchased an official Surf City beach towel, a pair of sandals and some Coppertone, before returning to the house for dinner. After supper Sarah walked down to the custard stand and got permission from the proprietor to start her own babysitting service in his lobby. The deal she made with the gentleman allowed her to meet lots of potential clients and gave her ready access to purchase ice cream and hamburgers for the kids. It was a win-win; Sarah had her own business and the owner sold more of his products.

Over the winter months I had saved up plenty of money, so I saw no reason to look for a job. Instead I took a walk up to the beach alone and found a bench near the top of a dune. Leisurely breathing in the salt air, I sat down on a green weatherworn perch and looked out over a peaceful turquoise ocean. The rhythmic sapphire waves were crashing on the beach in an endless procession of soft soothing sounds. Shrill honking sea gulls pierced the air as they patrolled the beach and systematically harvested scraps of discarded sandwiches and stale fries. Although the sun was setting on the bay behind me, it still illuminated a clear blue sky. A loud buffeting report betrayed the locations of nearby kites and the sea breeze muffled the shrieks of young children playing in the distance. Anonymously I watched with interest as parents rescued the airships of their panicked offspring, as they crashed the kites like dive-bombers into the sifted sand, which was littered with a collage of shattered sea shells.

When the sun finally set, the wind shifted its direction and a million mosquitoes began their nocturnal assault. Forced to walk back to the house, I found my younger brothers still up playing a game of Uno.[364] Too tired to join them, I ascended a single flight of stairs and collapsed onto my bed. A cool breeze hummed as it blew through the screen. The air was heavy with the scent of salt and a bouquet of pungent odors from the marsh that emptied into the bay. Low humidity and the distant din of crashing waves created perfect conditions for a deep restful sleep.

It was still dark the next morning when dad drove back across the Delaware. Much as he wanted to stay, he was needed back at the office to manage an ever-increasing quantity of orders for steam turbine parts for Westinghouse. After seeing him off to work and taking a few moments out for her daily cup of coffee; mom gathered her overanxious brood and took them to the ocean. Sarah quickly followed on her way to the ice cream stand to begin her babysitting service. It was great sleeping weather, so I stayed in bed till almost eleven, before making my way to the refrigerator for a swig of milk from the jug. Discovering a paperback copy of The Art of Loving[365] on a bookshelf in the living room, I retired to an over-stuffed chair in my bedroom to read the first couple of chapters. While mulling over the authors concepts, I put on a T-shirt and a pair of white cutoff jeans. Then I buckled up the new pair of leather sandals I had purchased the previous night. The ox hide straps, brass studding and oversized buckles made me feel like a Roman Centurion. Snatching a clean towel from the hall closet, I donned a pair of aviators and headed for the beach.

On my way to the ocean, I stopped off at the custard stand to see how Sarah was making out. She introduced me to a tall

---

[364] *Uno* – was a card game developed in 1971 by Merle Robbins. He invented it to resolve an argument with his son about the rules of Crazy Eights. The original decks were designed & made on the family dining room table. Merle sold them out of his barbershop until 1981, when he sold the rights to International Games for $50K plus royalties of 10 cents per copy. Today the game is produced by Mattel in 80 countries & has sold 150 million worldwide.
[365] *The Art of Loving* – is an international bestselling book, written by psychologist & social philosopher Erich Fromm. It presents love as a skill that can be taught & developed & was published in 1956 by Harper & Row.

dark handsome boy named Aaron Goldman. He worked behind the counter and I could see by their exchange of glances that there was chemistry between them. He looked older than she was so I asked her his age. When she told me he was eighteen, I told her to be careful. She rolled her eyes and barked back, "I can take care of myself; thank you. Besides, he's a nice guy."

Walking across the gravel parking lot, I stopped in at George's Pizza[366] for a soda. George was dressed in what looked like a white lab coat. As the screen door slammed behind me, he closed the oven and wiped the sweat from his forehead with a towel. The short rotund proprietor smiled gently and with a heavy Italian accent asked, "What can I get for you?" "Just a Coke please." Reflexively he wheeled around and in a seamless maneuver, grabbed a cup, filled it, capped it and placed it on the counter with a straw. "That'll be one dollar please." Sitting down on a heavy yellow pine bench by the window, I positioned my drink on a matching picnic table and marveled at what must have been a hundred coats of varnish. The marquee above the owner's head displayed a menu of sandwiches, hoagies and full course pasta dinners. Spying a vending machine in the corner, I asked the man behind the counter for change of a dollar bill. I bought a flip-pack box from the machine, which had a picture of the Marlboro Man[367] on the front of it. Looking around for some matches, George pointed to the end of the counter and I picked out a couple of books. When I finished my drink, I was just about to light up when I noticed a picture of a chef with a pizza on the back. It was the exact same one I had mistakenly put on the matches I sold to the

---

[366] *George's Pizzeria* – is a pizza & sandwich shop, located at 11th Street & Long Beach Blvd., in Surf City. George, a heavy-set Italian gentleman started the business & his pizza, ham hoagies & great service made it a favorite stop of mine for both lunch & dinner.

[367] *Marlboro Man* – was a figure used in tobacco ads for Marlboro cigarettes. It was used from 1954-1999. The manly icon was conceived by Leo Burnett & portrayed a rugged cowboy alone in nature with only a cigarette. The ads were designed to popularize filtered cigarettes, which at the time were considered feminine. The ads were considered one of the most brilliant ad campaigns of all time, because they transformed a feminine campaign, with the slogan "Mild as May", into one that was masculine, in a matter of months.

deli. On the bottom of the book I saw the words, Manufactured by Superior Match Company in Chicago, IL. What a small world. Finishing my cigarette, I threw the towel over my neck, walked out the front door and into the blinding sunlight. As soon as the screen door slammed behind me, I donned my aviators and crossed the sand laced boulevard.

Once I crossed the main thoroughfare, my footsteps were all that I heard. The sun's broiling temperatures brought back childhood memories of Death Valley Days,[368] albeit with the musty odor of melting macadam. In seconds my shirt was drenched in sweat. I passed a dozen weatherworn houses high atop cedar pylons and noticed that every one of them sheltered late model cars in between the creosote-soaked colonnade. The stillness and silence gave way to cheerful chatter, as I neared the end of the street. Scaling the shifting sands of the dune I was rewarded with a strong refreshing easterly breeze. I paused beside the park bench at the crest of the hill and looked out over a brightly lit seascape. My eyes feasted on hundreds of scantily clad women. Siren songs from the surf beckoned these babes on beach towels to anoint their bodies with the sacred oils of the annual ritual. Lying prostrate before the sun, these mere mortals were gradually transformed into gorgeous golden goddesses.

Although the sandals protected my feet from the scalding black tar on the street, they were absolutely useless in the shifting sands of the beach. Even after removing the heavy leather thongs, I still walked like a retard. The sifted soil was sun baked and deep. It wasn't until I reached the cool damp sand near the water's edge that it was firm enough to stand erect and walk normally again. Happily hiding behind the

---

[368] *Death Valley Days* – was a weekly television series set in Death Valley, CA. The show followed the lives of the teamsters who transported Borax from mines to factories, where it was made into soap. Wagon trains of mules pulled the heavy cargo across deadly deserts. These weekly television shows were sponsored by Twenty Mule Team Borax.

anonymity of my Foster Grants[369] I inhaled a visual smorgasbord of eye candy. I walked for almost seven blocks searching for a potential partner and then turned around to reevaluate the feminine inventory. Zeroing in on some of the best looking women, I found a piece of real estate near six tantalizing teens. Three giggling girls sat beside a skinny stoner on a king sized blanket. Lying quietly beside them was a couple of well oiled maidens tanning themselves on beach towels that were imprinted with romantic sunset scenes, on which they proudly displayed their grand teton bait. Rounding out this bevy of beauties was a lone bronze bikini goddess. She laid face down and peacefully slept on a bright white terrycloth towel.

After removing the horse collar from my neck, I held out the ends of the towel and gently lowered it close to the ground letting the wind unfurl the Surf City logo. The goddess continued to sleep, but her giggling girlfriends periodically glanced up at me and one even blushed when I locked onto her gaze. After covering my incandescent body with sun screen, I donned the shades and sat down on my towel. From behind polarized lenses, I discreetly observed the girls with little fear of rejection and wondered if they were doing the same. Nonchalantly placing a cigarette between my parched lips, I cupped my hand to block the wind. The breeze was strong and it immediately blew out the match. Striking a second time produced almost the same result. Again and again I tried to light the cigarette only to repeatedly fail. Had the girls noticed? Did they think I was completely inept? Were they secretly laughing at me? I couldn't just give up. Rolling over close to the ground and cupping the match with both hands; I tried one last time. Finally it lit, but just barely and it took a double death drag to keep the darn thing going. Now I really had to look cool. Modeling my behavior after

---

[369] *Foster Grant's* – references a 1960s sunglasses ad campaign, by the Geer, Dubois advertising agency, which asked the question "Who's that behind those Foster Grants?" It included such celebrities as Anthony Quinn & Raquel Welch, among others.

James Bond[370] I acted as if absolutely nothing had ever been outside of my control.

Although I went body surfing and swam in close proximity to the girls, I never could muster up the courage to speak with any of them. Whenever they looked my way, I simply pretended not to notice. I mulled over dozens of plans on how to introduce myself, but never actually made the move. Meanwhile the comatose cover girl maintained her mysterious magnetism by sleeping all afternoon. Feeling like a failure, I went home and stopped by to see how Sarah was making out with her new business.

Her new found friend Aaron was an orthodox Jew who always wore his yarmulke.[371] Since my sister had never seen one before she asked him about it. The inquiry was a great ice breaker and their frequently interrupted conversation lasted throughout the afternoon. Just before I arrived, he asked her out to a beach party with his friends. Sarah said she was doing well with her new business and I let her know about my bad luck on the beach. Sarah told me about her date and said that Aaron had a younger sister named Leah. She said she could probably arrange a blind date for me and that Leah and I could double date with her and Aaron. It was embarrassing enough to admit I couldn't meet girls on my own, but the thought of going on a blind date seemed even worse. Sarah said Leah was a nice girl and reassured me by saying she was kind of cute too. The only downside to the deal was that she was younger than me. Although still embarrassed about going on a blind date, I put my trust in Sarah's recommendation and decided to take a chance;

---

[370] *James Bond* – is a fictional character created in 1953 by writer Ian Fleming, who featured him in 12 novels & 2 short story collections. The 007 character has also been used in the longest running & most financially successful English-language film franchise to date, starting in 1962 with Dr. No. Bond is the quintessential fantasy hero. He does very little work, yet is filthy rich; he kills many, but he never dies; he casually dates many beautiful women, but they all pine for him alone & he always beats the odds.

[371] *Yarmulke* – a small beanie-like cap worn on the back of the head by Orthodox Jewish men. This cap serves as a sign of respect for God & recognition that its wearer submits to the will of a greater power above.

besides, it would give me an opportunity to keep an eye out for my little sister's safety.

Aaron's friends held their parties on the 2nd Street beach. Sarah and I met him and his sister at their house and then the four of us walked up to the beach together. There were about twenty people sitting in a circle and a pretty girl with long dark hair was sitting in the middle playing a guitar and singing ballads. We took up a position on the perimeter and sat down on the sand. Having been to a few drug parties back at North Penn, I braced myself and was fully prepared to leave if anyone pulled out a joint. To my surprise, the music was gentle and pleasant sounding. These teens were absolutely respectful toward the host and each other. In fact the entire group was so closemouthed; I could hear almost all of the words of the songs over the muffled modulation of the wind and the surf.

In between sets, Aaron introduced Sarah and I to the other members of the Second Street Gang. The leader of the pack was a girl named Sheryl Levite. She lived on the island all year round and seemed to set the tone for the way the rest of the group behaved. No one did any drugs and as far as I could tell, none of them were drinking either. They were just a nice bunch of kids, having a good time on their summer vacation. Later on that night the wind picked up and the temperature plummeted. I put my arm around Leah and covered her back with my windbreaker. She snuggled up next to me and after a while we began to gently kiss. When the party dispersed the four of us took a long walk down the beach. Things worked out so well for both couples that Sarah and I decided to meet up with Aaron and Leah at the dance the following evening.

Besides being the name of the town, Surf City[372] was also a popular song. The celebratory dance tune included the refrain, "three girls for every boy" and it accurately characterized the demographics of the island. Every firehouse dance ended with a chorus of exuberant teens, screaming the lyrics to the song at the top of their lungs. It didn't take long for me to learn the ropes and join in on the ritual. Our two-week vacation went by quickly, but our family enjoyed the shore so much that dad agreed to rent the same house again in the month of August.

On the way home from the shore I stopped in at Riley's house. Vinny and Chris were in the man cave listening to Black Magic Woman.[373] They told me there would be a party later on that evening; but then Chris added, "The only thing is that its for couples only. Vinny and I have dates. If you can get a date, you can come, but you have to have a date." I thought nothing of it and boasted, "No problem. I'll just call Mary Kate."

Vinny raised his eyebrows and glanced over at Chris saying, "You sound pretty sure of yourself Pat. Are you sure she'll want to go with you?" I was caught off guard by their tone and not sure why it had been put that way, but they both seemed to know something was up. Chris mockingly challenged, "If you're so confident, why don't you just give her a call right now." I was ticked off by his sarcasm, but still positive she would go with me. Pointing to the princess phone I said, "You mind if I use your phone?" Vinny nodded his head, "Yea sure, go ahead."

---

[372] *Surf City* – was the nickname Dean Torrence gave to his hometown of Huntington Beach, CA. Brian Wilson, of *The Beach Boys*, composed the original draft of the song about the town in collaboration with Dean. In 1963 *Jan and Dean* made it into a hit & Surf City, New Jersey adopted it as the closing song for all the teen dances at the firehouse.
[373] *Black Magic Woman* - is a song written by Peter Green, which first appeared as a Fleetwood Mac single in 1968. It became a classic hit by Santana in 1970 & reached #4 on their *Abraxas* album.

I dialed her number, while the two of them kept staring at me like NASCAR[374] fans leaning over the rail to watch a spectacular car crash. She picked up the phone and said, "Hello?" Now I would shut these two clowns up, "Vinny is having a party tonight for couples only. Wanna go?" Her answer was swift and firm, "No." My two jeering buddies were smiling with ear-to-ear grins. I wheeled around to face the wall and quietly asked, "What do you mean, No?" She softly responded, "I have other plans tonight." I was embarrassed, but I still believed I had sway over her. Pushing back hard I said, "Break 'em!" There was a long pause and then she quietly said, "I'm not going to do that, Pat... Good bye."

When I hung up the phone Vinny and Chris busted out laughing. Vinny turned back toward the stereo, picked up an album and looked sideways at me saying, "Not as big a hot shot as you thought you were, eh?" With that Chris fell on the black leather sofa hysterically laughing and jeered, "What's the matter, Pat. Cat got your tongue?" I had no idea what had just happened, but apparently the two of them knew all about it. I angrily fired back, "You knew, didn't you?" Neither of them let me in on what they knew about Mary Kate and what had transpired while I was away.

Mary Kate was a one-man woman. She needed to know in an ongoing way that her man cared about her. My escapades down at the shore had cost our relationship dearly. The whole time I was in Surf City I had not so much as given her a phone call. On our trip to Wharton Tract she had completely opened herself up to me in a last ditch effort to get me to commit to her and to her alone. I never did make that commitment and had been oblivious to the pain she felt

---

[374] *NASCAR* – the National Association for Stock Car Auto Racing is a family-owned & operated business venture that sanctions & governs multiple auto racing sports events. It was founded by Bill France, Sr. in 1947–48. Its roots go back to Prohibition when runners delivered moonshine in souped up cars, which gave the slip to the federal tax agents. Runners developed their reputations by outsmarting & out driving the law & held informal races to determine the fastest runner.

in my absence. While I felt somewhat guilty about not calling her, apparently I loved freedom more than I loved her. I wanted to meet other girls and wasn't ready to settle down. Additionally I could barely support myself, let alone a wife and kids. Even so, her decision to stop dating cut me to the quick and I never again enjoyed the privilege of seeing her or even hearing her voice.

Mary Kate was now out of the picture. Tom started his own house painting business and I was still miffed at those turncoat traitors who still claimed to be my friends. Their apparent betrayal left me with very little incentive to visit Jersey and that gave me plenty of time to work and build up my bank account. Throughout July I worked as many hours as I could and saved every dime for my return trip to Surf City. I washed mountains of dishes at the Holiday Inn and whenever I ran out of dishes I worked overtime to set up rooms for banquets.

The waitresses weren't even clocked in when I arrived in the kitchen for work at six in the morning. Yet already seated in the hotel dining room was a party of eight and my boss Linda asked me to serve them. Happy for the opportunity to finally be waiting on tables, I took down their orders and poured them coffee. A couple of drops spilled on one of the saucers and the customer flipped out. He demanded I bring him a clean cup. Shocked by both his volume and tone, I quickly apologized. However by the time I returned to the kitchen, my anger was hotter than the coffee and I came up with a plan to get even with the little bastard. Walking back to the table; I placed my index finger in the handle of the cup and when I set the mug down I flipped it over. When the scalding liquid poured into his lap I profusely apologized and feigning an attempt at wiping him down. Jumping back from the table he let out a string of obscenities and ordered me back into the kitchen. Franticly brushing the black coffee from his bright white shirt, the businessman tore off his yellow silk tie and blotted his pants with a napkin. I retreated through the swinging double-doors with a great big smile on my face. In a few seconds Linda burst through the door and shouted, "You did that on purpose didn't you?" "I sure did! He was being a jerk!" Rolling her eyes she urgently inquired, "Do you know who that man is?" "I don't care if he's the President of the United States! Nobody talks to me like that!" Hanging her head in utter frustration she followed through on her point, "That's Mr. Parven! He owns this Holiday Inn!"

Linda knew me to be a good worker and I believe she even went to bat for my job. I had treated Mr. Parven a bit less courteously than he was used to and it may have even led him to questioned Linda's ability to hire good people. The following Saturday afternoon, our chef set up a production line for a banquet and my job was to dish out the peas. In the middle of the task, Mr. Parven tapped my coworker on the shoulder and motioned for him to step back. The owner of the Inn took up the position next to me and silently stood there dishing out sliced carrots. After about ten minutes, he walked away without saying a word. I was sure I was fired, but it never happened. I assume all he really wanted to do was determine whether I was a troublemaker or just someone who had stood up for himself. I must have passed the test, because not only was I still employed, but a couple of weeks later I even got a raise.

By the time August rolled around I had plenty of money in the bank and was eager to return to the shore. Not only was I looking forward to seeing Leah again, but my Uncle Ray recently purchased a summer place on Lang Avenue in Harvey Cedars. Our family always enjoyed visiting with the Callahan cousins and since his new place was only a few towns up from Surf City, this promised to be one great summer!

I followed dad down to the shore in my car. Our family took up residence in the same house on 10th Street in Surf City. As soon as we unpacked, I drove down to 2nd Street to find Leah. I found her sunning on the beach and I used a towel to block her rays. Placing a hand over her forehead like a visor, she rolled over to see what was going on. When she saw that it was me she yelled, "Patrick!" Immediately jumping to her feet she gave me a big hug and asked, "When did you get here?" After some minor chitchat, we ran down to the surf with her raft to ride the waves. The gang had grown more numerous than they were the previous month and some of the group dynamics were a little different. For starters, I was instantly part of the in-crowd; not just with Leah, but with the entire Second Street Gang. Leah and I hung out on the beach till about four, and then headed home for dinner and showers. Later on that evening we reunited for a nice long walk on the beach.

Compared to the rest of the gang, I looked like an albino and they were not shy about letting me know they could spot newcomers a mile away. Day-trippers betrayed themselves with easily discernable characteristics. Tourists often had lily-white skin in the morning, bright red sunburns by lunchtime and smelled of Noxzema in the evening. To keep from being ridiculed I carefully worked on my tan. I began tanning early in the morning and made sure I was home before noon. I spent a couple of hours reading in the house and then returned to the beach late in the afternoon. Gradually increasing my exposure time, I soon had a golden brown tan and was eventually able to stay out in the sun for a full eight hours straight without getting burnt. Sarah and I frequented the teen dances every week and we always met up with Leah and her brother Aaron. In addition, we mixed it up on the dance floor with some of the other kids we knew and they in turn introduced us to other teens. We were getting to know an ever-widening circle of friends.

Dancing in the dark provided greater intimacy than the bright sunshine of the beach and with three girls for every boy, the demographics of the shore were clearly working in my favor.

One of the new girls I met at the dance was Leah's best friend Christina Nowicki. The slender brunette worked at the Surf City Pharmacy, which explains why I had not seen her on the beach during the daytime. There was something special about the warmth of her embrace and we shared several more dances together before rejoining the gang to sing the final euphoric rendition of Surf City. On days that Christina had off from work, she joined us on the beach. The three of us had wonderful times riding the waves and sitting on beach towels where we shared our stories and dreams for the future. Christina had already reached sixteen years of age, whereas Leah was just fourteen. The way that played out is that my conversations with Christina were a bit more satisfying than they were with Leah. Although I liked them both, I was drawn to each one for slightly different reasons.

Leah adored me and would have done just about anything to please me. Christina liked me too, but she was hardly inclined to start kissing my feet. As time went on I was drawn closer and closer to Christina. Gradually a strange dynamic began to emerge. I wanted to start dating Christina, but did not want to hurt Leah. Since I knew they were the best of friends and assumed they told each other everything, I was afraid to ask Christina out. The only opportunity I had to even broach the subject without upsetting Leah was when I was playing around with Christina in the water on her day off or when we were dancing together at the fire hall. During the day swimming with Leah steadily advanced to cuddling with her on a blanket, but Leah had a curfew. When the sun went down my slow dances with Christina morphed into romantic walks with her on the beach. Eventually the competition between the two turned sexual. Apparently they did talk with each other and eventually came up with a plan that included a playful game of striptease in the water. One day, out beyond the breaking waves they both proceeded to put me on the spot. Donning goggles, they challenged me to remove my swim trunks for a look-see. I was confused, flattered and embarrassed all at the same time. In order to get out of it, I issued a challenge of my own, "You first."

I thought it would get me off the hook, but to my surprise Leah handed me her goggles and the young women removed the tops of their bikinis. Diving down I saw a bland underwater world with a sandy bottom and drifting clumps of seaweed. Looking back towards the surface I saw the beautiful figures of two mermaids treading water. What a sight! I was awestruck and paused for a few seconds to admire their bosoms before surfacing. The giggling teens upped the anti by pressing their naked flesh up against either side of me, just below the waterline. Then Christina said, "Your turn." What else could I do? They had called my bluff. Still trying to control the game I said, "Ok, but you'll have to be the ones to take my shorts off." Much to my surprise they donned the goggles and like a well-rehearsed diving team, unzipped my white cut-off jeans and pulled the trunks down around my knees. When the two virgins resurfaced, they started laughing hysterically. Humiliated and assuming the worst, I quickly pulled up my bathing suit. The giggling continued unabated until Christina glanced at Leah and said, "He'll do." At which point the two mermaids burst out laughing again.

The Bohemian[375] ritual clearly put me on the spot. Although it may have satisfied their curiosity and broken the tension damaging their friendship, the relief would be temporary. From that day forward, I openly dated both of them. The competition for my affection inflated my ego, but it also tore away at their friendship. I liked Christina more than I did Leah, but I was afraid to tell her so, because I knew she would be devastated. Since I sensed Christina would feel any pain in her friend, I feared loosing them both; but I also knew that something would have to give. It all came to a

---

[375] *Bohemianism* - is the practice of an unconventional lifestyle, usually immoral & often done in the company of like-minded vagabonds.

head one day when they presented me with an ultimatum and came over to my house for lunch and a decision.

Dad had just finished another one of those touchy-feely seminars and knew about my dilemma. So when the girls came over for lunch he asked about their ultimatum. Trying out one of his newfound techniques, he set up a role-playing scenario to smoke things out. Obviously he was invading our personal space, but the girls loved having an issue so close to their hearts acknowledged. Near the end of the intervention dad asked, "Don't you think it's unfair to leave these two girls in limbo?" When I admitted it probably was; he followed up with another question; "Then, why don't you want to make a choice?" I responded by saying, "Because I'm afraid I'll loose them both." Even though the girls believed me, they still wanted me to choose. Dad glanced over at me and inquired, "Are you ready to face your fears, take a risk and make a choice?" I knew in my gut it would be stupid to open my mouth, but I felt trapped and emotionally exhausted. Giving into their demand I blurted out, "I'm sorry Leah, but if I have to choose, I choose Christina." Leah immediately burst into tears. We all hugged her till her sobbing subsided and then I drove them both home in silence. When I stopped the car to let them out, Christina started to walk Leah into her house and then turned back toward me and whispered, "Call me tonight." Later on that evening I did so and she told me that Leah cried on her bed for over an hour. Around eight I met Christina on the 10th Street beach, so that we wouldn't run into Leah. Sitting on the bench at the top of the dune, we talked about what had transpired until the mosquitoes started biting. So we took a walk out by the surf, where the wind kept the bugs at bay. Although Christina empathized with the pain of her friend, she was happy with my choice. Picking her because of her maturity seemed especially affirming to the young woman. We walked hand-in-hand for miles, occasionally stopping along the way to make out. We were growing closer, but only for about a week. Suddenly Christina wanted to break it off, because she felt disloyal toward her friend. I should have listened to my gut.

There wasn't much I could do about my relationship with Christina Nowicki, so when Chris came down to visit me we hung out with my cousins at Uncle Ray's house in Harvey Cedars. When I introduced Chris to my Uncle Ray and Aunt Joan they offered us some soda and made us feel welcome. Soon my cousins returned from a half-day fishing trip with lots of bluefish and my godparents asked us to stay for dinner. Aunt Joan led us out into the living room for some conversation and set her wine glass down on a clear glass coffee table. The view through the sliding glass doors looked out over a second floor balcony and we could see a panorama of sailboats gliding across the white capped bay.

Suddenly, my cousin Mariah appeared at the top of the stairs and said, "Hi Pat. Who's your friend?" I started to introduce Chris, but just as he turned around to see her she descended a couple of steps and stopped cold. Flicking her flowing brunette locks back over her shoulder she put one hand on her hip and giving her best impression of Mae West said, "How ya doin, big boy." Never had I seen Chris speechless, yet there he sat slack jawed. Without breaking any eye contact, Mariah kept up the offensive asking him, "What's the matter? Cat got your tongue?" Chris was usually a pretty cocky guy and downright handsome to boot. So it was extremely unusual for a girl to throw him off balance, but Mariah was audacious and her mystique made a lasting impression on him.

The Callahan household consisted of twelve of my energetic cousins, their friends and plenty of guests each night for dinner. Supper was generally a well-organized affair that was filled with good conversation and lots of laughter. Along with all that hospitality was the inevitable task of cleaning up. Each evening at least two of my cousins were assigned kitchen patrol. So whenever I visited I made it a point to help them out with the dishes. After dinner Mariah gave Chris the nickel tour of the house, while I was busy clearing the table. She showed him each of the rooms in the house, which were decorated with a theme color. That night, Chris and I were invited to stay over night and given the red room.

Mariah and Chris became an item for the week and my cute cousin introduced me to a friend she affectionately called Plain Jane. True to her name Jane Lowood was a smart albeit shy and simple girl, which turned out to be a very attractive combination. After dinner the twenty or so teenagers that made up the Lang Gang took a long walk on the beach. However, unlike the folks on 2nd Street, this crowd was loud and rowdy. They cracked jokes, told adventurous stories and laughed about all the good times they had experienced together over the years. Jane and I were a bit quieter than the rest and gradually lagged behind the pack where we were able to engage in our own private conversations. While walking down the beach in the dark I held hands with the Ivory Girl,[376] but since we both preferred to keep our budding relationship private we let go of our hands as soon as we approached the streetlights for Lang Avenue.

The next day we all went up to Pat's Steaks in Harvey Cedars for lunch. Spending the rest of the day on the beach, my cousin Peter tried to teach me how to surf. He lent me a ten-foot long board he called "The Log" and repeatedly told me not to put the board in between a wave and myself. Naturally I forgot about his warning after my first run. I was almost knocked out when I turned around to take another run and a wave hit the board and busted me in the mouth. Peter watched the whole thing happen and burst out laughing.

---

[376] *The Ivory Girl* – the Procter & Gamble Company name "Ivory" refers to a series of mildly fragranced bar soap. The 1st P&G ad "It Floats!" was introduced in 1891 & the "99 & 44/100% Pure" slogan, was based on independent chemical analysis demonstrating the purity of Ivory compared to its competitor castile soap. In contrast to hot sexy TV ads in the 70s, Ivory featured an innocent attractive young woman without any make-up, to indicate the health & purity of their product.

Giving me the kind of knowing smile that only comes from experience; he teased me saying, "I told you…"

Meanwhile, Natalie Larsen came down to visit my sister Sarah and brought along a bottle of whiskey. Chris and I met up with them at the dance and the four of us took turns swigging her Crown Royal[377] while making our way down the beach. Natalie downed the lion's share of the alcohol and for the next few hours we coupled off on blankets consuming a blissful quantity of hugs and kisses. The only trouble was that Miss Larsen seemed more interested in finishing her bottle than she did about spending time with me and she was soon wasted. Sarah and Chris on the other hand, had been trying to get together ever since that game of spin the bottle in the back of our moving van. Although they finally had the opportunity to share some of those longed for tender moments, it would all be cut short. It required all three of us to help Natalie walk upright and keep her quiet long enough to smuggle her into the house. However, once we got her into the bed she fell fast asleep and returned to Pennsylvania late the next morning.

Chris and I were extremely competitive and with the season coming to an end we challenged each other to a bet to see who could go out on the most dates within a twenty-four hour period. We started setting up dates with the girls we met at the dance. The rendezvous were kept separate so that the girls would not be able to find out about each other. I set up my first tryst on the 10th Street beach. The second girl I met at the custard stand and we went parking, down by the bay. The third was with a new girl from the 2nd Street Gang whom I secretly took to the Sand Piper restaurant for dinner and I even asked Leah out to the movies to see Diamonds

---

[377] *Crown Royal* – began production in 1939 to commemorate the first Royal Tour of Canada by King George VI & Queen Elizabeth. Seagram created a quality whisky in a crown-shaped bottle & dressed it in a distinctive royal purple bag. Like the packaging, the name was intended to reflect quality. It was sold exclusively in Canada until 1964.

Are Forever.[378] Chris made similar arrangements with his girls, lining up each date on a different street and finding a separate location for the date. As far as each of us knew, by the end of the night, the score was four apiece. Since my last date was with Leah, I dropped her off at her house and then walked up to the 2nd Street beach, where Chris and I had arranged to meet at midnight to compare notes.

Sitting on the park bench at the top of the dune was Sheryl Levite. The native islander had command of a communications network like nothing I had ever seen. She knew all about the dates Chris and I had been on and was intelligent enough to surmise that something other than love interests were involved. Sitting down next to her on the bench and looking out over the ocean she asked, "Have a good time with Leah?" I answered in the affirmative. Then she turned her head toward me and asked, "How about with Jeannie?" I was puzzled and asked how she knew about the other girl. She smiled and said, "I live here. I know everything." I looked at her half guilty and half laughing and said, "Not everything." She looked back to the surf for a second and then said, "You mean Carmen and Priscilla?" I couldn't believe my ears, "How do you know all that?" She smiled again and said, "I told you... I know everything." Turning back toward the ocean we both watched the surf for another minute. Then she turned back to me and asked, "So... who's winning?" At that point I was done questioning how she knew; it was just obvious that she did. So I said, "To the best of my knowledge it's a tie with four apiece and it ends at midnight. He probably picked up another girl by now." She looked back to the surf for a few seconds and then broke the silence saying, "I know someone else you can kiss tonight." I was floored that she would help me with such a

---

[378] *Diamonds Are Forever* – was the 7th spy film in the James Bond series & the 6th to star Sean Connery as the MI6 agent. The 1971 film is based on Ian Fleming's 1956 novel & directed by Guy Hamilton. Bond impersonates a diamond smuggler to infiltrate the ring, only to uncover a plot by his old nemesis Blofeld, to use the diamonds to build a giant laser satellite that would be used to hold the world for ransom.

dubious contest and asked, "Who?" A gentle smile came across her face and we began making out.

We were friends, not lovers. I knew she didn't love me that way and I could tell she was disgusted that Chris and I were willing to use girls to win a bet, but she also loved me as a friend. Chris, on the other hand, was a cocky guy that she had just met. So it was not so much that she wanted me or even wanted me to win the bet; she just wanted to see Chris loose. Something else was also going on here. For reasons I may never understand, this extremely popular girl was sitting at the top of the dune alone. Perhaps it was a comfort to her to know that she was needed and desired by someone whom she knew loved and respected her. The kissing only lasted a few minutes and then we both turned back to the sea and the serene sights and sounds of the surf.

Fifteen minutes later Chris walked up the dune from the beach. Without saying a word he sat down on the bench beside us and looked at the full moon that had risen above the horizon only minutes before he arrived. Sheryl smiled at him and said, "How'd ya do?" Chris might have expected a question like that from me, but he wasn't sure what to make of it coming from her. In a failed attempt at being nonchalant he said, "What do you mean?" Now she had him where she wanted him, "How many girls did you make out with tonight?" As Chris looked over at me I raised my eyebrows and said, "She knows about the bet." "Four... I guess we tied." Sheryl giggled and said, "Nope. Tom had five." Chris was shocked. "Who was the fifth?" Sheryl leaned back on the bench and impishly put her arms around me. Chris did an about face in the sand and started walking toward the ocean. "I can't believe it. I was hoping you were going to tell me that Leah bailed on you. I can't believe it." Realizing the contest was over and there was nothing left to say or do, Chris walked back up the dune to the bench and sat down beside us.

It wasn't just that the game was over; our whole summer was about to end. Sitting in silent reflection, we went back over all that had taken place in the last few months. We listened to alternating whispers of the gentle breezes of the quiescent evening, which were punctuated by the dull roar of approaching waves crashing from left to right across the shore line. A gigantic full moon hanging just above the horizon illuminated the beach and the moonlight shimmered like a speckled path across the dark blue waters. After about an hour of silent reflection, Sheryl leaned forward on the bench to stand. Raising her arms skyward she yawned. Her jacket fluttered in the wind and the sound of it reminded me of the kites in the afternoon. Turning toward us she said, "Well... see ya again next year." Chris and I both gave her long goodbye hugs. We stood there by the bench watching her walk down the dune beneath the street light. When she reached the bottom of the hill we heard the clicking of her flip-flops, as she traversed the sandy street and crossed the sidewalk that led to her home. A last wave good-bye and the silence was broken by the crack of the slamming storm door. Our vacation was over.

The next day we packed the car and headed for home. I came away with a black book filled with names and a heart filled with memories. My ego was in bloom, my confidence high and the equal status I once had with my friend Chris had been restored; but we had all paid a price. The overabundance of dating was flattering, but I felt a deep emptiness in the pit of my stomach. I was actually looking forward to going home. I had a great time in Surf City and met lots of girls, but I had also hurt some of them in the process. Most tragic of all, I had lost the affections of Mary Kate and Christina, the two women I cared most deeply about. Although it had all been very exciting, I was walking away with a hollow heart. Listening to the radio on the way home I lamented the losses.

Maggie May[379] reminded me of Mary Kate. How Can You Mend a Broken Heart[380] conjured memories of Christina and Go Away Little Girl[381] made me question my sexual indiscretions with Leah, who had been a fourteen-year-old innocent. I had not treated any of the women in my life very well and Sheryl had gently persuaded me to face up to that reality on the final night of my summer vacation. I vowed that the next time I met a woman I would make sure to Treat Her Like a Lady.[382] Although the two most popular songs of the summer had flattered my ego, Mr. Big Stuff[383] was hardly a title to be proud of and You're So Vain[384] had actually been a commentary on my pathetic behavior and meant to tame my arrogance, not to celebrate it.

I had been loved in spite of how I had behaved, not because of it.

---

[379] *Maggie May* – is a song written by Rod Stewart & Martin Quittenton in 1971, for the album "Every Picture Tells a Story" It expresses the contradictory emotions of a young man involved in a relationship with a mature woman & his struggles as he returns to school.
[380] *How Can You Mend a Broken Heart* – is a 1971 song written by Barry & Robin Gibb & performed by the Bee Gees. The song highlights a period of break-up & alienation.
[381] *Go Away, Little Girl* – is a song written by Gerry Goffin & Carole King. The lyrics tell of a young man asking an attractive young woman to stay away from him, so that he will not be tempted to betray his steady girlfriend. It made the American Top 20 three times.
[382] *Treat Her Like a Lady* – is a song by Cornelius Brothers & Sister Rose encouraging men to treat women better. The group hit the pop charts in 1971 & sold one million copies.
[383] *Mr. Big Stuff* – is a song by R&B singer Jean Knight & became a huge crossover hit. It song spent 5 weeks at #1 on Billboard's Best Selling Soul Singles & peaked at #2 on the Billboard Hot 100 Singles. The signature lines *Who do you think you are?* & *You're never gonna get my love*, made it one of Stax Records's most popular & recognizable hits.
[384] *You're So Vain* – is a song written & performed by Carly Simon. The song is a critical profile of a self-absorbed lover.

Chapter 19

Blind Ambition

When Nixon took the U.S. off the gold standard he shocked the world.[385] This reckless maneuver fundamentally changed the rules of business and turned the financial world on its head. Unfettered by the universal standard, the Keynesians[386] over at the Fed[387] began printing money with abandon and federal bureaucrats multiplied regulations and fees. Large banks and corporations had effectively taken control of our government and hamstrung their small business competition, without ever firing a shot. Thanks to the inflation of the dollar Callahan Machine Company had to pay higher prices for materials and taxes. As if that were not difficult enough, Nixon also instituted wage and price controls. Since it was illegal for any company to raise their prices, the losses came straight out of profits. A gangster government now controlled small business decisions. My father flipped out! Socially he was still a hippie, but dad was also determined to keep his business afloat. The owners fine tuned the manufacturing procedures and studied the tax code looking for every loophole that would allow them to hang on to their hard earned wealth. Down but not out, Callahan Machine worked aggressively to play by the new rules and make those same rubrics work to their advantage.

---

[385] *Nixon Shock* – On August 15, 1971 President Nixon canceled direct convertibility of the U.S. dollar into gold, ending the *Bretton Woods* system of international financial exchange. To combat the inflation, a New Economic Policy instituted wage & price controls.

[386] *Keynesians* - are followers of John Maynard Keynes. Keynesian economics argues that private sector decisions lead to inefficient macroeconomic outcomes & therefore, advocates active policy responses by the public sector, including monetary policy actions by a central bank & fiscal policy actions by the government to stabilize output over the business cycle.

[387] *Fed* – the Federal Reserve System is the central banking system of the United States. It was created in 1913, with the enactment of the Federal Reserve Act. It consists of 12 of the largest privately held banks. In July of 2012 the U.S. House overwhelmingly passed a bill sponsored by Texas Representative & Presidential Candidate Ron Paul to Audit the Fed.

The first fruit of this effort was the discovery of a tax shelter called CSY. Caribbean Sailing Yachts was a company set up as a foreign corporation. It purchased sailboats and then rented them out to vacationers in the British Virgin Islands. The beauty of the deal was that for an initial investment of ten-thousand dollars each of the four partners got a free week vacation so that they could inspect their foreign corporation. CSY provided the boat, the marina, the food, the booze and even airfare. Boat rental profits were plowed back into the company and new ships were purchased when the old ones aged. Everything about the plan was designed to be tax-free. None of the proceeds were ever returned to the U.S. and profits in the islands were only taxed at three percent. Since dad was a licensed captain and the boat slept six, he was able to take five guests with him on each and every visit. A Christmas vacation in the British Virgin Islands was soon on the agenda for my friends and me.

In September 1971 North Penn opened a brand new high school on Valley Forge Road. On the first day of his senior year Jon Baker walked down one of the freshly painted hallways and noticed me sitting in an eleventh grade homeroom. Poking his head in the door he asked, "What the hell are you doing in a junior homeroom?" I laughed and said, "I flunked." Clearly disgusted with my flippant response he said, "You idiot. Now you won't be graduating with our class." It was a much-needed wake up call for me. I quickly asked for a pass to the guidance office to lay my cards on the table. When Mrs. Binet opened her door I made my confession. "For whatever dumb reasons, I purposely flunked the eleventh grade. I realize now that I made a mistake and want to know what I can do to fix it?" She motioned me in to her office and helped me rearrange my schedule. Although it was easy enough to arrange she stressed how difficult it would be for me to succeed. "You're going to have to take two languages, three history classes, math, consumer economics and gym. You will not have a single study hall and you can't fail even one subject." It was a tall order, but I felt up to the challenge.

Sitting behind me in homeroom was Thelma Wilson. She was a pretty girl with long black hair and a smooth complexion. She had a soft pleasant voice, was kind, thoughtful and easy to talk with about anything. However, as soon as I told someone I wanted to ask her out I hit a brick wall. While it made no difference to me, Thelma was black. One guy said, "You can never date a black girl! If you do no other white woman will ever go out with you!" I didn't believe him, but when I asked others about dating her I got virtually the same response. So many people concurred with their assessment that I started to question my perception of reality. Although we remained friends and talked every day in homeroom, I never asked her out. How could I have been such a coward in the face of this dubious information and peer pressure?

Thelma was as sweet as honeysuckle, but her brother Wayne was quickly becoming a jerk. Wayne was in the click and almost everyone liked him. He was on the student council, ran track and dated several of the most beautiful cheerleaders. However, over the summer months he began working at the local McDonald's. Most of the row house tenants in Lansdale were Puerto Rican. Working with them twisted his view of the world. They convinced him he was a victim and that he would never get a fair shake in life, because he was black. Wayne went into an emotional spiral and shut down despite the reality he had experienced at school.

Mrs. Cash was my French teacher and she made Wayne Wilson my study partner. By the end of the summer Wayne had bought into the self-fulfilling prophecy of racism and he felt that studying was pointless. It was hard enough to learn a new language without trying to motivate a guy who flat out refused to work with me. I needed to pass every one of my courses to graduate and tried requesting another partner, but my French teacher refused the request. Although I put my best efforts into drilling with my mother and sister; I was unable to master the language.

While practicing my French flashcards one afternoon, I asked my mother about getting a dog. She absolutely refused, but I went ahead anyway and secretly bought a German Shepherd pup from a local farmer. Although barely weaned the dog's paws were as big as my wrists, so I named him Big Bear. Figuring my mother would never go out in the barn I tied him up in a room on the second floor with an old extension chord. One day when mom went out to get the mail and heard the puppy whining. When I got home from school I was in big trouble, but I begged her to let me keep the dog and to my complete surprise she said yes. I fed him some old freezer burned venison and kept him chained to the branch of a tree in our front yard. Predictably the novelty wore off quickly and the poor dog was sentenced to a life on the chain. Although Big Bear eventually lived up to his name in size it turned out to be a much more ferocious description than he actually deserved. Still, the mere site of him or the sound of one of his well timed deep throated growls kept our family safe.

Trying to motivate me again, dad gave me a set of vinyl records on personal development by Earl Nightingale.[388] The gift was timely and the next thing I knew I was writing down goals for my life, setting financial targets and devising plans on becoming a millionaire by the time I was thirty. I even made an appointment with the president of Pecora Chemical Corporation, which was the factory across the street from us.

---

[388] *Earl Nightingale* – was a motivational speaker known as the "Dean of Personal Development". At 17 he joined the Marines & became a drill instructor at Camp Lejeune. During the attack on Pearl Harbor, he became one of 12 men who survived the bombing of the USS Arizona. After the war he became a motivational speaker, hosted a radio program & was the voice of *Sky King*. His book *The Strangest Secret* became the first spoken-word recording & sold over a million copies, making it the greatest motivational record ever sold. (1921–1989)

Upon entering a solid oak paneled room a well dressed man asked me what he could do for me. I responded by saying, "I want to be a success. I feel you are someone who has made it and quite frankly sir, I'd like to pick your brains." Intrigued by my chutzpah, he spent the next hour telling me all about his career. Near the end of the interview I asked for one important piece of advice. He shook my hand, wished me luck and said, "When you are absolutely sure that you will fail, believe you will succeed, and you will."

I thanked him for his time and began reading the biographies of several successful men. The common denominator that seemed to emerge was that each one of them had failed an average of seven times before they succeeded. One of these men was a famous restaurant owner. Someone once asked him when he became successful and he responded by saying, "I was successful when I was sleeping on park benches without a dime in my pocket, because I knew what I wanted to do and that I would do it." These stories reminded me of the scene in Gone With the Wind[389] when Scarlet O'Hara cries out, "As God is my witness, I'll never be this poor again." I was coming to the conclusion that in order to get to the top, you had to hit bottom. It sounds stupid now, but I made it my goal in life to race to the bottom.

My friends came from a variety of family backgrounds, which influenced their perspective on the world and also affected my own. My dad had inherited a manufacturing facility, so I naturally assumed I would have my own business one day. Although Chris was smart enough to go on to college, he planned on going through an electrical apprentice program. His father was a union man and he believed that labor and management were bitter enemies.

---

[389] *Gone with the Wind* – is a 1939 film adapted from Margaret Mitchell's 1936 romantic novel. This epic film was set in the South & tells the story of the Civil War & its aftermath, on a fictitious plantation called *Tara*. The MGM release stared Clark Gable, Vivien Leigh, Leslie Howard, Olivia de Havilland & Hattie McDaniel. It was produced by David O. Selznick, directed by Victor Fleming with screenplay by Sidney Howard.

Tom's father was a professional musician with his own conservatory. In that family college was expected and business was simply a tool to make a living as an artist. Tom read the entire series of Tom Swift books and wanted to become an astronaut. To fulfill his dream he needed to maintain a straight "A" average in high school; he also started a painting business to pay for college. Vinny Riley's father was an executive engineer with RCA, who frequently worked with the CIA and the Pentagon. Vinny picked up on his nuanced people skills and organizational ability. Since Vinny had very little interest in going on to college, his father demanded that he get a job early and learn a trade. Vinny's father signed him up for baseball so he would learn the value of teamwork and refused to let him quit even when he lost all interest. In both work and play the pressure on him to perform was intense.

The circumstances of the friends I hung out with on my side of the Delaware River were also unique. Jon's father was an inventor who worked for Texas Instruments and the company had transferred his family to Pennsylvania. Jon could care less about science and was angry about being uprooted from his home state of Texas. This tough hombre was a hard worker and quite capable of taking care of himself. He was also determined to get out on his own as quickly as possible, so that he could return to the Lone Star State. In contrast, my friend Jessie's father was a drifter and a drunk. His mother worked countless hours as a low-level factory worker at Greene Tweede in Kulpsville trying desperately to make the ends meet. Their gypsy family lifestyle and trailer park mentality habitually shunned etiquette and absolutely despised the rich. In a twisted sense of fairness family members felt completely justified in taking advantage of anyone who had more money than they did.

Coming from a business family my ambition was much higher than that of my friends. When I spoke of setting goals, starting a business or making a million dollars by the age of thirty, they simply humored me. When I sang I've Gotta Be Me[390] at the top of my lungs, they thought I was delusional. It was pretty difficult for them to relate with my overwhelming desire to conquer the world when nothing so grand was tangibly in front of me. I was beginning to feel pretty isolated until I got what I presumed to be my big break.

George Rosellini was a good friend of my father. He invested in a company called Bestline Products and offered to shepherd me in at the direct distributor level. Dad loaned me three grand for some seed money to get started in my own business. Similar to Amway[391] the multi-level marketing company sold soap and personal care items, but it was just getting started so it seemed to be more of a ground floor opportunity. A few weeks later a tractor-trailer pulled up on the side of Wambold Road and we emptied half its contents into an empty room in the barn. I finally had the financial tool I needed to fulfill my dream. At least that's what I saw. Few others were as positive about the idea. Lesley's father called it a Ponzie scheme[392] and cautioned me to avoid it like the plague. Although upset with his negativity at the time, I probably should have heeded his advice. Once again it became obvious that I was too shy to engage in sales, let alone bold enough to invite people to business opportunity meetings. Worst of all, my attempts to

---

[390] *I've Gotta Be Me* – was a popular song, which first showed up in the Broadway musical Golden Rainbow, which starred Steve Lawrence & Eydie Gormé. Singer Sammy Davis, Jr. recorded his version of the song in 1968 where it became a surprise hit.

[391] *Amway* – is a direct selling company & manufacturer based in Ada, Michigan. It uses network marketing to sell a variety of products, primarily in the health, beauty & home care markets. American Way Company was founded in 1959 by Jay Van Andel & Richard DeVos. In 2010 the family of companies now known as Alticor had sales of $9.2 billion.

[392] *Ponzi Scheme* – is a kind of fraud & investment operation. Normally, if investments make a profit, this profit is shared & distributed among those people investing money, but a Ponzi scheme is different. It offers returns that are paid by the people investing themselves, or by other people investing & not from the profits made. It is named after Charles Ponzi, who became notorious for using the technique after emigrating from Italy to the U.S. in 1903. More recently, Bernie Madoff pleaded guilty in March of 2009 to 11 federal felonies & admitted to turning his wealth management business into a massive Ponzi scheme that defrauded thousands of investors of billions of dollars.

get my friends involved made them feel used and forced them to distance themselves.

During the first half of the seventies, multi-level marketing firms or MLMs, started sky rocking along with the unemployment rates. Unfortunately, all that rocketing started rocking some boats. The result was that more than five times as many MLM related law suits were filed between 1970 and 1974, than were litigated throughout all of the fifties and sixties combined. Scores of attorneys brought class action lawsuits against Koscot, Bestline, Holiday Magic, Culture Farms and others. Many of these civil actions succeeded, but even though the lawyers made millions, plaintiffs rarely recovered anything near what they had lost. I wholesaled off my product and didn't even come close to recovering the $3,700 investment. This millionaire thing was not working out very well.

While I was trying to start a business; my buddies were working on cars. Jon got a job as a mechanic at the Texaco station in Kulpsville. After working countless hours in our garage he put a vintage Jaguar[393] back on the road. He then purchased an old Chrysler New Yorker[394] which we cracked up after testing out a new speedometer cable. The totaled vehicle occupied the garage for over two years, until my father ordered us to chop it up with a torch and get rid of it piecemeal in the trash. Meanwhile Jessie bought an old Ford Falcon wagon[395] and adorned it with a new piece of chrome

---

[393] *Jaguar XJ6* – is a luxury sedan sold under the British Jaguar marque. The XJ6 was a 2.8 litre straight 6-cylinder launched in 1968 & it replaced the original saloon model, which had the input of Sir William Lyons, the company's founder. "Mr. Jaguar", along with fellow motorcycle enthusiast William Walmsley, co-founded the Swallow Sidecar Company in 1922, which became Jaguar Cars Limited after the World War II.
[394] *Chrysler New Yorker* – was Chrysler's longest running nameplate. The name defined the brand to be above mainstream cars like Ford, Chevrolet & Pontiac, but below full luxury vehicles like Cadillac & Packard. The 1956 "PowerStyle" model was designed by Virgil Exner & included leather seats, a pushbutton automatic transmission & a 280 hp V8 engine.
[395] *Ford Falcon* – was an automobile produced by Ford Motor Company from 1960-1970. Robert McNamara "the father of the Falcon" became U.S. Defense Secretary before its introduction, but his faith in the Falcon small-car concept was vindicated when record sales, handily outsold other compacts by Chrysler & GM.

every other week. The time we spent often seemed pointless to me, since dressing up a hunk of junk was an activity somewhat akin to placing pearls on a pig. I spent hundreds of hours handing wrenches to my motor-head mates while boring them with my latest scheme for making money, but none of it was a total waste of time. Working together gave us the chance to laugh, learn about cars and get to know one another. It all seemed like good stuff, but my highs school buddies had dark sides. Jon was prone to taking unnecessary risks. In addition to his unorthodox method of testing out speedometers, he liked filling his mouth with butane from a lighter and then blowing out fireballs into the air. One night he even set his mustache on fire and slapped himself silly trying to extinguish the flame, which sent Jessie and me into hysterical laughter. It was easy enough to forgive Jon for his recklessness, but Jessie turned out to be a shameless thief.

Jessie Allen felt completely justified in stealing just about anything he needed from anyone who was better off than he was and he rarely considered or even cared about the consequences. One day he needed a battery for his car, so he simply stole one from the pickup truck across the street. He even bragged about his thieving prowess, which is how I found out about the incident. While shocking to Jon and me, he felt we were being petty when we demanded he replace it immediately. Not only did his thieving ways cause potential problems with my neighbors, they soon maneuvered us into the crosshairs of the law.

Jessie had a bum knee, which he claimed was from an old football injury. He needed an operation, but his family had no health insurance. Melody Brook Ice Rink in Colmar was a great place to meet girls and so it became a regular hang out, but one night Jessie suggested we all go to a roller rink in Sanatoga. Roller-skating seemed kind of low class to us, but Jessie insisted and several of us piled into his Ford Falcon wagon for the half-hour drive. About midway through the evening Jessie fell down and faked a knee injury. We all knew he was bluffing and tried to get him to quit playing around, but he continued the charade. When the ambulance arrived, we all played stupid so that we wouldn't get in trouble. Meanwhile, Jessie shamelessly hammed it up and left in the ambulance. Later on he sued the rink for a free knee replacement operation. In spite of their character flaws, we all managed to maintain our friendship, but I always felt more comfortable with my friends from Jersey.

Chris and Tom periodically came up from Jersey to visit and I would pick them up at the North Wales train station. From there we headed out to North Penn high school for sporting events and dances. On one such occasion I met up with Tom to go to a football game with our arch rival Pennridge. We had planned on meeting Lesley and her girlfriends at the game, but when I walked past the grandstand a drunken guy kicked me in the head. Jumping up on the bleachers I tried to punch him, but ten guys stood up behind him. Even though my eye was bleeding and I was furious about being kicked, I had to back down. Tom and I reluctantly walked away and then met up with Lesley and her girl friends. After explaining what had happened and fuming for a while, I decided to take a walk under the bleachers where I found a six-foot board on the ground. Emerging from the darkness in front of the inebriated barbarian with my four-by-four, I raised it up to club him. He jumped up on the railing to pounce on me, but I swung the jagged edge of the board around and pointed it toward his chest screaming, "You just try it ass hole!" The next thing I knew the place was crawling with cops. I explained my behavior to a security guard who told us to go back and sit with our friends. The guards managed to keep us apart, but the drunk and his gang kept yelling, "I'll see you after the game." Walking out the main gate, I knew there would be a fight, but I was just mad enough to relish the idea. Feeling like I needed to handle this one myself, I asked my friends to stay out of it unless I was ganged up on. A crowd gathered around in a circle, as the two of us squared off in the shadowy field.

Suddenly one of the cowardly creeps went down on all fours behind me. The belligerent bully charged me and I was slammed flat on my back. Then the bloodthirsty brute knelt on my shoulders and repeatedly punched me in the face. A second guy held my feet making it almost impossible to escape, while the rest of the bombed bastards blocked Jon and Tom from helping me out. By the time it was all over my face looked like a piece of raw hamburger and I could barely sit up under my own power. A policeman helped me to my feet and took down some information, but by that time the rest of the gang had disappeared. While gathering my wits some sympathetic witnesses offered up the names of the other ruffians and the cop asked me if I needed an ambulance. I told him I had my own car and that I would be ok to drive.

Since my car was in the same dark field, Tom locked all the doors as soon as we were inside the vehicle. Within seconds the mob returned and was crawling all over my car. They jumped on the roof, ripped off the antenna and broke the side-view mirror. Following the attack they all disappeared into the darkness, as quickly as they had arrived. I started the engine and paused to catch my breath. Since I was parked on the grass in an overflow area, I started out of my spot slowly. When I turned down the aisle the guy who had just beat me up appeared in my headlights with a tire iron. I saw red and hit the gas! I had every intension of running the bastard over, but Tom stretched out his foot and slammed on the brake. I tried to push it away, but he overpowered me. Keeping his foot firmly on the brake, he yelled at the top of his lungs, "Right now you have everything on this guy! You hit him now and its murder one!" I didn't want to hear it and bellowed, "I don't care!" Tom didn't budge an inch. He kept his foot on the brake, until I broke down crying. When I regained my composure, his foot came off the brake and Officer Castle started knocking on my window. The familiar policeman had seen the entire incident and some other men in blue had already arrested several of the hoodlums. When I opened the window he asked, "Would you like an escort?" I told him I would not need one and then slowly headed for home. Tom and I headed for home in reflective silence, as my blood pressure returned to normal. Finally I broke the silence by questioning a statement he had made in the heat of the moment; "Murder One?" Tom just laughed as he back pedaled and said, "Well... maybe it would just be second degree."

On Monday morning, I was called out of class to identify the jackass and sign a statement regarding the incident that took place on Saturday night. I later submitted all my medical bills and the estimates for the damage to the car. All the bills were paid in full, but because he was a minor, no criminal charges were ever filed. I moved on with my life and forgot all about it for almost ten years. Then one day while driving home from work, I pulled into the left-hand lane to pass a jeep and recognized the bully. Like sheet lightening all my rage came flooding back in full fury. I immediately hooked my car into his lane and never even looked back. The next day I began wondering if I killed the guy and checked the North Penn Reporter for accidents, but I found none so I assume he survived. Some may call my actions depraved indifference, but I prefer to think of it as a kind of temporary insanity and quite possibly poetic justice.

While I busy was acting out on the world stage Lesley joined the drama club and performed in a high school adaptation of the Broadway play David and Lisa.[396] She later took on lead roles in avant-garde productions like Brave New World[397] among others. These plays introduced her to a whole new set of friends, most of whom had extremely odd personalities. The most bizarre creature all was the drama teacher herself.

---

[396] *David and Lisa* – is a play that begins with David & his mother preparing to go to a school for children with mental & psychological issues. His mother is depicted as overprotective & overbearing. David is afraid to be touched, but with the help of teachers, psychologists & a schizophrenic named Lisa, both of them are healed of their maladies.
[397] *Brave New World* – is a novel by Aldous Huxley, which anticipated developments in reproductive technology & other radical changes in a future society devoid of moral values.

Ms. Ellen Westheimer headed up the drama club and remained there for over thirty years, influencing hundreds of children. I myself went to one of the tryouts, but found the people and the culture so creepy that I bowed out before the first audition. Several members of the club developed homosexual lifestyles and decades later it was revealed that Westheimer herself was a lesbian. Ten years later she was forced to resign, amidst allegations of child molestation.

In October Jessie Allen talked my sister Sarah into becoming a member of the Civil Air Patrol.[398] The two of them encouraged me to join their Search and Rescue Squadron and I soon signed up. In addition to military protocol, we learned things like map and compass orientation, first aid and survival. The military discipline was refreshing to me and I proudly wore the dark blue uniform of the Air Force. Although the chain of command and discipline reminded me of good times at Valley Forge Military Academy, the familiar routines also brought back memories of Bordentown, where cadets with rank tended to abuse their authority.

Come December our CAP Search and Rescue squadron ascended the steep trails of Hawk Mountain for our survival training. Mother Nature decided to throw almost everything she had at us that weekend. The rain turned to snow on the way up the mountain and by the time we reached the pinnacle my wet canvas pup tent was frozen solid. It even made a crackling noise when I unrolled it. Once inside my tent, I tried everything I could think of to stay warm and dry. The top and bottom of my sleeping bag was wet from the rain, so I curled up in fetal position in the middle of the down filled bag. I had just about stopped shivering when the sergeant banged on my tent flap. A cadet forgot his tent and

---

[398] *Civil Air Patrol* – or CAP is the official civilian auxiliary of the United States Air Force. It is a volunteer organization with an aviation-minded membership that performs 3 key missions: emergency services, which includes search & rescue (by air & ground) & disaster relief operations, aerospace education for youth & a cadet program for youth.

sleeping bag. The sergeant ordered me to share my sleeping bag with a lanky nerd who was standing beside him in his soaking wet long johns. In addition to my natural revulsion to zipping in with another guy, this clueless kid drenched everything he touched. I was freezing cold and mad as hell. How does anyone just forget their tent and bedroll? The sergeant had the responsibility to check all gear before any cadets ascended the mountain. If anyone should have been inconvenienced it should have been the cadet or the sergeant. In the military everyone must follow orders, but the order made no sense to me, so I got dressed and went outside to sit by the fire.

The snow was almost two feet deep when we arrived at camp and the fire had melted a six foot diameter pit down to the ground. To stay warm we hauled trees from the surrounding forest all night long, which fed flames that shot up almost ten feet in the air. Our bonfire illuminated the entire camp and kept those of us who were feeding it warm while temperatures plummeted into single digits and the winds whipped up into a full blown blizzard. The old veterans said that they had never before seen conditions like that on Hawk Mountain. Eventually the storm passed and in the light from the morning the sun revealed a clear blue sky. I was exhausted from having stayed up all-night and still angry about the insane orders I had been required to follow. Descending the mountain half frozen, I pushed my leggings through a thick blanket of snow and ate my lunch from a small tin can filled with sardines. Mulling over everything that had transpired, I decided to withdraw my membership in the Civil Air Patrol. I also vowed that I would never again place myself in a position where I had to follow orders without question.

Apparently I was not the only one questioning authority. Soldiers dying in Vietnam made the electorate wonder why a man could give his life for his country at age eighteen, but could not legally drink until he was twenty-one. In January

1972 a newly elected legislature lowered the legal drinking age in New Jersey to eighteen. Naturally on New Year's Eve a bunch of us descended on a bar in Camden and started downing shots of Jack Daniel's. It was not long before we were feeling no pain. Chris noticed how attractive the shot glasses looked and suggested we take a couple of them home for souvenirs. Our little crime spree ended when the bartender caught me and demanded I put the glasses back on the bar. I sheepishly smiled and pulled a couple of tumblers out of my pockets, but the remaining six stayed in the kangaroo pockets of my corduroy jacket.

When the bartender announced last call, we were pretty well plastered. Piling into a station wagon our driver soon stopped the car to drop off one of the guys who lived in Camden. Jose was sandwiched in the back seat so Vinny and I had to get out of the car to let him out. Standing there in the middle of the street, Vinny asked me if I still had any of those shot glasses. When I pulled one out to show him he pointed to a second floor window and shouted, "Quick! Throw it!" Without thinking I threw it and the glass went crashing through a bedroom window. Vinny pushed me back into the car and yelled, "Go! Go! Go!" Bob Wallace peeled wheels and raced around the corner. How the vandalism affected the residents didn't seem to matter nearly as much as the risk it posed to us and we weren't out of danger yet. Bob slowed down after a couple of blocks to avoid drawing attention and then carefully followed the speed limit all the way back to Pennsauken. The rest of the trip was relatively uneventful until we arrived in Match Town.[399]

---

[399] *Match Town* – refers to a small black ghetto on the south side of Merchantville, NJ. It was so named because all the row houses are made of clapboard & a single match could easily send the whole place up in smoke. Good hard working folk lived there & one in particular became famous. *Arnold Cream* was the son of immigrants from Barbados. When he was 13 his father died & he quit school to work at Campbell Soup Co. so he could support his mother & 11 siblings. Arnold also began training as a boxer & took the name of his idol, Joe Walcott, the welterweight champion from Barbados. The pastor at St. Peter Church was also interested in boxing & became good friends with *Jersey Joe Walcott*, who went on to win his 1st heavyweight title by knocking out Joe Lewis in 1948. At the age of

Vinny Riley rolled down the window, hung his head out and let loose with a string of embarrassing racial epithets. We panicked, pulled him back inside the car, covered his mouth and told him to shut the hell up! Although none of us would ever have maligned a Negro to his face, we thought nothing of telling colored jokes in white company. So we hardly held the moral high ground with our friend Vinny, but he was clearly reckless and out of line. We never understood his rage and he never explained the story behind all this venom. We silenced our friend for the sake of safety and felt lucky to make it home alive. Sadly we never reflected on the damage such words did to the peaceful people who lived there.

Back home in Pennsylvania, Lesley was spending more and more time with her friends in the drama club, but she also wanted me and my friends to know that she still cared. In her whimsical poetic style, she saw us off on a camping trip by giving me her picture and a love note.

"This is me. Alive and living, learning, growing, seeking and finding, giving with a smile and a warm hand to one whom I love dearly. Go and climb your mountains and when your feet are sore and blistered, I will heal them. And when they are all better, and you can walk; you can carry me. Ok? Go grow, learn, love, understand, care, find, know, look and come again. With love always; this is my gift to you and your bud boys."

In addition to camping trips, we went skiing in the Pocono's and attended Philadelphia Flyers hockey games. Dad often got tickets from work, but only at the last minute. With four season tickets we could all go together whenever the tickets became available, but the last minute nature of the deal earned me the nickname "Guru" when Mr. Lang complained that every time I called, Chris dropped everything to follow

---

37, Joe won back the title for a 5th time against Ezzard Charles, also by knockout, making him the oldest man to do so, until George Foreman broke his record in 1994. (1914-1994)

me. These activities gave us many opportunities to bond and provided the security of knowing there would always be someone around with whom we could ask advice or blow off steam. Although hanging out with the guys in Jersey involved some risk, we generally emerged unscathed; but our adventures in Pennsylvania usually involved more serious consequences.

Dad bought me a set of flares for my car and Jessie decided to put one of them on my neighbor's concrete front porch as a harmless prank. What we didn't know is that buried in the front yard was a large propane tank. The newlywed bride was leaving the kitchen to bring her husband a cup of coffee when she entered the dining room and saw the whole front yard lit up in a bright pink glow. Assuming the tank had exploded she spilled scalding hot coffee all over her long beautiful legs. When my father found out he grounded me and taped an index card on to the steering wheel of my car, which read, "Patrick – Do not use this or any other car."

In retrospect it was probably an appropriate punishment, but at the time taking away my car befuddled me. The source of the confusion was that when my father first gave me the car he insisted it would be mine and that he would never take it away. So I felt duty bound to defend my property and immediately drove it to New Jersey. I stayed with Tom for my entire Easter vacation. Dad eventually called to apologize for going back on his word and asked me to return home. It had only been a two-week stay, but it was comforting to know that I always had a place to go, if I ever really needed one. It wouldn't be long before I would have the opportunity to do the same favor for another friend.

On the same day that the British were busy slaughtering the Irish on Bloody Sunday[400] I received a desperate phone call

---

[400] *Bloody Sunday* – on January 30, 1972 a British Parachute Regiment shot 27 unarmed civil rights protesters in Derry, Northern Ireland. Of the 13 who died, 7 were teenagers & the wounded included 5 shot in the back & 2 run over by army vehicles. The Widgery

from Vinny Riley. His dad had been riding him unusually hard that day and the pressure was overwhelming. He just needed to leave the house, get some rest and clear his head. Boarding a bus bound for Philly he transferred to a train and I picked him up at the station in North Wales. Vinny had left home in a hurry. The only things in his backpack were a couple of shirts, a few changes of underwear and a case of beer. The grain bin at the top of our barn made a perfect hideout for him. It was cold out so I gave him a sleeping bag, some winter clothing and a jug of hot chocolate to keep him warm. During the day I still attended school, but in the afternoon I rejoined him as soon as I got off the bus. I felt like Harriet Tubman[401] secretly bringing him food each night and ironically harboring him like a runaway slave. Vinny never did tell me what drove him to run away and I never asked, but after a couple of weeks he calmed down to the point that he was able to return home. Although he never revealed where he had been, his family was happy to have him back. Sometimes you just need a place to go, so you can sort things out.

Nixon announced a new Space Shuttle Program[402] and it became a proud moment for many Americans, but the glory would be short lived. Corruption was eating away at the oval office. Gradually it became apparent that our president looked more like the Godfather[403] than one of our Founding Fathers and by August 1974 Richard Nixon would resign.

Tribunal cleared the soldiers & authorities of any blame, but even Tony Blair called the investigation a "whitewash". "The Bogside Massacre" is significant, because it was carried out by the army in the full view of public & press.

[401] *Harriet Tubman* – Born into slavery in Dorchester, Maryland in 1820, she successfully ran away in 1849, but returned to slave country many times to rescue both family members and others from slavery. She became the most famous Underground Railroad "conductor," taking part in abolitionist gatherings and working with Union forces during the Civil War.

[402] *Space Shuttle Program* – was a NASA project designed to create a fleet of ships that could go into orbit like a space ship & return like a glider to an airstrip. The shuttle crafts carried all sorts of experiments & the cargo bay doors opened to reveal a mechanical arm that could launch satellites, deliver parts to build a space station & retrieve wayward satellites. The last shuttle in the fleet was retired in 2010.

[403] *The Godfather* – is a 1972 American gangster film based on the novel by Mario Puzo & directed by Francis Ford Coppola. The star-studded story chronicled the fictional Corleone crime family from 1945-1955. It received Academy Awards for Best Picture, Best Actor &

In April I became legally allowed to run machinery, so I quit my job as a dishwasher and went back to working for Callahan Machine Company. Summer was just around the corner and I would need a war chest of cash for my vacation at the shore. Machine operators commanded a much better wage than laborers, but work, school and homework were also taking their toll. The combination often exhausted me, but I enjoyed the precision machine work and it felt good to be pulling my own weight.

Most of my younger brothers rode motorcycles with dad almost every weekend. Although I was no longer interested in bikes, I liked listening to their tales of glory and calamity every Monday at the dinner table. One of their heroes was a dare devil named Evil Knievel.[404] I had seen some of his jumps on TV and decided to go down to the Spectrum in Philadelphia, to watch him jump the Snake River in a homemade rocket. The pay-per-view company filming it had no cameras set up inside the canyon. So when the parachute malfunctioned on take-off the audience could not see what happened. Like fog rolling into a valley, a creepy feeling drifted through me. I had just paid ten dollars to help some guy kill himself. Actually the parachute did open and the crazy daredevil landed on the rocky bottom of the canyon and a shock absorber on the nosecone broke his fall. Knievel survived just fine, but the guilt I experienced in providing the incentive for some guy to risk his life for my momentary thrill disgusted me.

Meanwhile back in Jersey, Tom got a job as a soda jerk at Friendly's Ice Cream. He met lots of people there and

---

Best Adapted Screenplay. It was also ranked as the 2nd greatest film in American cinematic history. Sequels included: *The Godfather Part II* in 1974 & *The Godfather Part III* in 1990.
[404] *Evil Knievel* – was a motorcycle daredevil by the name of Robert Craig Knievel, who is famous for his televised motorcycle jumps, especially his 1974 attempt to jump the Snake River Canyon with his X-1 Skycycle, which was more of a rocket than a motorcycle. The parachute accidentally opened on take-off sending him to the floor of the canyon. His achievements & failures, including a record 37 broken bones, earned him several entries in the Guinness Book of World Records. (1938-2007)

introduced me to a buxom young blond waitress named Heather. After he got off work, Tom and Kitty double dated with us and the four of us started spending some of our hard-earned cash on motel rooms. Although the encounters were sexually charged, technically we all remained virgins. Unlike other girls I had dated, Heather drew a strange boundary line. Whereas most girls let you go just so far and no further, Heather would either allow me to take off all of her clothes, or she would take off all of mine, but neither one of us could take a stitch of clothing off, once the other began to disrobe. At first it seemed exciting; no resistance and a complete striptease act accompanied by enthusiastic heavy petting, but it were also a bit odd. When I asked her about it she went silent. I guess it was just her way of making sure we never went all the way. I liked Heather allot, but didn't understand the game. After an aggressive questioning of the logic behind her gerrymandered foreplay, we had a big fight and stopped dating.

Whenever one of my friends lost interest in a girl, it was not uncommon for another one of us to begin dating her. Usually the transfer of title was amicably accomplished, but there were some pretty strict rules. One of the most basic rubrics was that you had to make sure of the breakup by asking permission. Tom began dating a really cute little blond named Marion Gerber after he and Kitty had a little spat. I was also attracted to Marion, but patiently avoided any flirtation until Tom lost interest and ended the relationship. I followed all the unwritten protocols to the letter and dutifully asked him if it would be ok for me to date the young woman. He initially said yes, but then we almost came to blows when Tom realized he still liked her a bit more than he thought he did. Just before he punched me in the nose, I risked enraging him still further by asking him to reevaluate his priorities.

I started out by saying, "Tom, this is me, Patrick, your friend. I'm going to be here long after this Marion is gone. Do you really want to do this?" He paused for a few seconds and then said, "You're right Pat; there's plenty of fish in the sea and he went back to dating his true love Kitty.

Chapter 20

Lazy Daze

Love is a profound mystery and many have tried to define it; but most have done so with precious little success. Carol King[405] plunged into the paradox by presenting the world with the painful follow-up question, Will You Still Love Me Tomorrow?[406] Although hard to describe, we are often able to recognize love when we find it. The popular expression "love at first sight" describes that mutual attraction, which is so powerful that it can break through all of our inhibitions and even override the man rules.[407] The instant our eyes shared that first fleeting flirtatious glance, Carol Stover and I were both twitterpated.

The lovely Miss Stover dearly loved Vinny Riley, albeit not in the same romantic way that he loved her. For weeks he had been telling us about his new girlfriend and every time he saw her, he was carefully angling to win her over. Although I was happy for his bliss, my own love life was on the skids. One night I dropped by Riley's house to commiserate with him, but he said he had a date with Carol Stover. There was no way he was going to cancel, but since they only planned on listening to records, he brought me along to show her off and figured the two of them could probably cheer me up. Shortly after he introduced me to Carol I forgot all about my troubles. We listened to several

---

[405] *Carole King* – is an American singer, songwriter & pianist. She & her former husband Gerry Goffin wrote more than 24 hits during the 1960s. Although most successful in the first half of the 1970s, her first hit was in 1960 at the age of 18 with, "Will You Love Me Tomorrow". Carole still tours today with fellow artist James Taylor. (1942-Present)

[406] *Will You Love Me Tomorrow* – is a song written by Gerry Goffin & Carole King. It has been recorded by many different artists & was ranked among Rolling Stone's list of The 500 Greatest Songs of All Time at #125. The song is famous for being the first song to reach #1 in the United States, by an all-girl group.

[407] *Man Rules* – refers to that unwritten code men abide by in their relationships with other men. It includes rules like not dating your buddy's girl & not ratting out a friend, etc.

of her albums and the three of us laughed our way through a playful game of Twister.[408] While listening to her newest album Tapestry,[409] Carol told us that her best friend had just informed her that she was engaged and would soon be married.

Somewhere in the middle of reminiscing about her lifelong companion she let it slip that the name of her best friend was Mary Kate O'Neil. When I learned Mary Kate was the one getting married, I began to cry. Vinny had only introduced me by my first name, so Carol was confused by the reaction, but when Vinny told her that my last name was Callahan she connected all the dots. The depth of my sorrow over the loss of Mary Kate both surprised and impressed Carol. Her attempts to comfort me created a kind of unspoken bond between us and for a split second our eyes locked, but neither one of us dared to say a word about our heartfelt connection. Vinny had been a good friend to me and I was under the impression that Carol was his girl. Although not romantically attracted to Vinny, Carol knew how he felt about her and did not want to hurt him.

After returning to Pennsylvania I anguished over how to handle the situation. I ended up writing her a letter and told her about a pretty girl I had recently met. Extolling the young woman's positive attributes; I let Carol know how much I wanted to date the girl, but said I had a problem because a friend of mine liked the same girl. In the last line of the letter I told her that she was the woman in question. Wondering if it was the right thing to do, I nervously walked

---

[408] *Twister* – was played on a large plastic mat with 4 rows of colored circles. A spinner attached to a board served as a die for the game, directing hands & feet to the colored circles. Invented by Charles Foley & Neil Rabens in 1966, it didn't become a success until Eva Gabor played it with Johnny Carson on the Tonight Show. The Milton Bradley game was called "sex in a box" by its detractors, probably because it was the first popular American game to use human bodies as playing pieces.

[409] *Tapestry* – is a pop album by singer-songwriter Carole King, released in 1971. It remains the longest charting album by a female solo artist selling over 25 million copies worldwide. In 1972 it garnered 4 Grammies: Album of the Year, Best Female Pop Vocal Performance, Record of the Year for "It's Too Late" & Song of the Year for "You've Got a Friend".

over to the mailbox to send the risky missive. To my surprise, there in the mailbox was a letter from Miss Stover. The love note gushed with similar sentiments of how she felt about me. Carol explained to me that although Vinny was a good friend, she was not his girl and only loved him like a brother. That evening I called her on the phone and ran up a nice sized long distance bill. The next day she sent out another letter and thanked me for the phone call. Freely expressing her feelings she told me how much she was looking forward to my next visit. No longer depressed and down-hearted; I was doing fine on Cloud Nine.[410]

Even though I worked hard at school all year long, I was still not sure I would graduate. Math class was a joke, my English teacher went away on maternity leave and my French partner was wallowing in self pity. By the time May rolled around I was exhausted and not only from school. Apparently I wasn't the only pooped out pubescent. Chris came up for a weekend visit and neither one of us had enough energy to do much of anything. With temperatures approaching 100 degrees, Chris and I found ourselves sitting on the floor in the garage. While drinking beer and smoking cigarettes we tried our level best not to exert ourselves too much. We made a game out of it and called it Lazy Daze. Sitting on the relatively cool floor we competed with each other to see which one of us could be the laziest slob. Every time we came up with a more extreme form of laziness we would exhaustively moan, "Laaaaazy Daaaaze." When Chris halfheartedly tried to light up his cigarette, he failed to accomplish the task and left the unlit cancer stick hanging from his lips. I asked him to pass me a beer, but it was simply too much of an effort for him to open the cooler. Eventually we even tried to stop breathing, but it was too much of an effort to hold our breath so we exhaled in unison, "Laaaaazy Daaaaze."

---

[410] *Cloud Nine* – was a 1968 hit single recorded by The Temptations for the Motown label. It was the 1st of Norman Whitfield's psychedelic soul tracks & won Motown its 1st Grammy Award. The song was written by Whitfield & former Motown artist Barrett Strong.

While Chris and I were savoring the self-indulgence of sloth, my industrious cousin Peter was overseeing a crew consisting of my younger brothers, who were painting a large smiley face on the side of the barn. Dad came out to inspect the project and found them all hard at work in the sweltering heat. On his way back to the house he caught sight of us playing our little game and the juxtaposition so disgusted him that he ordered us off the property. Half lit with no particular destination in mind; we threw some clothes and camping gear into the back of the pickup truck and headed for the Jersey shore.

The wind blowing through the wing windows provided some relief from the heat and helped us to do some much needed sobering up. Flying down the Pennsylvania Turnpike we soon forgot all about Lazy Daze and found our way to Belleplain State Park[411] where we knew Tom Reeves was camping with his family. Traveling north with us on the Garden State Parkway[412] Tom propositioned every pretty girl on the highway and arrogantly argued with any driver that dared to object to his exuberance. Tom suggested we camp at a place he knew called Pirate's Cove.[413] The campground was full, so we crossed to the other side of Route Nine and established a base camp at a place called Baker's Acres[414] in Tuckerton. Pitching a tent in one of the last two campsites of the overflow area, we walked back down a sandy road to their community pool. Our diving drew the attention of a few adoring teens and Chris began talking some of the girls and eventually invited them to join us back at our campsite. Tom

---

[411] *Belleplain State Park* – was established in 1928 by the State of New Jersey for recreation, wildlife management, timber production & water conservation. In 1933, the Civilian Conservation Corps built 3 camps, which provided jobs for 8 yrs.
[412] *Garden State Parkway* – is a 172.4-mile limited-access toll road that stretches the length of New Jersey from the New York state line, at Montvale, New Jersey, to Cape May at the southern tip of the Garden State, paralleling Route 9 & most of the New Jersey shore towns.
[413] *Pirate's Cove* – is a small family campground on Route 9 in Tuckerton, NJ boarding Barnegat Bay only a 10-minute drive from Surf City on Long Beach Island in NJ.
[414] *Bakers Acres Campground* – is a superb family vacation destination, located on Route 9 in Tuckerton, NJ, only a 10-minute drive from Surf City on Long Beach Island in NJ. Its oak & pine shaded sites include a pool, a recreation pavilion & a camp store.

sang songs and played his guitar by the campfire and one by one we each began sampling the kisses of the tantalizing teenyboppers. The girls had to leave by eleven and wanted to know if we could see us tomorrow. Since we had no idea where we would be we declined their invitation. We were feeling our oats and loving our freedom!

In the morning we drove over to Long Beach Island and dropped in on a girl that Tom knew in Beach Haven.[415] Wendy was very excited to see him and we drove down to the Wharf to eat lunch together. She worked at the Country Kettle Fudge shop and had to show up by 2:00 pm. So we dropped her off at work and left for the Surf City beach. Chris and I introduced Tom to the 2nd Street gang and Sheryl Levite instantly locked eyes with him. Chris soon paired off with a brunette sun goddess and I tried patching things up with Christina Nowicki. Maintaining tradition, the Terrible Triangle ate dinner at George's, before rejoining the girls on the beach for the evening. Tom pulled out his guitar again and was quickly encircled by a dozen delighted dames. In the meantime I was making a little bit of progress with Christina. Although she willingly sat with me we never did kiss or take any walks together. Several of the girls had curfews, so we headed back to Bakers Acres for some shut-eye. The next day we hung out with the camp girls by the pool until late afternoon and then headed for home. I dropped my friends off in Pennsauken and then continued on to Pennsylvania. When I pulled into the driveway the trip odometer read 632.7 miles. Not bad for an impromptu road trip.

A few days later, Jon and I were cruising for chicks in the country, when we passed a couple of girls near the Harleysville Hotel. In a vain attempt to impress them I peeled wheels, missed a gear and broke two of my motor mounts. From then on I was having all sorts of problems

---

[415] *Beach Haven* – is a shore town on Long Beach Island, just south of the causeway in New Jersey. It boasts Fantasy Island, the amusement park & arcade, along with a lot of neat shops over at Bay Village & Schooner's Wharf.

with my car so I traded it in for a van at Miller Chevrolet in Lansdale. I installed a new stereo system, built storage compartments under a bed and installed shag carpeting on the floor, walls and ceiling. There was only one problem; the transmission died. Since the sale was "as-is" the dealership refused to take it back. I put my hippy van up for sale in the side yard for one-thousand dollars. The customer who bought my lemon came back for his money the following day, but I gave him the same line that the dealership had given me. The swindled man looked at me with contempt and drove away in silent disgust. I felt guilty about cheating the man, but didn't know what else to do. Legally I was on sound ground, but ethically I knew I was dead wrong.

Conveniently located around the corner from Callahan Machine Co. was a used car dealership. Creagan Motors had a 1970 Ford Torino Brougham, which listed for two grand. The salesman knocked a hundred dollars off to make the sale and I plunked down my hard-earned deposit. However, when I returned to sign the paperwork for the loan he had changed the price. I was pissed and said, "I thought we agreed on nineteen-hundred?" He just laughed at me and said, "Everyone knows that nineteen-hundred means nineteen ninety-nine." I furiously objected, "You put it back to nineteen-hundred like we agreed." Unfazed by my theatrics he stood up, leaned over his desk and said, "That's the price. Do you want the car or don't you?" I had plans to go to Jersey on the weekend so he had me over a barrel for the time being, but I wasn't going to let him get away with it Scott-free. I signed the paperwork, stood up slowly and said, "Yea, I'm still buying the car, but I'm gonna to tell all my friends that you rip people off." He confidently laughed, handed me the keys and said, "No you're not. You just got done telling all your friends at school, how you Jewed me out of a hundred bucks. You're not gonna say anything. Enjoy your car." I was mad as hell, but everything that little weasel said absolutely was true. By the time I got home, the excitement about having a new car completely eclipsed any anger. Showing off my bronze colored vehicle with the black vinyl top, I gave rides to everyone in my family and then made a beeline for Jersey.

Tom and I drove over to see Vinny at the Hess station by the airport circle where he worked as a service attendant. Soon after we arrived, Chris dropped off a case of beer and then left to meet Sophia Romano for dinner. The three of us happily consumed the chilled golden brew, while we hung out with our friend and helping him to pump gas and check oil. Each time the bell rang we took turns servicing customers. Vinny had a thick wad of bills, which totaled almost a grand and he gave us each one-hundred dollars to make change. His coworker Kyle was a tall, lanky wanabe who helped himself to our beer and kept trying to join in on our conversations. At around eight o'clock, Tom left in my car to get a shower and pick up Kitty Carter, who by now was his steady girl.

While Vinny was out checking someone's oil, Kyle came into the office for another swig of his beer. Looking at the row of Miller High Life[416] bottles lined up along the back wall he asked, "Which one is Vinny's?" I pointed to one of the bottles and asked, "Why?" He laughed and said, "I've got an idea. Why don't you piss in his beer?" It was the last thing I expected, but I ignored the idiot until he went back outside. When Vinny returned I said, "Kyle is messed up. He just told me to piss in your beer. What do you think we ought to do about it?" Vinny looked up from his wad of bills, smiled and said, "Piss in his!" I immediately grabbed Kyle's bottle and filled it up. Vinny laughed and then changed the subject saying, "You better watch your time." Just then, Tom pulled in with Kitty and I took off with the two love birds to pick up my own girl Carol Stover and Vinny's latest squeeze Melanie Perry.

---

[416] *Miller High Life* – is Miller Brewing's oldest brand with distribution beginning in 1903. The pilsner category of beers were referred to as "The Champagne of Bottle Beers" because of their high level of carbonation, similar to champagne.

Rounding everybody up took awhile and by the time we returned, I had forgotten all about our little prank. While filling my gas tank I heard Kyle yelling across the parking lot, "Did you piss in my beer?" I smiled as he briskly walked toward me and I nonchalantly said, "Yep!" Suddenly he lunged in-between the pumps, got up in my face and yelled, "Why?" A bit irritated but still amused I said, "Cause you told me to piss in Vinny's beer and he's my friend." I thought it was over, but then he called me out. At first I didn't believe him and laughed right in his face, but that only made him angrier and he pushed me backwards while I was hanging up the hose. At that point I accepted his challenge and said, "Let's go." We walked out behind the station and I beat the crap out of him. Although I did take a few punches, it was over in a couple of minutes and it was the first fight I had ever won in my life. Fresh from the battle, I got back in the car and drove away with my friends. Everyone wanted to know all the details about the fight, but I drove on in silence until Tom told everybody to back off. Carol pulled out a tissue to blot some blood on my eye brow and then snuggled up next to me until we arrived at the theater. I had won the fight, but would pay a price with some sore knuckles and a goose egg over my left eye.

The movie we saw was Cabaret[417] and it was dominated with sexually charged deviance. I saw Carol as a good Catholic girl and was embarrassed to be seeing the movie with her. I even wanted to leave to protect her and treat her like a lady, but I did not want to cause a scene either. Everyone else seemed to be just fine with the movie. On the way home I trashed the immorality and perversion of the film and pointed out that the characters seemed to be too comfortable with Nazis. Tom and Vinny took the opposite side of the

---

[417] *Cabaret* – was a 1972 musical film directed by Bob Fosse & starring Liza Minnelli, Michael York & Joel Grey. The film was produced by ABC Pictures & distributed in the US by Allied Artists. The story is set in Berlin during the Weimar Republic in 1931, under the ominous presence of the growing Nazi Party. It was nominated for 10 Academy Awards & was selected for preservation in the U.S. National Film Registry, as being deemed "culturally, historically, or aesthetically significant".

argument, while the girls remained silent. After we dropped everyone else off, Carol let me know that she was embarrassed by the flick and appreciated me speaking out against it.

With the school year coming to a close, Christina Nowicki called me up out of the blue at my home in Pennsylvania. She berated me for mistreating her and Leah last summer and then promptly hung up the phone. Apparently I had not patched things up with her as well as I thought I did. I should have just apologized, but instead I wrote her a letter defending myself and tried to assure her that I never meant her or Leah any harm. There was no way of knowing whether my letter would communicate love or just make matters worse.

The onset of summer vacation brought me a mix of emotions. I wanted my friends to join me at the shore, but their lives were now moving in different directions. Tom had a painting business. Chris and Vinny were starting apprenticeships. Even my girlfriend Carol would be heading off to college. Dad only rented the Surf City house for the month of June, so the rest of the summer would cost me plenty. While I could probably live at Uncle Ray's place, inviting other guests over would be out of the question. There had to be another way to spend the rest of the summer at the shore. The trouble was that the fiascos with my cars had depleted my finances. I looked into campgrounds, motels and cheap apartments, but nothing at the shore is inexpensive and camping during the summer months isn't very comfortable. At the end of May I quit my job and tried to build my own trailer. The homemade contraption was an overly ambitious and ill-conceived project that had been doomed from the start. After my best efforts failed, I shifted gears and bought an old trailer from the Oak Grove Trailer Park. My five-hundred dollar Prairie Schooner may not have been very pretty, but it was all mine. I fixed up the inside and leased a space for it at Baker's Acres Campground. Things were starting to look up again!

Graduation[418] may have provided me with a sheepskin, but thanks to my abysmal grades community colleges were the only institutions of higher learning that would even take a look at me. Although I should have failed French, the teacher graciously gave me a "D minus" for the year and she even winked at me on my way up to receive my diploma. Dad was also in a generous mood and gave me a fresh start by canceling all of my debt. Although I had crossed the finish line, I had no way of knowing what the future would hold. I could also care less and would deal with it in September. The school year was over and I was ready for the shore.

The day after graduation, I drove to Pennsauken High School and picked up Carol right after she finished her last class. We drove down to the Wharton Tract State Forest where we stopped for lunch and took a quick dip in the Wading River. Moving on to Surf City, I introduced Carol to the 2nd Street gang and noticed that Christina Nowicki was now dating some guy named Harry. After she introduced us to her new boyfriend she left us and walked over to the 3rd Street beach. Carol knew all about the gang. She was aware that I had dated some of the girls and I'm sure she felt the vibes, but she was gracious with them and they were fairly courteous. Carol had no desire to join the gang; she simply wanted to put some faces to the names she had heard about and get a feel for the place. I was not all that comfortable with the encounter and neither was she or anyone else for that matter. Carol had always looked beautiful to me and she was; but next to the bathing beauties on the beach she looked kind of plain. The gaggle of goddesses gave her the once over and from the looks on their faces; they were wondering what it was I saw in her.

---

[418] *Class of '72* – on June 12, 1972 graduates of North Penn High School included some 800 students. Thanks to my decision to flunk 11th grade, I graduated in the bottom 8% of my class with 0.2 credits above minimum.

Carol played the clarinet for Pennsauken high school in the Big Red band; therefore I had to get her back in time for the graduation festivities. Although we continued dating throughout her freshman year in college, she never did return to the beach with me. After driving her home, I turned around and returned to our rental house in Surf City by myself. Generally I slept there at night and hung out on 2nd Street beach during the daytime. Occasionally I went out on dates with some of the new girls, but more often than not, I spent my time swimming and talking with the other members of the gang. In the evening I communed with my cousins, always making it a point to help out with the dishes. That single gesture was very much appreciated and insured that I was always welcome. Whenever I wanted privacy, I could crash at my trailer on the main land. I had plenty of options until the rest of my family went back home. I hung out on the beach during the day, ate dinner at my uncle's and usually attended beer parties at night on the beach in Harvey Cedars. My biggest expense was buying hoagies for lunch at George's Pizza. Life was easy going and downright peaceful, but all that was about to change.

Christina Nowicki failed to show up for work one morning and she had not called her boss. Disturbing speculation loomed even larger when someone noticed that there were no cars in her driveway. It all remained a mystery until I received a desperate letter from her. It was a heart-wrenching plea for companionship. Christina told me that an absolute war had broken out between her and her parents. The upshot of it was that her mom had accused her of acting like a thirteen-year-old, having sex with her new boyfriend and experimenting with drugs. Following a big argument over the phone between her mother and father, her mom drove down to the shore and forced her to return home with her.

Christina half agreed with her mother about being immature, but considered the other two accusations absolutely ridiculous. She was grounded from the shore, placed virtually under house arrest and banned from using the telephone. Depressed, lonely and struggling with an untenable situation, she even shared thoughts of suicide with me. Were it not for a part-time job working with some little kids in a park near her home, she probably would have killed herself. The general theme of her letter was that she was terribly lonely and had no one to talk to. She begged me to write or visit and ended her plea with a request that I ask others from the gang to write her as well. My friend Chris came down for the weekend and we drove up to see Christina, but we were unable to locate her house. I failed to write to her, because I didn't know what to say, but I let others know of her predicament and they did write and encourage her.

Miss Nowicki was grounded; I was running out of money; and like Christina, I was missing my long lost friends. A weekend was all I was able to arrange and unfortunately no one wanted to go to the shore. Chris had heard lots of war stories about the Poconos from the electricians he was working with and he wanted to spend some time in the mountains. During the winter months we had always made good use of our cabin at Arrowhead Lake, but we had never been there during the summer months. Four of us arrived at dad's cabin late one Friday night and played cards till well past midnight. Since Chris and Vinny had fake IDs they planned on going out clubbing the following Saturday night.

We slept in late the next morning and drove down to the lake to go swimming. The air temperature was in the high nineties, but the water in the lake must have been thirty-three degrees. Since the contrast almost produced heart palpitations, we decided to try the community pool. When we entered the gate we headed straight for the diving board. While waiting in line for our turns, we noticed a lone teenage girl amidst a sea of mothers and small children. In complete silence we skillfully planned out our strategies and competed for the young woman's attention using glancing eyes and cautious smiles. This fourteen-year-old flowering child had absolutely no idea the competitive energy she had just released.

Tom Reeves stepped up on the board first and although the youngest member of our band of brothers, he was built like Mr. America.[419] Walking forward with the seriousness of an Olympic athlete, he flexed his bronze muscle bound body drenched in Coppertone and tested the bounce of the board. Flashing a smile in the direction of the girl and winking with his clear blue eyes, he brushed his sun bleached blonde hair to one side and held his arms straight out on either side of him. A single bounce launched him straight up and over, into the most beautiful swan dive I had ever seen.

Chris Lang was next. He was slim, trim, well toned and dark tanned. He was the ladies man of our little gang. Women seemed to flock towards him and he always knew exactly what to say to them. He enjoyed life to the full and his zest for life was contagious. Before Tom had even made it out of the water, Chris stepped up smartly and with one bounce, executed a perfectly formed jack-knife.

Next up was Vinny Riley, who stepped onto the board and let out an awful moan that drew everyone's attention. Stumbling down the diving board in a goofy rendition of a man plagued with cerebral palsy, he fell off the end and shook uncontrollably like he was having some kind of a seizure. The competition had been steep! The swan dive, jack-knife and comedic act all won poolside notice and I was behind the eight ball.[420] What could I possibly do to top these guys and win this girl's attention?

---

[419] *Mr. America* – was a bodybuilding competition started by the Amateur Athletic Union. It was first held on the 4th of July in 1939 & the winner was named "America's Best Built Man". In 1940 this was changed to what is now known as the Mr. America contest.
[420] *Behind the 8 Ball* – when playing the game of Eight Ball on a pool table, a 'behind the eight ball' position leaves the player in a very difficult position. If his cue ball strikes the (black) eight ball first or the eight ball is potted by mistake the game is forfeited.

Slowly stepping up on the board, I paused for a second and then did a regular old dive to the bottom of the pool. There was nothing fancy about the maneuver and I returned to the surface. Popping up right in front of her I locked in on her bright blue eyes and intimately held her gaze in speechless silence. Scrambling for a line I blurted out, "Come on in; the water's fine." To my complete surprise she jumped right in beside me. We splashed, dunked and chased each other across the pool. There was a flurry of activity in what seemed like a fantasy world. This girl was fun!

After a while I introduced her to my friends and we left the pool area to go boating on the lake with the playful Wendy Kimmel. Tom and Chris launched the sailboat and were quickly underway, but Vinny had other plans. Although we had all known each other for quite a while, Vinny Riley had been a late addition to the tight inner circle we proudly called The Terrible Triangle. For him the contest for the girl wasn't over yet. So I maintained vigilance, as Wendy carefully boarded the canoe. Soon after we set the boat in motion Chris and Tom zipped by us a couple of times, showing off their sailing skills and perfecting their utilization of a fairly good wind. They weren't competing anymore, just playing with us and executing a little face-saving device, after their puzzling defeat.

Wendy sat in the middle of the canoe, while Vinny and I jockeyed for position. The tension filled ballet concluded with him paddling in the bow and me steering from the stern. Suddenly the stalemate was over. Vinny leaned over to watch a fish and his brand new glasses fell off into the ice-cold water. The normally stable canoe almost capsized when he panicked and dove to the bottom of the lake. Surfacing for air, he begged for my help. I mean, this guy was really desperate! Fearing his father would kill him for loosing the glasses; he didn't wait for an answer and quickly dove back down to find them. Clearly in the driver's seat, I stayed in the boat to gloat. "I'll steer the canoe. You keep diving... I think I saw them fall off over there." He knew exactly what I was doing, but had no time or desire to argue. Chris and Tom made several dives attempting to help him, but their efforts proved fruitless. The loss of the glasses put Vinny in a bad mood for the rest of the weekend.

Meanwhile, Wendy's parents were wondering what their daughter was doing out on the lake with a bunch of strange boys. The slender teen was a shy girl and kept quiet for most of our walk along the beach. In an effort to draw her out of that bashfulness I quizzed her about where she lived, shared a few jokes and told her how pretty she looked. The encounter was interrupted by ever louder calls from her family for her to return. Mr. & Mrs. Kimmel were picnicking across the field with two small children and getting impatient with her delay. I wanted to go over and meet her parents, but Wendy didn't think that was such a good idea.

Like a hard charging buffalo; Mrs. Marianne Kimmel came stampeding toward us, shouting and wildly waving her hands. The unusual behavior gave credence to Wendy's cautionary council. Since we were running out of time I told her to meet me at the dance by eight. Squeezing my hand she flashed a joyful smile and said, "I'll try." Then she ran across the field to intercept her angry mother. Mrs. Kimmel paused just long enough to give me the hate stare and then chattered on about all the awful things that could happen to young girls who wander off with strange men. Eventually they rejoined the rest of their family at a picnic table book ended by a cooler on one end and a Coleman stove on the other.

I kicked myself for not getting a phone number and wondered if she would even show. Meanwhile back at the cabin, Tom was busy chopping firewood and Chris was cooking hot dogs and beans. Vinny sat slouched in the overstuffed lazy boy chair drinking a can of beer and complaining about how I had not helped him to find his glasses. If he was looking for sympathy he had come to the wrong place. Chris reminded him that Wendy had made her choice and he should just get over it. Tom told Vinny that he would have done the exact same thing if the situation were reversed. Still sulking, he picked up a hot dog and dropped the subject.

I was the only one with a date for the evening, but the night was young. Their plan for the night was to pick up chicks in the bars and invite them back to the cabin. All the guys teased me about dating a fickle teeny-bopper and predicted that her parents wouldn't even allow her to go to the dance. I responded by saying that they were just jealous, but I assumed they were probably right. I was skeptical they could pick up any older women and was quite sure they wouldn't be bringing anyone back to the cabin. Chris smiled saying, "We'll see..." I smiled and agreed.

After dinner my friends went to the bars and I went down to the lodge. Arrowhead Lake was a family community and most of the kids at the dance were young... very young. I felt out of place, but leaned up against a wall and waited for Wendy Kimmel. Little kids ran around whipping each other with Twizzlers.[421] The DJ played juvenile tunes like Candyman[422] and Popcorn.[423] It was too much for me and I made my way to the door. Suddenly a flustered and out of breath, skinny little blond came running up to me, "You're not leaving are you?"

---

[421] *Twizzlers* – are a popular brand of fruit-flavored candy. The licorice candy was originally produced in 1845, by Young & Smylie, in Lancaster, PA & is now manufactured by a subsidiary of The Hershey Company.

[422] *The Candy Man* – was a song from the 1971 film Willy Wonka & the Chocolate Factory. Leslie Bricusse & Anthony Newley wrote the song. The Sammy Davis, Jr. version hit #1 on the Billboard Hot 100 chart in 1972 & featured vocals by the Mike Curb Congregation. Although he originally disliked the song, Davis eventually worked the song into his acts & it is now recognized as one of his signature songs.

[423] *Popcorn* – is a famous early synthpop instrumental, originally recorded in 1969 by Gershon Kingsley. In 1972, it was a huge hit in many countries, when a Danish instrumental cover band called Hot Butter re-recorded it.

"Well, I was about to; where have you been?" This young woman had kept me waiting and I was pissed. Being four years older than she was this girl was frantic about losing her chance to date an older man. Wendy claimed she had run into trouble getting away from her parents and told me she had to be back by ten. She profusely apologized for being late and seemed willing to do almost anything to make it right. Still angry about being kept waiting I tried to salvage the evening. I figured I could teach this naive little girl a lesson. "Wanna go parking?" Fear cascaded across her face, but she nervously agreed to the invitation. Opening the passenger door, I let her in the car and drove around the lake looking for a private place to park; finding none I returned to the cabin. The guys had already returned empty handed, so I walked in to the cabin with Wendy Kimmel on my arm to gloat. Chris was busy cleaning up the dinner dishes and Vinny was sitting at the kitchen table drinking beer and playing cards with Tom. As predicted they had been refused entry into the clubs, but Chris had managed to purchase a couple of six packs of Colt-45.[424]

Wendy needed to go to the bathroom and as soon as she closed the door I pulled Chris aside to let him know I would be in the driveway and was not to be disturbed. Promptly returning to the car Wendy and I started making out. I ran into some slight resistance when I started to feel her up, but when I began taking off her clothes she actively fought me. Pulling away abruptly I poured on the pressure. "Look, little girl. You were late coming to the dance and now there is not that much time. Do you want to be with me or not?" The poor young thing looked terrified, but she eventually acquiesced. Luckily for her we quickly ran out of time.

---

[424] *Colt 45 Malt Liquor* – is a brand of beer introduced by the National Brewing Co. in the spring of 1963. Previously, the only major national brand of malt liquor was Country Club. Through a series of mergers & acquisitions the Pabst Brewing Co now owns the brand. Its label was designed with a kicking horse & horseshoe, which is a subtle reference to its "extra kick" when compared to competing brands & contrary to popular belief it was named after running back #45 Jerry Hill of the 1963 Baltimore Colts & not the gun.

I drove her back to the lodge and pulled into the parking lot, where I took down her phone number. I was just about finished when her father spotted us. David Kimmel called across the parking lot and told Wendy to get into his car. When she hesitated Mrs. Kimmel began screaming. Terror overwhelmed the poor girl and she began to visibly shake. Although I offered to walk over with her, she convinced me that it would only make matters worse. Squeezing my hand again she haltingly walked toward her angry parents. Mrs. Kimmel glared at me again, but this time I stared right back at her. When their car disappeared into the darkness behind the lodge, I got back into my car and returned to the cabin.

Peering through the picture window I saw my plastered friends playing a serious game of bumper pool. When I opened the front door they hit me with one snide remark after the other about how I had been robbing the cradle. Returning the volley, I ridiculed them regarding their prowess with older women. Unable to think clearly enough to spar with me, the room fell silent before the ugly truth of my commentary and they returned their attention to the game. Breaking the stony silence before hitting the hay I added, "You won't believe it. She's from Cherry Hill."

After our weekend together in the mountains, I returned to the shore alone. The remainder of the summer seemed like an endless string of long lazy days on the beach, the occasional date and drinking parties on the dunes in Harvey Cedars. While I did use my trailer for dating, most of the time it was just a convenient crash pad. Near the end of the summer I started running out of money and began renting the trailer out to some of the guys, who paid me back by chipping in for gas and giving me food money. When the lack of cash went critical; I bought cases of beer and resold the six-packs to underage drinkers for double my original investment. Were it not for this black market merchandising, I would have been forced to end my vacation right then and there.

Occasionally Chris or Vinny came down for the weekend, but Tom spent the rest of the summer painting houses, to save up for his college tuition. No matter how much pressure we put him under; Tom remained a man on a mission and refused to take a single day off. Meanwhile, Vinny sweated away on construction jobs and studied for his professional plumber's license. Chris worked on some pretty big jobs in Philadelphia and pushed his way through a very formal electrical apprenticeship with Local 98. While my friends were hard at work on their careers, I was acting like a beatnik and living like Dobie Gillis.[425] I saw no reason to do otherwise and felt I was just making the most of my youth. I wasn't opposed to working; I just thought summers should be enjoyed and set aside for rest, relaxation and a time to reflect on and enjoy life. During the winter months I had worked hard and lived like a Spartan. I saved my money and felt like I deserved to enjoy the fruits of my labor. Although still on track to become a millionaire, my leisurely life at the shore was giving me pause. I watched Chris and Vinny slaving away at labor-intensive jobs. Tom's total commitment to his painting company demonstrated the startup energy required to go into business and the terrifying tab of tuition. No matter what career path was taken, it seemed to demand an enormous amount of work. I was beginning to question the return on the investment.

In the Summer of '72, life was beginning to morph. We band of brothers sensed the earth moving beneath our feet. The never-ending fun of childhood was being supplanted with the realities and responsibilities of becoming adults. Nostalgic notions of the past prompted us to hold on to those happy memories. In an attempt to concretize our companionship we

---

[425] *The Many Loves of Dobie Gillis* – was a CBS sitcom from 1959-1963. It was based on a collection of short stories, by Max Shulman & inspired the 1953 film *The Affairs of Dobie Gillis*. The series revolved around teenager Dobie Gillis (Dwayne Hickman), who aspired to have popularity, money & the attention of beautiful & unattainable girls. His lack of success became the story in each episode. His partner-in-crime was TVs 1st beatnik, Maynard G. Krebs (Bob Denver) who had a deep aversion to the term "work" & was convinced life is for enjoyment.

formed *The Fraternal Order of the "Ad Infinitum"*.[426] We even made a scrapbook for *The Terrible Triangle* and another one for *The Bud Brother's Association of America*. Like sand in the hourglass, the carefree times were slowly empting out. Our teenage years were coming to a close and we would soon drift apart, but not 'till the fat lady sang.[427]

Labor Day signaled the end of the summer for me. Once again I found myself staring out over the ocean in quiet reflection. The difference was that this year I sat on the bench of the windswept 2nd Street dune alone. I had almost given up hope of seeing anyone until next year, when Christina Nowicki walked onto the beach. Although she was still grounded, her father was down with some of his friends to play poker. Dearly loving his daughter, Mr. Nowicki had always been opposed to his wife's punishment of her, so he brought Christina along with him for his weekend getaway. It was Saturday around four in the afternoon and most of the gang had gone home for dinner when I walked down the dune to sit next to her. Christina and I sat there on the beach together and whatever had come between us melted away like butter in the warmth of the afternoon sun. She seemed serene and content to just sit quietly on the beach looking out over the surf. I asked her if she would like to go to the Wharf, which experience had taught me was one of her favorite places to go, but she gently refused my overture. Surely I deserved the rebuke, but I remained with her and listened to the sea gulls, as I struggled to find the right words to say next. Breaking the tension she said, "I'd rather just hang out with you on the beach, if that's ok." Startled and

---

[426] *The Fraternal Order of the "Ad Infinitum"* – is a Latin phrase, which loosely translated means "Brothers till the End".

[427] *Kate Smith* – was a singer, best known for her rendition of "God Bless America" by Irving Berlin. Smith had a radio, television & recording career for about 50 years, which reached its pinnacle in the 1940s. Her plump figure occasionally made her the object of derision, but later on, the Philadelphia Flyers hockey fans lovingly referred to her appearance before their games by saying, "It ain't BEGUN 'til the fat lady sings!" She became a kind of good luck mascot and during the hotly contested Stanley Cup Finals the saying got turned around to be, "It ain't OVER 'til the fat lady sings!" (1907-1986)

energized by the olive branch I smiled and whispered, "Sure!"

Combing back my hair with her fingers she asked if I would stop by her house around eight. Her eyes were glassy, as she studied the contours of my face and said, "Its good to see you again Patrick." Leaning in I gently kissed her lips and squeezed her arm to let her know how much I cared. Gradually the dunes began casting their shadows on the beach and cooling the air as the tide ran out and Christina stood up to shake out her towel. I gave her another hug and she smiled, as we said good-bye and she disappeared over the sandy ridge. Walking back down the hill to retrieve my towel, I paused to watch two small children playing tag with the waves, before heading over to Baker's Acres so that I could get ready for the evening. I scraped some quarters out of the ashtray in my car to use in the coin operated shower and then disappeared into my trailer. After the shower I splashed on some Old Spice, got dressed and snagged a blanket from my bed. Driving back to the island I walked into George's Pizza and ordered dinner.

All through the meal I searched my mind and my heart to get a handle on what I was feeling. I reflected on all Christina and I had been through. I looked forward to our evening together and hoped that our relationship could grow deeper over time. At exactly eight o'clock, I showed up on her front porch and knocked on the screen door. Mr. Nowicki motioned for me to come in and cheerfully introduced me to his friends. Listening to their conversations as they sat around the kitchen table drinking, smoking and playing cards, it was apparent they had been good buddies for many years. Christina asked her father for special permission to stay out late and her dad smiled affectionately and winked. "Sure hun. You two go out and have a good time." I thanked her father and we walked away hand-in-hand up to the end of the street.

There was a strong ocean breeze, yet it was still comfortably warm from the heat of the day. Straddling the edge of the surf we must have walked a good twenty blocks on the cold damp sand, until our feet were freezing cold. Ascending a sloping shoreline we warmed them up in the stored heat of the finely sifted dry sand. Finding a shallow depression beneath a weatherworn picket fence on the dune, I spread out the blanket.

Sitting down on our makeshift bed, I lit up a cigarette. As we watched the waves rolling in on the beach she started to speak. She spoke of her summer job back home, her bitch of a mother and how much she loved and felt sorry for her henpecked father. Christina shared how lonely it was being grounded and how depressed she had become. She shared how she struggled with our relationship and how much she had wanted to spend more time with me, but felt disloyal toward her best friend Leah. She even admitted that when I dated other girls, she felt jealous. Finally, she talked about the future and how she wanted to go to college to become a pharmacist. Christina went on to say that she remembered everything about me, even the smells. When I asked her what she meant, she said that she remembered the smell of my particular brand of cigarettes and Coppertone, of Old Spice and even my own unique smell, which was different than that of any other man. She claimed she loved that smell, simply because it was mine. I flicked the cigarette butt in the air and the ocean breeze carried it back to the saw-grass. Less than a week ago there was a dune fire, so I remained vigilant until the orange glow faded from sight.

Off in the distance we could make out the faint whine of a jeep. We momentarily looked up and saw the patrol headlights. I stayed silent and listened while she finished unburdening herself. When the lifeguards passed she paused the conversation and we watched the dull red taillights fade, as they journeyed southward. It would be several hours before they returned. Placing my arm around her I gently lowered her to the blanket and we began making out. After awhile we started touching one another with gentle caressing strokes. One thing led to another and although we took our time, eventually we discarded every stitch of our clothing until our naked bodies were passionately intertwined. Pausing to admire her beauty, I propped my head up on one elbow and marveled as the full moon illuminated the fullness of her form in a silvery glow. Our eyes locked and then like the flowering petals of a tender rose she spread her legs to invite me in.

More than anything else in the world I wanted her; yet something gave me pause. I rolled over on my back and looked up at a star filled sky. What if we had a baby? I was still not sure I could support myself, let alone a family. I was not prepared to marry her. We had to stop; and we had to stop now! Putting my clothes back on, I walked down to the water's edge and stared out into the darkness. There was no way to explain my behavior. Hell, I wasn't even sure I understood it myself. A few minutes later Christina walked up behind me and wrapped her arms around my waist. I turned around to hug her and gently kissed her lips; but we both knew it was time for me to walk her home.

The following day we both experienced the emotional pain and regret of our sin. What seemed so beautiful sweet and gentle in the glow of the moonlight, rotted like the seaweed on the beach in the noonday sun. Christina sat alone on the 3rd street beach starring out over the ocean and focusing all of her attention on a point well beyond the breakers. Feeling guilty, confused and unable to catch her eye, I found it impossible to approach her. Whatever reasons I may have had for walking away last night, appeared to be stupid and cowardly now. While I'm sure it was the correct decision, it was a decision that should have been made long before we ever crossed the dune. There was nothing left to say. The damage to our relationship was irreparable, complete and lethal. The only thing our hearts could do now was to ache for what might have been.

Once again my summer vacation was over and another year of my life was lost to the dustbin of history. I returned home from the shore with that old familiar admixture of marvelous memories and ruinous regrets.

Chapter 21

Love Unlimited

The music of Love's Theme[428] was pure adrenalin and Barry White's instrumental resonated with the emerging exuberance of the seventies. The Love Unlimited Orchestra gushed forth with soaring surreal crescendos that filled us with hope and enthusiasm for things to come. Unfortunately the pulsating piece only produced a temporary euphoria. The ever popular practice of promiscuity was an even greater rush for me, but my unrepentant sexual sins left me spiritually empty, socially isolated and slipping by default into the same cultural cesspool as the rest of my generation. Surreptitiously, the same serpents that enticed us with their siren songs of sexual freedom were also invading the Catholic Church and corporate creeps were compelling congressman to do their bidding. Both the clergy and the politician had breached the public trust. Lobbyists were using regulations to bludgeon their competition and churchmen were attempting to destroy the Ark of Salvation from within. Lots of adults were duped and disoriented by these societal upheavals. Many of our parents went missing in action and teachers encouraged students to establish their own morals with values clarification classes so we were left to figure things out for ourselves. If high school taught us anything, it convinced us we were on our own.

In 1971 John Cardinal Krol[429] became the president of the NCCB[430] where he had held the line against dissidents of the

---

[428] *Love's Theme* – is an instrumental piece recorded by Barry White's Love Unlimited Orchestra & was released in 1973. By 1974 it was one of the few instrumental & purely orchestral singles, to reach #1 on Billboard's Hot 100 chart.

[429] *John Joseph Krol* – was a Polish-American Cardinal and the Archbishop of Philadelphia from 1961 to 1988. He was elevated to the cardinalate in 1967. (1910-1996)

[430] *NCCB* – the *National Conference of Catholic Bishops* along with the (USCC) *United States Catholic Conference* combined in 2001, to form the (USCCB) *United States Conference of Catholic Bishops.*

Church in America. His nemesis, Bishop Bernadin[431] undercut his support and by 1974 replaced him as president. The NCCB was intended to provide a collegial gathering forum for bishops to discuss common problems and to share strategies. Instead, Joseph Bernadin created a sprawling bureaucracy, which usurped the ecclesial authority of individual bishops to govern their own dioceses. Harshly criticized in The Ratzinger Report the future Pope Benedict XVI called for the abolishment of what he termed corrupt conferences.[432] What eventually came to be known as the USCCB morphed into a virtual war room for the reassigning pedophile priests into different diocese around the country. The clandestine maneuverings of Bernadin's bureaucracy effectively dismantled and discredited the Catholic Church in America. Juxtaposed to this evil activity, Charismatic prayer groups started springing up all around the country and breathing new life into an ailing Church. One such oasis was called The Body of Christ Prayer Community[433] and in time it would become a new spiritual home for me.

Large corporations were cleverly sucking the life out of small businesses. In the Fifties and Sixties, giant look-alike companies began to appear. Franchises began showing up in small towns all across America. Most were financed on Wall Street and the Seventies brought with them even more cookie cutter enterprises. John D. Rockefeller[434] is often quoted as

---

[431] *Joseph Louis Bernardin* – originally Bernardini, was an American Cardinal of the Roman Catholic Church who served as Archbishop of Chicago from 1982-1996 and was for a time president of the NCCB. He was elevated to the cardinalate in 1983. (1928-1996)

[432] *The Ratzinger Report* – is the name given to a long series of interviews with Joseph Cardinal Ratzinger given to the Italian journalist Vittorio Messori. The book was very critical of the hermeneutic of rupture, often associated with the liberal spirit of Vatican II. A re-read is helpful in correctly understanding the mind of Pope Benedict XVI. The Ratzinger Report, by Joseph Cardinal Ratzinger, published by Ignatius Press, San Francisco, CA, 1985. *The Problem of Episcopal Conferences*, pp. 58

[433] *The Body of Christ Prayer Community* – was a charismatic prayer community founded on September 13, 1972, by Father Domenic Rossi, who at the time was a brother in the Norbertine order, at the Daylesford Abbey in Paoli, PA & its apex membership totaled 400.

[434] *John D. Rockefeller* – was an American business tycoon, industrialist & book-keeper, most known for his role in the early petroleum-industry & the founding of Standard Oil. Measured in today's dollars, Rockefeller is the richest person in the history of mankind. He was also the first billionaire in history. (1839-1937)

saying, "Competition is a sin." So along with the newest bonanza came legislation designed to regulate out the competition. Millions of corporate dollars supported politicians who reinforced the corrupt cabal between business and government. Serious competition had been eliminated, which is one of the cornerstones of the capitalist economic system. The government corporate cabal slaughtered small businesses by the millions. True capitalism had been hamstrung and crony capitalism was in charge.

As we attempted our journey into manhood, Chris Lang and I moved into the Hatfield Village Apartments. Chris was half-way through his apprenticeship with Local 98[435] and working on construction jobs in Philadelphia. I returned to the machine shop and ran a cutoff saw to make base plugs. We were the best of friends and had much in common, but living together also brought out our differences. Chris was a night owl and wanted to go to parties, dances and the bar almost every other night. I liked going out on the weekends, but after a hard day at work I wanted to kick back and watch nostalgic TV shows like The Walton's.[436] It wasn't long before we were fighting over stupid things like: not putting the cap back on the toothpaste, leaving dishes in the sink or deciding what the word "clean" meant in regards to the bathroom. While ecstatic over the independence of having our own apartment; things eventually got so bad we broke the lease in order to save our friendship.

Still too young to drink in Pennsylvania; Chris and I tried sneaking into a club known for its carding leniency in Lansdale. I met a beautiful brunette there named Irene Blair

---

[435] *Local 98* – is the Philadelphia chapter of The International Brotherhood of Electrical Workers (IBEW) a labor union representing workers in the U.S. & several other countries. The union primarily represents: electricians, inside wiremen for the construction industry, linemen & employees of public utilities. Today they also represent computer, telecommunications, broadcasting & other electrical workers.

[436] *The Waltons* – was a television series created by Earl Hamner, Jr., based on his book Spencer's Mountain & a 1963 film. The show centered on a family growing up in rural Virginia during The Great Depression & World War II. CBS ran the series from 1972-1981. It was produced by Lorimar Productions & distributed by Warner Brothers.

who loved to dance. Near the end of the evening she invited both of us out to King Arthur's Court in Quakertown. She said she knew the bouncer and that he would let us into the exclusive club. Although the cover charges and drinks were expensive, we all had a great time. Over the next few weeks I went out dancing with Irene in three additional clubs. The only trouble was that I soon realized she liked the dancing more than she liked me. I hated to lose such a good-looking dame, but I felt used and didn't want to waste any more money on her. But the real emotional one-two punch came through Carol Stover.

Carol attended the University of Maryland and had her own apartment in Baltimore, Maryland. I considered her a good Catholic girl and although we often got carried away with passionate kissing, I never pushed things sexually. So when she invited me to spend Christmas vacation with her, I naturally assumed I would be sleeping on the couch. Upon my arrival, we toured University Park, went shopping in an open-air market and cooked dinner together. Later on that evening we sat around talking and shared a glass of wine and some cheese. It was the perfect ending to a perfect day. Around midnight she offered to share her bed. Although I was excited about the prospect, I was surprised by the offer and so I figured she just wanted to cuddle. We gently kissed and spooned throughout the night, but in the morning things progressed. Although inexperienced and a little hesitant, she kept giving me the green light. The situation was all too familiar, but this time there was an additional twist. I felt an overwhelming sense of guilt and went limp. After a deafening silence Carol went into the kitchen to make breakfast. I was angry, embarrassed and scared, all at the same time. My failure to launch had everything to do with knowing I was doing wrong, but I silently blamed my mother for the dysfunction. I saw mom as the ice lady and believed she had somehow managed to inject her moralistic rules so deeply into my psyche that I was unable to function as a man. I was so angry that while Carol was making breakfast, I called up mom on the telephone and accused her of psychologically damaging me with her prudish teachings. Although the accusation was false it must have pierced her heart, but she stood firm behind the time honored teaching of the Catholic Church, insisting that all sexual activity was reserved for sacramental marriage.[437] During breakfast our conversation deteriorated into an intellectual discussion and although it was awkward, we both knew it was time for me to leave. The following year she married a man who truly loved her and went on to raise a beautiful family with him.

Nothing seemed to be working in my life. I was stuck in a dead-end job and one by one my relationships with women were falling apart. Old friends were moving on and it was apparent they would no longer be my traveling companions. Just when I thought nothing could get any worse, the other shoe dropped. I was loosing my friend Lesley and was all alone. On January 15, 1973, Lesley left to join the cast of Up With People.[438] Later that year she went to college at the University of Arizona. With no commitments and nothing left to loose, I started taking flying lessons at Montgomeryville Airport. A single flight lesson was all it took to get me hooked. I redirected my career efforts, setting my sights on becoming a commercial pilot. The prestigious position required a great deal of responsibility and many hours of study, but I was up for the challenge. "She took off to find the footlights and I took off for the sky."[439]

---

[437] *CCC 2391* – Carnal union is morally legitimate only when a definitive community of life between a man and woman has been established. Human love does not tolerate "trial marriages." It demands a total and definitive gift of persons to one another.

[438] *Up With People* – was a singing troupe, which traveled all over the country & indeed the world. They presented a feel good musical that advocated breaking down the barriers of race, country & religion, with the goal of universal brotherhood. However, just below the surface it was laying the groundwork for the attitudes embraced by the new world order. It advocated a live & let live lifestyle, with no absolutes & no objective moral boundaries.

[439] *Taxi* – the line is from a song written & performed by Harry Chapin on the Heads & Tales album released in 1972. It reached #24 on Billboard's Hot 100 list. Harry was inspired to write it, when he happened upon an old lover, as a cabbie in NYC. The nostalgic ballad was about a relationship he had with a college student named Clare MacIntyre. They

During the day I worked fulltime as a machine operator at Callahan Machine and in the evenings I was attempting to recoup my investment in Bestline Products, by wholesaling off inventory in hundred dollar lots. Although still banking what I could, I no longer lived like a Spartan. Chris made great money in the union and used his newfound wealth to purchase a brand new forest green Pontiac Formula 400 Firebird[440] and some top of the line ski equipment. We made frequent trips up to dad's cabin at Arrowhead Lake and went skiing at Jack Frost or Big Boulder.[441] On the way up the northeast extension we psyched ourselves up for the trip by listening to multiple sets of our skiing anthem, the Love's Theme instrumental. If we were every lucky enough to bring back snow bunnies, we broke the ice with them by playing the UnGame;[442] but truth be told we never met girls on the slopes and rarely even met them in the lodge. Once in a blue moon we brought girls from back home along with us, but most of the time we just competed with each other on the slopes and hung out in the cabin playing bumper pool. Skiing all day long left us exhausted and we returned to the cabin absolutely famished. After dinner we would play poker and drink to anesthetize our aching bodies. Competition on the slopes was extremely intense! Chris won almost all of the races, but one day his binding broke loose and I eagerly sailed on by him. I thought I would finally beat him in our friendly contest, but then he launched himself over a mogul and flew right over my head. Winning was everything!

---

met as camp counselors at neighboring summer camps & the relationship ended, when she went away to be an actress & he left for the US Air Force Academy.

[440] *Pontiac Formula 400 Firebird* – was built by the Pontiac division of General Motors. It was introduced at the same time as its platform-sharing cousin, the Chevrolet Camaro. This followed the release of the Mercury Cougar, which shared its platform with another pony car, the Ford Mustang. The sexy 1972 metallic green Formula 400 sported a sleek looking matching set of slender ram air hood scoops & they powered a 400 cubic inch V8 engine.

[441] *Big Boulder & Jack Frost* – are skiing destinations in the Pocono Mountains of eastern Pennsylvania. Big Boulder is located in Lake Harmony & Jack Frost is in Blakeslee, PA.

[442] *The Ungame* - was created in 1972 by Rhea Zakich. It is a non-competitive learning game of conversation that is supposed to foster listening skills & self-expression. Players progress along the board answering questions such as "What are the four most important things in your life" & "What do you think life will be like in 100 years?" Special spaces on the board also encourage players to exchange their thoughts & feelings or describe how they've been affected by past emotional experiences.

Most of Chris Lang's union buddies bragged about their predator prowess by telling glorious tales of how they acquired the trophies that adorned their living room walls. Chris soon wanted to go hunting and bag a deer of his own. So I asked my uncle if I could borrow Miss Hickey's Hut[443] for the weekend. Chris and I drove up to the sleepy little town of Waterville, where we spent the better part of three days hunting whitetail deer on the snow-covered mountain next to the Little Pine Creek. Getting up before dawn we braved single digit temperatures and patiently waited for our quarries. At midday we took a break and ate lunch in a bar where we listened to the patrons telling tales of the legendary stags that got away and the champions who had bagged the bucks with the biggest racks. Reinvigorated by these tall tales we braved the elements and tried our luck again until the sun disappeared behind the majestic mountain on the far side of the creek. Returning to the cabin we prepared hearty meals that included: a fresh sliced head of lettuce drenched in French dressing, thick juicy steaks and mountains of mashed potatoes. Hot brown gravy formed a lake at the top of the Irish staple and copious rivers of the luscious lava flowed down the soft sides of its slopes. These manly meals were simply irresistible! As soon as supper was over we stoked a coal stove, drank lots of hot chocolate and pulled out topographical maps.[444] Pouring over the familiar green charts we divined the migration patterns of the local deer population and then attempted to plan a strategy for our hunt the following day.

Each evening we studied the maps, cracked jokes, chopped firewood and engaged in serious conversations about the direction of our lives. Neither one of us ever saw a deer, but I assumed we were both having a great time, until he started

---

[443] *Hickey's Hut* – is a small cabin located on 30 acres along the Little Pine Creek in Waterville, PA, south of the Little Pine State Park & was originally owned by Miss Hickey.
[444] *Topographical Map* – is a type of map characterized by large-scale detail & quantitative representation of relief, usually using contour lines. The United States Geological Survey (USGA) charts or "green maps" are colored maps that show both natural & man-made features including: forests & fields, mountains & streams, roads & trails, houses & towers.

venting on the way home. In my mind hunting was all about having a good time; but Chris had come to kill a deer. After bragging all week at work that he would be bringing back the biggest trophy buck; he was sure his union brothers would not only ridicule his words as mere talk, but might even question his manhood. I had no idea my best friend was not enjoying himself. I had always looked up to Chris and was astonished to learn that peer pressure held so much sway over him. This concern over what others thought of him was crushing the life out of Chris, but it was very real and we never went hunting again.

"All that is necessary for the triumph of evil is that good men do nothing."[445] Bragging rights may matter in the macho world of construction, but the gold standard for manhood is recognizing evil and protecting the camp, even at the cost of our lives. But most American men were asleep at the switch on January 22, 1973 when the Supreme Court ruled in *Roe vs. Wade* that a woman had the right to kill her unborn child. Not only did the high court make a grievous moral error, they also usurped Congressional power by writing law instead of squaring it with the Constitution. Our founding father Sam Adams would have tarred and feathered them; at the very least Congress should have impeached the evil men in the black robes; but Americans did neither and neither did I.

I was unaware of Warren Burger's barbaric blunder. I had never even heard of abortion, let alone understood it to be a murderous act. However, two things brought the issue front and center. The first was a magazine article and the second was something shared by a close friend. Sitting in a waiting room I happened upon an issue of Life Magazine.[446] The

---

[445] *Edmund Burke* – is often credited with having made this statement. He was an Irish political philosopher, Whig politician & statesman who is often regarded as the "father" of modern conservatism. (1729-1797)

[446] *Life Magazine* – in the article "The Drama of Life before Birth" the April 30th issue of LIFE Magazine documented the fetal stages of development in vivid color, almost 8 years before the Supreme Court ruled on Roe vs. Wade.

article featured full color photos of human life in all its intrauterine stages. Shortly after I read the article, Lesley Wright returned from Brazil and informed me that she met a boy and had become romantically involved with him, while traveling with her new singing troupe. Although she would never again see the father of her child, the boy from Brazil had impregnated her. Faced with an ectopic[447] pregnancy she went ahead with an abortion. She shared all the gory details of the gruesome procedure she experienced, as I tried to help her through her postpartum grief. Despite the fact that her particular case involved the principal of double effect,[448] the death of her child still took a toll on both of us.

Helping Lesley through this heart wrenching time brought us closer together again, but the entire culture was in moral freefall and would militate against anything good coming from it. We went to a shocking triple feature at the Three-O-Nine Drive-In, which was yet another deviant sexual propaganda film. I still can't believe that we stayed for all three movies. Deep Throat,[449] The Devil in Miss Jones[450] and The Last House on the Left,[451] each had virtually the same message. The mantra running through the three-fold assault was that oral sex is a powerful way for a woman to get what she wants. Desensitized to any semblance of a moral code, I came away even more tempted to push the sexual envelope.

The next time my friends came up from Jersey we put together a party in the barn. Looking for dates we cruised

---

[447] *Ectopic* – pregnancy is one that occurs outside the womb. It is a life-threatening condition to the mother and the baby cannot survive.

[448] *The Principle of Double Effect* – means that sometimes one must perform an action that is in itself morally good, but may also have an unintended ill effect for which the person isn't morally culpable. Thomas Aquinas deals with Double-effect in his Summa Theologiae, IIa-IIae Q. 64, article 7.

[449] *Deep Throat* – was a 1972 pornographic film written & directed by Gerard & starring Linda Lovelace. It launched the porn chic trend, but was still banned in some regions & the subject of several obscenity trials.

[450] *The Devil in Miss Jones* – was a 1973 pornographic film, written, directed & produced by Gerard Damiano & starring Georgina Spelvin.

[451] *The Last House on the Left* – was a violent & pornographic 1972 horror film written & directed by Wes Craven & produced by Sean S. Cunningham.

through Lansdale and then went to the Astor Diner for dinner. While looking over the menus we noticed three girls sitting in a nearby booth. Suddenly, a waitress flew out of the kitchen and sat down beside them. Chris said, "Hey Patrick, isn't that Natalie?" I hadn't seen her since she got drunk on the beach in Surf City. I heard that she had gotten married, but there was also a rumor she was getting divorced. I waved to her and she came running over to our table. Throwing her arms around me she exclaimed, "Patrick! I'm so happy to see you. What are you up to?" She already knew Tom and Chris, so I introduced her to Vinny. Seizing the moment Chris said, "We're throwing a beer party up in the barn. Do you know anyone who might like to come?" She smiled and said, "Sure. I get off work in an hour and I'm sure my girlfriends would love to come." With that she ran back over to the other booth and when he saw their reaction, Chris smiled and said, "We're in!" Natalie came back to our table with the rest of the girls and introduced us. They all seemed pretty excited and were looking forward to the party. Natalie knew where I lived and she said she would show the rest how to get there. Now all we needed was some beer.

None of us were the requisite age to purchase liquor, but I stopped into a drive through beer distributor anyway and gave the attendant my order. When he asked for ID I handed him my driver's license. We all put on our best poker faces, waiting for the guy's response. Handing it back to me, he placed three cases of Michelob in the trunk and we drove out. As soon as we were out on the road again, Tom asked me, "What did you give him?" I smiled and said, "Confidence!"

Back at the barn we straightened the place up, cracked a few cold ones and played some pool until the girls arrived. After getting the ladies some drinks and playing a few games of pool with them, we turned out the lights to dance. Within the hour we were coupled off and making our way to the couches. Natalie must have been traveling with a different crowd lately, because this was all too easy. Although still in the same room, each couple had access to their own couch and to some degree of privacy. No one was attending the record player and when the last record ended the only sound in the room was the hum of the electric heater. It didn't take Natalie and I much time to reacquaint. Soon we were making out, feeling each other up and clothes were being shed. We rapidly traversed three of the four bases, including the one encouraged by the movie Deep Throat. I had gone as far as I wanted to, so I attempted to slow things down, but this hot to trot divorcee had no intention of tapering off. I thought about walking away, but we were not totally alone. I was afraid she might object. She might even loudly object! What would my friends say? What would the other girls think of me? Would they all start laughing at me? Without any warning, she rolled over, climbed on top and I let her have her way with me.

After a brief respite, we quietly got dressed and walked outside where I directed her to the bathroom inside our house. I sat on the edge of a knee-high cinder-block wall while a flood of questions filled my head and my heart became clouded with intense emotion. Why did she let me make love to her? More to the point, why did she push me to do something I wasn't even trying to do? Did she love me? It was the first time I had ever gone all the way. Although it felt pleasurable and seemed more intimate than anything I have ever known, I had been saving this gift for my wife. Should I marry her, to make it right? I sat there pondering the questions, smoking a cigarette and wondering what to do next. Whatever decisions there were to be made, I couldn't make them alone. There was someone else involved in this and I didn't have all the answers. I desperately needed to know how she felt.

When she came back out, I offered her a cigarette and she sat down beside me. I had to say something, which would transform this bad thing, into a good thing. I hesitatingly began a conversation saying, "You know... That was really special to me. It was my first time." I expected her to say something equally tender or romantic, but with a callous indifference that matched the cold night air she said, "Oh, I guess I shouldn't have done it." Taking a last drag of her cigarette, she walked back into the barn. My heart was more than just broken. All my hopes and dreams, my very personhood lay shattered on the ground, like thousands of tiny shards of glass. I was devastated! I had given all of myself to someone who couldn't have cared less. After a few days of soul searching I tried to salvage the relationship by asking her out again. She accepted the invitation and things seemed to be improving, until she said she missed her period. Now I was really in a pickle! I tried to comfort her and began thinking about marriage. Each time I saw her, I asked if her friend had visited. She seemed to warm up to me during the maternal panic, but once she knew there was no danger of a pregnancy, she drifted away and let me know through my sister that she wasn't interested in dating me anymore.

I told Lesley about the loss of my virginity and when I shared my shattered heart with her she seemed keenly aware of the emotional devastation I had been through. We seemed to grow even closer and thanks to some pretty candid exchanges I ended up learning a lot about gynecology from her. We started out just spending time together as friends, but things turned pretty physical after we watched a controversial movie called The Harrad Experiment.[452] Although it presented an outrageous concept at the time; the coed dorms it promoted soon became commonplace on many university campuses. Eager to try out what we had seen on

---

[452] *The Harrad Experiment* – is a 1973 film about a fictional Harrad College where the students are required to live together so they can learn about sexuality & experiment with each other. Based on the 1962 book by Robert Rimmer, it deals with the concept of free love during the height of the sexual revolution. In The Wonder Years 4th season episode "Growing Up", Kevin's sister is seen reading a copy of the book while on vacation.

the silver screen; I parked on lover's lane and we made love in the back seat of my car.

Lesley likened our friendship to the stability of an old oak tree. She claimed that lovers were like flowers, which were beautiful but quickly faded. We both had the same birthday so we celebrated it in the cabin behind my house. Drawing from her magnificent metaphor, I offered her a card with the picture of a tree with a blossom emerging from the bark. The inscription I wrote inside read, "Sometimes flowers grow on trees." After making love on the sofa bed Lesley smiled broadly and said, "Happy birthday Patrick." We dined at the Astor and watched a movie at the Drive In. The lovely lady's choice was The Way We Were.[453]

The subtle message in her selection was that we would not always be this intimate. She knew that Up With People would soon be on the road again and like the characters in the movie; our lives would take separate paths. I didn't like the message and in my anger I drove aggressively and ended up running a red light. Suddenly a car flashed in front of me and it was too late to stop. My mind went into hyper-drive and I threw my body in front of her. I watched with fascination as the window shattered and the hood crumpled up in what seemed like slow motion photography. Although we both emerged unscathed, she was shaken and the car was totaled. Cradling the woman in my arms I begged for her forgiveness.

When Leslie went back on the road I returned to the Caribbean in what came to be known as The Nautical Nitwits Trip. Dad was captain, Sean and Sarah were shipmates and I was allowed to bring Chris and Tom. Sarah

---

[453] *The Way We Were* – is a 1973 romantic movie staring Barbara Streisand & Robert Redford. It was directed by Sydney Pollack, with a screenplay by Arthur Laurents, who based it on his college days at Cornell University & his experiences with the House Un-American Activities Committee. The film was a box office success & was nominated for several awards including Best Original Song for *The Way We Were*, which charted 23 weeks on the Billboard Hot 100 list & sold over a million copies.

kept the ship's log, as we sailed from island to island. Snorkeling among the reefs during the day, we enjoyed fabulous evenings of dancing to the beat of steel drums. Pickled with rum for most of the trip, I continued to slide down the slippery slope of sinful behavior. It even became a community problem when I almost got our whole crew into a brawl after trying to make out with a married woman.

After returning from vacation, I spent the rest of the winter working hard to build up a nice bank account. Since my car had been totaled, I bought a used Corvair[454] Convertible for $250. Although it burned oil badly and the twin carburetors kept going out of sync, it was the perfect little shore car. The yellow babe magnet had a black interior, a 5-speed manual transmission and a 4-cylinder engine. Near the end of May I quit my job again and headed for the shore. Driving down in the middle of the night, I attempted to disprove Ralph Nader's safety theory by accelerating my little Corvair to over one-hundred miles per hour on route seventy-two.

The Terrible Triangle agreed to meet at Baker's Acres on Memorial Day. We kicked off our summer vacation by staying in the trailer overnight and then arrived at Surf City the following day on the 2nd Street beach. Tom and Chris quickly paired off with two new chicks from Florida, while I sat brooding and kicking myself for having walked away from the incomparable Christina Nowicki. After working up some courage, I made my way over to her towel to apologize for what had transpired last year. Judging from the look in her eyes, I was surprised she listened at all. Although she accepted my mea culpa, she said she wouldn't be hanging out with me or any of the gang ever again. I'm not sure what

---

[454] *Corvair* – was a car initially marketed by Chevrolet as a family economy sedan, but with the mid-1960 introduction of the 5-passenger coupe with bucket seats, the Corvair found a new sporty-car niche & in 1964 influenced Ford to produce the Mustang. A variety of factors contributed to a drop in sales after 1965. Safety issues had been raised in "The Sporty Corvair" chapter of Ralph Nader's book, where he called it *Unsafe at Any Speed.*

happened with the rest of the gang, but she was clearly done with all of us.

After dinner we drove up to Harvey Cedars to see my cousins. Chris got together with Mariah who was still calling him "big boy." I hooked up with Plain Jane and Mariah introduced Tom to one of her new girlfriends. I took the Lang Gang for a drive around town in my new convertible where we played some miniature golf. We walked down to the dunes and spent the rest of the evening drinking, telling stories and making out on blankets. On the way back home we scraped our toes across the cold damp sand of the beach revealing a spectacular green glow of luminous algae. Everyone had a light hearted good time and in the morning we drove back to Surf City for a hearty pancake breakfast.

The loss of love from Christina was heartache enough, but seeing the rest of the gang shun her, hurt me even more and was also puzzling. Whatever happened during my absence must have destroyed the ties that bind and she was not the only person they were avoiding. In a reverse of fortunes, my friends were made to feel welcome, while I was left sitting alone on the beach. No one asked me to leave; they just didn't include me in the conversations. Monday afternoon Tom headed back home with Chris in his Firebird. Their departure left me high and dry, wondering what I would do for the rest of the summer. The situation was so depressing that I smoked an entire pack of cigarettes in one afternoon. Late in the afternoon I asked Sheryl Levite to tell me why Christina was sitting all by herself and why I seemed to be getting the cold shoulder from the rest of the gang. She refused tell me what had happened, but gave the cryptic response, "What goes around, comes around." With the sun in my eyes I drove back to the mainland in my convertible. There in my ancient rusting Prairie Schooner I spent the first of many lonely nights; mourning my losses and wondering about what might have been.

I spent the rest of the week at my uncle's house, reading in the breezy comfort of the second floor living room, where I watched the sailboats gliding across the bay. Aunt Joan emerged with a glass of wine each afternoon and shared her crackers and cheese with me, while we discussed the meaning of life. My Godmother had grown up in a family of fourteen children. She shared with me the wisdom she had acquired from that experience and from raising twelve children of her own. I told her I felt like running away and starting my life over again, but had no direction. I asked her how I should go about deciding where to live. She smiled and said that most people stay pretty close to home, unless they are motivated by either a great love or a great idea. I had neither.

When not hanging out with my Aunt, I spent hours talking with Mariah. We shared everything and engaged in lots of intimate conversations. We pulled no punches with each other and offered candid observations about whatever we were discussing or sharing. No matter how difficult the topic neither one of us let the other one get away with not telling the truth. Peter loved sailing and occasionally took me out on the catamaran where we often pushed the envelope by skipping across the whitecaps at breakneck speed on windy days. Although it was exhilarating, our reckless adventures often led to unexpected, hilarious or even dangerous consequences. Sometimes in the evening I would slip away with Plain Jane to make out on the beach or take in a movie, but most of my nights were spent drinking on the beach with my cousins and the rest of their many friends. Although I enjoyed Jane's company, things never got too serious with us. Every few days I would return to the mainland to sleep in the trailer. Although it was once a frightful thought; more and more I was feeling the need to be alone with my thoughts.

Red Baker was the owner of Baker's Acres Campground. I got to know him and his wife fairly well. They ran the campground like a perpetual family picnic. Red was a tough old bird who took no guff from anyone, but most of the time he had a cheerful voice and a ready smile. If there was a problem in the camp, he knew about it and was quick to confront the instigators. He also had no qualms about throwing the bums out if need be. As tough as he was, he was a gentle caring soul and his patriarchal style was meant to protect those he loved and whom God had put in his charge. His willingness to guard the lives of others was also evidenced when he worked as a smoke jumper during the winter months.

One day Red invited me to the Tuckerton Fourth of July picnic. Sensing I needed to get back in the game, he talked me into entering a greased pig contest. The slimy little piglet looked easy enough to catch, but seeing and doing are two different things. My ineptness provided great entertainment for the gathering masses and the little critter left me covered in mud. It was all in fun so I took no offense and went swimming to clean myself off. The Independence Day celebration concluded with a spectacular fireworks display over Little Egg Harbor.[455] I can still taste the hot dogs and smell the homemade root beer.

Without the camaraderie of the 2nd Street Gang, the shore was becoming a very lonely place. So I drove back home to spend some time with my dog. I started taking long walks with Bear and his new canine companion Holly.[456] Traipsing through the fields and along creek beds with the dogs gave me some time to think. I started laying out a new plan for my career. I decided to cut my vacation short and return to work

---

[455] *Little Egg Harbor* – is a portion of Egg Harbor named so by Dutch sailors for eggs found in nearby gull nests, which were so numerous it was hard to walk without stepping on one. Captain Cornelius Jacobsen made the first known account of the town in May of 1614.

[456] *Holly* – was an adopted miniature collie that followed Neil home from school one day. The dog had a great disposition & the entire family loved her. Big Bear & Holly were both gentle dogs & had puppies together, but when they went out hunting they became vicious predators. Working together they double-teamed the game & became so successful at catching rabbits, pheasants & groundhogs there was no need to buy anymore dog food.

at Callahan Machine Company. Since I was once again running out of money I limited my vacation time to the weekends. Chris started bringing Vinny up to the farm with him. The three of us rode the go-cart, jumped motorcycles and went swimming at the Harleysville Community Center.[457] Sometimes we met girls there and managed to get dates with them, but most of the time we just hung out with each other and had fun. During the week I earned a steady income as a machine operator by day and continued wholesaling off the Bestline soap inventory at night. Eventually, I registered for school at Montgomery County Community College[458] and resumed my flying lessons at Montgomeryville Airport.

It was time for me to get serious and start working on a career.

---

[457] *Harleysville Community Center* – in 1955 the Harleysville Lions Club voted to make a contribution toward the construction of a community pool. Today the center includes 3 pools, a bathhouse, pavilions, refreshment stand, soccer & baseball fields, & a Scout Cabin.
[458] *Montgomery County Community College* – is a two-year community college offering associate degrees & technical certification in numerous fields. It also offers non-credit courses to the general public. The college was founded in 1964 in Conshohocken, PA & in 1972 opened a main campus in Blue Bell, PA.

Chapter 22

Flying High

In September of 1973 I decided to get serious about earning a living. I began work at a local airport and quit my job at Callahan Machine Co. The strategic move meant a cut in pay, but Montgomeryville Airport[459] offered it's line crew significant discounts on their flying lessons. The instructed time was by no means cheap, but it seemed worth the cost as an investment in my future. I was focused on becoming a commercial pilot, but I also wanted to be in business for myself. To accomplish these goals, I decided to offer transportation services to executives, by using a fleet of Lear Jets.[460] I would call my new company Tri-Star Aviation.[461]

After securing a job at the airport, I asked my father for some financial aid to help pay for flight lessons. Having been a flight instructor himself, he was familiar with the industry and saw the training as a good investment in my education. I used the money he gave me to purchase thousand dollar blocks of flight time, which netted me an additional ten percent discount. The task of the employees in the line crew was to gas planes, schedule lessons, mow forty acres of grass in the summer time and plow snow off the runway in the winter months. I assisted with the maintenance and

---

[459] *Montgomeryville Airport* – was a privately run general aviation airport with a single macadam runway. Like many others it is no longer in operation & the property at the intersection of Routes 202, 309 & 463 in Montgomeryville, PA is now a shopping center.

[460] *LearJet* – is a manufacturer of sleek business jets for civilian & military use. It was founded in the late 1950s by William Powell Lear Jr., as Swiss American Aviation Corporation. Learjet is now a subsidiary of Bombardier & marketed as the "Bombardier Learjet Family". In 1974, the worldwide Learjet fleet had exceeded one million flight hours & in 1975 the company produced its 500th jet and was the first manufacturer to do so.

[461] *Tri-Star Aviation* – the name of my business came from nostalgia over my affectionate for the Terrible Triangle, my dream of reaching for the stars & the business of aviation. In 1984 I felt the inspiration was confirmed when I sat down to watch a movie called *The Natural*. The show opened with a winged horse galloping & flapping its wings on to the screen. The subsidiary of Columbia Pictures was similarly named TriStar Pictures.

inspection in the shop, washed the customer's airplanes and secured the aircraft in the hangers when the sun went down. I took full advantage of every opportunity to be a co-pilot on air-taxi runs into Philadelphia and assisted on cargo flights to places as far away as Charlotte, North Carolina. These trips permitted me to receive instructed time, in high performance aircraft like the Arrow[462] and the Seneca.[463] To pay for this flight time on my own would have cost me thousands of dollars in plane rental and instructor fees.

Chris and his brothers rented a three-bedroom apartment in Cherry Hill, New Jersey. The Lang brothers held frequent parties that drew scores of women almost every Friday night. Saturdays were more intimate affairs and soon became known as date night. Unfortunately, initial contact intimidated me and I rarely ended up with a date for Saturday night. So I played the role of DJ and bar tender, but it soon grew old. Feeling like I was missing out on all the fun, I decided to give Wendy Kimmel a call.

Wendy jumped at the invitation and regularly came with me to the parties. Although we were sexually involved, I didn't pressure her and the relationship began to flourish. Trying to keep my budget in check, I occasionally took her out to the movies and we often ate meals at the local Burger King. I wasn't trying to be cheap or anything; I thought Whoppers tasted great and we both enjoyed going to the movies. Everything seemed to be working out fine until the day I met her parents.

Wendy invited me to her house for Thanksgiving dinner with her family. The house was a shabby looking split-level, but the table was decked out in fine China and Silver. David and

---

[462] *Cherokee Arrow* – the Piper PA-28 Cherokee is a family of light aircraft designed for flight training, air taxi & personal use. Built by Piper Aircraft, the Arrow is a complex trainer featuring 200 horsepower, a variable pitch propeller & retractable landing gear.
[463] *Seneca* – the Piper PA-34 is a twin-engine light aircraft, produced by Piper Aircraft since 1971 & used for personal & business flying.

Marianne Kimmel were eager to meet me and to find out who this man was that was dating their daughter. For better or for worse, the brief encounter would soon expose much more about all parties involved than any of us cared to know.

Albeit with a certain first encounter uneasiness, the afternoon began pleasantly enough. Wendy's father led a simple grace and then all eyes locked in on me. Thanks to a lack of proper training in etiquette, I happened to pick up the wrong spoon for the soup and was asked about my reasoning behind the selection. I recovered beautifully with a lighthearted joke about not having a big enough mouth. Although the adoring sibling twins quietly giggled, the whole family had conspired to deliver an airy joke of their own, which contained a serious salvo. The main course was served on large hand-painted plates from China and the food was covered with silver plated warmers. I had seen similar stainless steel covers at the Holiday Inn, but these heirlooms looked pretty fancy. Already feeling like a cave man visiting the home of Emily Post, I waited for the others to make the first move, but they continued to stare at me in silence. Mrs. Kimmel said, "Go ahead; open it." When I lifted up the silver dome it revealed a Whopper. When they saw the expression on my face, everyone fell over themselves laughing. Mrs. Kimmel said, "Wendy tells us that whenever you go out to dinner, you always take her to Burger King, so we thought this is what you would like for supper." I took it all as good humor designed to break the ice and laughed right along with them. Defending my fast food choice, I told them I liked Whoppers and had never heard an objection from Wendy. The rest of the meal went well, with almost boring conversation, while I eagerly tried to give her parents the best impression I could and get to know them. Although they were cordial, I was about to see a much darker side.

While helping to clear the table, Wendy's eight-year-old brother dropped a saltshaker on the hardwood floor and it broke. Mrs. Kimmel instantly flew into a rage, yelling at the top of her lungs at the poor little tyke. Six times she called him stupid and ridiculed him for breaking the doohickey. I was shocked at the abuse and felt for the little guy, who was crying hysterically and pissing his pants. I looked over at the father, hoping he would stop her, but the wimpy little coward just looked away. The situation demanded a response! So I shouted, "SHUT UP!" The room fell silent as Mrs. Kimmel wheeled around with a shocked look on her face. "What did you say?" "I said, SHUT UP! He's just a little kid and it's only a stupid salt shaker!" Firing her cannon in my direction she hollered, "You Shut Up! You're a guest in my house! How dare you talk to me like that! I think its time you left." Holding my ground I said, "No! You shouldn't talk to anyone like that, let alone a little kid!" Her face was bright red and it looked as if the veins in her neck would explode. Walking toward me she bellowed, "GET OUT!" I turned to the terrified teen behind me and said, "Wendy, get in the car." When the panicked girl picked up her coat, the maddened mother yelled, "Oh no you don't. Wendy Kimmel; you stay right here." Looking her in the eye I repeated the command, "Wendy… Get in the car and lock the door!" For a split-second, she hesitated, torn between the two titans, but recognizing the seminal moment she walked out the door. Now Mrs. Kimmel really lost it. Screaming all sorts of vile epithets at us, she demanded that her teenage daughter return and even threatened to charge me with kidnapping. Continuing to stand my ground, I physically blocked the raging maniac until Wendy was safely in the car. Then I briskly walked back to my vehicle and drove away. Although I'm confident I had done the right thing, it was still a hell of a first impression.

The rest of the world wasn't doing much better. Vice President Spiro Agnew[464] resigned after being accused of

---

[464] *Spiro Agnew* – was the 39th Vice President of the U.S. under Nixon, the 55th Gov. of Maryland & the first Greek American to hold these offices. In 1973, he was investigated by the U.S. Attorney's office in Baltimore, MD & was under investigation for extortion & tax fraud, bribery & conspiracy, before being formally charged for accepting bribes totaling more than $100,000. He plead no contest on condition he resign as Vice President. Agnew is the only Vice President in U.S. history to resign due to criminal charges. (1918-1996)

bribery and was replaced with Gerald Ford.[465] It was the first visible crack in the Nixon administration. Halfway around the globe OPEC[466] mandated a cut in oil exports to punish America for her role in supporting Israel. The resulting rise in oil prices led to the 1973-1974 stock market crash, which produced the most persistent economic problem for the U.S. since the Great Depression.

I may have been unlucky in love, but I had crystal clear financial goals and was making steady progress in my career. I placed a great picture of a Lear Jet above my desk to keep the dream of Tri-Star Aviation ever before my eyes. It takes commitment and hard work to turn dreams into reality and being part of the line crew gave me many opportunities to work on planes in the shop and get free flight instruction as a copilot. Soon I was checked out in the Piper Cherokee[467] and by November I had soloed. One month later I became certified in the Cessna 150[468] over at Pennridge Airport. During the winter months, when I could not fly because of weather, I hit the books and finished up my ground school.

Happy Days[469] premiered on ABC in 1974 and the reality was looking almost as hopeful and joy filled as it was portrayed on TV. To celebrate, we held a New Year's party in the barn. Tom gave Kitty Carter a pre-engagement ring, Chris and I split a bottle of Crown Royal and even Lesley happened home from her worldwide tour, long enough to

---

[465] *Gerald R. Ford* – was the 38th President of the U.S. & the 40th Vice President. He was the 1st person appointed to the Vice Presidency under the terms of the 25th Amendment, after Nixon resigned on August 9, 1974. (1913-2006)

[466] *OPEC* – is an acronym that stands for the Organization of the Petroleum Exporting Countries. It is a cartel of 12 countries made up of Algeria, Angola, Ecuador, Iran, Iraq, Kuwait, Libya, Nigeria, Qatar, Saudi Arabia, United Arab Emirates & Venezuela. They alarmed the developed world when they used the "oil weapon" during the Yom Kippur War by implementing oil embargoes & initiating the 1973 oil crisis.

[467] *Piper Cherokee* – the PA-28 light aircraft is an unpressurized, all-metal, 4-seat, single-engine land airplane with low-mounted wings & tricycle landing gear. it is designed for flight training, air taxi & personal use, by Piper Aircraft.

[468] *Cessna 150* – is a 2-seat, tricycle gear, general aviation airplane, that was designed for flight training, touring & personal use, by Cessna Aircraft Company.

[469] *Happy Days* – was an American TV sitcom that aired from 1974-1984 on ABC. The comedy presented an idealized vision of life from the mid 1950s to mid 1960s in America.

join us. We danced the night away and looked forward to a bright future.

The airport job ended on June 7, 1974, when I obtained my Private Pilot License. Dad bought another block of flying lessons for me and I sold off the last of my soap inventory. I recycled the proceeds into my training and started working on my Commercial Pilot's License. Once I had the license all I would need to start my company would be a Jet Rating and an Air Taxi Certificate. Working at the airport had given me inside information. So even after I stopped working there I was able to take advantage of co-pilot requirements and kept building up my hours in both the high-performance Arrow and the twin-engine Seneca. Shortly thereafter, the airport purchased a flight simulator. That let me log flight time at a fraction of the cost. I returned to the machine shop where I could make more money and attempted to build up my bank account. Buoyed by dad's financial help and encouragement, I was able to fast track my career in aviation.

With so much going on, it wasn't long before winter was back again. This year Chris threw our New Year's Eve party in his apartment and the celebration drew over forty people. Up against the wall in the kitchen was a plastic trashcan filled with punch. The vile brew consisted of fruit juice, soda and full slices of oranges, along with gallons of grain alcohol. Enshrined above the inebriating caldron was the album jacket of Goats Head Soup.[470] The demonic icon might just as well have been a scull and cross bones, but no one seemed to heed its warning.

The night air was bitter cold and blustery, when I left to pick up Wendy. Arriving back at the party, we filled our glasses with punch and walked into the living room. Wall-to-wall people made dancing difficult and it was so smoky we could

---

[470] *Goats Head Soup* – was the 11th studio album by The Rolling Stones. It was released in 1973 & spawned the hit single "Angie" possibly its best-known track, which topped the charts in both the US & the UK. On the jacket was a ram's head floating in its own blood.

hardly breathe. The two of us were looped from the punch and wanted some privacy, but every bedroom was already occupied. So Tom lent me his station wagon and Chris gave us a couple of sleeping bags. Squeezing past a plethora of people, we made our way outside to face the windswept freezing temperatures in the parking lot.

Flipping down the back seat of the car I made up a bed in the back and we climbed inside to get out of the cold. It had been six months since we dated, but we had consumed a lot of punch that night and I started putting pressure on her to come across. Although I worked hard on the seduction, I also waited for her to give me a green light. When she finally submitted we made love. She was a virgin and began to weep and was unable to stop sobbing. I thought I physically harmed her, but the injury was much deeper than that and she had no words to describe the inner ache.

Once the line was crossed, we made love often and although she seemed happy with our relationship, I was always worried about her getting pregnant. One night after making love on a sandy road in the middle of the pines, I panicked. I told her we had to stop or she was going to get pregnant. She saw no such difficulty, since she had never once missed her period. I rolled my eyes at the idiocy of her statement and started screaming at the top of my lungs, "What? Are you stupid? Don't you know that only means the odds are even worse?" She calmly replied, "We'll just get married." Her naiveté infuriated me and I got back in the car to drive her home. A few weeks later she told me she was joining the Army. I couldn't believe my ears. When I demanded she tell the recruiters she had changed her mind, she told me she had already signed a contract. One week later she left for basic training at Fort Bragg.[471]

---

[471] *Fort Bragg* – is a major U.S. Army installation near the town of Fayetteville, NC. It was named after Confederate General Braxton Bragg. The base covers over 251 square miles in four counties & is home to multiple divisions of the military including U.S. Special Forces.

The positive benefits of things like working hard were immediate and seemed pretty obvious to me, but the consequences of bad behavior were not always readily apparent. Writing checks with my body that I couldn't cash with my life had cost me the love of several women I cared about. Loosing Wendy to the Army was only my most recent loss. My sister told me that Leah Goldman became a drug addict and was now a patient at Norristown State Hospital.[472] Chris Lang totaled his new truck and lost his front tooth in a drunken driving accident. Americas were also having their comeuppance. Watergate ran its legal course prompting Nixon to resign on August 9, 1974. Gerald Ford became president, Tricky Dick was pardoned and any remaining political faith in America was lost. Jimmy Hoffa[473] had advanced the power of the Teamsters using mafia muscle, but without Nixon to protect him, he would mysteriously disappear in the summer of seventy-five.

Although Boobus Americanus[474] hated Nixon, they were also clueless as to what he had actually done wrong. Working at the Lansdale Theater, I saw All The President's Men[475] twenty-two times and I watched almost all of the Watergate hearings on television. When it was time for me to

---

[472] *Norristown State Hospital* – originally known as the State Lunatic Hospital at Norristown, is a psychiatric hospital located outside the city of Philadelphia. Leah Goldman became a patient there after experiencing a bad trip on LSD.

[473] *Jimmy Hoffa* – was the President of the Teamsters union from 1958–1971. He built up the trucker's union, into a powerful force & was beloved by his members. Unfortunately, he was also convicted of jury tampering & bribery, thanks to his alleged association with the Mafia. Richard Nixon, pardoned him in 1971 in exchange for his resigning as union president, but he mysteriously disappeared on July 30, 1975 & is presumed dead. Although his death remains a mystery, in the book The Weasel: A Double Life in the Mob, by Adrian Humphreys, his driver Marvin Elkind, claims that Hoffa was killed by a mob enforcer & buried in the foundation of the General Motors Headquarters building in Detroit, MI.

[474] *Boobus Americanus* – is a label created by Irv Homer, a longtime radio talk-show host from Philadelphia. Evil Irv used the term to describe Americans who have no knowledge of history & precious little understanding of how our own government is supposed to work, yet they frequently regurgitate media talking points & believe every bit of propaganda they hear. Today, Rush Limbaugh calls these same characters low information voters.

[475] *All the President's Men* – is a 1974 book by Carl Bernstein & Bob Woodward, which was subsequently made into a movie. The two journalists chronicled the Watergate break-in & the ensuing Watergate scandal for The Washington Post, which led to the resignations of President Richard M. Nixon, H. R. Haldeman & John Ehrlichman.

go to Vietnam, Nixon had canceled the draft, so it irritated me that the misled masses hated this man without knowing why. Making sport of these bubbleheads, I frequently exposed their ignorance in front of their friends. Although rarely winning any converts, I walked away from each argument satisfied that these idiots had been put in their place.

I finally passed the written portion of my Commercial Pilot License on February 26, 1976. Now all that remained was for me to secure an instrument rating and pass a practical exam. The new license would allow me to fly paying customers and begin to accept payment for my piloting services. Although Tri-Star Aviation was on track to become a reality a lingering teenage promise stood in the way.

In 1976 the Fourth of July marked the Bicentennial birthday of America. Back in high school five of us chose Independence Day as the departure date for our much discussed dream trip to California. In preparation, I quit my job, sold all of my precision machine tools and closed out my bank account. I used the proceeds to purchase an LTD wagon[476] and a brand new Coleman[477] popup tent trailer. The other guys in our party were supposed to chip in for gas and food, but when the date arrived every single one of them crapped out on me. I felt like I had been punched in the stomach and had no clue what I should do about it.

Elvis Presley had just finished touring the country and his last concert was scheduled for July 5th in his hometown of Memphis, Tennessee. The king of Rock n Roll was dog tired,

---

[476] *LTD* – the Ford LTD Country Squire is a full-size station wagon that was built by the Ford Motor Company from 1950-1991. Initially built as a "woodie" this family car featured an all-steel body & a tailgate with simulated wood trim.

[477] *Coleman* – the Coleman Company specializes in outdoor recreation products. Coleman is known for camping gear & was founded by William Coffin Coleman, who began selling kerosene lanterns in 1900 in Kingfisher, Oklahoma. He moved to Wichita, Kansas, in 1902. Their most famous products are the Coleman Lanterns, which originally burned kerosene or gasoline & used one or two mantles to produce an intense white light.

but as usual he gave his fans a great performance that included: Its Now or Never.[478] Listening to that song on the radio helped me to make a pivotal decision. I would go to California by myself. Jessie Allen and Sam Dillinger claimed they still wanted to go on the trip and asked me to delay my departure for a couple of weeks, but I was done with the talker brothers and refused. Insisting they could travel much faster on their motorcycles than I could with my trailer in tow, they asked if I would meet up with them on August 15th at Fishing Bridge campsite in Yellowstone.[479] I agreed to the rendezvous point, but also made it clear I would not hang around in camp waiting for them.

On July 10th dad gave me a gas credit card, which expired at the end of August. Loading up the station wagon, I set out for the Poconos and spent my first night at the Arrowhead Lake cabin. In the morning I picked up I-80 and headed west for The Golden State. After I left the green hills of Pennsylvania, the land flattened out across Ohio and then reverted back to green hills again in Indiana and Illinois. Driving through the Buckeye state I passed by endless cornfields for over eight hours. Farming obviously provided enormous wealth for the great state of Iowa.

Each night I would pull off on a lonely road to park. After entering the back of the station wagon, I opened the sleeping bag and crawled inside. Every few days I would stop off at a KOA[480] or some little out of the way private campground. As soon as I located the site I set up the trailer, went swimming

---

[478] *It's Now or Never* – is a popular song performed by Elvis Presley in 1960 & recorded on RCA Records. The melody is borrowed from the Italian standard, "'O Sole Mio", but the inspiration came from "There's No Tomorrow", recorded in 1949, by Tony Martin.

[479] *Yellowstone National Park* – is our 1st national park & was established by Congress in 1872. It is primarily located in Wyoming, but also extends into Montana & Idaho. Yellowstone is known for its wildlife & its many geothermal features, especially Old Faithful Geyser. The Lewis & Clark Expedition bypassed the region during the early 1800s & other than mountain men, organized exploration did not begin until the late 1860s.

[480] *KOA* – or Kampgrounds of America is a franchise chain of nearly 470 campgrounds throughout North America based in Billings, Montana, USA.

and got a nice hot shower. It took time to open up the trailer, so most of my nights were spent in the back of the station wagon. With no traveling companions to make use of the camper and needing to pay higher tolls for the trailer, I questioned the wisdom of bringing it along.

The rolling hills began to level out again and the landscape morphed from the lush greens in the rearview mirror to the dusty earth tones of the prairie ahead. Wheat fields seemed to extend all the way to the horizon and every minute rise in elevation revealed yet another panorama of magnificent beauty. The two-lane interstate bared little resemblance to the limited access highways back east. Half-height telephone poles lined the left hand side of the road casting their shadows across the gray sun parched pavement and something resembling bouncing ping-pong balls were actually herds of pronghorn[481] prancing in unison across the distant horizon to the north. Although an old black and white sign was rusty and riddled with bullet holes, it still let me know that I was approaching the remote town of Rawlings, Wyoming. The name of the frontier town reminded me of Linus Rawlings and I wondered if it was named after the great mythical mountain man, played by Jimmy Stewart in the epic movie How The West Was Won.[482]

One afternoon, while searching for a place to camp, I noticed a gravel driveway that led to what looked like an old deserted airport with a few dilapidated hangers. Turns out it was a fully functioning county airfield. The FBO[483] was an

---

[481] *Pronghorn* – is a species of mammal native to western & central North America. It is often colloquially known as Prong Buck, Pronghorn Antelope or simply Antelope, since it closely resembles the true antelopes of the Old World (Antilocapra Americana).

[482] *How the West Was Won* – is a 1962 epic Western film, based on the novel by Louis L'Amour, which follows four generations of the Prescott family, as they move westward, from New York state to the Pacific Ocean.

[483] *Fixed Base Operator* – is a provider of services to general aviation & FBOs are located at or adjacent to an airport. Barnstorming began after WWI, but the Air Commerce Act of 1926 instituted the licensing of pilots & regulation of aircraft maintenance & training. This prompted pilots & mechanics, who made their living on the road to begin establishing Fixed-Base Operations, at airports throughout the U.S. Today there are 3,138 in the U.S.

elderly gentleman who lived with his wife in a small bungalow behind the office. After showing him my license and log book, I inquired about renting their lone Cessna 150 for one hour, but he said that his insurance terms required that he go along so that I would not get lost. I was so close to getting my commercial license his judgment felt like an insult, but I still wanted to fly so I agreed to the condition. Once I saw how difficult navigation was on a landscape that had so few landmarks, I was happy to have the former WWII bomber pilot along. The wise old man was absolutely right; I would have gotten lost.

The prairie is a windy place and the kindly couple let me set up my trailer in one of the empty hangers and graciously invited me to join them for breakfast. At sunrise we ate eggs from their chicken coop and enjoyed crisp bacon, which they had purchased from a local pig farmer. Our conversation eventually turned political and I was astonished to learn that although they were well aware of the corruption in our government, they had absolutely no fear of socialism, communism or the inevitable slavery that follows. The totality of their faith was in Jesus Christ. The form of government that we lived under was a matter of complete indifference to them. The octogenarian couple had absolute trust that the Holy Spirit walked with them here on earth and that they could look forward to an eternity with the Father in Heaven. Their perceptions seemed awfully naïve, but I thanked them for their generosity and was soon on my way.

The Rocky Mountains looked like a purple haze on the horizon. Although barely able to distinguish peak from prairie, the monotonous hours of driving magically transformed the magnificent mirage into a well defined panorama of pine forests, granite cliffs and snowcapped peaks. At the base of the glorious Grand Teton Mountain[484] I

---

[484] *Grand Teton* – is French for "big tit" & at 13,775 feet it represents the high point of the Teton Range, as well as the fantasy of some lonely French trapper. The Wyoming Mountain is part of the Snake River drainage basin & is fed by several local creeks & glaciers.

turned north and headed for Fishing Bridge campsite in Yellowstone National Park[485] to meet up with Jessie and Sam. As luck would have it the camp was closed for the season due to bear activity. Prior to the invention of the cell phone, it was impossible to contact men on motorcycles. If it was Chris Lang or Tom Reeves, maybe I could have contacted a park ranger; but there was no way I was going to bat for the Talker Brothers.

On my way to Glacier National Park,[486] a bunch of teenagers passed me in an old rusty car. They were either drunk or high and they started throwing canned goods out the window. The cans were hitting the pavement and bouncing up in front of me. I swerved to avoid hitting the first can, then dropped back to avoid the second, but when I slowed down they threw out even more cans. Fearing for my life, I thought of pulling out the .30-30 Winchester, but it was all the way in the back and I had deliberately placed the shells in a footlocker. Since it would take too long to get at them, I would have to find another way to defend myself. The LTD wagon had a strong passing gear that kicked in at forty miles-per-hour. So I slowed down to forty and hit the gas. Flying past them on the interstate, I forced them off an exit ramp. Figuring they would follow I tried attracting the attention of a state trooper. Raising my speed to one-hundred and five, I maintained the illegal speed for almost to an hour, before realizing I was completely on my own in the Wild West.

I finally made it to the park where a ranger at the entrance handed me a bunch of brochures. They included beautiful

---

[485] *Yellowstone National Park* – was the world's first national park, set aside in 1872 to preserve a vast number of geysers, hot springs & other thermal areas & to protect the incredible wildlife & rugged beauty of the area. Most of the 3,472 square miles of the park are located in the northwest corner of Wyoming, but it also extends into Idaho & Montana.

[486] *Glacier National Park* - is located in Montana, bordering the Canadian provinces of Alberta & British Columbia. The pristine park encompasses over 1,000,000 acres 2 mountain ranges, 130 lakes & hundreds of species of animals. It was first inhabited by the Blackfeet & Flathead Indians & became a national park in 1910, but in 1976 both Yellowstone & Glacier were designated as part of the United Nations Biosphere Reserve.

pictures of the mountains, directions to campgrounds and lots of warnings about not feeding the bears. I wound my way up a long serpentine road that wove its way through tall pines, over pristine streams and alongside thundering white water falls. In late afternoon I pulled off to one side for a quick meal. Opening up the tailgate, I flipped up the lid on the cooler and pulled out a can of soda. Since I was quickly burning daylight, I dipped the cold hotdogs into a jar of mustard and skipped the rolls altogether. Resting on the tongue of the trailer I felt a cool breeze, as I watched the setting sun disappear behind the mountain. Throwing on a jacket, I looked up a steep forested mountain and pulled another link out of the plastic packaging. Suddenly, I heard a crack! It sounded like a deer coming down the side of the mountain, so I listened intently and quietly took another sip of my soda. I thought I heard hooves clicking against rocks and then hitting the soft pine-needled carpet with a thud. It sounded like several does were making a diagonal descent off to my right, but it was getting pretty dark.

Suddenly there was a really loud thud! I knew bucks usually followed the does, so I stopped chewing my hotdog and listen even more carefully. I wondered whether it was an Elk or the granddaddy of all Stags. Whatever it was, it was getting closer by the second and picking up speed. Finishing my Coke, I squinted and strained my eyes for a glimpse of the trophy buck. The sounds of his hooves were getting louder and more pronounced, but I still couldn't see the deer in the dimly lit forest. Quietly dipping my hotdog into the mustard jar again, a horrible thought occurred to me. What if it's a bear! Throwing the food back in the cooler, I closed the lid, jumped into the driver's seat and sped away. I never did see what it was, but I wasn't going to stick around and find out.

The next morning I found myself in a campground at the bottom of a steep granite mountain in the greenest pine forest I have ever seen. A pristine stream thundered over a waterfall and rushed along side a small creek by my camper. The water was so cold that there was a lip of ice along its bank. I lingered there for a day to rest, enjoying the fresh scent of pine and the familiar smoke of the campfires. Refreshed and ready to travel again, I pushed my way across dozens of steep mountain ranges. There were so many tall pine trees I started wondering where the Idaho potatoes were grown. My question was soon answered when I stopped at a trading post and one of the locals informed me that the spud farms were farther south and that the main crop of Idaho was actually lumber.

After hugging the northern border of Oregon, I attempted to drive up Mount Hood.[487] About halfway up the mountain my car began loosing power and I had to pull over to the shoulder. Having no idea what I was looking for, I popped the hood and removed the air filter to study the top of my four-barreled carburetor. Stuck on that lonely road in the middle of nowhere things went from bad to worse when it began to snow. Oh how I wish I had paid more attention to my friends while they were fixing their cars. Feeling utterly helpless, I looked up at a light gray sky and asked God for help. When I dropped my gaze, I noticed that there on the side of the carburetor was a large black plastic knob. Leaning in to see what it was I saw some writing on its circumference. Two opposing arrows were labeled "Lean & Rich". When I flew planes I always used a mixture control. Let's see now; the air is thin at this altitude, so I have lean out the mixture. I turned the knob all the way to the lean side and the car started right up. Either God answers prayers awfully quickly or I know a lot more about cars than I thought I did. The light snow turned into a blizzard and navigating down the other side of the mountain was like

---

[487] *Mount Hood* – originally called Wy'east by the Multnomah Indian tribe Mount Hood is an 11,249-foot high stratovolcano in the Cascade Volcanic Arc of northern Oregon. It is located about 50 miles east-southeast of Portland, Oregon.

trying to negotiate Donner Pass.[488] Once I made it down the side of the mountain, the temperature rebounded and I drove through Portland in the pouring rain. It was a long day, but I didn't want to stop in a city. So I pushed on through the night amidst the deluge and then looked for a secluded place to park my rig. Taking a small detour on one of the side roads, I discovered an old abandoned factory with a large parking lot in the rear. Exhausted and finally hidden from the road, I crawled into the back, slid into my sleeping bag and fell fast asleep.

About ten o'clock the next morning I woke to the sound of hundreds of singing birds, a glorious blue sky and not a cloud in sight. Driving to a restaurant just outside Fort Vancouver[489] I sat down to a hearty breakfast of bacon, eggs and home fries. Well rested, well fed and close enough to my destination to taste victory, I spent the rest of the day pushing on toward California. When I was able to smell the salt air, I took some scenic back roads and made the final push west to Eureka.[490] Stopping just north of the town, I looked out over the vast Pacific Ocean. To the north waves were crashing against large jagged boulders out in the water and the breakers repeated their sensational explosions of white foam against the rugged black cliffs. Looking southward I saw dark pumiced beaches littered with white-gray driftwood. I had traveled over three thousand miles to see the deep blue of the Pacific and inhaled the salty air. Like

---

[488] *Donner Pass* – is a high mountain pass in the northern Sierra Nevada, located above Donner Lake about 9 miles west of Truckee, California. It is a narrow pass with a very steep approach from the east & has a gradual approach from the west. In early November 1846, the Donner Party found the route blocked by snow & was forced to spend the winter on the eastern side of the mountains. Of the 81 emigrants, only 45 survived to reach California & some of them are alleged to have resorted to cannibalism to survive.

[489] *Fort Vancouver* – was a massive British outpost on the north bank of the Columbia River & the final stop on the Oregon Trail. Many of the emigrant pioneers who had made it that far, were very low on supplies & completely exhausted.

[490] *Eureka* – is a shore town, adjacent to Humboldt Bay in northern California. It is home to the world's tallest trees – the Coast Redwoods. The Pacific Northwest timber industry & fisheries have steadily declined since the 1950s. Overcutting & overfishing, increased regulation & the creation of parkland to preserve virgin forests, rivers & fisheries led to diminished profits & massive layoffs of blue collared mill workers & fisherman of the town in the 1970s. The term Eureka means, "I found it!"

a gold miner hitting pay dirt, I stood on the top of my trailer, looked out over that great big ocean and shouted, "Eureka!"

After watching my first sunset, I followed the coastal highway south until I noticed a quarter-mile wide beach dotted with dozens of bon fires. The flickering yellow flames revealed an even larger number of cars, tents, trailers and vans. I stopped at a roadside parking lot to investigate and followed the gravel pathway that led to the beach. The shadow cast by the light of the campfires alerted the campers to my presence and I was cheerfully invited to join them. The friendly strangers offered me food and my choice of beer, wine or grass. No one seemed worried about getting busted nor were they all that wasted. Some teenagers sat on a long gray log, which had washed up on the beach and several adults clad in Hawaiian shirts were relaxing on beach chairs. A pretty woman in a sundress quickly brought me a chair and her husband invited me to set up my trailer next to theirs. After accepting the invitation we sat by the fire talking, laughing and getting to know one another until about two in the morning. I had never seen a more welcoming and peaceful group of total strangers. To them everyone was acceptable and they seemed genuinely interested in getting to know me. Although I only consumed a few beers, the sounds of the surf and the camaraderie mellowed me out. I drifted off into a very restful sleep and woke to the din of squabbling sea gulls and the heat of a noonday sun. The trailers and the people were gone, the fog had long since lifted and the bright sunlight danced on the water like so many mirrors on a backdrop of the deep dark blue waters of the Pacific.

Following the costal highway south, I crossed the Golden Gate Bridge[491] and arrived in San Francisco. While fighting

---

[491] *The Golden Gate Bridge* – in 1937 it was the longest suspension bridge span in the world. The Golden Gate is located where the San Francisco Bay meets the Pacific Ocean & is one of the most recognized symbols of the United States. During construction a safety net

some horrendous traffic, I noticed my gas gage was on empty. A big sign read, "Last filling station before bridge". I planned on topping off my tank there, but had to wait for a light. A guy on the corner waved at me, so I politely nodded in return. However after glancing up at the red light, I noticed he was still looking my way. At first I didn't get it, but the pervert started walking toward the car and I realized the queer was hitting on me. Yuck! I had to get out of town and quick. The line of traffic made me nervous, but when the light turned green I bypassed the pit stop and took a chance. Luckily I made it across the Bay Bridge and filled up at a Gulf station. Anxious to leave the city, I followed a maze of Interstate highways out of the bay area and passed right through the concrete jungle they call Los Angeles.

Interstate-5 took me past the Marine Base at Camp Pendleton[492] where the Pacific coastal views were much more scenic than those in the city. Stopping for meals provided opportunities for me to get to know the natives, but the further south I traveled, the less I enjoyed their company. Everyone spoke Spanish and I had no idea what strange foods were on their menus. The diners looked progressively dirty and by the time I reached San Diego, I was afraid to touch anything, let alone eat it. Patrons started starring at me and I became concerned about their intentions. Figuring I had seen enough of Southern California I turned east to cross back over the mountains. I considered visiting Lesley Wright, who was now living in Tucson, Arizona, but I had no phone number and no address to go on. So when I reached Yuma, I turned north to check out the Grand Canyon[493] and the Hoover Dam.[494]

---

saved all but 11 lives & the men who fell on the net & lived are proud members of the *Halfway to Hell Club.*

[492] *Camp Pendleton* – is the major West Coast base of the U.S. Marine Corps & serves as its prime amphibious training base. Located in San Diego County, it was established in 1942 to train Marines for service in World War II. In 1944 Pendleton was declared a "permanent installation" & became the 1st Marine Division in 1946. It is named after Marine General Joseph Henry Pendleton, who advocated setting up a West Coast training base for Marines.

[493] *Grand Canyon* – is a gorge of the Colorado River, which is often considered one of the Seven Natural Wonders of the World. Grand Canyon National Park covers 1,217,262 acres

While camping alongside of Lake Mead[495] I met some other campers who had a jet boat. I offered them a few dollars to use for gas, if they would be willing to take me out water-skiing with them. We all had a lot of fun, but there was a stiff breeze that day and it made the surface of the water choppy. Coupled with the speed of the jet boat, these microwaves beat the hell out of my feet. Although I thanked them for their hospitality, I also concluded it was much more fun to watch them ski, than it was to do the actual skiing. Since I was only a half-hour outside of Las Vegas, I decided to try my luck at gambling, but I was worried about losing all of my money. So I filled the car with gas, left my wallet in the trailer and took a paltry forty dollars into town with me. That left me just enough money for dinner, parking and gaming at the Golden Nugget.[496]

I had never been to a casino before, so after enjoying a delicious complimentary steak dinner, I started out playing the slot machines. I spent twenty dollars worth of quarters on the one-armed-bandits and won three times that much money. However later on that evening I felt like a real looser when I learned that winning machines pay off twenty dollars in quarters, but you can also get another hundred and eighty from the attendant when you show her the blinking light. What an idiot! I had thrown away five-hundred and forty dollars in winnings. I tried a couple of other games like Black Jack and Roulette, but nothing was nearly as exciting as the Crap Tables. Cashing in a twenty dollar bill for some

---

of land in Coconino & Mohave counties. America's 15th oldest national park is located in Arizona & became a UNESCO World Heritage Site in 1979.

[494] *Hoover Dam* – is a concrete arch-gravity dam in the Black Canyon of the Colorado River. It is located 30 miles southeast of Las Vegas on the border between Arizona & Nevada. At the time of its completion in 1936 it was the largest hydroelectric power generating station & concrete structure in the world. Originally called Bolder Dam, it was subsequently renamed to honor President Herbert Hoover.

[495] *Lake Mead* – is the largest reservoir in the US. It is located on the Colorado River & formed by the Hoover Dam. The lake was named after Elwood Mead, who was the commissioner of the U.S. Bureau of Reclamation from 1924 to 1936, during the planning & construction of the Boulder Canyon Project, which created the dam & the lake behind it.

[496] *The Golden Nugget* – was a casino built in 1946, making it one of the oldest gambling establishments in Las Vegas, Nevada.

chips, I placed my first bet. Twenty dollars became forty, which grew to eighty, which multiplied again and became a hundred and sixty. The next thing I knew, I was rolling the die for three-hundred and twenty dollars. This was more exciting than sex! That is it was until I rolled snake eyes. The pounding in my chest gradually subsided, as I walked away from the table in utter disbelief. Although the gambling rush was replaced with emptiness in the pit of my stomach, I decided to try again the following night with an additional forty dollars.

The evening of ecstasy I experienced on the first night, expired in less than an hour on the second. Shocked and disillusioned at my lack of luck, I slowly walked away from the crap tables. The din of the crowd grew distant and dull, like the air being let out of a big balloon. Leaving the casino I took notice that the darkness had quickly eclipsed the bright sunlight and warmth of the daytime. Since I had no jacket to block a constant assault from the cool desert breeze I was left freezing cold. Worried about hypothermia I sprinted all three blocks to the parking garage, which left me physically exhausted in addition to being emotionally depressed. Shivering and waiting for the heater to kick in, I drove down the lonely two-lane highway disconnected from time and place. The disorienting stupor persisted until I rolled over some gravel, which let me know I was back in the campground. Climbing up into the trailer, I slipped into my down filled sleeping bag and fell fast asleep.

In the morning I traveled north toward Salt Lake City, Utah. Unlike most modern cities I found the place to be unusually clean and spacious. A strange monument to a seagull[497] caught my eye and I marveled at the grandeur of the Salt

---

[497] *Seagull Monument* – is a small bronze statue located on a pillar in front of the Salt Lake Assembly Hall. In 1848 Mormon pioneers planted crops for their first spring season in Utah. As the crops ripened, crickets descended on the farms & consumed entire fields. The harvest was saved by flocks of native seagulls, which devoured the ravenous insects. This event is remembered by Latter-day Saints as the Miracle of the Gulls.

Lake Temple,[498] which was prominently located downtown. Even the Great Salt Lake[499] was enormous and the white beaches at the water's edge betrayed an even larger lake in times past. Reversing course I traveled south across the high deserts of New Mexico. The beautiful day with its clear blue sky and almost Martian like landscape was the perfect backdrop for a plethora of pretty wild flowers, but the drive through Northern Texas would be endless and barren.

The state was huge and its landscape desolate. It took me forever to cross the Lone Star State[500] and with nothing to see but mesquite trees, tumble weeds and a dusty desert; I drove for hours at a time in a torpid trance. Although dead tired by the time I reached Louisiana, Interstate Ten was raised up on concrete stilts high above the bijou, it was pitch black and there was no place to pull over. So I pressed on throughout the night.

I had driven for over thirty hours straight and by the time I reached Baton Rouge I was road weary and running out of money. A defect in the radial tires[501] started cutting down on my gas mileage and it was wearing out the tread. Buying new tires would consume the last of my gas and food money. Scared, alone and exhausted; I decided to seek some help from Lisa Moore, who was my former nanny. She now lived in Tennessee, so I canceled my plans to visit New Orleans and drove northeast through Mississippi, Alabama and Georgia. When I arrived in Knoxville I turned into her

---

[498] *Salt Lake Temple* – is the largest temple of The Church of Jesus Christ of Latter-day Saints. It is the centerpiece of a 10 acre Temple Square in Salt Lake City, Utah & is the 4th temple built since Brigham Young, the city' founder, 1st Governor & the 2nd President of the cult, led the Mormon exodus from Nauvoo, Illinois to the promised land.
[499] *Great Salt Lake* – is located in the northern part of the state of Utah & is the largest salt lake in the western hemisphere.
[500] *The Lone Star State* – is a nickname that refers to the state of Texas. It originates from the star on the 1836 flag of the Republic of Texas.
[501] *Firestone 500* – during the 1970s, Firestone experienced problems with their steel-belted radials when tread began separating at high speeds. While the cause was never proved, it is believed that the failure of cements used to hold the tread to the tire, allowed water to penetrate the tire, which in turn may have caused the internal steel wire to corrode.

driveway and had a grand total of eight dollars left in my pocket.

Lisa was delighted to see me and wanted to know all about my trip and our family. When her two kids came home from school she introduced me to a terminally shy boy named Toby and a precocious little sweetheart named Shirley. The adorable children were fascinated to meet someone from their mother's past and begged me to tell them story after story about mommy. When her husband Simon Moore came home from work, he offered me a beer and we went outside for a smoke. I explained my financial situation to him and apprehensively asked, if he would mind my staying with his family for a while, until I got some work and made enough money to replace my tires and finish making the trip back home. To my relief he was more than open to the idea and let me know where the employment office was in town. The next day I secured a one-day job cleaning up some mud that had seeped into the back of a flooded out department store. The nasty smelling job lasted for a week and only paid minimum wage to each member of the crew, but it was a beginning. The following week I went back for some more work, but none was available.

Lisa Moore was a part-time bookkeeper for a beauty supply wholesaler. She thought her boss might have some work for me and was able to get me a job moving pallets around in the warehouse. Business was booming and the boss wanted to open a new warehouse on the other side of town. He wanted to build some offices in the front of the building and finding me a good hard worker asked if I knew anything about carpentry. Since I let him know I was a very good helper, but not really a master carpenter, he gave the lead for the project to another man. The tall, lanky, chain-smoking employee told the boss he knew everything about carpentry and he was put in charge of the project and became my supervisor. We both set about laying out the studding for the walls, drilling holes to run wire and hung the drywall. Every few days the big boss stopped by the empty warehouse to check up on our progress. He complemented us on our craftsmanship and never had a single complaint. Although initially unaware of my competition, I knew much more about construction than my supervisor. The shrewd southern scammer had a way of taking credit for everything and was therefore able to command twice my hourly rate. In hindsight I should have been more self assured about my own abilities.

One rainy Friday the redneck brought in a case of Pabst Blue Ribbon[502] beer and offered me a sixteen ounce can. I had no aversion to drinking, but thought we should wait until the end of the day. He convinced me that the chances of the boss stopping by on a rainy day were miniscule and so I accepted his gift. In a couple of hours the two of us were both buzzed. The more we drank the faster we downed the bubbly brew and before long crumpled cans were strewn all over the recently tiled floor. Murphy's Law[503] was obviously operative when the boss walked in, saw the mess and fired both of us on the spot. I returned home with my tail between my legs and told Lisa what had happened. Not only was she disappointed in me, but was embarrassed that she had recommended me. Simon on the other hand, thought the whole thing was hysterically funny. I didn't have much money, but had saved enough cash to buy new tires and had just enough cash left over to buy the gas I needed for the trip back home and precious little to spare. Ready or not; it was time to go.

Sadie Callahan was the eldest of my cousins and she had moved away from home as soon as she reached the age of eighteen. I had not seen Sadie for a number of years, but had

---

[502] *Pabst Blue Ribbon* – is a brand of beer sold by Pabst Brewing Company, which was established in Milwaukee, WI. PBR was originally called Best Select & Pabst Select, but the current name came from blue ribbons tied around the neck of the bottle, a practice that ran from 1882-1916. The Pabst Brewing Company is now based in Woodridge, IL.
[503] *Murphy's Law* – is a popular adage that states that "things will go wrong in any given situation, if you give them a chance," or more commonly, "Whatever can go wrong, will go wrong and usually at the most inopportune moment." There are several variants on the rule.

heard she was now living in Wichita. So there was one more stop I wanted to make on my way back. I called home for her address and made my way west through Tennessee, Arkansas and Oklahoma until I reached her home in Kansas. We enjoyed a pleasant dinner in her home and discussed all that had transpired since we last saw each other in Harvey Cedars and then reminisced for the rest of the evening. Around midnight I took up residence on her couch and the next day we went to a Blue Grass Festival.[504] Although I never heard Blue Grass music before, I enjoyed it and wound up buying a Jew's harp[505] from one of the vendors. The old man with a beard and overalls who sold it to me also taught me how to play it without breaking my teeth. The folks at the festival were as laid back as the people in northern California, but the culture was much more wholesome and their topics of conversation revealed a simpler way of life and a much slower pace. Sadie had to go to work the next day and I needed to get to Pennsylvania. So we gave each other a great big hug and I was back on the road again.

There were no more stops to make and very little money left for gas or food, let alone lodging. So I catnapped on country roads in the back of the station wagon whenever I grew tired and continued on as soon as I awoke. The so-called adventure of a lifetime with my friends, which had been planned since my junior year in high school, turned out to be a solo sojourn that depleted my savings and interrupted a promising career in aviation. I made good time on that last leg, but arrived home flat broke.

---

[504] *Bluegrass* – is a style of music that was developed during the mid-1940s. The style is an amalgam of old-time music, country, ragtime & jazz. Its beginnings can be traced to Bill Monroe the "founding father" of bluegrass music; the style was named for his band, the Blue Grass Boys, which was formed in 1939.

[505] *Jew's Harp* – or jaw harp is a lamellophone, which is in the category of plucked idiophones: It consists of a flexible metal tongue attached to a solid frame. The tongue is placed in the musician's mouth & plucked with a finger to produce notes. Changing the shape of the mouth adjusts the pitch & the amount of exhaled air controls the volume.

While I was touring the country, my sister secured a position as a secretary with IMS Health.[506] Sarah developed a friendship with the man who serviced their computers. Clark Woods lived at the Hatfield Village Apartments and had recently been looking for a new roommate. Sarah recommended me to Clark and we worked out a living arrangement. I went back to Callahan Machine Company, but because I had sold all my tools to go to California, I was not able to work as a machine operator. So Jim Cleaver gave me a job running the forklift. The position paid almost as well and gave me the money to begin flying again. Soon I was back on track. Once again I could pursue the dream of one day becoming a commercial pilot and owning my own executive air charter service. Every weekend I built up my hours and was progressing in both skill and knowledge. I was getting back into the swing of things until dad asked me to go out West again.

---

[506] *IMS Health* – is an international company that supplies the pharmaceutical industry with sales data & consulting services. Bill Froch & David Dubow founded it in 1954 & today IMS is in more than 100 countries, has 7,600 employees & boasts revenues of $2 billion.

Chapter 23

Wilderness Survival

Dad initiated this marvelous adventure by handing me a brochure for a survival training course with Outward Bound™.[507] The wilderness survival school had been developed as a response to the experiences of British rescue workers during World War II. Bomber squadrons returning from missions in Germany were being shot down over the English Channel. Although boats and seaplanes were often launched quickly, the survivors were giving up hope within hours of being rescued. The philosophy of the program is contained in its motto: "To Serve, To Strive and Not to Yield." After purchasing some winter clothing and spending a few weeks in physical preparation, I boarded a plane for Pendleton, Oregon. A van picked me up at the airport and my Ski Mountaineering Survival Course began the day after most people were celebrating New Years Eve. The next three weeks were spent learning how to survive in the snow-covered forests of the Wallowa Mountains.[508]

Splitting us up into three coed patrols, our class of ten spent the next few days in base camp. We learned about: first aid, cross-country skiing and how to climb shear faced cliffs. We were issued: skis, backpacks, food and camping equipment and taught the proper uses of each. Before leaving the base camp we spent a restful day learning map and compass orientation. Then we packed for a six day, six-thousand foot

---

[507] *Outward Bound*™ – is an international, non-profit, independent, outdoor education organization with 40 schools around the world & 200,000 participants annually. The OB programs foster personal growth & social skills through challenging expeditions outdoors.
[508] *Wallowa Mountains* – are a mountain range located on the Columbia Plateau in northeastern Oregon. The range runs approximately 40 miles between the Blue Mountains & the Snake River. The area is called the "Alps of Oregon".

vertical climb to the precipice of Sacajawea Peak.[509] All the skiing was uphill and we learned how to use different color-coded waxes that corresponded to the changing temperatures of our environment. Near the end of each day we set up our camp, built a fire, made dinner and sat around listening to our counselors tell serendipitous stories that taught us valuable lessons about the dangers of survival and the solutions used to overcome those obstacles. Each story reinforced and explained one of their directives. One such instruction we were given was to keep our tent flaps open at night, because an individual breathes out about a quart of water every eight hours. If a tent flap remains closed water droplets begin to condense on the walls and ceiling. As the water accumulates and the temperature drops, it begins to snow *inside* the tent. Amusing tales of wet sleeping bags and frozen campers broke the ice and warmed our souls, as we sat around the campfire. These stories let us know that our instructors were competent and that the discipline and guidance they gave us came from personal experience.

Stopping just short of the summit we were taught how to build an igloo. Worn out, sore and cold after five days of skiing uphill, we readily removed our sweat soaked boots and donned a pair of soft, dry, quilted bootees. Then we sat around the campfire and drank hot Jell-O to stay warm. The following morning, we left the skis in camp and ascended the pinnacle on foot. Upon reaching the summit we returned to the igloo and then skied, or should I say fell, back down the mountain to the base camp. After a weeklong expedition without showers we were all rather ripe. Although our survival settlement had outhouses, a barn and some cabins with stone fireplaces, there was no indoor plumbing in the winter.

---

[509] *Sacajawea Peak* – is the highest point in the Wallowa Mountains. It is located in the Eagle Cap Wilderness area of the Wallowa–Whitman National Forest & at 9,838 feet it is the 6th highest peak in Oregon.

The creek was frozen over with ice four inches thick, so our instructor used a sledgehammer to bust a hole through it. Our patrol was shown how to construct a sauna, because in the absence of a hot shower it is the next best way to get clean. The sauna was made from plywood that was covered in plastic and insulated with dozens of old sleeping bags. The interior was heated with an old wood stove and got so hot that breathing the air made my lungs ache. When our bodies became superheated, we ran down a snowy hill to the creek and took the Polar Bear Plunge.[510] After a speedy rinse we ran back up the hill to get dressed in the barn. Although it wasn't nearly as cold as it sounds there was something weird about the experience. The entire patrol entered the sauna together naked.

There were two females in our group and the sauna was so small that it forced me to sit next to one naked woman and across from the other. I found myself directly in front of a voluptuous brunet that was so close our toes almost touched. I struggled to avert my eyes so that I wouldn't get a hard on and pretended, along with everyone else, that nothing was out of the ordinary. In order to keep from passing out from the heat we took sips of water from a canteen and wiped down our grimy bodies with a wet rag and a bucket. When I could no longer stand the heat I ducked out of the hut and ran down the snowy trail to the creek. Jumping through a hole in the ice I started vigorously rinsing. Within seconds I was back out and high-tailing it up to the barn, where I put on clean warm clothing. That night we slept like little babies in warm cabins with crackling fires.

While Sunday was a day of rest, Monday began a three-day solo. Abandoned in the wilderness, with minimal food and gear, I was expected to survive using the skills I had just recently acquired. My backpack contained: warm clothing,

---

[510] *Polar Bear Plunge* – is an annual event where participants dive into frigid waters to raise funds for charity. The largest U.S. one is the Plungapalooza & it raises funds for the Special Olympics. It is sponsored by the Maryland State Police at Sandy Point State Park, MD.

half of a canvas pup tent, one bag of GORP,[511] a dozen kitchen matches, one packet of lemon-aid mix, a canteen and a single can of sardines. Finally we were given a pencil and a small journal. Dropped off at one-mile intervals, we were each ordered to stay within clearly defined boundaries on a map. In the event of an emergency, I was instructed to leave a note in a small stuff sack hanging from a tree by the trail and to stay put. Then the trainer and the rest of the patrol disappeared down the trail. I was all alone in the wilderness!

As my compatriots disappeared over the snowy ridge, I felt the full weight of responsibility coming down on my shoulders. Almost immediately the immortal words of John Wayne echoed in the caverns of my mind, "Mount up. We're burnin daylight." There was almost three feet of snow on the ground, the temperature hovered at forty degrees and it was raining. I trekked into the forest to look for a campsite and found an open area surrounded by dozens of towering Ponderosa Pines. Near the edge of the clearing was a three-foot diameter tree that had fallen over on its side. I constructed my shelter by using the trunk of this big tree as the back wall of my little hermitage. Using the upended roots as a starting point, I rolled two-foot diameter snowballs and piled them up in a row to use as the front and side walls. The canvas pup tent served as a roof and I pinned it in place with mortar made from the wet snow. Then I removed the snow from the floor of the interior and exposed a perfectly dry mattress of spongy brown pine needles. Having finished the waterproof and windproof shelter, it was time to work on building a fire.

I dragged six-inch diameter trees back to camp and piled up the fuel until it got dark. When the rain stopped I gathered dry pine needles from inside the shelter to use as tinder for the fire. I broke off branches from the trees I had gathered

---

[511] *GORP* – is an acronym for trail mix, which means "Good Old Raisins & Peanuts" or "God's Only Real Perfection". This survival food includes: carbohydrates, protein & fat.

and in no time the fire sported three-foot high flames. After piling on some of the bigger branches, the flames reached over my head. Finally, I drug the logs over the fire and let the fire burn them in half. After about an hour I had a nice warm star fire with glowing orange embers. Whenever a log burned through, I pushed it across the fire and burned it in half again. An unusually shaped pine tree made a perfect lazy boy chair and pointing my wet boots toward the fire, I stretched out to relax and enjoy the evening. Outside my camp the weather was cold and clammy, but inside I was toasty warm, snacking on peanuts and looking forward to a good night's sleep in a warm dry bed. I wasn't just surviving in the wilderness, I was downright comfortable.

The next morning the sun lit up a sapphire blue sky adorned with soft puffy white clouds. I threw a handful of pine needles and some sticks on the embers that were still glowing orange behind a dusty gray ash and watched my campfire burst forth with new life. I melted snow in an aluminum cup and then mixed it with the powdered lemonade, so I could wash down a breakfast of GORP. Gathering wood and tending the fire was hard work. Although it consumed most of my day, in between each haul I rewarded myself by taking a rest on the easy chair. In the afternoon the temperature climbed into the forties so I discarded my parka and sat on the edge of a cliff. A thousand feet below me was a beautiful snow-covered valley punctuated by outcroppings of granite and dozens of generously spaced Ponderosa Pines. A handful of eagles completed the panoramic view and as they soared overhead with almost effortless grace, they reminded me of their emblematic importance to our nation. They are the symbol of our strength and our freedom.

I began recording my impressions in the little journal. I sketched pictures of the beautiful view and reflected on my life. The writing gradually revealed that something was missing in the spiritual dimension of my personality. I once felt close to God, but now I was feeling out of touch. Where was He? Why did He let bad things happen to me? When did I become so selfish? I had no ready answers, but I began a quest to reconnect with God. On the third day, my councilor arrived in camp to go over my solo experience with me. I rose from the makeshift lazy-boy to greet him. He was shocked by the size of my shelter and chided me for having such a big fire. "You were supposed to survive, not build the Taj Mahal!"[512] Not only had I conquered the elements, I had made myself comfortable in the wilderness. I really enjoyed my time alone and had discovered that spirituality is what was missing in my life. The solo was a tremendous success and my only regret was that it was over. The rest of the course centered on leadership and group dynamics, but it was anti-climatic. On January 23, 1977, I received my Certificate of Completion.

After graduation we loaded our gear into vans and were driven back to our hotel rooms in Pendleton. For the last three weeks we had been living on TVP.[513] I lost so much weight I poked three additional holes in my belt. Absolutely famished, we carpooled to an "all you can eat" buffet. The scrumptious looking food easily seduced us and we stuffed ourselves silly, going back for two and three helpings. By the time we returned to our hotel rooms we were holding our stomachs and moaning in agony.

I loved learning how to survive in the wild and relished the solitude of the wilderness. I enjoyed the experience so much I wanted to stay. I even thought of trading in my airline ticket for some camping gear and food, so that I could go back up into the mountains for the rest of the winter. For the first time in a long time I was happy. The last thing I wanted

---

[512] *Taj Mahal* – is a tomb built in the 17th century by Mughal ruler Shah Jahan in memory of his wife, Mumtaz Mahal. It is in the city of Agra, Uttar Pradesh, Republic of India. Widely thought of as one of the most beautiful buildings in the world, it is one of India's biggest tourist attractions.
[513] *Textured Vegetable Protein* – Our instructors claimed it was freeze dried food, but we were sure it was Gravy Train dog food, in little plastic bags.

to do was leave, but my mountain top experience had come to an end. The steep decent of the departure would prove even more brutal than skiing down the mountain. Problems at home, mental and physical limitations, as well as an accident, would all militate against my career in aviation.

A few days after returning from Outward Bound™, I ran into my first setback. Although I had acquired the requisite two-hundred fifty hours of flight time; I still needed forty hours of instrument time. Under IFR[514] conditions every rule tightened up. Altitude and heading parameters were cut in half. Every single maneuver had to be reported to and directed by the air traffic controllers; on and on ad infinitum. Flying was no longer independent or fun. After every lesson the muscles in the back of my neck felt like rebar. There dozens of things to keep track of and I was unable to keep all the details straight in my head. I discussed the problem with my flight instructor, but it soon became obvious I lacked the mental agility to fly under instrument conditions and without an instrument rating; I would never be a Commercial Pilot. Unwilling to accept defeat, I looked for a medical solution, but the doctor diagnosed me with hypoglycemia[515] and I was grounded. Despite my best efforts my flying days had come to an end and I had run smack into the Peter Principal.[516] I had to face the fact that Tri-Star Aviation would never get off the ground. "Tell me why, oh why, oh why can't my dream come true?"[517]

---

[514] *Instrument Flight Rules* – or IFR is one of two sets of regulations governing civil aviation; the other is Visual Flight Rules or VFR. The Federal Aviation Administration has rules & regulations that are designed to govern flight conditions when flying by outside visual reference is unsafe. IFR flight depends upon flying by referencing to instruments in the cockpit & navigation is accomplished by instruments that pick up electronic signals.
[515] *Hypoglycemia* – is the medical term for a state produced by a lower than normal level of blood glucose. It can produce a variety of symptoms & effects, but the principal problems arise from an inadequate supply of glucose as fuel to the brain, resulting in impairment of function & effects can range from vaguely "feeling bad" to seizures, unconsciousness & although rare it can sometimes cause permanent brain damage or death.
[516] *Peter Principle* – is the principle that, in the world of business a man continues to be promoted, until it becomes obvious he does not have the ability to go further.
[517] *If I Can Dream* – is a song performed by Elvis Presley & written by Walter Earl Brown, as the finale to his 1968 Comeback Special. Although not technically gospel, Presley

Apparently my dreams were not the only ones turning into nightmares. Dad returned to Esalen and mom joined an Ashram.[518] President Jimmy Carter[519] implemented disastrous economic and foreign policies that bankrupted farmers, sent interest rates soaring and for an embarrassing four-hundred forty days the Ayatollah Khomeini held Americans hostage in Iran.[520] Even Elvis Presley died of a drug overdose.[521]

When my father returned from California, he went to something called *est*.[522] Erhard Seminars Training was all the rage in the counter culture movement. As usual dad tried out his newfound techniques on the kids. I generally resisted and resented the pop psychology hoops he wanted us to jump through, but this time he made no attempt at manipulation with me. What he did do was urge me to go to an *est* seminar. He promised that if I did, he would never again bug me about psychology. Seeing it as a way to finally get him off my back, I agreed.

The *est* seminar began with the presenter telling us, "Everything I am about to tell you is a lie; so don't believe it." He then proceeded to redefine the meanings of words in Webster's Dictionary saying, "Webster says this word means, [and he would read the definition], but in this seminar we will use it to mean [and he would read a different definition]." The presentation was held in the ballroom of the

---

performed the song 2 months after King's assassination, with the same intensity & intonation of southern gospel, expressing the anguish of a lost dream.
[518] *Ashram* – is a hermitage led by a guru & remotely located in surroundings conducive to spiritual instruction & meditation. Residents act out spiritual & physical exercises of Yoga.
[519] *Jimmy Carter* – was the 39th President of the U.S. from 1977-1981 & served 2 terms as State Senator. He was Governor of Georgia, from 1971-1975 & prior to that he was a peanut farmer & naval officer. (1924-Present)
[520] *Iran Hostage Crisis* – refers to the events following the seizure of the US embassy in Tehran, Iran on November 4 1979, a crisis that lasted over a year until January 20 1981.
[521] *Elvis Presley Dies* – at the age of 42, prescription drug abuse had severely compromised his health & he was found unresponsive on his bathroom floor. Attempts to revive him failed & death was pronounced at 3:30 PM on August 16, 1977 at Baptist Mem. Hospital.
[522] *Erhard Seminars Training* – founded by Werner H. Erhard the 2-weekend course known as "The *est* Standard Training" was billed as a way for participants to achieve, a sense of personal power & transformation. The $300 *est* course was offered from 1971-1984.

Waldorf Astoria Hotel in New York City, with over 300 of us sitting on chairs in a banquet room. We were not permitted to have a watch and were even forbidden from going to the bathroom, until the end of each session.

This brainwashing continued for three days and then picked up again on the following weekend. It was like some kind of emotional boot camp. Come graduation day we were so mixed up, tired and submissive that the leader had us walking around the room gobbling and believing that we were turkeys. Having utterly destroyed our ego, they then hit us with the clincher. "You are God. You have been denying it for your entire life. Now is the time to just admit it." The room fell silent for a few minutes and then someone shouted out, "I get it!" One by one the emotionally starved attendees fell like dominos. Most of us bought into the lie that we were a bunch of little gods. My reaction was no different than anyone else's. I didn't just *think* I was a god, I *knew* I was an all-powerful being. There was nothing anyone could do to stop me from accomplishing anything I wanted to achieve. From that point on this existential philosophy became the controlling influence over my life. The new mindset colored every aspect of my religious, physical, emotional, moral and financial being.

Despite my Caesarean powers, I had my third car accident in as many years. The totaled car threw my insurance into the high-risk category. With the money I spent over the next three years on the insurance premiums, I could have purchased a brand new car. One thing *est* taught was that each individual is one-hundred percent responsible for the creation of every success and failure in his life. Following that line of reasoning to its logical conclusion, I presumed that I must not really want to fly for a living, own a business or drive a car. So, I decided to change direction and pursue a college degree instead.

I went back to Montgomery County Community College, bought a ten-speed bike and moved into an old springhouse on my teacher's farm. After living there a couple of days, I sensed my new landlord was probably gay and quickly moved out. Then I bartered my painting services with an adult classmate of mine, in exchange for renting a room in her barn. I finished out the semester living in her second floor studio apartment. While I was able to ace Business and Politics, I fell flat on my face in Math and Economics. I had grown up in a business family so conceptually I grasped economics, but algebra was used for calculating trade advantages and I could not handle the equations. The upshot was that I withdrew failing after a month. Poor academic preparation in high school was beginning to cut the legs out from under me.

The painting job may have earned me a place to stay, but I still had to do odd jobs to put some extra cash in my pocket. So I helped my cousin Peter Callahan put a cellar door in dad's cabin at Arrowhead Lake. The job was pure ditch digging and removing the huge boulders required brute force to the point of exhaustion. Peter and I had both gone through *est* so we reinforced in each other the idea that we had each chosen this type of strenuous labor. Nice work for a couple of gods, ehh? But that night I began questioning the teachings of *est*. If I was god, why would I create a world where kids became addicted to drugs, government leaders were corrupt and daredevils tried to kill themselves on motorcycles? It was the first of many questions I would begin to ask myself. Although I still considered myself a god, I didn't like what I was seeing.

The second thing I noticed was an attitudinal shift in my relationships with women. I used to go out with girls because I liked them, but ever since I lost my virginity to Natalie, I had become callous and angry. Somewhere along the line, I resolved that if that's the way things are, Fine! I'll treat women the same way Natalie treated me. I satisfied my lustful appetites and could care less who I hurt. In this vengeful fury, I deliberately started using women on a regular basis. I had no qualms about getting women drunk and lying to them, so long as I got laid.

Financially I was down, but not out. I still had every intention of reaching my goal of becoming a millionaire by the time I was thirty. There were only seven years left; but since I was now a god, I saw no reason to give up the dream. Westinghouse cut back on orders to Callahan Machine Company, which meant there was no work for me in the shop, but Uncle Ray asked me if I wanted a job as a prospector. I was to call customers on the phone, until I interested one in our machining services. Then I was supposed to turn the sale over to Uncle Ray and he would close the deal. He offered me a choice between an anemic hourly rate and a straight forward commission. I wanted the security of a paycheck and I opted for the hourly rate. He advised me that there was a lot more money to be made working straight commission and suggested I take a percentage of the sale, but I still went for the wage. As my Godfather, he was also looking out for me and therefore he asked a third time, reminding me that straight commission is always a better deal than an hourly rate. Uncle Ray told me to think long and hard, because this would be his last offer. Once I made a choice, he would not allow me to change the terms of our agreement. Again I chose the hourly pay arrangement. He knowingly smiled and said, "Ok... Its your choice."

For the next six weeks I poured over the Thomas Register[523] and the Dalton's Directory.[524] I mailed out hundreds of brochures and followed up with a plethora of phone calls,

---

[523] *Thomas Register* – is a multi-volume directory of industrial product information covering 650,000 distributors, manufacturers & service companies within 67,000+ industrial categories & are also known as the "big green books". They were first published in 1898 by Harvey Mark Thomas, as "Hardware & Kindred Trades".
[524] *Dalton Directory* – contains information on 14,000 businesses in the Delaware Valley & includes the names & titles of 40,000 executives & key personnel.

before finally getting my first prospect. Uncle Ray and Allis Chalmers[525] closed a deal for ten grand. The commission on that sale would have covered most of the wages I had already received. A second sale for sixty grand was with Caterpillar Tractor.[526] My godfather had not steered me wrong and because his word was his bond, neither would he allow a change in our agreement. Every time I got a sale he smiled and said, "Straight commission is always the better deal." He wanted that lesson to be burned into my brain. My final sale was with General Electric[527] and it was for over a million dollars. Although not nearly as profitable as Westinghouse, the repeat business provided steady work and there was no longer a need for my services.

The Callahan Machine Company sales job had come to an end, but I still maintained the dream of making my fortune. In the course of prospecting for the shop, I had discovered that Houston, Texas was the fastest growing city in the country. The oil, petrochemical and real estate markets had created a virtual boomtown. Rather than stay at Callahan Machine Company and take a job in the machine shop, I decided to relocate to Houston and go make my millions. I finally had that great idea my Aunt Joan had spoken to me about, but I needed some seed money to get started. KCS[528] was a tax shelter for the owners of Callahan Machine Company. The partnership was a separate company that owned the building and the machinery, which it then rented to Callahan Machine Company. KCS was designed to produce an income stream for the children of the owners.

---

[525] *Allis-Chalmers* – was a manufacturing company with diverse interests & is most famous for their bright orange farm tractors. They divested their manufacturing interests & today Allis-Chalmers Energy is based in Houston, TX.
[526] *Caterpillar Inc.* – designs, manufactures, markets & sells machinery & engines. Also known as "CAT", they are the world's largest manufacturer of construction & mining equipment, diesel & natural gas engines & industrial gas turbines.
[527] *General Electric* – is an American electric co. founded in 1890 by Thomas Edison & is now the world's largest multinational conglomerate, headquartered in Schenectady, NY.
[528] *KCS* – was a partnership that was set up as tax shelter for my father's company. The acronym stood for Kowalski, Callahan & Smith, the last names of the owners, which rented the building & machinery from their children who were the owner/partners in KCS.

There were thirty kids involved and each one owned a percentage of the company. Although none of the kids had ever tried to sell their ownership, as a partner I had the option of selling my shares. My percentage was worth about twelve grand. Following Uncle Leon's advice, I sold my shares to the other partners for ten grand and maintained the option of buying my way back in at a future date.

Moving to Texas, would mean that Clark Woods would loose me as a roommate. Since my brother Murry was looking to get out on his own, he took my place with Clark in the Hatfield Village Apartments. I stuffed all I owned into my 1968 Camaro[529] and drove straight through to Houston. On this particular pioneering adventure, I hit the road filled with hope, ambition and the security of knowing I had ten grand in the bank.

Signing a one-year lease on a two-bedroom apartment, I put a sleeping bag on the floor and started looking for work. On my third interview I received an offer that was four times larger than anything I had ever made as a machinist. While considering my first offer, I received another call. The man from my second interview was offering me a thousand dollars more. I decided to hold off on accepting any more offers, before first finishing the rest of the interviews, which I had already scheduled. A third company that sold loans to drilling companies said they would sweeten that pot with a company car, an expense account, a five-thousand dollar base salary and a commission on top of everything else! The experience was heady and made me wonder what other opportunities were available in this tremendous Texas town. Although I had three good offers in hand, I kept holding off making a decision. "Greed is good!"[530]

---

[529] *Chevy Camaro* – was a car manufactured by GM under the Chevrolet brand & is often classified as a pony car or a muscle car. It went on sale in 1966, designed to compete with the Ford Mustang & shared the same platform & major components as the Pontiac Firebird.
[530] *Wall Street* – is a 1987 film released by 20th Century Fox. It is directed by Oliver Stone & stars Michael Douglas, Charlie Sheen & Daryl Hannah, with the screenplay by Stanley Weiser & Stone. The film tells the story of Bud Fox, a young stockbroker who is so

Houston is horribly muggy, so I just assumed the electric bill for the air conditioner would be my biggest expense, but I was severely mistaken! In spite of the success I was having, loneliness dominated my mood and I soon came down with a severe case of telephonitis. Most of my calls were to Lesley Wright. She had just earned her BA from the University of Arizona, purchased a home in Tucson and was pursuing a graduate degree in extraterrestrial phenomenon. The cost of an airline ticket was actually cheaper than my phone bill, so I canceled the next day's interview and flew out to see her on the next available flight. Lesley met me at a Tex-Mex restaurant inside the Tucson International Airport, where we talked for hours. She then invited me back to her modest home on the outskirts of the city. The house had no air conditioner, but it had some kind of a water-cooled system and every backyard included a pool. Lesley was very matter-of-fact about sexual encounters and although we never engaged in intercourse, we slept together every night.

Each day I slept in late and went swimming in the afternoons, while my friend attended her college courses. In the evenings we went out to quaint cantinas and engaged in non-stop conversations over fine southwestern food and tequila until almost midnight. Knowing my plans to become a millionaire she celebrated with me over the apparent success I was having in Houston, but she also saw that despite some fantastic job offers, inside I was dying. After listening to me pour out my heart one night she empathized with the depth of my pain saying, "You know Patrick, you've always been a little uptight. Why don't you smoke a little dope or do a little cocaine." She clearly meant well, but it seemed like a case of the blind leading the blind. Reflexively rolling my eyes I said I needed to take a walk. The truth is that I was so low I was actually considering her suggestion. Walking along a white gravel path I looked out

---

desperate to succeed, he gets involved with Gordon Gekko, a wealthy, unscrupulous corporate raider. At the Teldar annual stockholder's meeting, Gekko gives his infamous "Greed is Good" speech.

over the Painted Desert and chain-smoked while I thought about her suggestion. After awhile I came back inside and said, "Lesley, I have no idea which way is up, but I'll be damned if I'm going to put something in my body that I know will hurt me, to make me better. It just doesn't make sense." Now she was the one rolling her eyes. Trying one last time to help me she said, "There's only one other thing I know of; your cousin Karl talks about the Lord. I don't buy everything he says, but he's got something."

Neither one of us had any interest in sex that night, so we just held each other tight and cuddled. The following morning I thanked her for being a friend and flew back to Houston. Although I picked up where I left off in the interview process, my heart wasn't really in it and no better offers were forthcoming. My cousin Peter Callahan was getting married and I had planned on attending his wedding, so after concluding the last interview for the week, I boarded a flight bound for Pennsylvania. Since Lesley had once dated my cousin Karl, I gave great weight to what she had to say about him and wanted to know more. So I scheduled a three-hour layover in Chicago, where I could visit with him and reconnect with my long lost cousin Karl Kowalski.

Chapter 24

Amazing Grace

My family rarely visited the Kowalski's and we were not as close to them as we were with the Callahan cousins. It had been over five years since I last saw my rabblerousing cousin. Karl Kowalski sold marijuana, before most people even heard of it. He was thrown out of the parish grade school at St. Monica's, Conestoga high school and Villanova University. The rebellious space cadet was frequently in trouble with the law and his bedroom always looked like a disaster area. So, even though Lesley had suggested I talk with him, I wasn't really expecting much.

Karl agreed to meet with me at the Chicago O'Hare Airport.[531] When I departed Houston[532] the powerful DC-8[533] pressed my back firmly into the powder blue chair, as we rolled down a very bumpy runway, rapidly picked up speed and rotated for take-off into the magnificent sapphire sky. Many memories flooded my mind, as I anticipated the reunion with my crazy cousin. I was apprehensive about what would happen when he picked me up, but Karl was more than happy to see me and even suggested I lengthen my layover. He said I could spend the night at his place and go on to Philadelphia in the morning. Strapping my luggage to the back of a moped, the two of us putted along residential roads at the break neck speed of forty miles-per-hour. Although his choice of a vehicle was quirky to me, it also

---

[531] *Chicago O'Hare International Airport* – is a major airport located in the northwestern-most corner of Chicago, IL. It is the primary hub for United & American Airlines. It began as a manufacturing plant for the Douglas C-54 Skymaster in 1942-1943, which produced a 4-engined transport for World War II. The site of the 2M sqft. factory was picked for its proximity to Chicago's workforce & easy access to its extensive railroad infrastructure.
[532] *Houston Intercontinental Airport* – is 2nd only to Dallas/Fort Worth in Texas. It opened in June of 1969 & was re-named George Bush Intercontinental Airport in 1997 after the 41st President. Houston is home to Continental Airlines & averages 700 daily departures.
[533] *DC-8* - was a 4-engined jet manufactured by McDonnell Douglas from 1958 to 1972.

seemed pretty normal for Karl. I expected a total mess when we got to his pad, but the apartment was immaculate and fastidiously organized. Something had really changed.

In the late seventies disco was in vogue and Donna Summer[534] was the queen of the night. So Karl invited me to attend a dance lesson with him and his dance partner. After the instruction a group of us went out to the local Holiday Inn to practice the steps we had just learned. One unique thing about the disco culture was that your dance partner was not necessarily your girlfriend. She was simply the girl you practiced your routines with so that you could compete in dance contests. Karl and Stephanie tried getting me out on the dance floor, but with only one lesson under my belt it was intimidating. The graceful couple put on quite a show, gliding across the floor and their perfection even drew the applause of the audience. The precision of their exhibition drew a sharp contrast with the hapless scraggily haired rockers in most bars that jumped around freestyle in their faded jeans and tie-dyed T-shirts. Every disco dancer was dressed to the nines. Clean cut men wore three-piece suits with gold-chained watches in their vest pockets and the women were decked out in flowing satin gowns with captivating chiffon sleeves.

After a few sets Karl and Stephanie returned to catch their breath. Stephanie was a drop dead gorgeous woman and had just demonstrated almost flawless perfection. Karl kept insisting I dance with her and the next thing I knew she was pulling me out of my chair and onto the floor. I was mortified, but with a disarming cheerfulness she patiently went over three simple steps and reassured me by saying, "You keep doing exactly what you're doing and I promise

---

[534] *Donna Summer* – is a singer & songwriter who gained prominence during the disco era of music, earning her the title "The Queen of Disco". Trained as a gospel singer, she is best known for her "powerhouse" vocal delivery. Her repertoire also includes gospel, R&B, rock & pop. In the 1970s she had 3 consecutive #1 double albums on Billboard & was the 1st female artist to have 4 - #1 singles in a 13/mo. period. Donna has sold more than 130 million records worldwide. (1948-2012)

I'll do all the work and make you look good." I kept doing my three little steps and she pirouetted around me like a spinning top with her long flowing gown gracefully unfurling behind her. True to her word, she made us look so good that we cleared the floor on our first dance. From that moment on I was hooked!

We left the club around midnight and then Karl and I stayed up until almost four in the morning. Sitting there at his kitchen table we reminisced for hours and drank spring water, which he had imported himself from Hickey's Hut. Karl had been attending the National College of Chiropractic[535] and would soon be graduating with a physician's license to practice the healing arts of chiropractic. Finally I broached the subject that was most important to me. I told him what Lesley had said about his relationship with the Lord and suddenly the conversation took an abrupt turn. He launched into an exuberant litany of all the things that had brought him into a relationship with Jesus Christ. He shared about all that the Lord had done for him and how he had gone to a Catholic Charismatic Convention, where he saw a crippled man jump up out of a wheelchair. He enthusiastically shared that he had given his life over to Jesus and that his whole life had changed. I had heard many people speak of God, but never with this kind of enthusiasm. Karl went on and on about the Lord and all that He had done for him. Although he gave many details of how God had turned his life around, nothing spoke so powerfully to me, as the dramatic witness of the change in his own life.

Reminding me that I had an early flight in the morning, Karl called it a night. Leading me into the living room, he handed me a sleeping bag and laid his sofa cushions on the floor so

---

[535] *National College of Chiropractic* –was founded in 1906 as the "National School of Chiropractic" in Davenport, Iowa by John Fitz Allen Howard, DC. In 1908, he moved it to Chicago, seeking a more rigorous academic culture & access to the anatomical study of cadavers at Cook County Hospital. In 1920, a 5-story building was purchased & the name was changed to "The National College of Chiropractic" & today the school is known as "The National University of Health Sciences".

that I would be comfortable. Before disappearing into his bedroom, he invited me to join him at an upcoming Catholic Charismatic Convention in Atlantic City, New Jersey. I told him I would think about it and got ready for bed in the dark. I stared up at the ceiling of his den and tears started running down the side of my face. Whatever it was he had, I wanted it! For the first time in a long time I fervently prayed to God. I asked Him to give me the same deep faith and love that Karl seemed to have and then I peacefully drifted off to sleep.

The next thing I knew, Karl came running into the den to tell me that the taxi driver was outside beeping his horn. I ran out the door in my bare feet and put my sox and shoes on in the cab, while the driver raced down the highway to the airport. We arrived just in a nick of time and I ran down the concourse to board a United 707[536] and find a window seat for the last leg of my journey. The passenger jet rolled slowly through a maze of taxiways, before revving up her engines on the rain soaked apron at the end of the runway. In a New York minute it taxied into position and I willingly surrendered to the forty-thousand pounds of thrust needed for take-off. Tiny beads of water streamed backward on the window until the plane burst through the overcast ceiling. Another sapphire blue sky replaced the dreariness of the world I was leaving behind. The contrast between how I had been living my life and the hope of what could be in the future was overwhelming. As I marveled at God's creation, I ordered a few drinks. Not only was I numbing the pain in my heart, I was trying to clear the lump in my throat and use the napkins to wipe away the embarrassing tears from my eyes. Dad picked me up at Philadelphia International Airport[537]

---

[536] *Boeing 707* – is a 4-engine commercial passenger jet airliner developed by Boeing in the early 1950s. It remained common throughout the 1970s & is credited with having ushered in the Jet Age leading to a later series of aircraft with "7x7" designations.

[537] *Philadelphia International Airport* – is located in Philadelphia, PA & is the international hub of US Airways. In 1925, the PA National Guard used the site (historically known as Hog Island) as a training field for its airplane pilots. The site was dedicated by Charles Lindbergh in 1927, but there was no terminal there until 1940, so airlines used the Camden

and wanted to know all about my experiences in Houston. I told him about the job offers and then about Karl and how much I wanted whatever it was he had. Dad said nothing, but nodded his head with a kind of knowing smile. I told him I wanted to go to the convention in Atlantic City and asked him if it would be ok for me to stay with him for a couple of weeks. He readily agreed and I was soon back in familiar surroundings.

I visited friends, caught up with my mail and handled some finances at the bank. I got so busy taking care of business that the trip to Atlantic City became just one more item on my "to do list". I ran into my Aunt Mary Kowalski at Peter's wedding and she invited me over to her home for dinner. After the meal I pulled my Uncle Leon aside and asked him if he could get me tickets to the Charismatic Convention in Atlantic City. Anyone could have gone and there were plenty of tickets available, but my uncle made it sound as if he were calling in a marker when he whispered, "I think so; let me see what I can do." A couple days later he gave the tickets to my father, who brought them home to me from work. When I called my uncle to thank him, he offered to drive me down to Atlantic City with their family. He asked me if I had ever been to a convention like this and when I told him no he asked, "Would you like to go to a prayer meeting first, so you can get a feel for it?" I agreed and met him in Paoli, PA, at The Body of Christ Prayer Community.[538]

After eating dinner with the Kowalski's we all drove over to the Abbey. Alana my eight-year-old cousin led me to a pew and sat down next to me. She had long platinum blond hair and a smile so warm it could melt the ice off of the Alaskan

---

airfield in NJ. Once the terminal was completed, American, Eastern, TWA & United started flights to the airport.

[538] *The Body of Christ Prayer Community* – was a Catholic Charismatic Prayer Community, which met at the Daylesford Abbey in Paoli, PA. It was founded on 9/13/72 & at its apex; there were 400 worshipers at Wednesday night prayer meetings. A core of 100 faithful formed several ministries, camped out on Intense Weekends & even discussed living together. It was destroyed by the teachings of a heretical priest & no longer exists.

Pipeline.⁵³⁹ The charismatic prayer meeting began with exuberant songs and the service was punctuated with spontaneous prophecy and the strange utterances of people praying in tongues. After a silent period, a man stood up and said, "I got this in prayer last night and it's for someone who has traveled a long way to be here tonight." My ears perked up as he read from sacred scripture. "I am the vine: you are the branches: he that abideth in me, and I in him, the same beareth much fruit: for without me you can do nothing."⁵⁴⁰ A second man prophesied, "I am the vine and you are the branches. Your branch has been severely trampled so that only a few strands survive, but the root is strong and out of that will grow a new vine that will be stronger than the first ever was." The gentleman was describing my faith. I burst into tears knowing I had trampled the faith of my childhood. Alana leaned over and put her arm around me whispering, "Patrick, Jesus really loves you." Her tender words of comfort unleashed the floodgates, turning a restrained trickle into a raging river. Her squeaky little voice let me know I was loved and God used those dainty little arms to make His touch real for me.

Three days later I found myself listening to a talk on Sexuality at the Atlantic City Convention Center.⁵⁴¹ The boisterous priest giving the talk read the same scriptures about The Vine and The Branches and even repeated the same preamble, "This scripture is for someone who had traveled a loooooong way to be here tonight." I was utterly unprepared to be sitting amongst thirty-thousand people for

---

⁵³⁹ *Trans-Alaska Pipeline* – is a 48"diameter 800 mile pipeline that delivers oil from Prudhoe Bay near the Artic Circle, to the Valdez Marine Terminal in Alaska. It sports 11 pump stations & several hundred miles of feeder lines. It was built between 1974 & 1977, after the 1973 Oil Crisis caused a sharp rise in oil prices; making exploration economically feasible & subsequent legislation removed legal challenges to the project.
⁵⁴⁰ John 15:5 – "I am the vine: you the branches: he that abideth in me, and I in him, the same beareth much fruit: for without me you can do nothing."
⁵⁴¹ *Atlantic City Convention Center* – is located in Atlantic City, New Jersey & is most famous for being the home of the Miss America Pageant. It was built to make the city a year-round destination rather than a mere summer resort & the same considerations later led the city to become the #1 gambling center in the United States, outside of Nevada.

such an intimate encounter. Choking back the tears, my nose was running and without any Kleenex on me I was reduced to wiping the phlegm on my jeans. I desperately wanted to give myself completely over to God, but thought I would lose what little was left of my personhood. I had already done that with *est* and seen disastrous results. However the Franciscan[542] was not finished with his prophecy. "You are a wild stallion and you think God wants to geld you." Bingo! It was the very reason I was holding back. Friar Tuck[543] went on to say, "God doesn't want to geld you. He wants to put a bit in your mouth and keep you from running in circles." Suddenly God's message made all the sense in the world! My heart exploded with the submissive sentiment, "Yes Jesus! Come into my life! I've made a mess of it. You tell me what to do and I'll do it!" Although my yes was in no way audible, it ratified the sacred commitment I had long ago made at my Confirmation. Quickly finding a priest, I made a general confession and after receiving absolution, an overflowing sense of joy and freedom washed over me. I wanted nothing but the opportunity to do the Father's Will and to please my Savior.

On Monday morning I flew back to Chicago and attended some classes at the college with Karl. In the evenings we took turns dancing at the disco with his partner and the three of us talked like magpies about the Lord. After a couple of weeks, I had a serious heart-to-heart talk with my cousin about where I should go from here. All of the reasons I had for moving to Houston seemed invalid now. I wanted to reorient my priorities. Serving God was primary and the relationships I had with my family and friends came in a close second. Houston was extremely far away from all of that so I wasn't sure what to do next. After praying with Karl

---

[542] *Franciscan* – refers to members of a Catholic religious order, founded by Saint Francis of Assisi. They are an order of priests & religious, serving God though the vows of poverty, chastity & obedience. The order focuses on spiritual direction & serving the poor.

[543] *Friar Tuck* – is the companion to Robin Hood in the Robin Hood legends. The character of the clergyman is depicted as a jovial friar & one of Robin's Merry Men.

about it he smiled and said, "I think you know what you have to do. God will work out the details." I flew back to Houston ready to pay dearly for breaking my lease, but another tenant had been on a waiting list and I was released without penalty. I tried sight seeing in Texas before leaving, but the oppressive heat and humidity drove me back indoors. So I spent my last week in Texas reading a bible Karl had given me. When my landlord gave me the final paperwork to sign, I packed up my Camaro and headed northeast toward Chicago.

I spent the next two weeks auditing college classes with Karl and he introduced me to one of his classmates. Gloria Morrow was a beautiful Catholic woman with jet black hair that ran all the way down to her waist. We saw some movies and went dancing with Karl and Stephanie. Although we often hugged and kissed, any sexual displays of affection remained comfortably out of bounds. Our relationship grew and we both looked forward to her graduation. She intended on taking over her aging father's practice in Valley Forge, as soon as she obtained her license.

I wondered aloud whether my car would last, where I would live and what I would be doing for work. Karl assured me that God would take care of such things, if I would just seek first His Kingdom.[544] The month before I returned to Pennsylvania, Murray totaled his uninsured van and needed

---

[544] *Matt. 25-34* – "Therefore I say to you, be not solicitous for your life, what you shall eat, nor for your body, what you shall put on. Is not the life more than the meat: and the body more than the raiment? Behold the birds of the air, for they neither sow, nor do they reap, nor gather into barns: and your heavenly Father feedeth them. Are not you of much more value than they? And which of you by taking thought, can add to his stature by one cubit? And for raiment why are you solicitous? Consider the lilies of the field, how they grow: they labour not, neither do they spin. But I say to you, that not even Solomon in all his glory was arrayed as one of these. And if the grass of the field, which is today, and tomorrow is cast into the oven, God doth so clothe: how much more you, O ye of little faith? Be not solicitous therefore, saying, What shall we eat: or what shall we drink, or wherewith shall we be clothed? For after all these things do the heathens seek. For your Father knoweth that you have need of all these things. Seek ye therefore first the kingdom of God, and his justice, and all these things shall be added unto you. Be not therefore solicitous for tomorrow; for the morrow will be solicitous for itself. Sufficient for the day is the evil thereof."

to move back home to pay off the bills. That meant Clark Woods needed a roommate and I moved back to Hatfield Village Apartments. Using a portion of my money from the sale of the partnership, I bought a brand new VW La Grande[545] and a set of precision tools, so I could go back to work as a machine operator at Callahan Machine Company.

Returning to the Abbey, I went through a Life in the Spirit Seminar[546] and became a member of The Body of Christ Prayer Community.[547] For the next fifteen years the Daylesford Abbey became my spiritual home. Eventually I was asked to be a Youth Group leader, drove a van for a homeless shelter called My Brother's House[548] and served on the team for Life in the Spirit weekends. The next two years were like a honeymoon; not only was it easy to avoid sin, but I wasn't even tempted. Desire for alcohol and cigarettes evaporated. Anger and self centeredness were transformed into caring for others. I treated all women with dignity and never allowed my sexual attractions to deteriorate into lustful desires. Filled with His Grace, I wholeheartedly submitted my will to the legitimate authority of the Catholic Church, fell in love with my family and pledged to follow Christ anywhere he wanted me to go.

After the honeymoon the stink of sin began creeping back into my life. A heretical priest brought doctrinal errors into

---

[545] *La Grande* – was the last of the Beetle cars produced by Volkswagen. Although the "Bug" was virtually the same economy car first introduced to the US in 1938, this model was larger, sportier & had a more powerful engine. The first model of the "People's Car" was manufactured when Hitler called for a basic vehicle that was capable of transporting two adults & three children at 62 mph & was to be made available to citizens of the Third Reich for under 1,000 Marks. Over 21 million Beetles have been produced in all.

[546] *Life in the Spirit Seminar* – is a weekend retreat designed to introduce someone to a personal relationship with Christ & to release the power of the Holy Spirit in their lives. It was also used as an opportunity to welcome newcomers into the local prayer community.

[547] *The Body of Christ Prayer Community* – was a Catholic Charismatic Prayer Community, which met at the Daylesford Abbey in Paoli, PA. It was founded on September 13, 1972 & at its apex there were 400 worshipers at Wednesday night prayer meetings. A core of 100 faithful formed several ministries. They camped out on Intense Weekends & even discussed living together, but it was destroyed by the teachings of a heretic priest & no longer exists.

[548] *My Brother's House* – is a shelter for homeless men in Philadelphia. It was founded by The Body of Christ Prayer Community & is now run by the organization Bethesda Project.

his teachings and they drove me from the Abbey and eventually destroyed the entire community. I even left Holy Mother Church for a time, but by the Grace of God I am Catholic again. The spiritual detour was not a total loss, because it taught me never to let bad men steal my faith. I now meet regularly with a good holy priest who absolves me of my sins, guides me spiritually and helps me to sort out moral dilemmas. Although the charismatic movement was instrumental in bringing me back to Christ; my faith does not exclusively rely on the spiritual milk of emotional highs. I now know with absolute certainty that the true Ark of my Salvation is Jesus Christ and the One, Holy, Catholic and Apostolic Church, which He established and sustains.

Several personal and emotionally charged encounters with Christ have encouraged me throughout my lifetime and I remain grateful for them. Although precious and few, I cherish the memory of these intimate visits. The ecstasies let me know and recognize the voice of my Shepherd. Movements of the Spirit, by their very nature, are powerful and short lived interventions. They are meant to accomplish a specific purpose, but they are not mere emotional events. My faith is now expressed in a much more traditional manner.[549] The Church calls me to listen to God through daily prayer, study of the Sacred Scriptures and participation in the Mass. Although I still struggle with sin,[550] Confession is readily available to reconcile me with the Father. Finally I recognize that heaven is not assured[551] and that I must utilize every tool Jesus gave me in His Church.

As the autumn of my life approaches, I see that the political predictions of our founding fathers have come true. No

---

[549] *Tradition* – "And we charge you, brethren, in the name of our Lord Jesus Christ, that you withdraw yourselves from every brother walking disorderly and not according to the tradition which they have received of us." (2 Thessalonians 3:6)

[550] *Psalm 50:5* – "For I know my iniquity and my sin is always before me."

[551] *Heaven Not Assured* – "Wherefore, my dearly beloved, (as you have always obeyed, not as in my presence only, but much more now in my absence,) with fear and trembling work out your salvation." (Philippians 2:12)

longer a moral and religious people, we have lost our freedom. The lack of discipline in our society is reflected in the spending habits of congress, the overreach of bureaucrats and the degenerate decrees of the court. The American civilization has all but collapsed and in anticipation of the approaching anarchy; federal, state and even local governments have surrendered our sovereignty to the administrators of a global tyranny. If our culture is to survive, we must first be worthy of freedom. In addition we must be willing to fight and die if necessary, to defend our faith and our republic! Things will not just magically manage to work themselves out. We dare not dabble in doctrines that tell us that heaven is assured, when two-thousand years of Catholic teaching say otherwise. Christians will need to get serious about their walk with the Lord. Our families will not survive unless husbands sacrificially love their wives; wives respect their husbands; and parents fully embrace their responsibility to discipline and educate their children. Make no mistake; we are at war! America will die if we fail to reform our lives or dare to ignore the safeguards of our Constitution. Regardless of whether we are discussing religion, politics or economics; for far too long we have been *Asleep in the Light*.

When I awoke this morning I made my coffee and sat down to watch the news. Pope Benedict XVI had just announced he would abdicate the Chair of Peter at the end of the month. Wow! I didn't see that one coming; but it makes sense. Church teaching is often about balance. John Paul II used his waning years to give witness to the intrinsic value of the elderly. Pope Benedict XVI is now showing us how to humbly accept our limitations. I also think his timing was picture perfect. Obama's State of the Union address has been upstaged and liturgically it's Lent. The cardinals will soon be down on their knees begging the Holy Spirit for guidance. Hopefully by Easter we will have another good and holy pope to energetically lead us. *Onward Christian Soldiers!*

Made in United States
North Haven, CT
09 August 2024